I, ARNOLD

Also available from Millennium

(Rounds One and Two of the Galaxy Game)
The Galaxy Game
Fission Impossible

I, ARNOLD

Round Three of the Galaxy Game

Phil Janes

MILLENNIUM
An Orion Book
LONDON

The right of Phil Janes to be identified as the author of
this work has been asserted by him in accordance with the
Copyright, Designs and Patents Act 1988.

First published in 1995 by
Millennium
An imprint of Orion Books Ltd
Orion House, 5 Upper St Martin's Lane
London WC2H 9EA

A CIP catalogue record for this book is available
from the British Library

ISBN: (Csd) 1 85798 101 4
(Ppr) 1 85798 102 2

Typeset at The Spartan Press Ltd
Lymington, Hants
Printed and bound in Great Britain by
Clays Ltd, St Ives plc

This book is dedicated to
Judy Martin, Charon Wood, Deborah Beale and Caroline Oakley;
the people who have given me the chance to grow

Prologue

Richard Curtis didn't mean to kill his father; it was just one of those things, and one which left him owner of the Arnold Curtis Space Research Centre and its collection of suddenly very nervous staff. He *did* mean to invent a method of interstellar travel of use to beings with lifespans less than those of bristlecone pines (which make quite awful astronauts), but he couldn't. Until he found, in his kitchen cupboard, next to the cheesy biscuits, a device which cancelled inertia.

The Champion of the Game for the last seven eons had, like all its race, left its body behind on some planet so long before that the descendants of the worms which ate it had now signed non-aggression pacts *which they really meant*.

It and its kind had then done the usual Most-Powerful-Beings-in-the-Universe bit – exciting stars into novae; creating a planetary system or two, through kinetic influence over the ensuing clouds; dropping a few amigo acids;[1] clearing the rock strata of any 'missing'-link fossils, and so on. But, a few immortal millennia after losing their physical form, they'd also pretty much lost interest. They could do anything, but they'd already done it.

What was left to prove?

And who to?

All that remained was internal competition, except that with omnipotence you simply get a heap of no-score draws.

The Game was therefore initiated, with the combatants using teams from lesser species – they weren't exactly pushed for choice – to dilute their powers, as a way of deciding just who was *the* Supreme Being.

[1] Experimenting with essentially friendly life forms.

Winner takes all, loser dissipates its energy into the gaps between normal- and hyper-space, and becomes nothing.

The ultimate accolade or the ultimate defeat.

The game was everything.

What else could there be?

In the latest contest, the Champion had drawn humanity as the race from which it must choose its team, which was a bit like a swimmer getting the lane with the shark in it. And its Challenger – the swimmer who got the lane that sloped downhill – had drawn the six-armed, multi-muscled trands.

The first round had demanded that the team travel from their home to another planet across the vastness of interstellar space, and the Champion considered that its fortune was looking up when it came across the human Richard Curtis, busy building a spaceship and wanting only for something to get over the problem of inertia, which the Champion duly provided, next to the cheesy biscuits.

If its fortune *was* looking up, though, it was to see storm clouds gathering as the human team was formed.

The crew of the anti-inertia silver dart that was the spaceship Pioneer didn't know they were taking part in the Game. What with all the bickering going on (Curtis's stowaway secretary, Gloria, having taken a shine to the Pioneer's pilot, then having it dulled by his dismissive attitude and judging that the first officer – who apparently thought he was starring in a novel – was *the* one for her, thus putting several noses out of joint; and with Arnold the ship's computer gleefully throwing data-spanners into the works at every opportunity) the inaugural trip was dangerous enough without all the obstacles thrown in their way by the Challenger. But the Champion had not remained the Champion without having a few tricks up the sleeve it didn't need, and the crew finally arrived at their destination to be met by the elegant, patience-challenged Biondor, the Keeper of the Galaxy.

Biondor exercised his office by confining humans to Earth until they grew up enough not to keep trying to kill each other, but he had orders where Curtis and team were concerned, and even Biondor didn't mess with the likes of the Champion.

He explained what had been really going on, and told the team that they were not returning to Earth, but had to continue playing until the Game was won and lost. They could then go home, whatever the result, but winning carried the advantage that they could do so while still alive.

Failure in any round where the opponents succeeded meant death.

So did refusal to play, which would have been their first choice.

The trands had completed their journey so far with all the apparent problems of a yogi meditating on his third straight lottery win, so the humans were currently scraping a draw.

The rules allowed one change of personnel, and Fission was brought from 24th century Earth to join in the fun before Biondor presented them with the challenges that made up the second round. They had no choice but to set out, armed with no plan, little optimism, much trepidation, and as usual a superabundance of argument.

Their new team member had enthusiastic views on how things should be done – her way – but they managed to get through anyway, with luck and a following wind. The Champion engineered much of the luck, and the team – Curtis leading by example – easily fulfilled the other requirement, stimulated by challenges which held quite enough danger to provide the death that failure to complete them already promised.

The trands sailed through by dint of their unquestioned ability to beat things to a pulp at the first sign of resistance, and sometimes well before then.

Still a draw.

But still alive.

Just.

Thanks to a Champion who is straining to keep its title and its existence, in the face of a group who are to competent teamwork what Marx was to stirring political speeches . . . Harpo Marx, that is.

So on to the Challenger-devised third round, of which the reluctant humans have been given scant details by Biondor.

They might not know very much about what's going on, but they're pretty used to that by now. *They're* going on, because they have to.

If they fail; well, they could try to console themselves with the fact that it's only a game.

But they know it isn't.

It's *the* Game.

And it's hard to feel consoled when you're dead.

3

I

When antigravitons were isolated and their use became viable, among the first to benefit were a large number of people called Smith who frequented thin-walled motels. Antigravitons don't squeak.

This was no motel and, being largely underground, it was soundproofed by an entire planet, but no-one would have noticed squeaky bedsprings in any case because the voice of the woman supported by the straining subatomic particles had risen to a crescendo that would have drowned an argument in a monkey house.

'Oh, yes! Oh, Rudy! Yes!'

She had long green hair, brown eyebrows, blue eyes, ever-pinkening flesh – currently basting itself – and presumably no eye for colour schemes. He, silent, had jet black hair, olive skin that, apart from a mark on one fast-moving buttock, appeared not only unblemished but unresponsive to his efforts, and eyes that glowed deeply crimson, concentrating on the bobbing larynx of the stretched-back neck below him with no apparent emotion whatsoever.

'Oh, RUDY!'

He made no sound. Actions speak louder, even, than screamed words.

'Rudy! That's it! THAT'S IT!'

And it was. Rudy stopped immediately and rose from the couch in an easy, flowing movement.

'Oh!' The disappointed 'Oh' that slips out when it slips out. 'What are you doing? I didn't mean that was *it*, I meant . . .'

Too late. Rudy's readiness relaxed instantly, as though he had thrown an internal switch; which, she presumed, he had.

'Oh.'

Clothes, such as they were.

'Rudy.'

The door, such as that was.

'Rudy! Where are you going?' She pushed herself to a sitting position, a hard edge in her voice. 'Come back here immediately!'

He didn't. Ignoring the order, his red eyes sought the contact to remove a door that didn't appear to be there in the first place, and his hand found it.

And then the eyes changed. The red faded, deepened, became brown, and the brown contracted to irises. From robotically expressionless, they became intense, the eyes of an animal; one you'd throw a stick at, not for. Primeval, feral, eyes showing no sign of deliberation; only of instinct, to survive, to fight.

But not, apparently, to mate.

He walked through the doorway, the voice calling him back in anger and in vain.

Still the eyes changed, intelligence now welling up like tears, pushing the bestial ferocity into the background, diminished with distance, yet shining through like a magnesium flare in an Hadean pit.

'Rudy, where are you going?' The woman leaned against the wall, clutching an inadequate covering at her neck, and watched the receding back. The anger of her disregarded order was now the plaintiveness of loss. 'What are you doing? You're *mine*.'

But he walked up the spiral slope that led away from her and never looked back.

II

If someone had transplanted the Taj Mahal into the main spaceport, any visitor to the planet would have wondered what the shabby little building in the corner was for; and those from the less advanced worlds of the Federation would probably have made a pee line for it.

Magnificent, lavish, and opulent were discarded from incomers' thoughts as inadequate descriptions. Impressive, or what! was the one that best fitted.

You are entering a world that has the lot.

It was enormous and gleaming. No expense had even been considered, it said, let alone spared. The walls and the floor glimmered in mother-of-pearl swirls, and the ceiling would have made Michelangelo sigh and chisel a moustache on David's lip. Any number of archways, corridors, and tunnels led off the main hall, promising so much for the well-heeled travellers that their eventual destination would have to be a let down.

The purposeful movement of people through this vastness, from spaceship bays or restaurants to rest rooms, sports areas or entertainment centres, resembled hundreds of platelets sliding smoothly past each other in a blood sample on a microscope slide.

Except for one enormous clot.

Richard Curtis – Captain Richard Curtis – paused before entering the main concourse and allowed his crew of five to gather round him.

Above them, a sign hung in the air with no visible means of support. 'Welcome to Earth', it said.

Curtis looked at it, knowing that there was no logical reason for it to say 'Welcome to Earth Five Zero', since it didn't know it was, but feeling, nevertheless, that it should. He shrugged the matter away inwardly, and turned a smiling face to his crew.

'Right, we're here.' They looked at him silently, but more than one expression passed comment on his perspicacity – always one to hit the nail on the head as soon as he ran out of thumbs. 'Now remember, I'm as much the Captain on the surface of this planet as I am on the spaceship.' The android in the party raised a knowing eyebrow, and smiled the smile that should have met Custer's prediction of victory.

'Was there something, Arnold?' Curtis asked him. Arnold shook his head and said nothing, but the smile spoke volumes. Curtis consigned any doubts to history. 'All right, follow me!'

He led them boldly under the welcoming sign; spearheaded the adventure of turning a corner towards the hubbub of the spaceport; and walked into a walrus.

It was a big walrus, a male, lying on the shale beach with the sort of lazy shift-me-if-you-can manner that comes so naturally to three tons of fat, tusks, and foul breath, and it ignored Curtis completely. Around it lay a number of females, petite only by comparison, reclining in the sated manner of those who don't smoke. They, too, seemed oblivious to the presence of their off-world visitor.

Which was odd, since, by the time his reactions had kicked into gear and stopped him, Curtis was standing not only in the middle of the harem, but in the middle of a walrus.

He eeked! and scrambled out, looking down at his jump-suited legs to ensure they weren't covered in walrus insides, then paid attention to the sensible bit of his head that was muttering 'hologram' to any other bit that would listen.

He straightened his jump-suit, ignored a deep and somehow androidian sigh, and looked around him, retrieving his composure and air of authority in equal measures.

'Now, how do we get out?' he mused, then held up a hand in case this musing should be seen as a sign of indecision. 'Don't worry, I'll find out!'

Thomas Wilverton, the diminutive First Officer to Curtis's Captain, looked toward several large signs marked Exit which hovered thirty feet up, about fifty yards away from them, but held his tongue. He lightly touched the arm of the not-so-diminutive woman who stood indecently close to him and pointed out their immediate destination – should Curtis need to ask it would come better from Gloria; Wilverton had no cause to belittle his Captain, and, besides, he was trying to work out what book he was in.

Curtis did need to ask, apparently, but instead of utilising Gloria's new-found knowledge he utilised his hand to stop the nearest passer-by, who thereby relinquished the description, but instantly looked as though he wanted to re-qualify.

'Excuse me. Could you tell me where I might find the exit?'

The man pointed. 'I think you'll find they're just over there under the enormous Exit signs. I don't know why they have to make it so confusing.'

'No, nor do I,' gushed Curtis. 'Thank you very much.'

'Please don't mention it,' replied the now reinstated passer-by, throwing a 'Dick!' over his shoulder as he went.[1]

'It's Richard, actually,' Curtis corrected the retreating back half-heartedly, then turned to his expectant crew, and indicated the exit. 'It's over there. Come on.' They followed like seventeen-year-olds pretending not to be out shopping with their mothers, while Curtis kept a surreptitious eye open for a toilet – he knew he should have gone on the ship, but he had been afraid they would leave without him. They halted in front of a barrier across an archway professing another Welcome to Earth.

'Where do you wish to go?' came a pleasant, neutrally sexed voice from the gateway in front of him.

We should have thought of this, thought Curtis. Bother.

'Er,' he replied, typically, and paused while he waited for his brain to come up with something convincing and Captain-like. Sadly, while his crew looked on with interest, his brain completely ignored his discomfort and just got on with something else.

'"Ur" was an ancient city of Sumer, as it was then known,' responded the gateway. 'But it has not been inhabited since the fifth century BC. The site of the former city *is* known, however. Is this the site you wish to visit?'

'Er,' he confirmed.

The silence from behind him was the loudest he had come across, and he could hear breath being held prior to bursting out in a snigger. Especially Arnold's, who didn't have to breathe, but who had taken a good deep one for that express purpose. He could hear the word 'Captain?' in their minds in *that* tone of thought.

It was more than Curtis's irresolution could stand.

'No! No I don't want to go to Ur,' he said, as near to triumphantly as it is possible to deliver that particular phrase.

Behind him, a young male walrus dragged itself across the shale. The harem owner hauled its head off the ground and watched the approach, snorting loudly by way of warning or sinus trouble.

The sound filled a pause during which the gateway waited to see if anything was following the Triumph of Curtis, and when it became

[1]Not as in 'Going to the fancy dress party as a petrol pump'.

obvious that nothing was, asked, 'Where do you wish to go?' It slightly stressed the 'do', but did not quite add the word 'then'.

Curtis's mouth opened automatically, and 'Er' started rushing from wherever words start towards the aperture. A more than averagely alert part of his brain – not that it had much to beat – realised that 'Er' would be exactly the last thing a proper Captain would say at that moment and ordered the bottom jaw up, bloody quick. 'Er' saw the light fade rapidly from the end of the tunnel until it cut off altogether, just moments too soon; and Curtis said, 'Um', instead.

'Um?' asked the gateway, with a trace of irritation. They could imagine it frowning, pursing its lips a touch. 'Did you say "Um"?'

'Er,' said Curtis before he could stop himself. 'Oh shit! I didn't mean "Ur"! I don't want to go there.'

Behind him someone made what sounded *so* like an heroic effort not to snigger which had only barely failed that Curtis just *knew* it had to be Arnold.

'There is a world gazetteer on the terminal to either side of the portal where you can make a decision.' The gateway dropped back into the smooth antiseptic tone it had first used. 'There are others waiting. Please clear the portal.'

'They're with me. They're my crew.' There, that sounded good. That would show it.

The subordinates felt the gateway studying them, weighing up their worth in the light of the news that this was their leader; but it passed no comment on what it saw, which was unfortunate for Curtis, as he then had to make the next gambit as well. He wasn't very good at gambits, which thereby qualified for membership of the astonishingly populous Curtis-not-very-good-at Club.

He had to do something; the gateway was making him look really stupid in front of everyone. He glanced, distracted, at the young walrus plucking up enough courage to approach its elder, then turned back to the gateway, standing a little straighter.

'Look, it really isn't as simple as you try to make out. Let me explain.' He paused momentarily. Smooth so far. 'We are taking part in a Game played by super aliens, and in this round – er, we're the Champion's team and the trands are the other one. And in this round there's a great danger facing the Earth – or this version of it anyway, because it's not actually the real Earth, the one that we come from – though I expect it feels like the real Earth to you. Anyway, it's a renegade household robot and we've got to stop it reducing the planet to barbarism . . .'

'Ruling!'

The thought had pulsed through the ether from the Champion's being and vibrated the Lessers beneath the two combatants in a maelstrom of high energy radiation. The Third Elder had risen slightly above the rest, flashing the purple of respect but drifting inexorably into ultraviolet as the enormity of having to convey an umpiring decision to this most powerful of its race got the better of it.

The Champion hung tightly above it, and though it had no eyes with which to stare coldly, it could give anything an impressively frigid sense.

'These trands do not employ robotic labour, First Elder. The Challenger – the Second Elder,' it threw in, ingratiatingly, its tone that of the worm addressing the record-breaking python, 'is therefore entitled.'

The Champion showed no reaction, although far away in a corner of the Galaxy, an old red giant star surrendered to gravity and collapsed, before bursting forth as a super nova, and the First Elder's mien lightened indefinably.

Despite the clues it could provide, its team on Earth Five Zero would be tested in locating the quarry – especially since, in its opinion, locating the Sun would only be a half-decent bet if they had three guesses on a summer's day – and this ruling would give the Challenger's team of trands an enormous advantage.

Maybe enough to win the round, and therefore the Game.

Which would mean death.

The Champion knew that it would fade and dissipate its energy to nothingness across hundreds of parsecs, rather than rejoin the Lessers from which it had emerged when it Challenged so many eons before. Some things it could not do.

'Very well,' it pulsed, and the visible orange was a monumental effort of calm emanation. 'But the two will be identical in appearance.'

'Agreed,' came the tremulous thought of the Third Elder, before the briefest pulse of gamma radiation sent it flooding back into the Lessers with the very sure knowledge that its agreement was as superfluous as a Grendarian zilchipede's new socks.

'. . . Except we don't know how it's going to do it. But Biondor says it hasn't got the basic laws like the ones, you know, that Asimov said they should have so they wouldn't hurt anyone, and it might try to hurt everyone for all we know. He's the alien who's sort of in charge of the Game, only he's not one of the ones that's playing it. Biondor, that is. Not Asimov.' Curtis paused, a little breathlessly. That seemed to have gone all right. 'So it's really quite complicated.'

Behind him, the smiles sagged a bit as cheek muscles began to ache.

There was a pause, during which, off to one side, the young male reached the old bull, and both reared up on whatever bits walruses rear up on, before diving for the neck, hitting targets that hardly demanded precision, before backing off momentarily.

The gateway ignored it all, remaining non-committal; non-admittal for that matter. The team could imagine it staring at Curtis with tight lips and cold eyes.

'Do you understand?' asked Curtis.

'I understand the words.' The irritation had clearly become the sort of itch which you just have to scratch despite the lack of privacy and its position at the top of your inner thigh.

The gateway scratched, in a voice that did not express awe for Curtis's mission, 'Tragically, I am but a simple portal, albeit to every conceivable destination on this planet, and I am not the Earth-based representative of Intergalactic Rescue. I would, however, point out that this has proved historically sufficient for every one of my customers.

'Unless you actually wish to choose a destination on the globe, or even within it where such exist, and then begin to travel there by following my directions, then I am afraid I cannot be of very much assistance to you, however fascinating I may or may not find your explanation, and whatever danger this planet, or any other version of it for that matter, might be in.

'I do have a colleague across the hall I think would be more suited to you, however. It is marked "Departures".'

Arnold wondered if it was kinky to fall in love with a door, before his amour was interrupted by the bull walrus delivering a monstrous blow to its challenger's throat, and the younger reeling backwards.

The gateway seemed suddenly to remember itself, and its squeaky clean voice.

'Please feel free to use the gazetteer on the terminals to either side of the portal.'

Curtis suddenly slumped. His shoulders were the only visible sign of it from the rear, but they were joined by the corners of his mouth, his eyebrows, his heart, and his thoughts.

Whether it was the supposed members of his crew, a dragon, a bunch of hungry fleas, or anything else he had come across since leaving the bosom of Mother Earth Prime four hundred and something years before, everything had done nothing but abuse him, and enjoy it.

He was having one of *those* lives.

All through this Game thing everyone had ordered him around like . . . like . . . like someone who's terribly easily ordered around, and he wasn't really Captain at all and now this gateway had proved once and for all that he was just a complete and utter, total, hopeless, ignominious, insignificant, ineffectual, useless little second-rate failure and it just *wasn't fair*.

He hoped fervently that his father wasn't watching from whatever after-life Curtis had inadvertently despatched him to by tipping him through the penthouse window.

His father wouldn't have been pushed around by a door.

His father was never pushed around by anyone.

Not only, Curtis thought, was *he* pushed around by *everyone*, he hadn't even got the measure of inanimate bloody *objects* yet; and, in front of his crew, they purposely made him look *stupid*.

'Where do you wish to go?' asked the gateway.

'Look, why don't you just *piss* off, you . . . you, *door*!'

The worm turned on his heel, aware of several people on the concourse giving the quick once over to someone having a row with a door – and losing – and would have clomped off had he been wearing the sort of footwear able to provide a good clomp, which he wasn't, so he sort of squeaked off instead, rather pathetically, in the direction of a bloodied and bowed young male walrus, pulling itself back to the safe obscurity of the sea. The two, hologram and human, seemed to catch each other's eye, and share a moment of life at the bottom.

I bet, said Curtis through his eyes, that big walrus in the middle is your father.

He's everyone's father, the walrus didn't reply. That's the point. That's the point of everything.

Gloria watched Curtis's sagged shoulders raise and lower again in a deep sigh. Her expression immediately betrayed a heart as full as her figure, which Wilverton noticed since she was the almost constant subject of his gaze. He squeezed her hand, and she turned to him.

'I do feel sorry for Richard,' she said, quietly. 'He tries ever so hard.' Wilverton nodded, and squeezed again. Such a soft heart, he thought, and so well protected. A derisory, very androidian, snigger from his left expressed an alternative view of Curtis's efforts.

Curtis didn't hear, intent as he was on putting distance between himself and his tormentors. Though he doubted if *anyone* could find so isolated a place. He stared at the ground – sulking with head held high destroys the poignancy – walked in a straight line, at least forcing people, clutching their glowing direction markers, to detour around him, and wandered under a 'Play Area' sign. He did not register a child's excited voice crying out.

'Mummy! Look at Wind flying, Mummy!'

'Yes, dear. Isn't Wind clever?'

Then a buzzing sound forced its way through Curtis's current thoughts of Earth Prime – home. He glanced in the direction of the noise, and saw something flying towards his head, tiny wings flapping frantically.

He instinctively waved an arm at it and, for the first time in a long career of ball-game disasters, he connected. The thing clattered onto the ground at his feet, and its outer casing broke away, taking the wings with it and leaving a small cuboid box, which struggled back into the air and hovered forlornly a couple of feet up.

This time he did hear the child's voice, as did much of the concourse.

'Mummy! That man broke Wind!'

She was at his side in a second, child in tow.

'What did you do that for, you stupid man? Haven't you ever seen a toy bird before?'

Curtis shrank towards the defensive, but bumped into the shade of his father before he reached it, and bounced off.

'It startled me. You really should . . .'

'Well, that's no reason to go smashing it, is it?'

'Excuse me! But the reaction was purely instinctive. It has been a part of the human racial make-up since we were monkeys swinging in the trees. We can't change our basic animal instincts!' Let her argue with *that*, he thought.

She slapped him hard across the face, and his ego pushed his father's ghost out of the way and pulled the covers over its head.

'How dare you use language like that! Especially in front of my daughter! You offworlders should learn how to behave before coming here. You pervert!' She yanked the child's arm like a dog's choke chain. 'Come on, Krela, your father's ship should be landing.'

Curtis looked after her in amazement. What had he said? The woman was mad!

It was probably the Challenger thing influencing her mind.

Except that this sort of thing seemed to have been happening to him since the midwife first swiped him.

He looked briefly for his friend, the walrus, but he was nowhere to be seen. Probably drowned himself, thought Curtis.

'Man's a nerd,' said Fission, turning back swiftly from the latest Curtis débâcle to the matter in hand. Wilverton suspected that she referred only to Curtis and not to 'man' in general, but with this blue-haired, red-blooded member of their party – plucked by Biondor from Earth Prime at the end of the Game's first, time-dilated round – it was dangerous to make that particular assumption. He was certainly not going to risk a question on the matter.

He wondered if the people on Earth Five Zero would differ from Fission – not that they had ever managed to determine if she was the norm in her own time on Earth Prime. Wilverton somehow doubted that; it seemed unlikely that any version of a Universe could hold too many Fissions – there wouldn't be enough insults to go round. No, that wasn't being fair; she was just a bit intense, and she had hidden qualities. Hidden by an expert, perhaps, but qualities, all the same.

They seemed to speak normally here, he thought, which was one difference. There were fifty, Biondor had told them, between this quantum version of the Earth and their own.

'We should make some sort of plan before using the gateway,' he said, steering his thoughts back.

'Well, *you'd* better do that, Thomas,' said Gloria. 'You're the cleverest.'

'Speak for yourself, mega-mams,' commented Fission. Gloria blushed.

'Don't call Gloria that,' snapped Wilverton, and almost looked as though he was going to confront her physically. He remembered his gentlemanly manners just in time; since otherwise he would almost certainly have been writhing on the ground seconds later with his hands in his lap. Fission opened her mouth and bared her tusks but it was Peter Carlton, the last member of their crew, and erstwhile pilot, who replied.

And he sounded happy.

Because he felt happy.

Since they had left the bosom of Mother Earth, this feeling was a visitor so rare it made Halley's comet look like a lodger.

15

Why, then? Because the female occupants of Earth Five Zero, he had noted, were simply gorgeous. And they were dressed either in some lightweight and otherwise nondescript shirt and slacks, presumably for space travel, or a sort of chiffon drape that was as close to nakedness as made no difference. His spirits had immediately risen, and they weren't alone.

'Hey, come on!' he said, holding his hands up in the traditional peace-making sign, having to stop smoothing his hair back in order to do so. 'Let's not start off like this, eh? We managed to get through the last round by working as a team, and that's our best bet in this one. Just winter it a bit, okay?'

Fission glared at him for a moment. He was only acting the diplomat to gain the moral high-ground. She decided to let him have it for the time being, and conceded the peace like she would give up her favourite tooth to the dentist.

'Okay, Mr-fonking-reasonable. What's plan?'

'Good question,' replied Carlton. 'What's the plan, Wilverton? You're the cleverest, if slightly unbalanced.'

'I haven't got one.' Wilverton ignored the insult, though Gloria threw a glance at Carlton. 'The spaceship is impractical as a base, so I guess the first thing we want to do is get to an hotel or something. Then we can discuss what we do next.'

'That means we need money,' said Carlton.

Wilverton shrugged. 'We have money.' Then he changed the subject as though the answer also contained the explanation. 'It would be handy to find out what year it is.'

He looked around as though the answer was hanging in the air as conspicuously as the exit signs. Gloria and Carlton frowned in puzzlement but knew better than to question him – he *was* a little worrying at times, thought Gloria; he *was* a raving nutter, thought Carlton; but he had proved right too often before not to be given the chance. Fission had a different opinion.

'I *know* what year, you short dibble! 2453. I *come* from now, remember?' So much for peace. Wilverton ignored her, still apparently searching the horizon. 'Look,' Fission appealed to the others, 'you wait see what this loon is up to, or we make intelligent decision on what do next?'

'He's not a loon,' said Gloria.

'He thinks he's in book, melons. He thinks none of this real and sometime he'll reach page with big The End written.' Why couldn't these people see sense?

'What I think on that particular matter is irrelevant to what we should do next,' Wilverton told her, with infuriating logic, and still looking around.

'You think this book?' she pressed.

'I am not prepared to dismiss the possibility.' He wasn't prepared to admit that the notion might have been planted in his brain, either . . .

Fission turned back to Gloria. 'Where's that fit in your definition of sane, eh?'

Gloria thought for a moment. 'I haven't got a definition of sane.' Nor of an awful lot of other words, for that matter, she reflected.

'If you children have quite finished . . .?' invited Carlton, adultly, attracting stares on various hate levels.

'You're doing it now, are you?' Arnold was using his innocent voice. It always wound them up. 'Working as a team? I like to get these things straight, you understand.'

The barb pierced their hot air balloon, and the four team-mates settled back onto their beach.

'What makes you think this isn't 2453, like Miss Insult three-years-running suggests?' Carlton asked, getting the last one in. Fission forced herself not to react to any extent greater than an expression promising imminent death, which he studiously avoided.

'Because when Fission joined us it was 2453, and then we spent some time chasing across the Galaxy in at least four dimensions.'

'It didn't take long though, did it. A couple of days at the most.'

'It's not how long it is that matters.'

'Don't you believe it!' Carlton told him, with a peacock smirk.

Gloria moved to put a protective arm around Wilverton's shoulders, but he saw her coming and continued.

'We were travelling in the fourth dimension; time. Biondor did tell us we would be coming to Earth Five Zero in the current time, but he did *not* say what the current time was.'

Fission fumed silently, like Etna. Why didn't they just do what she wanted? It would be so much easier, more efficient, quicker, sensible . . .

She took a deep breath. It didn't help.

Wilverton suddenly found what he was looking for, reacted with an 'Ah!' and pointed to an Information sign hanging over the concourse some hundred yards away. He made his way towards it, and the others followed on behind in a straggling line, hardly noticing their Captain joining at the rear, still trying unsuccessfully to clomp, and rubbing his cheek.

Then Curtis was stopped short by a voice; the manners installed by his father's right hand overcoming his current need to mope.

'Good day, sir.'

That made a change.

He turned to the sound and was confronted by a bald figure in a long white robe and simple sandals. The only adornment to this basic garb was a gold chain around his neck, hanging from which was a trinket of some kind.

A small dog sat at his feet, looking as bored as a dry oil well. Curtis took a step backwards; he was allergic to dogs, and, indeed, most other things that could get up his nose.

His father once told him it was one of God's little role reversal jokes.

'I wonder if you would like to make a small contribution to the Foundation Foundation?'

'The what?' asked Curtis, not really caring, now that the 'sir' was confirmed as an advertising ploy.

'The Foundation Foundation.' He looked serious.

'What are you, science fiction fans?'

'No, sir, we are very far from fiction. We deal with fact. And science has done us little good. The world has for too long been concerned with material things, with greed, with the advances they think can be gained through the creation of devices that were never meant to be present on this world, because had they been so meant then they would have been put here in the beginning, and . . .'

It was an odd trinket, thought Curtis, as his eyelids began to droop. It was silver and it looked inescapably like an extremely large needle jammed up the bottom of a chimpanzee. Odd, he thought. I mean, a St Christopher maybe, or your name in little gold letters, but an anally intruded monkey . . .?

'. . . is why the prophet sent his sign to us, telling us to revert to simple ways, from the days when materialism had not taken over our thoughts, days when . . .'

'No,' said Curtis, 'I think it's silly.' And he wandered off after the rest of the group, feeling bigger, better and guilty.

The man watched him go, mouth agape in mid-plea, and not as in pleased. He clenched a fist, causing the word 'LOVE' to stretch across its back.

He looked down at his dog, who was eyeing Curtis's departing leg with a thoughtful, but nonetheless randy, expression, and wondered

18

whether to kick it. He didn't, but spoke to it instead.

'Life's a bitch!'

The dog looked up. I wish, it thought.

Then the man's eyes narrowed.

The Foundation needed the money to keep the election drive going and it was people just like the blue jump-suited figure shuffling away from him who threatened not only the result, but the Foundation's very existence.

Because they think the Foundation is '*silly*'!

Yes, came a much louder voice in the fore of his mind. Unless they learned to respect the Foundation, they would destroy it. They just thought it was silly, nothing to be taken seriously.

It's you against them. Life or death.

The Champion glanced electromagnetically to where the Challenger hung beside it, and pondered, with the wisdom of countless eons, with the knowledge of an infinite variety of Universes at its sensor tips – it didn't have fingers, or anything else for that matter – just what the Challenger was buggering about at.

It entered, lightly, the human's brain, and learned.

Tricky.

'It's time they learned,' he told the dog. 'We shall start the crusade. Come on, Stay.'

Stay glanced at him. 'You still think that's funny, don't you?' he thought, but faithfully followed his pack leader as he moved stealthily towards the shadow of a microbe shower. Once there, the hand covered with LOVE stole inside the robe, then emerged again, holding something that looked a lot like a weapon, and for the very best reason.

III

His crew had gathered underneath the Information sign as Curtis caught up with them, but there appeared to be nothing there, except a slightly brighter light than that which infused the rest of the spaceport, which was going some, given the scintillating reflections off the crystal roof so far above them that Carlton reckoned you could join the mile high club without going out of doors.

'How do you make this work?' Wilverton asked, looking around for buttons or something.

'Just ask what you will, and I will reply as best I can,' answered a voice which seemed to come from the light all around him.

'Oh, right. What year is it?'

'It is 2457.'

'Thank you.'

'Don't mention it. No problem at all. Have a nice day, now.' Wilverton moved away a little. 'Missing you already,' said the light.

'Human lover,' muttered Arnold in passing.

'Okay,' said Fission, pre-empting anyone who might dare to point out that she was wrong. 'So 2457. Four years. So what?'

'Did you have any savings?' asked Wilverton. Fission considered, and her eyebrows rose slightly as she did so, then fell like an anvil off a cliff as the implications reached their logical conclusion.

'Not having my money! I worked for that!'

'At twenty dollars a time,' muttered Carlton.

'What!'

'Nothing.' And he gave her a smile sweet enough to make his teeth fall out. Wilverton interposed his voice between them.

'I don't want your money.' He knew that Fission was more likely to donate her grandmother's in-use intestines. 'My savings will still be in their various accounts so long as the companies still exist on this version of Earth, and they've been there for over four hundred years. I reckon I've got all the money I want. So has Peter, so has Richard, and so has Gloria.'

He started walking back to the exit gateway, and the rest followed respectfully.

'Where do you wish to go?' asked the gateway.

'The nearest luxury hotel, please,' replied Wilverton.

'Thank you, sir. That will be the New Church Street Hilton. Please follow the blue line.'

Curtis gave the gateway a hate-filled glance as a blue line dutifully appeared on the ground in front of him. He shuffled along at the back of the group, dragging his feet, which you have to when you're shuffling. The floor of the spaceport was quite free of obstructions, so there was nothing to trip over, but when you have the poise of a pissed penguin you don't need anything to trip over, and Curtis suddenly missed his footing and plummeted.

To his left, another traveller made her way toward the Exit, walking at a far brisker pace, clearly in a hurry to get somewhere.

She never made it.

As Curtis hit the floor, the top half of the woman disappeared, to be replaced by the smell of singed flesh. The bottom half kept going for a bit – not a big bit – then, in the absence of instructions from above, downed tools in a messy heap.

Curtis landed on his side, painfully, and rolled off his bruised hip just as the floor where he had been bubbled under the heat of the beam which hit it. He heard someone scream in panic, and realised it was him.

A man moved with clearly robotic speed to the incident and searched somewhat redundantly for something to which he could administer resuscitation techniques.

Wilverton didn't know how some enemy could have discovered their whereabouts, or even if the attack was aimed at them at all, but he was damned sure he wasn't about to stick around to find out. After the moment of paralysis, any number of people were running in all directions, and he was keen to become one of them while he was still attached to his legs.

'Come on!' he yelled, grabbing Gloria's hand and running, and finding Arnold, magically, in front of them. More robots and one human with a peculiar light above her outstretched wrist strode into the centre of the confusion.

Carlton paused, gave Fission a gee-up push on the back, then helped Curtis scramble to his feet, and gave him the same treatment. The Captain staggered as a result, bent double, but managed not to fall, while the air above his back sizzled. Someone running towards the scene simply exploded in a shower of sparks, wired components, flexible chitin joints and positrons.

Curtis regained his balance and ran, and Carlton, glancing briefly at the eyeball that rolled along beside him, formed the team's rearguard.

A few people stood still, too shocked either to think of moving or to be capable of it once they had thought. Only one had remained motionless out of conscious choice, and now he moved off in the same direction as the jump-suited figures, tucking a weapon inside his white robe as he went. The material concealed the LOVE on his hand, but nothing hid the hate on his face.

Stay followed, wondering idly what they were going to do with all the spare bones . . .

A hundred yards away, Wilverton led and the others followed without demur, running in a crouch and looking like so many Groucho Marx's searching for cigars, following a blue line that was now less a directional aid than an escape route.

The line took them into a wide tunnel, walled and floored in what looked like marble, dotted with posters that seemed to be made of light. Carlton got the impression of a bald man on one of them and a woman with enough hair for both of them on another, but he didn't stop to study them or read what was written underneath. Time enough for art and literature when imminent death wasn't on the agenda.

Dodging frowns, they ran past a sign to the stripway, which turned out to be a wide, underground, moving walkway made of a number of strips, each about three yards wide, and each moving slightly faster than the one outside it, the farthest reaching about thirty miles an hour.

Wilverton hesitated, and Fission overtook him, leading them onto the first strip with the confidence of an expert. She noted with relief that the stripway's existence was not one of Biondor's fifty pivotal differences. He had told her – all right, *them* – only that in this version of the Universe Curtis and company had failed in the first round of the Game, which surprised her as much as summer sunrise in the Sahara. As regards the other differences, since they probably didn't have any bearing on getting through this round, winning for humanity, and, just maybe, staying alive, she didn't give a donkey's fonk.

Towards the middle of the stripway were a number of seats, some occupied, and she headed for these.

Carlton, Gloria, Wilverton and Arnold were following with no great difficulty – the difference in speeds between strips was no more than two or three miles per hour – but she noticed that Curtis seemed to be having some sort of problem. She ignored him.

He concentrated. His legs were managing fine while his brain let them get on with it. But then it clearly thought it should take suitable control of its motley collection of body bits, and messages started flashing around that they – the motley collection – were moving really quite fast, and that it could be ever so dangerous if they didn't all hang together.

Which was a pretty dumb thing for the brain to say.

As Fission approached the seats, she heard a slight thump behind her and glanced over her shoulder to see Curtis sprawled in the prat-fall position which might well have been named after him.

She sighed, strode a couple of paces back to her leader and yanked him to his feet as though he were a seven stone weakling – which he considered really unfair since he was an eleven stone weakling – and threw him into a seat, while Arnold looked on with a smirk, and Wilverton and Gloria just looked.

Carlton ignored them, looking round at the people and frowning; an odd reaction given the possibility that – give or take the presumed attempt on his life – he was in his favourite dream and wasn't going to wake up.

And fifty yards behind them, the white-robed figure with LOVE on his hand lowered his weapon again, waiting for Curtis's involuntary ducking and diving to stop, and began to wonder what strange quirk of fate was protecting him.

The Champion looked on and could sense the Lessers growing restless beneath it. It opened its being for the briefest of instants and the Lessers knew all they needed.

It was not assisting.

It could do almost anything, but where the Curtis human's unco-ordinated movements and ability to raise ineptitude to an art form were concerned, it could not improve on Nature.

Curtis looked up to thank Fission, but screamed, instead, as a lioness leaped straight for his throat, paws outstretched like a furry Superman, skin stretched over its ribs like a xylophone in storage;

23

though he saw only a mouth almost as wide as his own and thirty-seven sharp yellow teeth.

It landed on a young deer just to the left of Curtis's head, buried its teeth in the fawn neck, and lay there panting, seeking the energy to live a little; but he didn't spot that bit, either, since he had thrown himself sideways across several of the seats, and only now looked up to where his crew members were looking down.

Neither did he spot a beam of terribly excited photons rushing through the air towards where he had been a moment before, completely ignoring any medium through which they could pass unmolested. And if someone got hurt, it wasn't their fault; the particles[1] were just following the orders of physics.

'Is he *really* with us?' Carlton asked no-one in particular.

'He's not with himself most of the time,' Arnold replied. 'And I wish you wouldn't say "us"; it's most distasteful.' He sounded like his ears had stepped in something brown. Carlton ignored him.

Curtis was about to pull himself upright when the woman in the next seat slid sinuously sideways and settled on top of him. It might have been something that had happened to Carlton once or twice in the distant past, but for Curtis the possibility of anyone being suddenly overcome by his sexual attraction was one that made turkeys voting in favour of Christmas a racing certainty.

So, with a worldly-wise squeak which would have lowered his street cred had it not already been on about the same level as the stripway, he squirmed out from underneath, and felt something warm and sticky on his hand as he brushed it against the woman's body.

Body being the operative word.

Warm, sticky and red.

He held up the hand for the others to study while he did his verbal impression of a timid mouse awakening in the middle of a cat convention.

'Come on! No profit here!' yelled Fission, just beating Carlton to the shout. He hesitated, and Fission stared at him momentarily – she had the intensity of vision that could manage a momentary stare – before bursting. 'All right, stay then! Luc!'

She took off across the stripway and, after a brief glance at the dead woman, Carlton joined the back of the group, preparing to leap over Curtis when he next hit the deck, but Curtis's panic was overriding

[1]The dispute as to whether photons were particles or waves was resolved when it was realised that they move much too fast to have time to wave. And anyway, who'd see it?

even his body's apparent need to fling itself to the ground every few paces.

They ran towards an exit, jostling fellow passengers and attracting some 'Well, really!'s along with frowns suggesting that these outings should be better chaperoned, then up a slope towards daylight, blinking as the sun greeted their arrival.

LOVE's white-robed figure made to follow them, but he wasn't quick enough – Stay was being stubborn, preferring the traditional, but slow, way of walking, in which his paws occasionally touched the ground – and cursed as he missed the exit. He looked for the next one, but it wasn't in sight, so he cursed again and moved back to the fast strip.

Above him, the holo now showed a close-up of another bald-headed member of the Foundation Foundation, addressing any who would listen; a close-up that included his silver trinket. LOVE fingered his own, feeling the slight flare at the base of what some assumed was a needle, but what he knew to be the long thin silver dart shape of a sacred spaceship.

He sank into a seat and smiled up at the leader of his Foundation, warmth momentarily replacing the righteous fire that filled his being.

Try as he might, somehow this man above him was even more holy, more committed to past values. Balder, even, as though hair didn't dare to grow, defiling the smoothness of his hallowed head. 'I'm doing this for you,' thought LOVE, as the man's voice rose in excitement.

'. . . until the promised day when the prophet himself returns; when the great and revered Richard Curtis decides that this sinful and gluttonous world has given up sufficient of its decadent ways for him to reappear, and the Pioneer brings him back to the Earth.

'Then can we rejoice in the knowledge that our humble efforts have been rewarded by the reappearance of our spiritual leader; that, unworthy as we are, we have received the blessing of the glorious and sainted Curtis.

'We must ever prepare for that wonderful day!'

Breathless, thought Wilverton, is an oxymoronically excellent yet inaccurate description. He didn't say so out loud, which was probably just as well, because he was too busy taking in not less, but much more breath and trying to ease his aching muscles, while checking that they weren't being followed.

The Great Escape had a chase in it, didn't it? Admittedly, not from a public transport facility . . .

'Well, I think we've found our renegade robot.' Carlton interrupted his thought, having taken several surreptitious deep breaths to ensure he could talk quite normally.

'I think robot find *us*!' Fission corrected, also speaking normally, as much as ever. 'Hope we've lost it.'

There wasn't a lot to say to that – Carlton could only think of agreeing, which didn't seem appropriate – so they looked around them, to wheeze accompaniment.

Earth Five Zero was green. It didn't come as any great surprise to Wilverton – when he had left Earth there had been more 'green' movements than you'd get after a vegetable curry banquet – but there was certainly a lot of it.

On the green were people, sitting around, reading, eating, playing with balls that had clearly never heard Newton's ideas, or if they had, didn't believe them, as they hovered between what were presumably contestants.

And, over there, animals. He couldn't tell what they were, but unless some of the people had more than their fair share of legs, this was some sort of zoological garden. He assumed there were invisible fences keeping animals and humans apart, because no-one looked to be concerned.

Least of all the couple who sauntered past, hand-in-hand, gazing into each other's eyes. They were dressed largely in nothing, as far as Wilverton could see, and in the warmth of the sunshine that was all they needed. He glanced sideways at Carlton, noticed the frown on his face, and frowned in turn. Before he could ask the reason for this odd reaction, Gloria gave a squeal of delight.

Just behind them, two small tiger cubs were rolling over and over in the grass, flailing at each other with harmless paws and gumming each other's throats with mock ferocity; tiny balls of brown and orange and dirty white fluff.

Gloria noticed the look on Fission's face. It wasn't one that promised cuddles and feeding bottles, and the others were looking round nervously. Why was that?

'They're so sweet!' Gloria informed her, in case she'd missed the implication of the squeal.

'*They* might be. Only thing sweet about mother will be taste of last meal.' And what the fonk were tigers doing wandering around at the top of a public stripway?

'I hadn't thought of that.' Gloria looked about. 'I can't see any tigress.'

'Present company excepted,' Carlton threw in, with a glance at Fission, but she smiled thinly at him. Stony ground.

Then the animals looked up at them through the artificial crimson of their eyes. Gloria looked momentarily disconcerted and almost backed away, but when the cubs broke off and bounced up to her, she was all high pitches again. They rubbed around her legs and she stroked them. One trotted to Curtis and mewed plaintively at him, so he leaned down from a sudden position of superiority and tickled its ear, whereupon it turned its back on him, lifted its tail and sprayed his leg, before gambolling off, apparently dragging the supports from under his shoulders as it went.

'Why have they got robotic animals?' Wilverton wondered out loud, trying not to smirk.

'Who gives pile?' demanded Fission, her tone suggesting disinterest as much as her words. 'Let's get on.'

'Well.' Thomas had asked a question and Gloria was going to answer it. 'I think it's either because robotic animals can live happily together without killing each other, or because they've realised that you shouldn't keep real animals in captivity so they use robot ones and leave the others where they're meant to be.'

In case the animal protection societies should falter, God had invented Gloria, thought Wilverton. A Gloria who thought laterally with ease, but did have a bit of trouble with the straightforward stuff, bless her.

'By "where they're meant to be", I presume you mean on the dinner table?'

And the devil had retaliated with Arnold.

'That's different!'

'Why? Because they haven't got fur on when you stick your fork in them?'

'Don't be horrible, Arnold! You've been in a bad mood ever since we landed. What's the matter?'

'This Game's the matter! And humans!'

'Will you two quiet!' Fission sounded no longer asperated. 'We here to get robot.'

'And the robot looks like it's here to get us,' Carlton pointed out, but somewhat distractedly this time.

He was looking around again and frowning again.

27

Just like the ones in the spaceport, all the people he could see were perfect.

The women had finely sculpted features above bodies which had no visible flaw; and there wasn't much left invisible where a flaw might lurk.

Which would have been great, except that the men all looked as though they had just walked off the set of 'Rambo Tries Ballet'; two hundred pounds of muscle moving like the gazelle that's just won the Most Graceful Gazelle in the Jungle contest by a country mile.

It made Carlton feel like Wilverton. If these were the norm, then in comparison he would be . . . he would be . . . *scrawny*.

'Where do we get money, then?' he snapped, as a way of interrupting his brain's preparation for the downhill.

'Bank?' Point to Fission.

'Well, where's a bank, then?'

'How the fonk should *I* know?'

'Excuse me!' Gloria stopped a medium distant passer-by with two words, a big smile, and at least two other major attributes, but the red eyes which turned towards her said that just the words would have done it. She met him half way. 'Can you tell me where the nearest bank is please?'

He pointed to a low building quite some way behind them, the backdrop to which was the more substantial, if still largely underground, spaceport. Outside the bank they could just make out a large sign hanging in the air, promising point six of a ding for your wollar.

Judging from the reaction of Carlton and Fission, Wilverton assumed that this was either a spectacular deal on the currency market, or they had a rampant ding fetish, because they immediately scampered towards the building, before braking to such a slow pace that it denied they had ever been hurrying. Wilverton and the others followed. The robot watched their progress for precisely no time at all, before continuing on its way.

Curtis took up his position at the rear, head down, and Gloria hung back until she was walking next to him.

'Are you all right?'

'Fine.' Or, no.

They walked in silence for a few moments.

'I know it's nothing to do with me, and you used to be my boss and everything' – in another life – 'but you shouldn't try to be something you're not, you know. It doesn't matter if you're not the leader; it doesn't change who you are, and it won't make anybody think any less of you.'

A few paces ahead, Arnold turned his head briefly to contribute. 'Chance would be a fine thing.'

'Be quiet, Arnold,' Gloria told him, then lowered her voice. 'We do better working as a team, anyway.'

'How do you know? We never have!'

Gloria thought about it. During any displays of teamwork Curtis probably *had* been just an observer. 'Yes, well, we *probably* would. But anyway, you should be able to look in the mirror and find a faithful friend. That's what my grandmother used to say; unless she'd taken her teeth out. We should all just be who we are and not who we're not. I'm quite happy to be , , ,'

'Brain-dead?' floated back from in front, and Gloria threw a look at the back of Arnold's head.

'. . . who I am.' At least, so long as I've got Thomas, she added silently. 'I don't try to be a leader. It's not who I am and it isn't important.'

She waited for a response, and when none came she patted his arm, smiled the smile that had made many a man's blood rush from his knees to his groin, and moved forwards to Wilverton, watching, as she went, two large deer in the distance locking horns.

Curtis looked down at the green grass under his feet, and travelled most of infinity to a park in his childhood. To a bench where an old lady in a seemingly even older overcoat sat and fed the birds from a paper bag of breadcrumbs. And he sat next to her and took the crusts he had brought from his pocket and they shared the feeding and they shared their troubles. He comforted her in her old age; she comforted him in his youth.

But the memory didn't make him smile.

He had stolen those crusts from the kitchen bin, and used his pocket because his father would see a bag. And he'd had so many troubles to share.

He knew who he was.

And he knew it wasn't good enough.

He looked up to see how near they were to the bank, and found that it was blurred. He wiped his eyes angrily, set his shoulders in determined mode, held his head up, and tripped over a worm, which stared at the soles of his feet through tiny red eyes and ducked back under the surface to get on with its work, supplementing the natural inhabitants.

★

29

The Champion kept any electromagnetic comment on the Challenger's worm strictly inside its being, but couldn't help thinking that it was a nice touch.

It was learning, this Challenger, and it was also getting the better of this round.

The Champion had to act.

It gave the matter more thought in the next instant than most humans manage in a lifetime, from yogis right down to prop forwards.

IV

'I don't think it *is* the renegade robot who's been shooting at us,' Wilverton commented. Beside him, Gloria looked confused.

'If all we have to do is to stop the thing,' he explained, 'and to do that all we have to overcome is a physical danger, then that doesn't seem like the style of these aliens. There's no cerebral element, is there?'

Beside him, Gloria looked confused. And worried, with Arnold's last word ringing in her mind. Thomas kept saying things she didn't understand, because he was clever, and he wasn't going to want to spend the rest of his life with someone he couldn't talk to. But Carlton passed comment from just in front before she could think of some intelligent response, which didn't necessarily demand split-second timing.

'Logic,' he said. 'If you're right and we've still got to find the thing, then logic would be the key, because that would be anathema to a renegade robot. Robots are incapable of doing anything that isn't completely logical. Isn't that so, Arnold?'

'A fish,' said Arnold, looking serious.

Carlton's eyes hated him for a moment, but Fission did not appear to notice his slip down a couple of pegs; she had more fundamental concerns in mind.

'Fonking aliens!'

Gloria transferred her gaze to the other woman.

'You mean the Champion and the Challenger things?' Fission's expression – may-they-rot-in-a-boiling-cess-pit – confirmed the fonking aliens' identity. 'It might not be their fault, you know. It might be just instinct for them to do this, to play this Game thing. We shouldn't blame them too much.'

'The humans have grown soft and weak; some of your team dangerously so,' the Challenger commented with amused micro-waves.

31

The Champion shrugged the shoulders it didn't have with a mild emanation of green light.

'They have grown. There are different ways of doing so.'

'Intellect is not enough. Especially at that level. And compassion cannot aid them!'

'Opinion.'

'Fact.'

One group of things that disappears when the matter Universe is left behind by a metamorphosing race, is playgrounds. The Champion let a long radio wave answer for it, closing the matter.

The Challenger did not respond for a moment and, given how much response it could fit into a moment, this was an inaction of some moment. When finally it did so, the electromagnetic spectrum rippled with the possibilities of the suggestion.

'The trand way will always prevail,' it concluded. 'They have not forgotten what they are, and it keeps them strong. Dare you risk the swap?'

'Of course.' No pause from the Champion, indicating bravado. 'It will be interesting to see the result.'

'Your Wilverton Player will not survive.'

'You have much to learn.'

'Course we should blame them! They all powerful – they don't do *anything* don't want to. *Instinct!* Most powerful thing in Universe, not amoeba!'

'Well, you and Peter have been squabbling over who should lead the group ever since we landed,' Gloria responded, and ignored Carlton's immediate expression of denial. 'That's the same sort of thing – instinct – and you're not meebers either.'

'Nothing like same! If I lead we get things done. I good at it. You don't understand. You . . .' Not have four brothers for a start, she thought. You never knew Lucky Larna . . .

'Stupid.' Gloria knew that was the word Fission had swallowed. 'You thick.' She tentatively sought Wilverton's eyes, afraid to find contempt, but knowing that she had to look.

Wilverton was staring at her. She *was* an enigma, this woman. Simple, with her meebers, but more common sense than many brilliant scientists he had met. He felt his heart swell, which was slightly uncomfortable given a rib-cage that couldn't hold a well-built gerbil.

It was a pity that none of this was really happening. Or was it a pity? In real life he would have loved her as much as he did in whatever work of fiction they were in, but he knew that she would never look twice at him in the cold world of fact; there wasn't enough of him to warrant a second glance. Sad. Still, it didn't mean he couldn't say something nice to her . . .

Gloria looked at the sad expression, waiting for the verdict. She watched him open his mouth to say something . . .

And he disappeared.

'*THOMAS!*'

The Champion watched the scene and a slow radio wave drifted to the Lessers.

'It is done.' Now to see who was right!

'*THOMAS!*' Gloria looked around frantically, snapping her head in all directions, and yelling at such volume as to attract the attention of a lot of people, a number of animals, and quite possibly a few previously slumbering dead.

'*Where is he? Where's he gone?*' She was sobbing, wringing her hands.

'What happened?' asked Carlton.

'*He disappeared! Where's he gone?*' She was distraught, and only Wilverton's reappearance could make her traught again.

'I don't know.' Carlton spoke quietly, gently. 'Calm down. What did you see?'

'*I didn't see anything!*' she screamed. '*He disappeared. You don't see anything when someone disappears! That's what "disappears" means! You can't see it any more!*'

'She's hysterical,' explained Carlton, avoiding Arnold's get-out-of-that-one smirk.

'Just 'cos made you look stupid?' asked Fission.

'*THOMAS!*'

'Look, she's hysterical.'

'Slap face then.'

'*I'm* not slapping her face. She's a woman. *You* slap her face.'

'*THOMAS!*'

Fission shrugged, swung, slapped.

It went quiet.

They all looked down.

'Oh, well done!' Arnold congratulated her, as they studied Gloria's inert form. 'That's two down. Three more and you can do all

33

the leading you want.'

'Fonk off, quark-brain.' She looked around, scanning quickly for any clues as to where Wilverton might have been transported, finding precisely none, and arriving at the nothing-to-be-done conclusion in a second. 'Let's get some money.' She looked towards the bank, now only twenty yards away, then down at Gloria. Problem. Well, she wasn't going anywhere . . . No. Maybe not. 'Arnold, bring her.'

'*You* knocked her out.'

'And *you* gonna carry her!'

'Now, now. You tried that without the magic word!'

Fission sighed, a lick of flame just failing to appear as she did so. 'Please, Arnold.'

'No.' Arnold smiled. They stared at each other for a moment, the silence only broken by the clash of antlers in the distance.

Curtis was on his knees, patting various bits of Gloria in a medically meaningless way. If any of them actually did the job of reviving her, thought Carlton, her first reaction would probably be to knock *him* out.

A small chimpanzee trotted up on knuckles and feet, chattering to itself. It stopped on Gloria's free side and looked at her through its red eyes. Carlton and Fission looked on with suspended judgement, as it watched what Curtis was doing, then turned its gaze on him.

He stopped.

Something in the chimpanzee's attitude suggested foolishness on his part. He wasn't sure how, but it was an attitude he had come to recognise.

'I am programmed in all medical matters,' the chimp said, and Fission nodded shortly. It picked up Gloria's arm, put it down, reached over and picked up her other one, as Curtis immediately gave way to superior medical skills.

'Where is her wrist?' asked the chimp, putting down the arm and looking up at Curtis.

'Er.' Just between her hand and her forearm? Too simple.

'Her wrist. She does not appear to have a wrist.'

'Er.'

The chimp held up its wrist and pointed, then made a circular motion, indicating that there should be something around it.

Curtis stared at it as though it were wearing a big pointy hat covered with stars.

'Wrist,' said the chimp, pointing.

34

'Wrist,' mimicked Curtis, and the chimp nodded encouragingly. It moved its finger around the wrist.

'Device,' it said, and Curtis frowned.

'She not have one,' Fission told the chimp, quite satisfied as to which of the anthropoids was more likely to get them moving again. 'If you want talk to him, you should start with "me hungry" point.'

The chimp ignored the advice – or maybe it just didn't want to talk to 'him'. 'He' wouldn't have been surprised. 'I will administer such help as I may.'

It laid a hand on Gloria's forehead, and they could see a faint glow where skin touched whatever the hand was made of. They couldn't see the stream of particles bouncing off various bits of the inner woman, nor the second, concentrating on those areas where the echo had shown something wrong, but within thirty seconds Gloria opened her eyes and looked groggily at the chimp.

'Thomas?' He hadn't shaved. And he'd shrunk a bit, unlikely though that seemed.

'It's the doctor,' Curtis told her.

'Oh.' It looked like a chimp.

'You should acquire a wrist,' the doctor told her.

'Yes, doctor.' She thought about this for a moment. It didn't help. 'I expect a spare is always useful.'

'Not really,' the chimp reported, then turned and scampered off.

'So what's a wrist?' Carlton grudgingly asked Fission.

'Someone in spaceport had light above wrist device. Guess it tells state of person wearing. Used to have on Earth.'

'You don't have them any more?' He helped Gloria to her feet, and she stood swaying. Built as she was, the body had its work cut out to avoid toppling at the best of times.

'No. Have internal microcomps; study body constantly, perform repairs all time, stop cancers at cell one, that sort thing.'

Carlton opened his mouth for another question, fascination suddenly overcoming everything else. And he wanted to take advantage of Fission's openness; so far she had been as forthcoming as a clam on a glue diet.

Too late.

'We get money or swap small talk 'til get killed?'

Given the choice, they entered the bank.

About twenty yards away, from the cover of a tree against which he leaned nonchalantly, a man with slicked back black hair, and

35

wearing a lightweight, but opaque, smock and slacks watched them go. He frowned, and waited.

'Next!'

As the last customer moved away, stowing a small plastic rectangle in a pouch since the clothing he was just about wearing couldn't stretch to a postage stamp, let alone a pocket, Fission led the charge of the fight brigade towards an ordinary looking counter, on the far side of which sat a woman wearing purple hair and not a lot else.

'In or out?' the woman asked, with the semblance of a smile.

'What?'

'Are you offworlders coming in or civs going out?'

Sieves?

'Want money,' Fission told her. The woman's expression slipped from uncommitted pleasantness to something approaching animosity; it was difficult to tell if that was a request or a hold-up.

'Excuse my associate,' Carlton interjected with his best come-to-bed smile. 'I'm afraid her definition of tact is "affixed to something by means of a tack". We *are* from off-world, but I do have an account here, I think.'

'Give me a hand,' she instructed, disinterest now uppermost in her voice. He frowned at her, wondering both what had caused an obvious lowering of her regard, and what on Earth Five Zero she meant. 'Well, come on!'

The customer/supplier relationship appeared to have become a little strained here, he thought, still frowning, and feeling smaller by the moment.

Behind him, a swaying Gloria started clapping, a little uncertainly. Fission said something with a quiet 'fonk' in it and Arnold looked at the ceiling. Curtis wasn't risking an overt opinion.

Then the outline of a hand appeared on the counter in front of the woman, Fission pointed at it, and Carlton laid his hand on it, feeling a light scrape across his palm as he did so.

A screen in front of the woman brightened, and the woman behind the screen paled.

'It has been a little while, er, sir, hasn't it,' she commented.

Carlton smiled inwardly. It was 'sir' now. 'About four hundred years, yes.'

'Yes.' She paused uncertainly, moved a hand towards the screen, then moved it back again.

'If you could react before it reaches five hundred?' Arnold

suggested, helpfully, but the brain inside the woman's ears was apparently busy.

'Why aren't you dead?'

'If don't hurry, we will be,' Fission told her.

'I'll just have to check with Central,' she said, making the decision that she wasn't about to make a decision. 'If you will excuse me.'

A bald head emerged from the stripway exit, with, underneath it, a face as red as a robot's eyes, and further down, a dog taking a deep breath while it had the chance. Looking around, Stay brightened considerably at the sight of trees, but LOVE could immediately see no-one at all who looked anything like his prey, and his colour deepened to something that threatened seizure.

He would just have to rely on a hunch.

The Challenger allowed a brief wisp of ultraviolet to escape into the ether, for the sole purpose of riling its opponent.

Hunches were easy.

LOVE smiled.

Where did people go as soon as they left the spaceport? They went to the bank to change their dings. He yanked Stay off his current tripod. The dog glanced backwards, sadly. So many trees, such a small bladder . . .

'Well, Central says it's okay, so I guess that means it's okay.'

'Well worked out,' Arnold congratulated her. 'Mind like a rapier.'

She frowned at him. 'I don't *have* to do this, you know. I'm just sitting in for someone else today. I make my money painting.'

Arnold looked impressed. 'Walls? Doors?'

'What?'

'Arnold!' hissed Gloria, groggily.

'Can we get on?' Carlton asked, and the woman was back with him in an instant. Sea change? he thought; this is the whole Pacific. Amazing what money can do.

'Sorry, sir. Do you want a key?'

'To the vault?'

Well, it was possible, the woman thought, looking at the figures on the screen. He probably owned the thing.

'Key – chitin key – is . . .' Fission searched for the words, '. . . credit card where you come from. Not everywhere has DNA facilities. Don't need one yet.'

'Apparently not,' Carlton told the woman.

And that was that. He made to turn away.

'Excuse me.'

She had found a reason to continue the conversation – they all did. And to think he had been worried! He turned back, smiled again.

'I don't mean to be personal, but are you all right?' She looked concerned.

The smile faltered. 'Yes, fine. Why?'

'Well, you don't look very well, that's all. You look a bit sickly.'

He frowned his weak, grotesque frown, and Fission chuckled for the first time since they had met her.

'Next!'

'What now?' asked Gloria. 'How do we find Thomas?' Her voice was as plaintive as an orphaned kitten's miaow. Carlton shrugged, wondering if he could get some plastic surgery somewhere. Curtis wasn't going to risk a suggestion because they would just shout at him. They stood just inside the bank's entrance and looked miserable.

Most of them. Fission looked frustrated.

She glared about her at the downcast faces. They had to get moving. No time for self-pity. Never was.

Must try some man-management.

'For fonk's sake snap out of it, you bunch povvos!' she managed. 'Nothing we can do about skinny little nutter,' she motivated. 'If he's dead, he's dead. No profit moping. If don't get move on soon, we'll *all* be dead!'

There. Did that do it?

No. Apparently not.

'Luc! We got Game to win for humanity! For us! We got *do* something!' Fission looked around. Suggestions were scarcer than nun jokes in the Pope's Easter message.

'I think we should attack,' said Carlton. He couldn't attack the woman sitting behind him, now dealing – smilingly – with some semi-naked Adonis and his luggage-lugging robot. Not that that bothered him. 'Whether Wilverer Thomas is right or not, whether it's the robot or not, we can't just wait until it gets us. We should get it first.'

'How do you know it's just one?' asked Gloria.

'Because only one person gets shot at a time,' Carlton told her, shrugging. She nodded slowly, sadly, he thought. 'I reckon it's some sniper.'

Then Curtis risked it. He wasn't completely sure if he believed it, but he thought it would be nice to be on the same side as Carlton and Fission.

'I agree . . .'

'Thank God!' Arnold oozed relief, but Curtis still flowed.

'I think we should turn the tables and attack. He's sort of like the lone predator and we must be . . .' Damn! Never start a metaphor unless you know how it's going to finish. '. . . Jackals. The pack always wins in the end; it's the law of the jungle.' There. He smiled inwardly. '*Ow!*'

He spun round, grabbing his leg, which someone had just kicked. There was a familiar face staring at him; two, counting the tear-stained visage of Krela. As he rubbed his leg, Krela's mother kicked it again.

Behind mother and child, a perfect specimen of manhood looked at him, tight lipped, chitin key in hand.

'He's the one from the spaceport that I told you about,' she informed the man.

'What did you do that for?' Curtis asked.

'You're disgusting!'

'Why?' He sounded like his chin was going to pucker at any moment.

'You and Krela wait over there, Marqa,' the man said.

Oh, bloody hell, thought Curtis. Now what? He looked round at his crew, his colleagues, his friends. Some of them smiled at him. Gloria wasn't smiling at anyone – she was still having enough trouble stopping her body from falling over, let alone getting bits of it to move independently.

'Now listen . . .' The man's face was visibly reddening. 'It isn't clever talking like that, you know. If you want to talk dirty, you don't do it in front of my partner and child. All right?'

'But . . .' He looked round again. He'd have got more support from a meringue. 'But . . .' This wasn't fair!

The man leaned close, and there was real anger in his eyes. 'You offworlders may be throwbacks, but we're decent people here!'

He stalked off, collected his partner and wide-eyed child, and ushered them from the bank.

'They're weird,' Curtis complained.

Fission shrugged. 'This their planet. We play by their rules.'

'But what did I say?' Every time he mentioned animals, he upset

39

someone. Every time he mentioned *anything*, he upset someone.

The episode had at least dragged Carlton to the surface of his slough of despond, even if he just floated there like scum. 'We'd better find this hotel.' He led the way outside.

Then the bank fell on them.

Not all of it.

Just bits of it.

But that's all you need where banks are concerned.

An arch blown to medium-sized smithers flew in all directions with exactly the aerodynamic ability normally associated with wingless masonry, while the five staggered in nearly as many directions with their heads pulled rather uselessly into the collars of their jump-suits.

Carlton put a protective arm around Gloria's shoulder – about as protective as a head scarf in a flood, but it's the thought that counts, and she was grateful for it. Curtis thought he saw a terrified Fission darting off to one side, but then felt a rough push in the back and received the advice to 'Move butt!' and, even in the confusion and noise, recognised the much more Fission-like behaviour.

Animals screamed in terror, the smaller ones darting out of the way with robotic speed, disappearing into foliage. A group of red-eyed meerkats suddenly forgot some internal squabble and rushed for the safety of their burrows.

Two people were moving towards the building, suggesting that they weren't people – or if they were, that they didn't want to be for much longer.

Customers either threw themselves on the ground, or were knocked there by bits of bank, and were immediately tended by humanoids and the larger, remaining animals, who ignored role-playing and impacts while they protected their human masters and began administering first aid.

More bits exploded off the building as it was hit again by something, and a cloud of dust made escape more luck than judgement.

But then it was quiet and the dust began to settle, to reveal, despite their headless-chicken defence tactics, the Champion's team, completely untouched.

Unbelievable.

Not for the Challenger, it wasn't. Annoying, certainly, but quite believable.

40

The Champion could not directly affect the trajectory of the masonic missiles – well, it *could*, but the Lessers would have no choice but to declare a foul and disqualify it – but it could interpolate the trajectories of the various bits subject to impact, and affect the direction of the particle beam so that it hit the arch in the right place.

Or, to be more exact, it could affect the muscle twitch which, in turn, determined the precise angle of the gun barrel.

Or, to be even more exact, it could affect the outcome of a thought concerning the choice of food in LOVE's last meal such that the absorption of nutrients into the body, coupled with the body's chemical reaction to those nutrients, would result in precisely the right twitch by precisely the right muscle at precisely the right time.

If the Champion had possessed an arse, it would have been a really smart one.

The Challenger did take some consolation from the fact that the Champion had apparently missed a trick. It should have been possible to direct a particular piece of disintegrating bank at the LOVE human, and put him out of the Game, and yet the Champion had not done so.

The Challenger was satisfied.

But so was the Champion, if its radio waves could be believed.

The Challenger frowned suspiciously at that, utilising a brief and controlled burst of visible yellow, since evolution had withdrawn the eyebrow facility.

All of which was lost on the team. They neither knew nor cared how sartorially elegant was the Champion's metaphysical bottom; they simply knew that the crashing all around them had *been* all around them, and they shuffled together into some semblance of a group.

Just off to one side, a male gorilla with a silver back effortlessly lifted a bit of bank from his leg. His smaller mate brushed herself down while, safely clinging onto her via a handful of fur, a youngster watched the upside down world gone mad through rose coloured eyeballs. The male collected his partner and wide-eyed child and ushered them from the ex-bank.

'You want go on attack now?' Fission asked Carlton and Curtis.

Carlton smiled grimly. Curtis tried the same thing, but his lips were too busy quivering to bend upwards with any panache. There was a time to be a jackal, he thought, and time to be . . . something that runs very fast in the opposite direction.

Carlton pointed to where a crowd appeared to be gathered on the

grass a couple of hundred yards away. 'Come on. Safety in numbers.'
They hurried across the grass, trying not to tempt fate by thinking
that no-one appeared to be shooting at them any more.

It occurred to Carlton that 'safety in numbers' would not apply to
all the others they were about to draw into the fray – more like
'extreme danger in numbers'. He shrugged. Now was perhaps not
the time for philanthropic sacrifice.

It occurred to Arnold as well, but then the phrase 'human shield'
didn't hold any shameful connotations for him – on reflection, he
thought it was probably at least as good a use for the creatures as
anything else.

LOVE watched them go, then looked accusingly at the power gauge
on his gun. Stay gazed at him confidently. The pack leader had great
magic; he would know what to do.

LOVE shook the weapon and thumped it against his free hand.

Great magic.

The gauge failed to respond.

'Come on, Stay. The stripway, and we must hurry.'

Can't we walk?

V

They mingled with the crowd, heads down – superfluously so, since they were an average couple of inches shorter in any case. Carlton absent-mindedly picked a few bits of masonry off his jump-suit before remembering that in this body-built company it wouldn't matter how smart he looked. Then someone brushed against him and his hopes immediately rose until he turned to see Gloria looking for support from the two people in front of her that looked like Peter. He held her arm and she smiled lop-sidedly.

'Your family only manages to acquire degrees by instructing a higher temperature!' came a strident voice, and the crowd clapped appreciatively. Carlton stretched on tip-toe, pausing only to hate the God of Little Stubby Legs, and saw two men facing each other on a raised dais. Red facing each other.

One was bald and dressed in a long white robe; he looked pleased with himself. The other wore the more normal, chiffon very little, with green swirls, and his olive skin blushed. At least, the olive skin on his face did – Carlton would let Gloria check out the rest of him.

Which she did when she caught sight of him through a gap in the crowd. But she saw only Thomas; although the similarities between this physical triumph and Wilverton surely ended with the coincidence of limb numbers. Or maybe not, through the eyes of love – especially the unfocussed eyes of love.

'If I were to cast aspersions on your intelligence, you would probably thank me for the flowers,' Chiffon told Follicle Defeat. The crowd rippled with muted applause – clever, but lacking something.

'What's going on?' Gloria asked the back of Fission's head as the words of the protagonists worked their way through to her brain and confused it.

'It's an election debate,' came the reply, but not from Fission. The man standing by her side had slicked back black hair, topping off another perfect bloody body. A pace behind, Carlton managed not to snarl at him.

'Election?' he asked.

'Election,' the man confirmed in a slow drawl, turning towards him. While the body was no less well formed than all the others, the face showed lines, and the expression would have better suited the centre of attention on a scaffold. It was a face worn by worry, a sad face; it reminded Carlton of a slow saxophone solo. 'For World President.'

'There's a World President?' Carlton split his attention between the man and Fission, experts on two different worlds. Fission shrugged and Arnold answered.

'Perhaps they just like elections.'

'Yes, there's a World President,' the man confirmed, giving Arnold a doubtful look, still somehow tinged with melancholy – sort of dubious lugubrious – then turned back to Carlton. 'You're not civs, are you, or have you just been out of circulation for a while?'

A moment of thoughtful silence, then:

'We come from Earth Prime, four hundred years ago, in a different quantum Universe and we've been sent here to find a renegade robot, who is some sort of danger to this planet, as part of a Game played by super aliens who will kill us if we lose so long as we don't die anyway while we're losing.'

Said Curtis.

Well, he thought, he was the one who always got disbelieved, so it was obviously his job to say the things that sounded idiotic so that he could maintain the tradition.

Gloria wondered what she could do to cheer him up, but was too miserable herself to find an answer.

Curtis *was* trying to snap himself out of it. Ever since he was a boy, he had imagined that he had a little man on each shoulder, one who said positive things into his left ear, while the other spoke negatives into his right.[1] Whenever he felt miserable, he tried to listen to the positive and ignore the negative. Right now, all he could hear from the plus side was the gun being loaded with a single bullet.

'Ah,' said the man, and his expression took on a sub-layer of . . . something. 'I see. Yes, that *would* explain it.'

'You believe me?' The surprise showed in Curtis's voice a bit like Everest peeks above sea level.

'I have no reason not to believe you. Just because what you say sounds . . .' Bollocks? Like the ravings of a lunatic? '. . . a little unusual.'

[1] At least it gave him someone to talk to.

'Why, thank you!' Curtis pushed a hand at the man, who looked at it as though it smelled of germs that had gone off. 'My name's Richard Curtis.' He smiled, and withdrew the hand, untouched, not letting the slight twitch of the man's nostrils push him off this new path of friendship.

'Tamon.' He *didn't* smile. Possibly never had, thought Carlton. 'So, you are over four hundred years old?'

'Yes, I suppose so,' Curtis admitted.

The sub-layer of expression pushed its way to the surface momentarily, and Carlton saw – what? Revulsion, fear? But then it was gone again, and he just looked plain bloody miserable.

'What do you mean, "renegade robot"?'

'Hasn't got basics. Been removed.' Fission backed up Curtis's story; she, too, was studying his reaction. Tamon's eyebrows rose, pulling some of the creases from his face like a child hoisting trousers that are far too long.

'The only reason you like whale song is that your grandmother is shaped like one,' said Chiffon, to loud applause and the odd 'whoop'. The team ignored it, bar Curtis, who looked up and began to point at the Foundation member.

'This isn't helping us find Thomas, you know!' Gloria was sounding better, on the verge of anger. Guilt immediately failed to overwhelm them.

'We've got to find the robot, first,' Carlton told her. 'That might give us some clues to where he is.'

'Who is Thomas?' asked Tamon.

Tamon was not acting like someone who normally met Curtis and company, Carlton thought, in that he was still there.

'He's the cleverest one in our group,' said Gloria defiantly. 'But he just disappeared after we'd got away from the airport.'

'Spaceport,' corrected Curtis automatically, still pointing.

'It's the same thing,' said Gloria, irritably. 'Air is space, isn't it!' Curtis noticed that this was not a question. Gloria turned back to Tamon. 'We need Thomas because he always comes up with clever answers.'

'Sounds useful.' Tamon didn't sound sure. 'I could do with a few clever answers myself.'

We've picked another winner here, thought Fission. His outlook on life seemed to originate from a window ledge.

'He's from the Foundation Foundation,' said Curtis into the pause, pleased to be able both to lower his aching arm from

45

indicating Follicle Defeat, and to impart a bit of personal knowledge.

'The what?' Carlton frowned. 'Science fiction fans, are they?'

'They're standing in the election,' said Tamon. 'I don't know much about them, but then I don't go in for politics; I've never seen the point in gambling. Not with my luck. They talk about simple virtues, going back to the past, stuff like that. Bit kinky if you ask me.'

Carlton frowned. 'What's that round his neck?'

'I wondered that,' said Curtis. 'It seems to be a monkey that's had an enormous needle stuck up its . . . well, you know.'

'Rectum?' ventured Tamon.

'Well, it wouldn't have done them any good,' said Arnold, then adopted the punchline pose and added, 'Ta ra!' Tamon gave him a glance of pure disbelief. He wasn't alone. Arnold shrugged.

'Look, this isn't helping us get *Thomas* back.' Gloria nearly stamped her foot. 'When I got kidnapped he was the first one to come and look for me.'

She was right and there was the little matter of a Game to the death. Carlton addressed Tamon, still with a frown, but one of puzzlement as much as unhappiness.

'Have you any idea where we could start looking for a robot?'

'Anything to go on?'

'Nothing. Biondor just said a household robot had gone renegade.'

'Well, we can check with Central, see if one's been reported missing.'

'Let's go for profit!' Fission clapped her hands together in the distressingly eager way she had whenever there was a chance to get up and at 'em. I bet she's got a big 'S' tattooed on her chest, thought Carlton. 'How we get there?'

'We don't have to get there.' Tamon's hands moved toward each other, then stopped. 'We just need to find a terminal. There'll be one in the bank, but I guess that's out of action. I think there's one over there somewhere.' He indicated an area some distance away where a group of trees provided shade from the strong sunshine. 'Come on, I'll show you.'

They followed him away from the crowd, Carlton bringing up the rear, his face bearing not the semblance of a smile, but not, currently, due to the fact that it wouldn't attract a mate in a brothel. It was very fortunate, he thought, that they just happened to meet someone who not only was gullible enough to believe them, but had now offered to help them.

More than fortunate.

Someone, also, who, although he said he didn't go in for politics, had happened across them in the middle of a crowd watching an election debate.

Either the Champion was working overtime, he concluded, or the Challenger was working overtime.

VI

He was walking through grass lush enough to be proud of it, in bright sunlight.

Then he was . . . nowhere; blackness and no feeling, for how long? A moment? A year?

Then a sharp bump to bony buttocks and he was . . .

Given that some of it had started with wings and the ability to get airborne, there was a certain full-circle element to the food flying through the air, but the individual bits of bird would never get together to flap a wing again; and, anyway, the atmosphere a couple of feet above the table was just as full of ex-ground-based unfortunates.

Mr and Mrs Average Trand and family were breaking their fast, their wind, several tankards, a good part of their furniture, and the only thing that saved the plates was the fact that there weren't any. While the table may not have been clean enough to eat off, they were doing just that.

If the food ever managed to drop down that far.

With five family members, and thirty arms between them, smash and grab took on the aspect of a macabre, fast moving, stationary sport. The rules appeared simple – the biggest arms got the biggest bits of food. None of your 'please sir, I want some more' here; you wanted, you took, or suffered a compound fracture trying.

Until suddenly all activity stopped when the centrepiece of the feast revealed itself as a small, blue jump-suited, bipedal creature rubbing a bony buttock.

. . . in the middle of a breakfast table.

Fine, he thought.

What book am I in now?

Wilverton took in his surroundings in an instant. He was in the centre of an enormous table, and around him were what looked like the bits that the abattoir would make into fertiliser if they could find anyone with a stomach strong enough. He didn't recognise the animals – and they sure as hell weren't going to recognise him – but the remains didn't look terrestrial.

Around the table sat a number of creatures, or squatted – it was hard to tell, and, for Wilverton, irrelevant. The upper bodies were of more interest, because they contained the bits that could grab him.

Lots of them.

Six such bits each; big enough to qualify for the description of arms only in the same way as could siege engines. Covered in what looked like armour-plating that was beginning to lose interest in the battle against rust, they were all holding various bits of various animals, preparatory to stuffing them into their mouths.

Which were currently open, pointing at Wilverton, and displaying semi-masticated body bits.

These were not wimps, he thought – or 'povvos' as the word appeared to have become in Fission's world. These were not the sort of creatures who took a vacation by the sea and got sand kicked in their faces. These were not the kind of creatures who took part in a galactic Game played by bodiless super-beings and lost easily.

These are trands, he thought.

'Cor! Live meat! How'd you do that, Mum?' The first creature to react, after the moment of stunned silence, dropped what might once have been a vital organ – now the exact opposite – and reached out.

Wilverton flinched, but another hand from a larger creature slapped the youth away.

'What do you say, smaller?'

'Grub up?' he ventured, and an incorrect guess was indicated by a smack round the head. 'Want?' Whack. 'Gimme?' Wallop.

'You want new food you ask the biggest's permission. You go to college and what happens? Where's your manners gone?'

Manners? thought Wilverton, perversely, and his mind flashed him a picture of a Sunday afternoon tea table in Hertfordshire, with cucumber sandwiches, best Doulton china, and the hosts being torn into mouth-sized chunks by peckish trands.

He looked around quickly with exit in mind. The room was spartan, just simple and rather shabby stonework – it looked less like it had been built up than dropped down. There was a door in the far wall, past a supposed trand the size of a small brontosaurus, and a window a couple of yards away from the table's edge, devoid of glass, through which he could see up to a dark mass of storm clouds, but

49

not down. He couldn't see the ground.

Still, he thought, that was the obvious way to go. Just leap through it.

Not only because it was a better bet than the door.

But because . . . well, because he was one of the heroes, and he wouldn't get hurt.

Simple.

'Please, biggest, can I have its head?'

'Org gry.' Swallow. 'All right, but I want the teeth. Nice crunchy. Mother get squishy middle. Daughter, smaller son, leg each.'

It takes weeks of patient training to get a dog to jump through a hoop, thought Wilverton, in mid-air. Put it in the middle of this lot, threaten to eat it and it would learn damned fast or not at all.

He described a gymnastic arc, at the same time thinking that a dog wouldn't understand trand speech; was through the window without touching the sides, and he frowned at the thought, because he *had* understood; performed quite the most exquisite somersault so as to land on his feet, and thinking back they *were* grunts he had heard and not proper words, let alone in English, and instead, crashed back-first into a muddy hollow four feet below the window ledge, which temporarily concentrated his mind. He might not have made the final of the competition, he thought, but at least he was alive to feel the disappointment.

It had been the ground floor, of course.

He looked around and saw a jumble of low buildings that gave ruins a bad name, but no creatures.

Those grunts, then. It must have been trandian, and he had understood it.

He moved quickly away from where he was in the direction of something that looked like exactly where he was only somewhere else – there wasn't a lot to choose from in the homogeneous dilapidation. Vague noises of life knocked on his ears but he didn't know where they came from so he ignored them while their creators stayed out of sight.

If he understood it, did that mean he could speak it?

He tried to formulate a few words, knowing in his mind how they should sound, but managed only noises reminiscent of someone bending low over a toilet and clutching their stomach.

He noticed, through a gap between two buildings, what looked like a featureless plain, and made for it, reasoning that these creatures would be easy to see where there was no cover. They'd be

50

easy to see in a tank factory, come to that, but he didn't know where he might find one of those.

He ducked past a window. At least he didn't have to argue about who should lead and he almost smiled at those he had left behind, until he recalled that Gloria was one of them.

If only she was real . . .

She is, came a voice in his head. So are you. You come from the real Earth, Earth Prime. You *are* real. This *is* happening.

It's not! It's a book, and you're the hero. If it was real life you wouldn't be. You're not the hero type.

He stopped short as he cleared the last of the buildings, the thought pushed from his mind by another. A featureless plain might be bottom of the trand hiding-place list, but it wasn't all that high on the Wilvertonian one either. Small he might be, but he wasn't quite invisible, even if he turned sideways.

He squatted down and leaned against the side of the building – carefully; it was already leaning enough for both of them – took a deep breath after the exertions of his seventy metre dash, and pondered.

Drifting to his ears, and being noticed now he had stopped, were the noises of what he presumed was everyday trandian life – if it *was* Trand – grunts and shouts of anger and challenge, the sound of multiple fists slamming into craggy skin, and an unceasing animal keening, which Wilverton guessed came from animals who were anything but keen. On the other side of the ramshackle stonework, he guessed he would find some sort of animal market in full swing, and a load of arms the same way. He wasn't about to check.

At least he was safe for now.

Safe on Trand?

'I bet this *is* Trand,' he muttered to himself.

'It is,' replied a voice just behind him, making him jump.

Well, making him flinch a bit; had he jumped from the crouching position he had adopted he would have looked less like he was hiding as doing calisthenics, and he was leaving those to his heart, which suddenly was trying to find any old way clean out of his chest – favourite being the southerly route which his stomach was about to vacate.

He looked up to, from his position, a rather disconcerting view of a naked, fawn-coloured alien who stood calmly and looked down at him in an unspoken invitation to rise. He rose, but even knowing that Biondor was far more knowing, he still kept his neck as short as

51

you can without the help of Henvy VIII's divorce lawyer.

'Biondor,' he said, which in this situation was his equivalent of 'er'. 'I presume you are behind my transportation here?'

Wilverton's heart slowed to danger level as Biondor's calmness suggested safety. The two unseen craggy faces watching them from a window across what was either the street or the result of a localised earthquake – trandquake – suggested anything but.

'Indirectly. It is required by the Champion and Challenger.'

'Why?'

'They did not see fit to furnish me with a reason.'

It was odd to think of Biondor as an inferior being, when, to Wilverton and the rest, he was so patently superior. It was also time-consuming to think that, so Wilverton only did it for an instant.

'And this is Trand, is it?'

'It is Trand, although it is not Trand Prime. It is a version of the planet which is rather more . . .'

'Hurrrggghhh!!' came a comment from a window.

'. . . primitive than the more "real" version.'

It wasn't the fault of the inhabitants of Trand Whatever; they just hadn't got the conventional kick start towards scientific knowledge . . .

The mamble tree sucked moisture from the soil and split it into its constituent gaseous parts, discarding the oxygen and using the hydrogen as a fuel for its growth and also as a rather nifty way of distributing seeds via its distinctive purple fruits.

Under a mamble one day sat one of Trand Whatever's leading scientists, pondering the workings of the universe – why the sun seemed to revolve around Trand and not go wandering off on a trajectory all its own; why the moons faithfully clung to their mother planet instead of striking out for the wide black yonder, and why the nearer of the two moved so much quicker.

As he was thinking, a fruit detached itself from the mamble, and would have fallen into his lap had it been, say, an apple. As it was a mamble fruit, full of pips and hydrogen, it shot straight upwards instead.

The scientist watched it go, discarded the embryonic gravitational theory that was growing in his mind, and stomped off for a few beers.

(Such is history.)

Wilverton nodded from an instantly resumed crouch position, wondering how Biondor could remain unperturbed; convinced as he was by the noises from across the way that now would be an excellent time for a quick perturb.

'I saw it first!' floated across the street, like a brick.

'You're younger. It's mine.'

'I'm bigger!'

'I'm stronger!'

'Are not!'

'Am too!'

The sibling debate immediately moved from the word stage to the pummelling-with-great-ferocity-and-little-finesse technique, and Biondor still looked as troubled as the tabby in the tufted.

'They will be busy for a while yet.'

Wilverton rose again, gingerly, every instinct telling him to run, but the brain trusting Biondor just enough. 'So if I'm here, does that mean there's a trand loose on Earth Five Zero?'

'It means there is a trand *present* on Earth Five Zero; or that there will be – the passage of time on the two planets may not be the same, according to the decisions of the Champion and Challenger, so tenses become somewhat confusing.'

Fair enough, thought Wilverton.

'Whether he is loose or not is something I cannot say.'

Not fair enough. Judging from what he had seen so far, Wilverton had little doubt that the thing was loose. He had more important things to worry about.

'Are any of the others here?'

'You are the only human on the planet.'

Wilverton thought for a moment. 'Do the others know I'm here?'

'They do not know. As far as they are concerned, you simply disappeared. There is no way of them finding out for sure that you are here, although it may be possible for them to deduce the fact. I judge it unlikely, however.' Which, Wilverton knew, was Biondor's alienly euphemistic way of saying he wouldn't trust them to deduce the presence of an elephant from an elephant-shaped shadow and the sudden juxtaposition of four tons of elephant shit.

'Can you get a message to them? Can you tell Gloria that I'm all right. And . . .' He paused, embarrassed, and a part of his brain studied the phenomenon for its rarity value. 'And can you tell her that . . . that I love her?' There. He'd said it.

'No. Sorry.'

'Oh.'

'It is not my decision, you understand.' Biondor was not given to explanations – when he ventured one he generally made it as non-sensical as possible and then playfully called it a Revelation – but this human team was, he admitted, growing on him. A bit like a wart in the shape of a smiling face; you'd be better off without it, but there was something . . .

Wilverton flinched slightly as a shard of stone exploded from the window surrounds in front of the brothers and pinged past his ear. He glanced nervously across the street.

'What am I here to do? Are you allowed to tell me that?'

'I am sorry. All I can say is that the Champion chose you, especially, for this task.'

What should I make of that? Wilverton wondered. Peter would smile and grow a bit; Fission would probably punch the air – and anything else that happened to be in the vicinity – but I'm not like that. Which is probably the point . . .

'I see. Or rather, I don't, yet.'

'The Champion will no doubt furnish you with all advantages allowed within the Rules of the Game.'

'Which are?'

'Well, normally next to nothing, but you never know your inadvertent fortuity.' He paused momentarily. 'I must now visit the planet Moros and turn a certain unrepentant recalcitrant into a pillar of salt. Or pepper. Or possibly mustard.' He shook his head. 'Well, some sort of condiment, anyway. I must leave you now. The fight is about to finish, and the attention of the juveniles will return to yourself. It would be wise, when they approach, to be somewhere else.'

Having said which, Biondor disappeared in that frustrating way that aliens have, leaving Wilverton with a head full of questions that only he himself could now answer. Except that he couldn't.

VII

'Why are all these robot animals here?' asked Gloria, as they followed Tamon across what she presumed was a park. Tamon glanced at her, a little uncomfortably, she thought.

'As opposed to where?'

'No, I don't mean they should be somewhere else. Why are they robots? Is it because you leave all the real animals where they belong?'

Tamon didn't answer immediately, and Gloria saw the discomfort increase.

'There aren't any real animals. Not any more.'

Gloria stopped. She looked like she was about to sway again, and Carlton moved forwards, but it was only her chin that dropped.

'What happened to them?'

Tamon looked at her, watching the blood drain from her face. 'I guess you really *are* four hundred years old, aren't you,' he said quietly, to himself, before raising his voice only just enough for them to hear. 'They all died out. Mankind expanded when the robots were able to do everything for us, when Central was created, and their natural habitat disappeared. They followed. Obviously our ancestors were nowhere near as civilised as we are today. We make the animals,' and he paused almost imperceptibly, 'so we know what they were like.'

'That's horrible.' Gloria was looking accusingly at Tamon. 'That's awful!'

'No more hamburgers,' added Arnold, but she ignored him.

'Those poor animals. Aren't there *any* left?'

'Well, there are pets;[1] their habitat got bigger with man's. Apart from that, hardly any.'

'How could you!'

'We didn't! Back then, humans were, well,' he lowered his voice

---

[1] So you could presumably still get an old-fashioned curry.

55

again, even looked around, 'little better than animals themselves.'

'Is there a . . .' began Curtis, looking uncomfortable, then clearly had an idea. 'Is that why people keep hitting me?'

'Could be hundreds of reasons,' Arnold pointed out.

'No, I mean when I mentioned animals, and people being like them.'

Tamon looked sick. Sicker. 'Such a suggestion is quite obscene.' There was an edge to his voice. 'And for obvious reasons, since we clearly are nothing like animals any more.'

'But . . .' Curtis stopped in mid-argument. 'Look, I'm sorry, is there a toilet around anywhere? I've been meaning to go ever since we landed.'

'Er.' The change from historical global catastrophe to Curtis's bladder seemed to catch Tamon unawares. 'I don't think there's one very near here . . .' He looked round, as though a toilet might suddenly sprout.

'Use tree.' Fission pointed to a small copse off to their left.

'You *will* wait?'

Fission's expression sent him on his way before Arnold could deny the existence of a chance, and he trotted off, with the little voice from his right asking if that was *exactly* the parting question for a Captain . . .?

The Champion studied the planets in the Milky Way galaxy of this quantum Universe. Took about a third of a nanosecond.

'Vansasians,' it thought to itself, for no apparent reason.

A slow smile of relief spread across Curtis's face, as a dark stain of relief spread across the base of the tree.

He fastened the jump-suit, managing not to catch any important bits in the zip, wiped his foot on a nearby leaf,[1] and turned to face the semi-circle of gorillas who sat staring at him out of big brown eyes.

He turned the other way, to face the other semi-circle of gorillas.

Two semi-circles.

He was good at maths.

He wasn't good at gorillas.

Now, they're only robots, said the little man on his left shoulder.

Very large robots, mean looking, said the right.

---

[1] The only animal in the multiverse that can pee against a tree and keep its feet dry is the male Bostal, whose main attribute is extremely obvious, if a little unsavoury in polite company. Suffice it to say they have very long arms, as well, and need them.

Don't show fear. They can smell fear. Even through pee-covered tree bark, they can smell fear.

Curtis believed that – he could smell fear himself just then; it was very like rotten eggs.

Be bold. Show them who's boss.

Look, they *know* who's boss!

Bluff them.

Bluff them?

Go on the attack, most of it's all show with animals anyway.

I don't believe it! Okay, have it your own way; I don't know why I bother, I really don't!

Curtis stood as tall as God would allow, stared the biggest gorilla straight in the eye, puffed his chest out like a sparrow fluffing its feathers, and beat his fists against it. He launched into a spirited 'Singalongatarzan' to go with the action, but almost immediately segued into 'Coughalongadick', before heaving a wheeze in between the fast-forming bruises.

The gorilla in front of him reached into an unlikely pocket and withdrew some half-moon spectacles, which he placed delicately on his stub of a nose. He scrutinised the convulsed Curtis for a few moments, then turned to the slightly smaller creature next to him.

'What in heaven's name is it doing, do you suppose? And what is it anyway?'

The other looked around, frowning at Curtis, the foliage, and up at the sky.

'I don't think we're on Vansas any more, Momo.'

Momo shook his head contemplatively, and his glasses fell off. Curtis looked up in some confusion as he replaced them.

'We should do *something*,' said another, a dark brown animal off to Curtis's left. He looked that way.

'What?' asked Momo's neighbour. Curtis looked back. Wimbledon wasn't in it.

'I don't know. Whose turn is it to decide?'

'Momo? Is it you?'

'I decided yesterday. I chose bananas for dinner.'

'You always choose bananas for dinner.'

'I *like* bananas!'

'*Everyone* always chooses bananas for dinner,' commented a fourth, from the other side.

'Well, someone's got to decide. Shouldn't we kill it or something?' suggested Brown.

'Well, we could, I suppose . . .'

'Why do you want to kill it?' asked Neighbour, in a tone that did not completely dismiss the idea.

'I don't, necessarily. It was just a suggestion.'

Curtis watched the rally continue for a while, without anyone attempting a winning shot, then started shuffling towards the biggest gap between the smallest gorillas that he could find.

When she stood still, Gloria noticed, she thought more. Her brain obviously didn't have as much to do.

When she thought more, her mind filled with dead animals and Thomas.

She looked around for something to occupy her attention, because the alternative was to start hopping from foot to foot, and that would make people think she was funny.

A big hologram was the first thing she saw; of the bald head of a Foundation Foundation member, captured while wearing a smile that struck her as not having quite as much gorm as it might. Under its neck was a caption.

'Miron is a Complete Wanker. Vote for Pomona.'

Next to it was another, showing a woman whose purple hair was gathered into tresses which didn't just defy gravity, but held up two fingers to it for good measure. She was caught in the act of stifling a yawn. The caption read,

'Pomona has the Social Grace of a Fart in a Library. Vote for Miron.'

At least animals never try to belittle each other, she thought. What if they could, though? she wondered. Would the walrus pull itself up to its full height and be really sarcastic? It was the same thing, really.

'All the people seem to be very, er, fit,' Carlton said, quietly, to Tamon.

'Yes, I suppose so. Not unusually so, I wouldn't have said.'

'No. That's the point. Not unusually so. They *all* look *extremely* fit.' Carlton lowered his voice even more. 'Not to mention physically, sort of, perfect.'

'How can you be "sort of" perfect?' asked Arnold from behind him. Thanks to some inadvertent improvement to his auditory mechanism by Curtis way back on the old Pioneer, Arnold could hear a beetle belch in a burrow.

'All *right*, perfect, then,' Carlton corrected. He threw a glance over his shoulder at the android, who smiled sweetly. Carlton knew better

58

than to rile Arnold too far; while Arnold refused to believe that it was *possible* to rile anyone too far.

'Well, they're meant to be perfect,' said Tamon, as if that explained everything.

'But how do they manage it?'

'They're built that way.'

'Built? You mean they're robots?' Hope dawned in his voice like the first day of spring.

'No, they're human' – it was a wet spring – 'but they've been engineered that way.'

Engineered?

'Genetic engineering?'

'Of course.'

Did that make it any better? Well, not here it didn't – he still felt like the runt of the litter – but what about on Earth proper, Earth Prime? He glanced at Fission, and tried to think of a way of putting it that might elicit just an answer.

'They don't have it on Earth Prime, then.'

He hadn't thought of one.

Arnold beamed. This was going to be excellent.

Fission looked at Carlton with a neutral expression – but then a metal container is just a metal container until it detonates.

'No,' she said calmly. What might have happened if they did? she wondered.

'Oh.' Well that's good, he thought. But as Fission looked away, he felt somehow that he had lost, and they lapsed into a silence so awkward it made Curtis look lithe. Carlton tried to find something with which to break out of it.

'You still play football, anyway,' he commented, indicating a game some twenty yards away where several people were throwing an oval ball to one another. But they weren't catching it. It was stopping when it got to within a few inches of their hands, and they never touched it – it was like they had four-inch thick, invisible gloves on.

As he watched, the ball flew high over the intended receiver's head, and aimed straight for Tamon, who was clearly not paying attention. Carlton was about to offer a 'Look out!' when it was too late, but the ball bounced off, four inches before it reached Tamon, and flew straight at Carlton instead, arriving before he had a chance to react. And, inevitably, arriving half way down him, right *there*.

He doubled over, clutching himself, as Fission's chuckle pushed him the rest of the way off the ladder of allure, and anger rose to vie with embarrassment, both still trailing well behind aching agony.

He looked up to find some blonde git from a Cornflakes advert trotting up to him, looking apologetic.

'Hey, sorry about that!'

'Why don't you watch what's going on?' Carlton snapped vehemently, or as vehemently as he could manage in a hoarse croak.

'Well, I was. I watched you get hit.' He smiled, trying to lighten the atmosphere. Carlton stood upright.

'Are you trying to be funny?' he challenged, ignoring the small insistence in the back of his mind that, yes, he looked like a prat and there was nothing he could do about that, but now he was acting like one as well.

'Hey, I'm sorry, guy! What can I do? You want me to rub it better?' The sarcastic suggestion did not improve matters.

'You can be more bloody careful, that's what!'

Tamon stepped forward, his hand hovering above his wrist, but not touching the device there.

'It's okay,' he explained to the footballer. 'They're offworlders.'

The man immediately took a step backwards, and Carlton felt unclean and contagious, on top of everything else.

'Oh, right,' said the man. 'Okay. Yeah. That explains it. Right.' And with what sounded like the staccato of alarm, he backed away, snatched the ball from the ground and ran off.

'He did not understand your reaction. Civ . . . er . . . Earth people do not . . .' Tamon searched for the right words, always a sign that they're the sort best kept hidden. 'Display aggression. It is all but eliminated.'

'What call that then?' Fission pointed towards the footballers, and Carlton's black mood was suddenly lightened by the fact that Fission was on his side.

'What?' Tamon looked confused.

'Sport. Channelled aggression.'

'No it isn't. Football is about choosing the right plays at the right time. It's an intellectual pursuit with an athletic base.'

'They hit each other intellectually?'

'They have shields so that no-one contacts. It is perfectly safe. In fact, it's a good example of just how far we've come. We are not aggressive any more. We are *civilised*.'

There was an implication there, which no-one missed. Least of all an evilly-grinning Arnold.

'Touchdown!'

'Civs,' said Fission, in a tone suggesting that anyone who qualified had better keep an eye out in case she poked it that way. Tamon looked a little uncomfortable.

'How come *you* wear a shield?' asked Gloria, and Tamon looked as comfortable as a battery hen.

'I, er . . .'

'So you don't have to *touch* us?' Gloria's tone had turned nasty.

'Have you got a spare?' asked Arnold.

VIII

'It's trying to get away.'

'Well, should we stop it, or let it go?'

'What do you think?'

'I don't know. Anyone?'

A general rumble of gorillan disclaimers, and the shrug of countless massive shoulders – well, they were very countable in fact, but Curtis had other things on his mind – accompanied his progress towards the gap.

'Shall I stop him?' asked one.

'Er.'

The smell of what he didn't recognise as gorilla sweat and very old banana bits . . .

'Anyone? What do you think?'

The feel of gorilla fur brushing against his fast moving hand . . .

'Well . . .?'

And he was through.

Touchdown!

The only problem was that he needed to go to the toilet again.

Tamon searched for a response. He was out of stock of excuses, and spares, apparently. 'Look, I'm sorry. It's hard to explain. Shall we get on? Here comes the other one.'

The other one ran up to them, looking over his shoulder nervously. A gorilla shuffled out of the trees and stared at him through deep, red, expressionless eyes.

'You'll never guess what happened!'

They thought about the possibilities.

'Never *care* either.'

They followed Tamon in silence, Carlton bringing up the rear. It seemed to be still his turn, quite apart from the fact that he was trying to walk with his legs bowed.

He caught sight of a brightly-coloured bird sitting on a branch and preening its turquoise feathers. It glanced at him through its red eyes, and he scowled at it.

Uncivilised offworlder; him? No way!

He glanced at Tamon. Bastard.

Uncivilised people didn't sponsor two kids in an African village to keep them in school and clothes, because their father had died and so had the crops. That was hardly the act of someone who was *uncivilised*.

Not that he was going to admit to it.

He frowned, smoothed his hair down, and walked straighter. The bird watched him for a moment, then went back to its feather tugging.

A new thought pushed its way to the fore of Carlton's mind, now that there was room, and he looked again at Tamon. If this man was so disgusted by a bunch of backward offworlders, if he couldn't bear to touch them, what the hell was he doing offering to help them?

'I hear your last partner died. Three days before you met her!'

'While yours killed herself for a quiet life!'

The muted applause suddenly died as the two debaters were joined on the dais by a third, and the expressions on the front of the audience suggested that they were going to go the same way as the applause.

The newcomer orated by waving its six arms around and screaming abuse at everyone. Not that they understood it, but anything at that volume and with that blood-vessel bursting effort just had to be abuse, and a lot better than what had been produced by the candidates' supporters . . .

. . . Who conceded defeat almost immediately by leaping off the platform in opposite directions like a synchronised penalty-save competition.

The trand jumped off like a four-hundred-weight toad, and would have landed on the outskirts of the crowd had those skirts not been instantly gathered up and moved a lot further out. The visitor spun round, his arms flying out centrifugally as he did so, and found himself at the centre of ripples of humankind as the crowd headed for a number of homogeneous vehicles in neat rows a little distance away.

The trand watched them go, and looked puzzled. Why were they running away? *What* were they? Where was he? What could he usefully hit?

Then, beside him, appeared the form of Biondor. The trand saw the elegant alien through the prismatic shield which distorted his appearance to lend it several arms and a rather rougher skin texture. Biondor explained in the rude gutturals that passed for speech in a trandian throat, exactly what was expected.

Central was busy.

They arrived at the clump of trees and found that a number of them had panels set into the bark, which, according to Tamon, were access points to Central. All had people in front of them.

'What is Central?' asked Fission, hating the need to question this oh-so-superior Tamon, but needing to know. Tamon's face softened.

'Central is . . . Central. The Central computer. It runs everything, from the stripways to the grabs, from orbital hydroponics to robot production. Everything.' He shrugged. Central *was* everything. 'It's the whole world's household robot.'

'Not very good at phone lines, is it?' Arnold noted, leaning against a tree. His crossed legs indicated boredom, rather than tiredness, but he doubted that their perspicacity would stretch that far.

Gloria leaned – because she *was* tired, and emotionally drained, and her jaw hurt – against one of four legs which supported what looked like a gazebo a few yards away from them. Brightly-coloured in a reticulated orange and beige pattern, it provided welcome shade along with the trees next to which it stood.

Tamon looked slightly embarrassed at Arnold's comment – and everyone else felt slightly better; less inferior, thought Carlton – then approached the nearest man.

'I wonder, are you going to be long?'

The man turned to him, and looked him slowly up and down in just that disparaging a way as to make even Mother Theresa's sandalled foot itch with the need to kick his testicles into the middle of next week.

'I *really* don't know. I am doing research, and it cannot be hurried. If you *don't* mind.'

Tamon looked instantly trite, and muttered something that could have been an apology. Judging from the cringing body language, Carlton thought, watching their 'guide' back off slightly, it could have been a plea for mercy. The researcher noticed as well, with a slight smirk.

Mother Theresa would have smiled as she did it.

64

'Into what?' asked Arnold.

'I *beg* your pardon?'

'Granted. What are you researching?'

'The launch of the first tachy-gluon starship takes place in a few days. I am studying the propulsion method. It really is a quite fascinating advance, for those who can make sense of it.'

Arnold shrugged. 'It was always the next logical step after tachyon travel had been invented. I remember saying just that to Nanny. Wouldn't you agree, Fission?'

'Obvious.'

'Really.' He wasn't convinced. He wasn't the only one. 'Perhaps you can circumvent some of my research for me?' He smiled at Fission, who looked him straight in the eye and moved not a muscle. 'If you could just re-iterate the basic principles?'

She stared at him. She's going to rip his throat out, thought Carlton. With her teeth.

She didn't.

'Gluons bosons; zero mass and charge, one spin, strong forces holding up and down quarks together in triplet baryons – protons and neutrons. Got to be broken down before tachyons can be liberated, carefully, to maintain integrity of sub-atom beam. So, tachy-gluon. Makes long distance travel reliable.'

Gloria took all this in and mulled over it for a while. Fission might as well have said 'Bucket growers make pink tree wibbly plungers'. Perhaps she had. I bet the others know what she's talking about, she thought, though fixed expressions of non-description offered long odds.

The man's face set in a way that suggested Mother Theresa had achieved a successful gland transmission. Then he turned back to the tree.

'*If* you will excuse me. I'm rather busy.'

And they moved off, as a group.

But as they did so, Gloria gave a little cry of surprise, because the gazebo support shifted slightly. Then the whole gazebo shuffled. Moving to one side, she looked up, and the gazebo was a giraffe.

It had its nose plugged into a tree.

'Ah!' said Tamon, apparently steered back on track by what Gloria saw as somewhat atypical giraffean behaviour. 'This robot reports back to Central on the state of the area, so it can send repair robots and so on. We can use its terminal.' He walked up to the animal and slapped it on the leg, then stood back as it unplugged its nose and looked fifteen feet down at him. 'We need to ask a question of Central.'

The giraffe considered this for a long moment, then it said, 'Pardon?' and cocked an ear.

'I said: WE NEED TO ASK A QUESTION OF CENTRAL, THROUGH YOUR TERMINAL.'

The giraffe shook its head. 'One moment, please.'

It stepped back, spread its legs slowly and bent its neck down so that its red eyes were on a level with Tamon's. He repeated the request.

'We need to know if any household robots are missing and, if so, if Central knows where they might be.'

The giraffe nodded – one hell of an acknowledgement with a ten-foot neck – then struggled back to its full height and stuck its nose in the tree.

A moment later, it took it out again.

'Chanta has reported her household robot missing. Its where-abouts are unknown because it is missing.'

Arnold nodded slightly; that was more like it. These robots were far too obsequious for his liking. But Tamon did not take offence – the tone had held none. He turned to the group.

'Do you want to see Chanta?'

'Of course,' Carlton answered. 'How do we get there?'

'Grab?'

'Sorry?' Why did people keep saying things that he couldn't possibly be expected to understand? To make him look stupid, of course.

'Grab. A ground cab. As opposed to a flyer. I could take you if you want.'

Carlton's eyes narrowed. So did a number of others.

No-one said, 'You've got a cab?', and Arnold stowed his response.

The badge of office of the trand team was quite large, made of metal, and was affixed to its wearer by means of the sort of needle you'd stick in a horse if you were a sadistic vet. There was no catch into which the needle would fit safely, and painlessly. Just a needle.

On the outside of the badge was a crude drawing of a six-legged trand, famed through all of Trand Prime for his musculature and his prowess at transforming lives – into memories.

Currently the needle was embedded in the craggy skin of the trand captain, by definition, and a little dried trickle of blood announced that he had kept the title for a respectable time. It wasn't that trandian blood congealed slowly, rather that it was pretty much congealed already. For some of it actually to seep out of a hole with its cause still embedded was not the work of moments.

How long it would remain there would depend on the latest leadership contest.

Edwina[1] was challenging. Rupert had held the position for long enough, and while his decision to send Sam on the mission alone might have been a good learning experience for the youth, the others – Edwina herself, especially – were itching for a good fight. Hence the challenge.

She smacked Captain Rupert round the side of his head with a hay-making right hook from her middle arm. He made no attempt to dodge, of course, but left the ground and travelled sideways to smash a bulge into the rough hostel where the team had gathered.

He struggled to his feet, but it was no sign of distress – trands struggled whenever they wanted to get upright – then glared at Edwina and nodded his head in what could have been a bow by an ancient courtier. Good blow, his nod said, as Edwina watched him closely. But not good enough.

A bit of wall sagged into the room and expired with a little puff of dust.

Edwina stood to attention in front of Rupert, as she had twice already. Maybe the third blow would betray tiredness. She would see. He swung an arm a couple of times like an athletics hammer, whirled his fist like a discus, and despatched Edwina through the air like a very large and lumpy javelin.

She did see. Lots of things; stars mostly.

A rough sculpture might have broken her fall, but the reverse was certainly true, and lots of smaller rough sculptures was the result.

Edwina rose, even more slowly than had Rupert, and took a saggy step to one side to maintain her balance, while waving all six arms around, exactly unlike an Hawaiian dance. Not knowing whether her team-mates had noticed her distress, she stood to attention, then dropped to one knee and touched her Captain's foot. She was bested. It was over.

The Captain nodded to his second-in-command, then addressed Sam, the challenge already forgotten.

---

[1] Aliens are usually called Tpwenggjr or Sdewgt. Trand names herein are translated. You can't pronounce Tpwenggjr or Sdewgt, or, if you can, you deserve sympathy, not to mention surgery.

'Understand?'

Sam frowned in concentration. 'It is pink, with only two arms.'

The Captain thought for a moment, then nodded.

'Go,' he said. He might have added something along the lines of 'be careful out there', but in this case, there was really no need.

Something pink with only two arms satisfied himself that the building next to him was going to defy gravity for a while longer, and wondered what to do. He looked upward in response to a rumbling of thunder which he could easily imagine was the Champion and Challenger wrestling in the heavens.

The sky was a heavy mass of clouds, rolling as Wilverton watched, torn apart and folded inwards by a wind which gusted across the plain and flapped his jump-suit. Every few seconds lightning flashed high in the depths, followed by an immediate cacophony, as though a beast of fire was trying to escape from an all-enveloping, smothering prison. So far, it was dry, but the clouds threatened a deluge to make Noah rush for his varnish.

Hadn't he read a book once that started with someone being transported somewhere between one footstep and the next? Could he be in that? he wondered.

You can't think which book it is, because it isn't, and there are no heroes in real life . . .

It would be nice, sometimes, he thought, not to have a brain that continually worked overtime on anything and everything; to be, not thick, but not having to analyse, just able to accept things as they were.

He took as deep a breath as he could with so shallow a chest, and let it out in a worried sigh.

The sigh's end brought not silence but the absence of the near sounds of pummelling struggle. As Biondor had predicted, the fight had finished. He had to get somewhere else, and fast.

Another challenge, he thought, since he and fast went together like Charles and Di.

Except, of course, he didn't really have to worry, because heroes always won. That's why they were heroes.

That's why they didn't exist. For you, anyway.

You're from the *real* world.

You're real.

You can fail and die.

Not necessarily in that order.

★

Wilverton wasn't particularly big, nor did he conform to the much-held belief that greater intelligence meant a larger brain. His brain just filled the hole that was left for it inside the cranium, rather neatly; and rather fortunately, given the alternatives of rattling or seepage.

There *was* enough room inside it for two bodiless super-beings to engage in a bit of a skirmish.

On one side, and with the effort of competition against the Champion producing a visible blue emanation – in the blue corner, as it were – the Challenger reinforced the thoughts which would calm Wilverton, reduce the tension, let him know that everything would be all right and thereby stop him from panicking.

With slightly less visible effort, and therefore in the red corner, the Champion suggested just the opposite.

The Champion *wanted* its Player to have a bit of a panic. It was eminently possible to be over-confident. It had happened to Players in the Game many times before, and it didn't last long.

A let's-get-the-hell-out-of-here reaction to any danger meant that an animal lived to breed another day, or night,[1] and if the Wilverton human wanted to breed another night, then complacency would prove a perfect, and permanent, contraceptive.

Wilverton shook his head. Whether he was going to survive or not, there was no harm in giving fate a helping hand by moving his bum while his legs still stuck out the bottom of it. The sound of an opening door and a grunt of what sounded like anticipated mayhem agreed with him.

Of course, the young brothers might just be excited about seeing their first alien.

One of them threw a rock at him.

Of course, they might not.

He ran, not venturing on to the coverless plain now on his right, nor back through the buildings to where any number of trands awaited anything they could stuff into their mouths.

Brothers, said his brain. Why do you assume they're male?

Shut up and work the legs, he told it, as the siblings' grunts reached his ears.

'Let's get it!'

---

[1] The alternative strategy is displayed by those whose only defence is to remain perfectly motionless. This is fine until the dominant species invents juggernauts.

'Yeah! What is it?'

'Don't know, but it's not trand.'

Thump, thump.

It sounded like elephantine running to Wilverton, if elephants suffered from gout. He wasn't about to stop and check. He glanced to each side, in the vague hope that there might be something he could use, like a getaway car, or a mega-blast neutron-emission trand-basher laser . . .?

Nope.

Thump. Thump.

'It . . . might be . . . dangerous.'

'*I'm* not . . . scared!'

'Nor . . . am I!'

I am, thought Wilverton.

He could hear them breathing, or reaching the climax of an award-winning sex session.

Thump.

Thump.

But further away? Or wishful thinking? Could he really have come across a species with less athletic ability than himself?

Why did they want to 'get' him anyway? Hunger? Fear, maybe? That didn't seem likely – but then Curtis had killed an innocent robotic bird . . .

He darted round a corner, wondered whether to duck into an alley between two buildings apparently intent on meeting, and decided against it; it worked in films because the hero didn't wheeze like an old vacuum. He kept running, the significance of his reasoning not being able to keep up.

From the sound of it, neither could the trands.

Thump.

But not a running thump. A hitting thump. Then muffled voices from far behind.

Sam picked himself up and glared at the two youngsters for a moment before delivering several corrective blows to their heads. Young trands had to learn to respect their biggers.

'Chasing what?' he asked when the explanation was bubbled between temporarily swollen lips.

'Don't know. It was pink.'

'With two arms?'

'Yes.'

The big trand was pleased, they could tell. The parting slaps were hardly even concussive.

Wilverton slowed to a halt when the legs no longer had the energy to challenge the brain.

No problems, he thought, barring possible seizure. He looked out towards the plain.

What to do now, then?

Not that it mattered.

He kicked a stone, devil-may-care. It flew away, he saw not where.

Sniff. Time for breakfast. Stretch. Hind leg up. Scratch behind the ear. Use the teeth; tease the tummy, fur that is. That's better. Something tastes good! Have another go. Mmm.

How about some sex?

No; breakfast first. Then sex.

Up the passage. Pattering feet. Pause for a sniff; check the walls. Here, and there. No real reason. Just to check. Just in case. Towards the light. End of the tunnel. Dimmer than usual. Why was that? The sky would be dark. Poke the head up. Look around. Another sniff. Just to make sure. No threat in the wind. Head up further. Out of the hole. Another quick sniff. Now, over there. Maybe some . . . What the f . . .?

Thud!

A flying stone whanged into the head of a small rodent which had just ventured into the sweet morning air preparatory to the daily breakfast search. It was a short and unequal contest – the animal would never need breakfast again.

Swoop through the air with a rush of the wind in the wings.

> *Currents of warmth take you high then the ease of a glide;*
> *down and around. But the desert is different today*
> *as the storms and the gales make the effort of flight such*

a strain.

> *Beating the wings for the height that you need to survive*
> *in this wasteland of pebbles and stones where the food is*

so rare.

> *Oh, so tired.*
> *Must survive.*
> *So you cannot give up or the desert will claim you for*

bones

to feed to the carrion eaters that wait in their lairs.
Now movement, below! See! It twitches, comes out of its
hole.

Can it be reached, though, before it retreats? But it
stops!

Moving no longer it lies, dead but warm, easy food.
Gliding down, speeding down, swooping down.
Will survive!

A huge bird, massive, coarse, like the early terran reptilian flyers, landed heavily on the ground just next to the rodent, took hold of it in one talon and started feeding. It didn't take long, and having fed, it struggled, labouring, back into the air . . . in *that* direction, it decided. It would last for just a few more miles yet.

What are you doing? the Challenger considered in ultra-violet, observing stone, rodent and bird.

Watch and find out! – the infra-red answer.

Easy, thought Wilverton, predictable.

So, where to?

He could head for the plain, where a trand would stand out like a trand on a plain.

But if he was here for some specific purpose, then it was less likely to involve doing something in the middle of nowhere, alone, than in the middle of a city full of trands.

So that was where he would stay.

Protected.

Safe.

IX

The grab was quiet, inside and out. Carlton had managed to get into the front seat next to Tamon, consigning Fission to the back. Tamon had asked the grab's computer where Chanta lived, then verbally instructed the vehicle to go there, touched a couple of buttons to confirm what his voice had demanded, and off they went.

They learned quite a lot about the two prospective candidates for the post of World President during their short journey, from the hanging holographic posters dotted about. Apparently, Miron was a junkie with the intellectual capacity of a small heap of excrement, while Pomona would make the Whore of Holona look like a Sunday school teacher who had swapped her nappies for a chastity belt. It was a reminder of the politics at home, except that, according to Tamon, these more 'colourful' – as Gloria's mother called such words – comments were from the candidates' supporters. Miron and Pomona would not adopt quite such direct comparisons.

Still, it lightened the mood, but no more than a pall-bearer treading on a banana skin.

Looking to his left, Carlton spotted two civs sitting on the grass, holding hands and smiling at each other, using sets of teeth so brilliantly flawless that they probably threatened the vision of anyone who looked with unprotected eyes. He turned away and adopted the tragic expression of the ugly duckling who has finally come to accept that when it grows up it will turn, miraculously, into an ugly duck.

Gloria saw Wilverton everywhere and nowhere, and contemplated a life without him as empty – to borrow a phrase from the uncle her mother rarely spoke of – as a Japanese jock-strap. And if they *did* find him, there was no guarantee that he would want with her what she wanted with him; a lifetime – assuming they *had* a life left after this Game thing. They were so different. She had to know, and she had no way of knowing.

Curtis was looking out for gorillas acting funny, but had to make do with a pack of monkeys sitting in the shade and searching each other's hair for whatever robots kept there – little robotic salt grains, presumably. One suddenly screamed and lashed out, and the rest of the group watched the scuffle as the grab left them behind.

'Why do they make gorillas who can't decide what to do?' he asked no-one in particular.

A couple of them looked at him. It wasn't a question for which an answer sprung readily to mind. Gloria ran 'To get to the other side' through her head, but it didn't fit.

'What?' asked Fission, the tone implying that he'd better get it right this time.

'I met some gorillas and they couldn't decide what to do with me.'

'Know how they feel!'

'What's *that* supposed to mean?'

Fission looked at him. It wasn't his fault. 'Nothing.'

She sighed. She could take anything except frustration, but she shouldn't take it out on others – especially helpless others.

'No. Please! I'm sure we're all interested!' Curtis's dander was up and about. Don't, whispered the little men on both shoulders, for once in complete accord. Well, it *was* like hearing the man with the blindfold and the cigarette telling them not to answer the ringing telephone until they'd got this over with. 'Is there something I should know?'

'Oh dear,' said Arnold. 'Now, where to start . . .'

'Shut up, Arnold.'

'Okay, everyone just take it easy,' Carlton advised smoothly, the peacemaker in control.

Curtis subsided, and stared out of the window again, looking for walruses. It was probably the Challenger, he thought. Why didn't the Champion give them some help – a clue or something?

Had it possessed eyes; had it possessed lungs; had there been a sky in a direction which could meaningfully have been described as above it; the Champion would have sighed and glanced up at the sky.

It didn't, and there wasn't.

So it smashed a meteor into the planet Farger instead, and felt no better at all (which still left it considerably better off than the flattened inhabitants of the planet Farger).

A clue, Curtis pondered.

A cl . . .

He looked towards the front of the grab, where Tamon sat

expressionlessly miserable. And he frowned.

A minute or so later, the grab slowed to a halt, and Tamon checked the display.

'This is it.' To their right was a convex swelling in the ground, a slightly lighter green than the fine grass which surrounded it. Like many others they had passed, it was the roof of a dwelling, and in it, according to the grab's computer, lived Chanta.

'I will stay here, of course,' said Tamon.

Carlton nodded. 'I think I should go, with Gloria to give a reassuring feminine presence and Arnold, in case things get hairy.'

'What about me?' Fission's was the first voice raised in protest. She couldn't let them do it on their own, they'd only screw . . .

'We want to reassure the woman. If I need anyone to come and shout fonk at her a few times, then you'll be the first one I turn to.'

She scowled at him; not at the insult – that was just words. She *had* to go; she couldn't trust *them* to do it right. She wouldn't trust them to fart through the right hole.

She ground her teeth. That's always been the problem. You're in a flyer, you feel better if you're the pilot; you're in a fix, you only trust yourself to take control; you're in a relationship, you can't hold only one half of the reins. And you lose Janiel.

And Carlton was right about not having too many people – that was sensible.

Give them a chance.

She turned away and stared out of the window without a word, and Carlton had his victory, but he didn't know how it would echo.

'Well, of course *I'll* stay here,' said Curtis. 'I'm absolutely no use at all to anyone so I'd just get in the way. Don't you worry about me.'

'Okay,' said Carlton, obeying him instantly.

He *was* the Captain after all.

Carlton, Gloria and Arnold emerged from the grab and looked around. The entrance to the home lay at the end of a downward sloping pathway, the start of which was camouflaged even better than the building's roof, so that it blended in to the surrounding shrubbery almost perfectly.

'How do we get in?' asked Gloria after a while. Carlton shrugged his shoulders. 'Arnold?'

Arnold immediately stopped his frantic search for the entrance and pretended to be looking elsewhere for something else and with entry to the building the furthest thing from his mind.

'Sorry?'

'I saw you looking. Have you found out how we get in?'

Arnold scowled. 'No.'

Carlton and Gloria both flashed unashamedly smug smiles at him in perfect unison, savouring the moment briefly, before Tamon's voice came through the open side of the grab, followed by a pointing finger.

'It's over there.'

Over there was what looked like another shrub until they got close to it, when it revealed a hole leading onto a green pathway sloping gently downwards in a spiral. They followed it and then couldn't find the door. It wasn't that it was concealed; it just wasn't there. A conventionally rectangular hole in the chitinous wall led onto what was presumably a hallway bathed in a green light.

They stopped anyway, convention putting the door before them where carpentry had apparently been a bit lax, then Carlton moved forwards to stick his head inside and have a quick look. It was preceded by his hand, which found the door after all. It was soft, and yielded inwards slightly, but not all that much; as if it really did sympathise with a visitor's wish to gain access but had to respect its owner's territorial claims as a higher priority. Terribly sorry, but . . .

'What do you want? Who are you?' came a woman's voice from somewhere around the door. It didn't sound like the door itself, somehow, and Carlton knew that the occupant had been alerted. He also felt that she was looking at them as she spoke. He put on the best smile he could manage, but it was hardly top drawer – more like the back of the cupboard behind the old trainers and the jeans covered in paint.

'We're here about your robot. I'm Peter Carlton, this is Gloria Parkson and this is Arnold.'

'Why have two of you got silly names?'

'Er.' He put his smile back in the cupboard. 'I don't know really.'

'Brilliant,' whispered Arnold. 'Good answer.'

'Shut up, Arnold!' hissed Carlton, but it was too late. 'It's because we're time travellers from four hundred years ago and back then they weren't all that silly.'

'Yeah.' Pause. They could feel themselves being studied. 'You look it. I didn't know Central had done time travel.'

'It hasn't, as far as I know. It was dilation – we were travelling very near light speed.'

Another pause. They could hear her frowning. 'I heard of that.

76

Waste of time, I thought.'

'Me too,' Arnold chipped in.

'Have you found him, then?'

'Who?'

'Rudy. The robot. That's what you said you've come about, remember?'

'It isn't here then?' Carlton asked, hope fading.

'Of course he's here; that's why I asked if you'd found him.' Carlton looked embarrassed. Arnold smirked. 'Look, you'd, er, you'd better . . . You're from four hundred years ago?' She sounded uncertain.

'Yes.'

The pause that followed sounded curious, judgemental, and Carlton felt like an exhibit. 'You are, er, sort of, clean and all?'

The lips on two faces tightened to something resembling a four-year-old dental patient, while Arnold smiled broadly. Humans were such . . . 'prats' seemed to fit the bill, with their jostling for position and who's better than who.

Why didn't they realise they were all lower than earth-worms and have done with it?

There again, they wouldn't have been any fun that way.

'We do bathe,' Carlton told her. 'Even four hundred years ago there was running water and soap.' In his head a childhood memory was triggered – 'I washed me face an' 'ands before I come, I did . . .'

'Yeah. Sure. Sorry. You'd better come in.'

The door disappeared, which was a neat trick given that it hadn't been there in the first place, and a green line materialised on the ground in front of them, leading them through the hallway and into a living area lit by the sun because there didn't appear to be a ceiling. There obviously *was* one, because ornaments were hanging from it in a couple of places, but it was so perfectly transparent, from the inside looking out, that it might have been a scene from an agoraphobic's nightmare.

The room was maybe thirty yards by forty and contained what Carlton recognised as lounge furniture and dining furniture, although nowhere was there a simple angle; everything was all curves. Soft holograms of nothing more than shapes hugged the walls here and there, and Carlton assumed they were a sort of light sculpture, but other items baffled him completely.

In one corner, a small holographic Miron, leader of the Foundation Foundation, was addressing anyone who would listen.

'. . . urtis. We must ever prepare for that wonderful day.'

'Computer, start. Holovision off. Music on. Finish.'

In an armchair, her legs drawn up to one side and her feet hanging over the edge, was a youngish woman, early thirties, with dazzlingly green hair which might or might not have been natural since her eyebrows were brown. She had a half-full glass of some peculiar looking purple concoction in one hand, and a chiffon handkerchief draped over a small part of her body. Nothing else.

Carlton swallowed saliva and anger, and suffered a tired look from Gloria.

The woman also had about her the half-lidded eyes and loose-limbed look of one who has maybe indulged in the purple liquid just a touch more than was good for them and is now coming down the other side. She looked like tears had been only recently stemmed.

'Chanta?' Carlton asked. She tipped her glass and inclined her head slightly by way of reply. And looked him up and down. But he knew it was curiosity, not attraction.

'You're really four hundred years old?'

'It depends how you measure it.' Why did he feel like a lower species? It was ridiculous. 'Physically, I'm not as old as you are.' She didn't react, and he knew that one had missed. Just get on with it, Peter. 'We're looking for a robot, and were told that you might be the owner.'

'Well, I might have *been* the owner.' She waved her glass in the direction of some of the other furniture by way of invitation. 'You'd better park your arses.'

Gloria lowered herself to a seat while her eyebrows tried to remain at the same height as when she had been standing up. As she sat down, the chair seemed to reach out to her bottom and cuddle it in a way that she found rather unsettling because, even in her current state of misery and tension, she couldn't help but enjoy it.

'I suppose, legally, I still *am* the owner,' Chanta continued, 'but I sure ain't the possessor no more. Rudy left me.' She delivered this last sentence in a mumble of unmistakable self-pity, and her chin rested heavily on her chest.

'Rudy,' Carlton said by way of seeking confirmation.

Chanta smiled in melancholy reminiscence. 'Yeah, Rudy. That's what I called him.'

A sound like the dripping of water into partially filled milk bottles rose to a crescendo and subsided again. Carlton assumed that the computer was either playing music or torturing a Chinaman.

'Do you know, by any chance, where he's gone?'

She shrugged. 'I don't got no idea.' She shook the glass so that it confirmed her rather elegant denial.

'Oh.' Now what?

Chanta took a sip of whatever the verbose glass contained.

Arnold watched Carlton come to a halt and decided to be helpful for a change, partly to remind himself what it was like, partly to keep the humans off balance, but most of all so he could stop playing this stupid Game as soon as possible.

'It must be unusual for a robot to leave,' he suggested.

'You can say that again, buster!'

'It must be unus . . .'

'We was in the sack, quite happy,' Chanta interrupted him before Carlton's sideways look made a doomed attempt at shutting him up. 'When all of a sudden he's stopped and he's up and getting dressed. Didn't say a word all the time he was doing it. And ignored my orders!' She shifted herself upright in the chair. This was important. 'He always did whatever I told him, right away, no question. Anything I wanted. But when I told him to come back . . .? Nothing.' She slid down again. 'Just walked out the door and that was the last I saw of him. Seven, eight months ago that was and I ain't heard no sound from him since.'

Gloria was doing an impression of a bush-baby.

These are animals with overly large eyes.

In the case of the bush-baby the cause is somewhere in their evolutionary past, when the bush-baby with the biggest eyes saw the sabre-toothed tiger coming and got the hell out of there, while other, sadly myopic little bush-babies squinted into the near distance until they were carnivorously prevented from reaching bush-infancy, let alone bush-adulthood.

In Gloria's case the cause was her interpretation of 'in the sack' and 'he's stopped'. She wasn't sure if this interpretation was correct, but she was very sure indeed that she wasn't going to ask the question which would have solved the problem one way or the other. At least they had Morals four hundred years ago. With capital letters.

'Have you any pictures of him?' asked Carlton. 'Any holograms?'

'Why would I take a holo of a robot?'

'Well, if he was special to you.'

'Oh, he was special all right! but I'm not going to take a holo of *that* bit am I? I mean, holos only *look* three dimensional, you know!' She took another sip of the drink and chuckled to herself, while Gloria added '*that* bit' to her list of incriminating phrases, and sat a little straighter.

'Well have you any idea how we might find him? Did he have any distinguishing features?' I wish I hadn't asked that, he thought, even before Chanta burst into a fit of drunken giggles that had Gloria pursing her lips in anticipation.

'Well, apart from the ex*tremely* obvious bit, he's got a strawberry-shaped birthmark on his right buttock.'

'A birthmark,' confirmed Carlton. 'On a robot.'

She shrugged. 'It was in the moulding, they told me; something got into the plasti-whatever it is that they're made of.' Another shrug. Another sip. A further droop of the eyelids before: 'They asked me at the time if I wanted to accept him like that and I didn't mind. Especially when I saw what was round the other side! And when I found out what he could do with it!' She winked at Gloria. 'That's why I called him Rudy.' If Gloria had pursed her lips any tighter she would have swallowed her cheeks.

'Right,' said Carlton. 'And that's it?' Chanta nodded. 'Well, thank you for your time.' He rose, and the others joined him.

'If you find anything, you let me know right away. Oh . . .' She raised her free hand as he made to walk to the door; looked at him again, sort of sideways. 'Look. Er. Can I, er, can I touch you?'

Carlton looked down at her. At her perfect limbs and her perfect breasts and her beautiful face. How many times had someone who looked like this asked him a question like that?

Never.

At least, not while he was awake.

And while he was asleep, it was due to some sexual attraction, which was never going to be the case on this damned planet.

'No,' he told her. 'We wouldn't want you to catch anything, would we?'

And he led them out, with Gloria's shocked gaze boring into his back.

'Well?' Fission sounded as though she was still piqued at not being picked. Along with Curtis and Tamon, she was leaning against the side of the grab in the sunshine. A few people sat or lay on the grass nearby, in various states of undress, but Carlton ignored them. Only one, a woman, appeared to be paying any attention.

'The robot wasn't there.' He gave the report, ignoring for the moment the challenge in Fission's voice. 'It disappeared about eight months ago apparently. Just upped and left.' Or downed and left, more to the point.

Curtis narrowed his eyes and looked for all the world like he was thinking, like he had experienced an idea. The eyes took on a furtive appearance, as if they knew the secret and didn't want to give it away. They darted this way and that, and settled briefly on Tamon, narrowing even more. Fission watched him with limited interest; it looked like Let's Play Secrets at the neighbourhood crèche where she helped out occasionally.

'Do we know where it went?' Curtis asked.

'No. Chanta's got no idea. She hasn't seen it or heard from it since it went.'

'Great,' commented Fission, before her attention was re-taken by Curtis.

He nodded, as if Carlton's was the answer he had expected, and his eyes narrowed again. He obviously liked this secret he had somehow managed to acquire, Fission thought, and it sure as hell wasn't going to get out through any optical orifice. And it couldn't escape from that orifice through which he usually elucidated his ideas, because he had his back to the cab.

'Rudy, it's called,' Carlton said, with one of *those* grins. Gloria's lips immediately adopted the pursed position like a plastic regaining its original shape on cooling; the atmosphere around Gloria was suddenly icy.

'Rudy!' said Curtis, his attention dragged outwards once more by the incongruity of the name.

'Disgusting!' muttered Gloria.

'Why?' Gloria pursed and glanced at Curtis. She looked back to the front. It was going to be easier to say if she wasn't looking at someone.

'She used him as a . . . as a . . .' Maybe it wasn't easier. Gloria was not going to get any further than 'as a'. Arnold came to the rescue, gallant as ever, a knight saving his Lady from any trace of distress.

'Dildo?'

'Oh, really! Arnold!' It hadn't sounded any better even when spoken with all the innocence Arnold could muster.

'Sorry.' He was immediately trite. 'Vibrator?'

'Arnold!' The red of Gloria's blush spelled danger. She stared resolutely into the clean distance, at a cheetah lying under a hologram which informed her that 'Miron Only Has One Testicle' and that therefore she should 'Vote for Pomona'.

'Why disgusting?' asked Fission.

'I'm not rising to the bait, you know!' warned Gloria. 'I'm not that sort of woman and I don't wish to . . . to further my education in such matters.' Anger lent her a power of speech she did not normally possess. She replayed in her mind what she had just said, then showed what a short term loan it was by adding 'Yes, that's right.'

'Not trying bait you. Robots are companions. In lots of cases they're all people got. For lonely people, they're most important things in whole world. They're friends, helpers, become lovers. Inevitable. Lovers who never leave you, always be there when you want them, lovers you never have to impress, never have to worry about annoying or upsetting.' And don't need 'their own space', and don't want to be king of castle, she added silently.

'I'm sorry,' said Gloria. 'I was being oversensitive. I suppose I'm just a little old-fashioned.'

'You're four hundred years out of date, melons. Don't tell us how live.' Fission slammed shut the door to her soul as though she had suddenly realised that it was ajar, and letting out all the heat.

'Not *all* androids are like that, I should point out,' said Arnold.

'No-one would want *you*, tin man.'

Arnold smiled. 'Present company excepted, *if* I remember rightly, which, of course, it is impossible for me not to do.'

Fission prepared to fire a broadside, but Tamon interjected.

'Arnold is a robot?'

'Android,' he corrected, even though the question had not been put to him.

'But . . .' Tamon was a study in disbelief. 'But you talk back. You're obstructive, rude.'

'Rude? *Me?*' Arnold was clearly shocked at the unfairness of it all. 'I merely tell the truth.'

'But robots aren't like you, they're . . .'

Curtis stared at Tamon, knowing exactly what robots were like. He ticked off points in his mind.

They would stand no chance of finding the renegade robot unless the Champion gave them some help, and there had been no clues, up to now, as far as he could see.

This Tamon character didn't like politics and had met them at an election debate.

He hadn't gone in to see Chanta, who would certainly recognise her own robot.

And he had been too helpful; especially so in marked contrast to everyone else they had met.

Tamon was a robot.

The robot.

No doubt about it.

But he couldn't just challenge it, because it would run away with robotic speed and then he'd have to ask Arnold to catch it and Arnold would claim all the glory, or just as likely give him one of those looks and refuse . . .

He had to immobilise it. He clenched a fist. He would knock it down, and then sit on it and call the others to help.

And he'd be a hero.

He'd show them.

'. . . obedient. Helpful. They don't speak unless someone asks them a question. They're everything you're not.'

Arnold smiled.

Curtis swung. With a look of quite massive enthusiasm on his face, he described an arc that dwarfed Noah's, and let fly at Tamon's chin.

And he connected, four inches before he reached it. Then he bounced off and fell over backwards, where a twig waited to add injury to injury by piercing both jump-suit and bottom when he landed on it.

He pointed and tried to rub his bottom at the same time. 'He's the r . . . aaa!' He toppled over sideways, pushed himself up, sat on his pierced buttock, gave a yelp, shifted his weight at speed to his other buttock like a demonstration of bummerobics, and pointed again.

'He's the robot.' But by now it was less an accusation than an anticlimax.

'All right, enough!' said Tamon. Carlton tore his eyes from the fascinating antics of his Captain, expecting anger on Tamon's face, but what he saw was pure relief.

Tamon touched his wrist device, and a miniature holographic Tamon appeared above it, holding a glowing cobalt-blue scroll in its tiny hands. 'Security.'

The woman sunbather who had been watching their antics immediately jumped to her feet and came to join them, fastening her chiffon covering as she did so, and holding out her wrist, above which a miniature her held the same scroll as Tamon.

'Dano,' Tamon said to her, 'get in touch with Central. I've done what it said but now I'm struggling. It'll know what to do.' To Carlton he looked like he had finally found the ecu that would gain

83

him entry to the public toilet outside which he had been standing uncomfortably since they had met him.

'So that's why you've been helping us?' Gloria asked while Curtis struggled to his feet, and gingerly rubbed his bottom. There was nothing he could do about his pride or his shattered reasoning.

'I was told to keep an eye on you, after I reported Fission knocking you out; and then the bank reported that you had an account over four hundred years old. Central thought I should check.'

'So, will you help us find the robot?'

Tamon looked at Arnold.

'You're looking for a robot that acts like a robot's not supposed to? I'd say you'd found one. Whose is it, anyway?'

Curtis broke off from inspecting the blood from his bottom, but Arnold beat him to it. 'I'm not anyone's. I'm mine.'

'You mean you're unowned?'

'If that's the word you use to mean self-possessed, unique, then yes, I suppose so.'

'He's mine!' claimed Curtis.

'Oh, please!'

'I made you!'

'You couldn't make a bed.'

Tamon looked uncertain. 'Well, I'm not sure we can have an unowned robot . . .'

'Android.'

'. . . wandering around. Central will have to decide what to do with you. Just stay where you are.'

He might as well have asked the bull to hold the red cape for a moment.

'You know,' Arnold commented, conversationally, 'I've had just about enough of dumb humans, and this Game.'

His arm flashed out. Carlton felt a scrape across his forehead, Tamon found himself suddenly deposited on his backside at the insistence of the other arm, and then Arnold was off and running at a pace that put distance between himself and humanity in more ways than one.

X

Wilverton heaved in a deep breath, and blew it out again. For someone whose athletic experience had been limited to reading the back pages of newspapers – and getting a bit breathless if he did that too quickly – he had, he thought, done remarkably well. And not unnecessarily so; even if death wouldn't visit him, nothing precluded a considerable amount of damage paying a call.

He checked what he could see of the city from where he now was, hidden by a tree trunk. None of the buildings was more than a couple of storeys high, and each looked as though an apprentice bricklayer had thrown them together first thing in the afternoon following lunch from a large bottle with a red warning on its label.

He could just glimpse a market-square at the far end of an alley. Any number of large quadrupeds shuffled around, steam rising from sweaty bodies. Other, smaller animals, and birds strutted between them, while trands walked among them all, prodding the largest beasts, lifting occasionally, grabbing a bird, arguing with each other. He saw one hold out a hand with what he assumed were coins in it, indicating an animal next to him that looked like a cross between a cow and a hippo. Out of sight, the owner must have shaken his head, and the customer closed his fist around the coins before hitting the vendor with it. A returning fist flew into view and the customer staggered backwards, before nodding and adding some more coins, which were accepted. He grasped the animal's neck and led it away, until its legs gave way through this suffocation method of transportation, and it was dragged out of Wilverton's sight.

He raised his eyebrows. Interesting way to haggle. He wouldn't be able to afford a loaf of bread!

What a planet! He wondered what Trand Prime might be like. They certainly did not seem to have moved very far from the survival-of-the-fittest dictum, and the thought of beings like this inventing interstellar travel did not ring quite true. He shook his head. Intellectual snob!

85

What to do then?

He leaned against the tree trunk and blew out another deep breath.

And the Champion caught it.

The eddy rose to the branches above it and dislodged a leaf, carrying it from its ancestral branch – some of its friends gently waved it goodbye; with respect, it thought – and dropping it, some considerable distance away from its birthplace, over a low wall.

On the far side of which, sheltering from a wind still doing its best to be Wagnerian up in the grey broiling mass of clouds, was a harg, the trandian equivalent of a dog. Given the trands' predilection for the more robust way of life, this, unsurprisingly, was not an animal which could sit at someone's feet and resist the temptation to remove them at the knee. Built like a muscle-bound pony and with a deportment which would have lowered the tone on any death row, it made a pit bull terrier look like a sickly gerbil on valium.

The creature's natural demeanour – demeanour the better as far as the harg was concerned – was of little import to the leaf, which had hardly any experience of life beyond sucking sap and wafting, so it bounced off the animal's nose and settled down to some serious deterioration.

The creature was now well and truly roused, however, and after a futile search for an irritant that couldn't be killed as an assertion of the innate superiority of harg over leaf, it tried to get comfortable again, by circling a few times and flopping back down to the ground.

As it flopped, its tail disturbed a small stone, which took advantage of the slope on which the harg was sleeping by rolling away from it, and gathering speed. And gathering more stones as well, so that, after a few moments, a little cataract of pebbles was rushing headlong like an advancing cavalry, and picking up still bigger brethren, and bigger yet, until the whole mass of a mini avalanche was brought abruptly to a halt by the wall which marked a right angled turn in the pathway.

All appeared still for a moment, but then the wall began to topple, infinitesimally, lazily, succumbing to the suggestion that vertical was really no way for a trandian wall to be, and it crashed to the ground.

While all this was preparing to occur, Wilverton looked at the buildings in front of him slumping against the backdrop of the grey skies, looking less inviting, and less colourful, than the green furry bits on the cheese in his bachelor's fridge.

Bachelor.

Gloria.

No. Not now. *Con*centrate.

What was he supposed to do in an alien city on a prim . . . barb . . . alien planet to help win the Game . . .?

And not even a *real* alien planet; just a *version* of an alien planet. The only real thing on it was probably Wilverton himself, he thought.

The only real thing on it was him . . .

Why did the thought have to sneak up on him like that? He banished it.

In Westerns they run from building to building without ever being seen, he knew, so that was the opted plan. Admittedly, the cowboys rarely reached the next building along the line wheezing like an obscene phone caller on sixty Gitanes a day, but that couldn't be helped. He was here to help win the Game, not audition for True Grit II, and those going to and from the market might be too engrossed to notice him.

He scampered from his tree to the first building in line, carried on past that, ducked round a corner, and ended up against the unwindowed wall of a second house, clutching his calf which had just suffered a severe attack of cramp, and looking down at the unattached head of a trandian chicken, which glared at him in now permanent surprise.

Duke Wayne never had this trouble! he thought, wincing. Heroes weren't as vulnerable as lesser mortals.

'Get off your horse and massage my bloody leg . . .'

Peter Carlton wouldn't have this trouble, either, and he was rather more hero-shaped. But Peter wasn't here. So whatever the Champion had in mind demanded brains and not brawn, he concluded, with a logic that had no interest in whether being brawny or brainy was better.

In the first house he had passed, a young trand was bent over his studies in what passed for his bedroom. He paused, the niceties of deltoid mechanics – in his opinion there weren't many – on the page in front of him finally becoming too much, and gazed out of the window instead, towards the hustle of the market-place.

He smiled as he thought of Ingrid, and the way the muscles in her middle pair of arms had rippled impressively during that drinking house brawl the other night.

His face cracked in a smile – and trand faces very nearly did just that when bits of them were forced to move – but the smile froze as the shape of a small, crouched, scampering Wilverton shot past his window.

He hadn't seen a Wilverton before, and it was only after a moment or two of stunned immobility that he hoisted himself to his feet, crossed to the window and looked out. There was no sign of Wilverton by then, but that hardly lessened his excitement. He very nearly ran – well, he very nearly shuffled at a speed which would have blurred a long-exposure plate – into the main living room where his mother was tenderising an animal hide. The animal had given up its futile but traditional struggle quite early in the process.

He told her all about it in breathless grunts.

She smacked him round the head with a fist that would make a troll blanch and told him not to make up such stupid stories just to get out of doing his homework.

He shouted at her that biggers were so *stupid* and that he *had* seen something and how he wished he didn't live at home any more and how as soon as he was strong enough to set up his own family he'd leave, so there!

She hit him again.

He stormed out of the house, forgetting in his anger all about Wilverton, and stalked hotly down the streets towards his favourite drinking place, wishing that Ingrid wasn't housebound for a week after her exploits there the previous night.

In the following hours, he was to sink a few trand equivalents of bourbon – only with a rather greater blood content – to prove a blurred point, have a couple of short scuffles before closing time, and then stagger out feeling just as angry as when he went in and determined that next time the bigger tried he'd beat her senseless; then she'd respect him . . .

On his way down through the square in which the drinking house stood, he would pass a door that was open over the cobbles where he was walking.

'Biggers!' he would grunt, and punch the top third of the door shut with an action which on earth would have propelled the world karate champion into the next life. He would hear an 'Oomph' from the other side of the door as he did so, and would hurry past in case the owner of the 'oomph' caught him, and his mother found out.

★

88

Meanwhile.

Wilverton moved into the road again, heading for the next wall, and didn't see, at the end of a passageway, a trand remove some sort of gun from the belt around his waist and take careful aim at Wilverton's back.

It was a small back, but Sam was a good shot, and knew he wouldn't miss. He would have smiled as he took aim, but the noise might have alerted his target.

He squeezed the trigger, just as the wall behind him succumbed to the suggestion that vertical was no way for a trandian wall to be, and it crashed on top of him.

By the time Sam had shrugged its components off, Wilverton was nowhere to be seen. He kicked a piece of the wall angrily. Why had it chosen that moment to collapse? he wondered.

The Challenger extrapolated the falling leaf through the higher probabilities of future events and arrived at falling masonry. It sensed the Champion hanging in the ether a little way off, and clamped down on the feeling of respect which threatened to broadcast itself in visible purple; the Champion was quite aware enough of its own abilities without the Challenger confirming the opinion.

It turned back to the planet beneath.

Wilverton moved with a quiet confidence from wall to wall, risking some with windows and even the occasional door, becoming more certain with each step that nothing untoward would occur as the sound of the market faded behind him.

It came as a bit of a shock, therefore, when, pausing to regain a bit more breath, he felt a hand gripping his shoulder.

XI

'Damn!' Tamon looked after Arnold, struggling to his feet. 'Have you got through to Central yet, Dano? I need to know what to do.'

The erstwhile sunbather, who had paused in the action of touching her wrist device, frowned slightly.

'Shall we follow in the grab while we're finding out?' she asked, making it sound as much of a question as a suggestion. She's got the measure of this guy, thought Carlton.

'Good idea. Everybody into the grab.'

They moved to both sides of the vehicle, but froze at the sound of thundering hooves from behind them. Animals of all shapes and sizes were charging towards them, fleeing something; they couldn't see what.

Suddenly they were an island in the middle of flowing fur, as the fastest of the creatures reached them, and cheetahs and lions rushed past, not even pausing to let Gloria stroke them. Following them, elk, gnu, moose, and wildebeest were just some of the creatures Carlton didn't recognise, as he shielded his eyes from the cloud of dust with one hand. Curtis shielded himself with one Carlton. Fission stood just to the side of the grab and stared at the animals with an impatient frown on her face. It contrasted nicely with the worry and quiet squeaks in which Gloria was dealing.

'It's all right,' came the calm voice of the woman – Dano – into Gloria's ear from close range. 'They're robots; they're just acting scared. They stampede occasionally for authenticity but the last thing they would do is harm a human.'

Gloria believed her, even tried a wan returning smile, but still tried to become one with the paintwork.

The sunbathers and walkers had more faith, knowing that robots can avoid hyperactive gungas,[1] but that faith was shaken when the

---

[1] Reaction-sharpening toys that leap around the bedroom followed by reaction-sharpened children. Origin of name unknown, possibly from parental shouts referring to constant din.

animals were closely followed by several humanoids with eyes looking wide, scared and distinctly un-red. While the animals carried straight on, the people found trees to shelter behind, and those who had noticed the tell-tale eye colouring looked, concernedly, to see what they were running from.

Then it was quiet for a moment.

'Right,' said Tamon. 'Into the gr . . .'

He stopped. He couldn't say '. . ab' with his bottom jaw that far down.

The trand followed the animals and people at a distance of some fifty yards and wasn't getting any closer, which was probably the way they liked it, thought Carlton. *He* liked the way it was passing by, about thirty yards away, without giving them a second look, and he arrested his first reaction, to move to the far side of the grab.

'What is it?' Gloria asked the woman, but Dano shook her head and shrugged.

'Alien,' said Fission, in a tone suggesting it was the sort of alien you could tread in. Her team-mates knew of Fission's dislike for all races able to roam the galaxy at will while humanity on Earth Prime were confined to quarters for fighting among themselves.

'An alien! Here? On Earth?' Tamon sounded excited. 'We must make it welcome! Don't do anything hostile!'

Carlton looked at the creature, its six arms swinging like sledgehammers and flanking a body that the Incredible Hulk would have needed a month's solid work-out to achieve. Arnold would have had a suitable response, he thought.

He caught Fission's eye and they smiled slightly at each other. Inexplicably, the heavens were not rent asunder.

Then the trand was past them and dwindling in the distance and they had managed not to do anything hostile at all. There's lucky, thought Carlton.

'I reckon that was a trand,' he said.

'What would trand be doing on Earth?' asked Fission.

'Well, just about anything it wants!' The quip slipped out and withered as Fission's stony stare declared this was not the time. Her funny bone's so small it's a wonder her arm isn't all wobbly, Carlton thought, his slight internal bruising adopting the best form of defence. 'If it *is* a trand then it was transported here as part of the Game – must have been. And if that's the case . . .'

'Then Thomas is on Trand!' cried Gloria, shamelessly stealing the punchline.

'Yes.' Carlton's mind tried to flash a picture of Wilverton reciprocally rampaging through the cities of Trand Whatever, and came up with a hedgehog rampaging across an eight-lane motorway.

Gloria did not seem to have reached the same conclusion, judging from the optimistic gleam in her eyes. She turned and looked to where the trand had vanished – or, at least, was lost to sight; trands have a massive problem with vanishing.

We could catch up and ask it, she thought. We could ask it what it's doing here and then we might know what Thomas is doing on Trand.

It would break us into little bits, she thought.

Yes, she thought, but . . .

And there was no but.

She turned back, miserably sensible.

'Shall we follow it?' Dano asked, but Tamon shook his head.

'We're not authorised. We'll follow Arnold.' He looked around, to make sure that nothing else was about to countermand his orders, while Dano looked disappointed. 'Right. Er. Into the grab.'

Then the world exploded with a deafening roar and a blast of light that was even louder.

The grab jumped backwards as though it had been taken as much by surprise as its would-be occupants, and landed on solid ground, proving that at least part of the planet was still there, to anyone with the presence of mind to think about it.

But presence of mind was not the concern; it was the presence of body in a place under sudden attack that worried them, as another thunderclap – more like a standing ovation – and lightning flash performed a couple of yards in front of the vehicle.

The grab seemed to be the centre of attention and they moved away from it like the spokes of a wheel, joining sunbathers and passers-by in single-minded flight, so that the flow of humanity looked like a herd disturbed by a low aircraft.

Carlton, further perfecting his Groucho shuffle, looked round for the others, and found only Dano close by. Further off to his right he could make out Tamon and Gloria. When the sound of the latest detonation cleared enough for a tightly-controlled shout to be heard, he made use of the fact.

'No aggression, eh?'

If he did hear, Tamon saw fit not to answer.

Above them, hidden from their sight while they stared at the ground, an angtron[1] flyer hovered, wobbling slightly as the shock waves rushed away from all the commotion. A hand held something out the side of the craft, and then it didn't, the opening fingers wrinkling the word LOVE.

A second later, the screen in front of the pilot showed the flash of light and then the bodies scrabbling away from the cab and, incidentally, each other. The bald head leaned a little closer so that he could distinguish the figure of the blasphemer . . . whose headlong flight had quickly turned into a headlong dive, and who was now flush with the ground and not able to fall over or duck at the last moment. More; on his own and not endangering others by unjustly, selfishly, getting out of the way when someone was trying to shoot him. In fact, as a bonus, hugging the ground like it was a seventy billion square yard security blanket, and not moving a muscle.

A lying duck.

Curtis had passed the point where the brain was capable of sending messages to his various moving bits, because they were all bumping into each other in a frenzy and never got further than his head. His arms and legs just lay there and waited, while his brain consoled itself with the recognition that it couldn't see anything.

Fission ran out of the light and noise, trying to see where the others were as she did so, but unable to find them. Each time she paused to look around her, another detonation forced her further away, and she ran for a small sheltering copse where, she had already decided, she would regroup and attack. The details she'd work out when she got there.

At ninety degrees to Fission, Gloria followed Tamon as closely as she could. Getting even closer, she grabbed something four inches from his arm and pointed at a bush.

'Bush!' she managed to shout above the din. He kept moving, glancing distastefully at her hand, then at her eyes.

'Very good,' he told her.

'Shelter!'

'I intend to.'

She took a final look at the bush, as another detonation stripped it of most of its leaves, and followed Tamon towards some trees before missing her footing and sprawling with a cry and a small, unavoidable bounce.

---

[1]From antigraviton. The 'jingle' people in Marketing were absolutely thrilled.

Tamon ignored her completely and ran on for a couple of paces, encouraged by more explosions from not nearly far enough away, but then stopped and darted back to where Gloria lay. He yanked her to her feet and pulled her with him until she ran on her own. He headed again towards the trees, wondering, all the while, what had induced him to go back for the offworlder.

The Champion smiled with a curl of microwaves, and the skies of the planet Farger cleared miraculously.

The angtron flyer manoeuvred until it was directly over Curtis's prostrate form.

LOVE reached down and grasped the last of the devices, this one with a distinctive red dot on it, as in danger. He smiled. This would prove that LOVE hurts. At his feet, Stay watched with an expression of trust, doubt and air-sickness.

On the screen, the blasphemer finally moved. He brought his hands up and laid them on the back of his head.

Holding his arm out rigidly, with its handful of retribution, LOVE looked upwards, and offered a silent prayer to the most holy Curtis.

The soon-to-be most holey Curtis felt his collar gripped by something and his jump-suit dragged across the ground with his body inside it.

'I rid the Earth of one who would destroy us.' The hand released its grip and he waited, still peering upwards, and therefore not seeing that his screen was now empty. LOVE was blind.

Curtis rolled over, sat up, and looked up into the branches of a tree and Fission's face. He opened his mouth to say something when another explosion rent the air, and a bit of roadway flew past his head. He didn't notice the metallic impregnation of the material, both because it was travelling too fast, and because he was pitched forwards by the blast once more onto his face.

LOVE looked down at the screen, and saw just a big hole where the threat had lain. With a quiet smile he instructed the machine to travel.

Stay shook his head, and barked his knowledge.

'Quiet, Stay.'

Stay shrugged. Suit yourself.

The Champion pushed a quiet pulse of satisfied orange and yellow into the ether, matching exactly the wavelength of the visible light in the explosion on the planet below, a detail not missed by the Challenger.

The Challenger did not react, which took considerable effort, and caused a nearby star to dim appreciably. It apparently turned its attention to Trand.

The Champion stayed with Earth for a moment, studying the position of its team members. Then it searched the galaxy once more.

Curtis raised himself off the ground with a push-up – incidentally equalling his record – and Fission was gone. He did not see her ducking into a copse some two hundred yards away on the far side of the grab, and would have been greatly confused if he had.

What he did see was the head of some kind of large deer bent towards him, brown eyes fixed steadfastly on his own, and, in them, a look of something other than vegetarian intent.

Deers were supposed to be nice, affable, dewy-eyed things that made friends with rabbits and munched grass, Curtis thought to himself, as the unfairness of this latest situation mirrored the unfairness of all the other situations he had encountered since landing in this quantum Universe, and yet still managed to surprise him. Deers didn't frown at you like this. They didn't bare their teeth. They didn't waggle their antlers in a way that made you very aware of them.

It wasn't fair.

Behind the animal were a number of others in two groups, watching with apparent intellectual detachment.

'Leave this to me!' the deer snarled, its breath hot in Curtis's face, and smelling of grass, acorns, and a lack of dental floss.

It bent slightly, even closer, tilting its antlers towards his nose as if taking aim with a hammer, then lifted its head in the air, reared up on its hind legs, and Curtis shut his eyes tightly at the first downward movement, waiting for the blow.

Gloria and Tamon slowed to a stop when they ran through the trees and found themselves on a carpet of brown grass which covered any number of undulating hills, all dotted with leafy trees. Tamon snapped his head round and stared back the way they had come, finding the copse several hundred yards away, as if it had been running in the opposite direction. He frowned and looked at Gloria, presumably for an explanation.

95

She copied his glance backwards and shrugged.

'It's probably the Champion or the Challenger or Biondor or something,' she told him, covering most of the possibilities without getting them much further forwards.

'But . . .' He looked confused, pointing his head this way and that. Gloria couldn't help thinking that he looked a bit silly, but knew it wasn't his fault. She had seen quite enough since leaving Earth not to be fazed by a few unexpected hills. She wondered momentarily if she looked as silly when she was confused . . .

Where's Thomas? she thought, sadly.

Tamon turned and began to make his way back to sanity with determined steps. He didn't care how or why it had happened; he was just interested in stopping it happening as quickly as possible because it had never happened before and therefore wasn't meant to *be* happening.

'Stop there!'

He stopped immediately at the order, looking around frantically again for the owner of a harsh if high-pitched voice. It presented itself, as Gloria caught up with him, by jumping from the branch of a nearby tree and landing squat in front of them.

It was about two feet tall, covered in brown fur, with a lighter brown on its stomach, and it held a short, reasonably straight, sharply-pointed wooden spear.

It was a koala.

Possibly, Gloria thought – the spear preventing her from going all gooey and trying to tickle it behind the ear – a killer koala.

Several more of the creatures jumped down to join the first, forming a rough circle. Gloria noticed that they all had leaves on their shoulders, mostly just one, but the first animal, two.

'Rule four,' the bear barked at them, thrusting its spear forwards. 'No antelopes!'

'Interlopers!' hissed the koala next to him, one with, Gloria noted, one whole leaf and one torn in half on his – or her – shoulder.

'Interlopers!' the first corrected. 'No interlopers! Punishable by death.'

'They're not robots.' Tamon spoke quietly, almost with a sense of wonder. 'They're animals, real animals.'

Gloria watched. The real animals were edging towards them, spears first. It didn't seem, to her, much consolation that they were about to be killed by real animals as opposed to robot animals, even cute, furry real animals. What could they do? she wondered, looking around for some sort of weapon.

They looked very uncertain, nervous, even.

Did that help?

No.

'Wait!' she shouted, and they did, quickly. Too quickly? She had no time to think about it, assuming the talent. But at least they weren't advancing. So far so good. Now what? 'Er. We didn't mean to interlope. We're sorry.'

Two-leaves looked her up and down – from his height, mostly 'up'. Uncertainly, she thought, again.

'You're sorry?'

'Yes. We didn't know the rules and we're sorry. Will you let us go?' Even to her, it didn't sound the sort of impassioned defence that normally won over someone intent on killing you, but the koala seemed to be considering it.

'Well, I don't know what the rules say about that. If the ante . . . interlopers are sorry . . .' He turned to his slightly less beleafed lieutenant, who shrugged furry shoulders and looked around anxiously. 'I suppose we could just give you a warning and . . .'

'*NO WARNINGS!*'

The koalas very nearly jumped straight back into their trees at the bark from over to Gloria's right. She turned to see a much larger specimen, its fur darker and more patchy than the others, its nose almost split in two by a scar down the middle, and one ear practically missing. It wore two leaves on each shoulder and carried a spear twice as long, and, Gloria would have bet, twice as sharp as those of what she already knew to be its subordinates.

'Lord Kerl!' said Two-leaves in a wet-crotch sort of voice. 'I wouldn't have let them go. Not really. I was . . . I was taunting them.'

'If we let one of the creatures go, they'll be back for our trees.' Kerl clearly didn't believe him. Nor did Gloria; but then she didn't believe Kerl either. What Tamon thought was difficult to tell from his open jaw and uncomprehending expression. 'This is *my* territory, and it's death to any who enter without my permission!'

He had drawn level with Two-leaves by now, and without pausing, or even appearing to glance at him, he brought the spear round in a flat arc, catching the animal just behind the ear. Two-leaves hit the ground like a sack of rice and lay unmoving, only the steady trickle of blood coming from his head showing that he was still alive.

Gloria took a step forwards, and immediately the spear was levelled at her, held in paws that ended impressively in long black claws. Kerl stared at her through hard little eyes, and, looking into them, she saw madness. This one would chew a eucalyptus leaf to hear it scream. She hesitated, and something approaching a smile spread across the animal's face.

'You want to take me on?' Kerl asked.

She stared at three foot of cuddly, homicidal, cute, insane koala bear, and considered.

Carlton looked at three foot of grass that surrounded him and Dano, stretching into the distance across an impossibly flat, ridiculously wide plain, and wondered vaguely which planet had quite such a purple sky, making the grass rather darker than the orange which it seemed naturally to be. It was just a passing thought; another planet was just another planet these days, and there didn't seem to be any imminent danger.

He looked around, and saw, some two hundred yards behind them, a group of green trees, under a unique patch of blue sky. That, he thought, must be the doorway back to Earth Five Zero. And that was all his senses noted, dulled by all the lunatic experiences thrown their way.

'Where are we?' asked Dano, her voice unable to disguise the uncertainty.

Carlton glanced at her. While he recognised that, in all probability, it was the first time she had been transported from her planet to somewhere unintelligible by bodiless super-beings, he couldn't bring himself to feel too sorry for her. Mainly because it was also the first time he had been one up on a 'civ' since he arrived.

'I don't recognise the planet we're on now, but I guess that's the way back.' He pointed, and started walking, pushing his way through the grass. Dano followed automatically, eyes searching the horizon from under a deep frown.

If she had looked a little nearer she might just have caught a localised rustle of the grasses that couldn't be explained by a gentle breeze occasionally managing a half-hearted puff. And there, another rustle. And there.

'How did we get here?' she asked.

'Probably the Champion opened some sort of spacial wormhole in the woods to get me out of danger.' He wondered why he was talking about spacial wormholes, which he had only ever come across on the vidivision,[1] and didn't particularly like the answer. Dano accepted the gibberish with apparent respect.

'Tamon's report mentioned the Champion,' she muttered, distractedly.

They walked in silence for a short while. To both sides, the grass shifted ever so slightly as something moved under its cover, and moved faster than the two walkers, edging ahead of them. More disturbances followed behind, just keeping pace. A circle was gradually forming.

Carlton had other things on his mind, the distractions of the past few minutes giving way once again to the mood he had established.

Not that he was one to bear a grudge.

'Don't let being off-world upset you too much.'

There again . . .

Dano caught the tone, and her own was colder than a flu-ridden penguin's beak. 'I think I can cope for a little while. I won't breathe too deeply.'

The grass rippled unnoticed.

'Are you *all* snobs?' He didn't favour her with a glance, despite the appealing prospect.

Dano could have bristled. He expected her to; wanted her to, he admitted.

She didn't.

Instead, she wrinkled her nose and smiled tightly to herself. 'Well,' she said, and Carlton turned towards her at the sound of the smile. 'Most of us, I'm afraid.'

His balloon of anger sprung its first leak, and he sought to bolster it with mention of his current bête noire. 'Especially that Tamon.'

Her smile was a little more grim. 'He can be a bit much at times.'

The ripples in the grass were now directly in front of them – as well as all around – and suddenly stopped about ten yards ahead, as if preparing. Glancing alternately at each other and the copse, now about a hundred yards away, the two noticed nothing untoward.

'Doesn't it bother you having a boss like that?'

'Like what? Snobbish?'

'Not just that. Like he'd love to shoot himself if only someone would give him an order to do it.'

Dano smiled and shrugged. 'Why should it? It doesn't stop me from doing what I want to do, and someone's got to be the boss –

[1]"Star Trek XIX – Shawl and Slippers', in which Kirk and co. had to be beamed up from a chair, let alone a planet.

that's what a civilised society is all about.'

Carlton immediately reverted to his shaving brush stance. 'Don't start all that again! I'm sick of hearing how you're all so bloody civilised!'

She would have responded, but the grass erupted in a dozen different places around them, and all they could see were creatures leaping at them. Carlton got the impression of dark fur on some, while others appeared pink, as though furless, but with their skin flapping loose as they came.

That was all the time he had before he felt claws and teeth on the backs of his legs and on his arms. He was nearly knocked backwards by something which clung to his chest, a dark furred, almost spherical ball of an animal, with intense little brown eyes, aiming sharp teeth at his throat. Next to him, he saw Dano going down into the grass, the weight of creatures and her own efforts to rid herself of them destroying her balance.

Then he, too, felt his legs buckling under him, as the creature on his chest clawed its way higher, and he stretched his neck away, seemingly trying to detach his head from the rest of his body before the animal did it for him.

As the world turned orange and reedy, a voice floated up from down by his legs.

'Will you hurry up and get its neck, for Joop's sake – I'm totally shagged down here!'

Fission leaned heavily against the tree in front of her while she sucked in a few deep breaths.

Right, she thought, now for it.

Her plans were not much more advanced than that. She knew she was going to get right back into the fray and attack whatever she found there. It was just the 'what' and the 'how' that she had to work out, and she would do that as she went along. So long as she kept a firm grip on the 'why', she'd win through.

She pushed herself off the tree, spun round towards the grab, and looked over the edge of a cliff no more than a dozen feet behind her. At the bottom, a battering river of white water made a complete mess of its bed, and threw spits of spume ten feet up at her, but uselessly, as they never reached more than a quarter of the distance between them.

The rift was about fifty feet across, and the far side was dotted with trees. In the background, a small stand of them seemed to shimmer somehow, as if they were not quite there at all. By the cliff's edge, several had been torn from their roots, or had been broken off and thrown like a sacrifice to the waters, so that only their stumps remained. A strong breeze blew from behind her, across the gorge, and bent the trees and bushes. Except those that shimmered, which ignored the wind completely.

'Fonk,' she muttered quietly. The shimmering trees, she reckoned, were her doorway back to the Earth, never mind the fray. Her first target, then.

She looked around her.

She was at the edge of a wood, thinly made up of tall trees. Through them she could see another cliff edge, maybe twenty yards away. To right and left the twenty yards tapered to a point. She quickly trotted through the wood to another ravine, this one much wider than the first, and confirmed that she was on an island, presumably formed by the river rushing past on either side.

'Fonk,' she muttered again. It didn't get her any further forward, but it regulated the stress a bit. She looked up at the trees, apparently the only resource available to her, and there were lianas hanging down from them all, long ropes that shouted lasso to anyone who had ever watched a Western. Fission hadn't, but she heard the shout in any case.

She quickly selected a good long one and gave it a yank.

It broke somewhere high in the branches and fell to the ground with a high-pitched scream of panic.

Or so it seemed. But as the rope fell, it was followed by some sort of animal, tumbling head over heels, and crying out as it came. Fission moved forwards instantly to try to catch it, but, about ten feet off the ground, it suddenly stretched out its four limbs, and an expanse of webbed skin from ankles to wrists slowed it so that it only hit the ground with a moderate thump.

Reddish brown, and obviously rodentate, its most distinguishing feature was a long, bushy tail which arced over its head even as it lay there.

It sat up and looked at Fission.

'What did you go and do that for?'

'Needed rope. Sorry.'

It rubbed its head, then suddenly stopped, paw still raised, and stared at her. 'How did you get here?' It sounded eager.

'Don't know. Matter transfer, probably.'

It slowly lowered the paw. 'Have you got it here?'

'What?'

'This mat thing.'

'Not mat, matter . . . it . . .' How did you explain matter and TMT and alien beings to a flying squirrel? she wondered, and the answer came instantly. You didn't, unless you had a lot of time and more patience. She had no time, and less patience. 'Doesn't matter.'

It frowned at her, clearly trying to understand. 'Matter doesn't matter?'

'Forget it. Just want to get back over there.' She pointed over there.

'Don't we all!'

'Huh?'

'We all want to get back over there, but there's no way. Can't you get back the same way you came?'

'No.'

'Oh.'

The wind gusted from behind her, and she had to take a step to keep her balance. Out of a corner of her eye she saw movement, as more squirrels edged down the trees and approached them. She ignored them.

She looked at the liana, trying to measure its length against the width of the chasm. Would it be long enough once she had tied a noose at the end to lob over one of the tree stumps on the far side? Would it be heavy enough to be thrown across? She walked to the edge of the cliff, and the animals followed.

'What are you going to do?' asked the first. She told it, and it shook its head, pursing its lips.

'Ooh, I wouldn't do that. That sounds too risky, that does.'

'No alternative. Except stay here.'

Now it looked scared and wrung its hands. 'Can't stay here either. The island's . . .'

The piece of ground where Fission stood, tying what she hoped would be a secure slip knot in the end of the liana, suddenly shifted under her feet, and she jumped backwards just in time to see it plunge into the waters below.

'. . . disintegrating.'

Fission took a deep breath, then paused in her knot-tying to stare at the animal, and the dozen or so that surrounded it.

'You saying you stuck here?'

The creature nodded, and made to reply, but, instead, only managed to squeeze a tear out of one eye. It looked wretched, and so

102

did its fellows, suddenly a pathetic collection of despair.

'But you flying squirrels, for fonk's sake. You fly across. Climb tree; fly.' Carrying a rope, she thought to herself.

The squirrel looked as though she had suggested doing something terminal to its nuts. 'It's too far. We'd never make it.'

'We're flying squirrels,' said another. 'Not smacking-into-cliff-face squirrels.'

'Nor swimming squirrels either,' came a third confirmation. 'If we tried that, we'd be drowning squirrels.[1] We can't risk it.'

'We should have tried it when the chasm wasn't as wide,' said another, to those around it. 'We could have made it then. I'm sure we could.' It looked at Fission. 'It's too late now.'

And Fission went white.

The squirrels didn't spot it, nor the widening of the eyes and the quickening of the pulse. If they had, they would probably have found the cliff edge and made like lemmings.

Larna.

Lucky Larna . . .

When she was a kid, and Larna had been her best friend, they used to play around in the seas off the Gulf Coast. They had these brilliant wet suits that were blue with fish holoed onto them so that they looked just like a small shoal. They could swim with the fish, who accepted them, and they could scare the hell out of the fishermen – a whole shoal leaping out of the water and screaming Fonk! at them . . .

They were out in a small boat they had found abandoned on the shore – it had been Fission's idea – when the water started seeping in, then dribbling in, then pouring. And the current was taking them out as quickly as their paddling could take them in.

They had to swim for it, Fission had said, already moving. But Larna said it was too far, and just sat there whimpering.

Fission pleaded.

Larna cried, and clutched the side.

It was the only way, Fission had insisted, but Larna wouldn't move.

So Fission had jumped in and swum towards the shore, intent on getting help if Larna would not help herself. As soon as she could

[1]Quantum evolution had once come up with drowning squirrels, who lived on fish but couldn't swim. They didn't last long. Nor did the equally unlikely fish that fed on squirrels, as soon as they found out that they were not only woefully under-equipped to climb trees, but also sadly deficient in the lung department while they gave it a go.

stand, she looked back out to make sure Larna was still all right, and by now it *was* too far to swim. The boat was all but submerged.

As Larna disappeared into the water, Fission had fumbled with the thruwater glasses tied round her neck, and had turned up the magnification. Blurred by her tears she could see Larna swimming, fighting the current, getting nowhere.

She had cried out to her friend, knowing there was nothing she could do, that any help she might get would be far too late now.

But then, miraculously, that piece of luck for which Larna was ever after known. A school of fish, akin to the dolphins, saw what they must have thought was a small shoal of the young of their own kind struggling, and they massed beneath her, and pushed her back towards the surface. Without their help she would have drowned in seconds, but now it looked like she might make it.

And then . . .

Then . . .

Then a dozen sharp-beaked pelicans saw her, and made the same fonking mistake.

Lucky Larna, they called her, behind their hands, thinking that Fission couldn't hear.

She left it too late because she couldn't make a decision.

Fission had never, ever afterwards risked that mistake. And she had never forgiven herself for letting Larna make it. She should have tipped her over the side.

She had left a bit of herself on that beach, and knew, deep down, that it was the bit that not only could take a back seat, but which appreciated many of the joys of life.

Well, there was nothing she could do about it now.

She looked at the squirrels on the ground in front of her, and roughly wiped her eyes with her sleeve.

'It's *not* too late,' she told them, and something in her tone told even squirrels that contradiction just now would be their last diction. 'Not while I'm here.'

XII

Aglaea, of the Montana Aglaeas, could recount her American ancestry back to the town mayor who welcomed the passengers off the Mayflower, and when she met someone whom she had not met before, someone who was therefore ignorant of their honour, that was precisely what she did. At length, and largely without pause.

She vacationed, along with Shether – a small weed of a partner whose express purpose in life had been to initiate an heir to the Aglaea name, and having done that to follow his senior partner around in case she needed something to shout at – on the same very exclusive beach on the St James coast of Barbados. And terrestrial Barbados, not one of the rather cheaper – like, free – orbiting pleasure parks which reproduced every delight of any destination you would care to mention, including sand, sea, palm trees, and ski slopes, but excluding, of course, its authenticity.

Aglaea vacationed for the same six, ludicrously extravagant weeks every year, staying in the same hotel, which owned the beach, and even eating at the same dining table. A creature of habit was Aglaea.

Also a creature of such proportions that one could be forgiven for assuming that since her ancestors had set foot in the country, the family had done nothing *but* eat, whether at the same table or not.

She was returning from her lunchtime binge – 'snack', she called it – to her allotted place on the beach, reserved by the monogrammed towel on her reinforced sun-bed. The sun-bed was there, but the towel was not; it lay in a little monogrammed heap in the sand.

In its place lay a man, a smaller towel draped over his head in the bright sunshine. Aglaea came to a shuddering stop like an ancient super-tanker thrown into emergency reverse, while Shether dutifully halted a few paces behind her. Gasping for breath at the audacity of the unspeakable little person on her sun-bed, and resting a hand on her bosom for a moment to still a heart which pounded at the very effrontery of it all, she closed her parasol, momentarily, and poked the man with it.

Arnold pulled the towel from his face, and pointed a frown up at her.

'What?'

She all but swooned.

'What' indeed!

Shether looked on with a worried expression, knowing that 'what' came close to an obscenity in Aglaea's book – he had known her to feign dizziness when someone in her hearing said 'botty-pops'.

Given which information, she might just have poked the wrong person.

'What do you think you are doing?' Aglaea asked, using what Shether recognised as her imperious tone. She had a number of them, each containing varying levels of disapproval, and each a source of pride.

She had no notion that the tone king lay before her.

Arnold looked from Aglaea's face to his own shorts-clad body, then up to the almost clear blue sky, with only a couple of cotton wool clouds and the odd seabird vying with the sun for occupation, then, after a quick pass of the other sun-bathers on the beach, back to Aglaea's face.

'I'm conducting the San Francisco Philharmonic Orchestra,' he replied, raising his head slightly from the bed and indicating, with a sweep of his hand, the musicians arranged in a semi-circle in front of him. 'Oops, they've gone.' He laid his head down again.

'Don't be impertinent,' instructed Aglaea.

Arnold's eyebrows twitched. 'If you're a waitress, get me another ice cream would you?' He reached for his head-covering towel again. The tip of Aglaea's parasol stopped the towel's movement while her heart threatened to stop its own.

'How *dare* you! I am Aglaea. *The* Aglaea!' This was supposed to mean something to someone with sufficient financial clout to warrant a place on this particular beach. Arnold reacted not. 'You are in my personal space.'

Arnold looked her up and down, and sideways.

'Not all of it, surely?'

Aglaea clasped another hand to her bosom, which was in danger of becoming severely bruised by this time. Her complexion reddened much more quickly than would normally be occasioned even by exposure to the Barbadian sun.

'I shall have you thrown out, you impudent little upstart! You obviously have no idea of whom you are talking to.'

'I am talking,' Arnold stated with great clarity of diction, 'although I have absolutely no wish to do so, to a frumpy, late middle-aged harridan with delusions of grandeur and physical proportions not normally associated with land dwelling mammals. If there are any particulars I have omitted, then I'm sure they are insignificant ones. Have a nice day, now.' And he replaced the towel on his head.

Aglaea could not speak, could hardly take a breath, and she reached behind her for Shether, propelling him forward so he could stand up for her. He wiped the smirk from his face as his feet inscribed two deep ruts in the sand at the insistence of his beloved's fistful of shirt front.

'Er, just who do you think you are?' he tried. A muffled voice came back to him from beneath the towel.

'I am Arnold. *The* Arnold.'

That seemed to end the matter.

The Arnold had left Tamon – a nerd even by human standards in his objective opinion – and the others behind him, holding one hand protectively close to his body so that the grease from Carlton's brow would not dry.

After running for about a mile he had slowed and ducked behind a bush, half expecting Tamon to be following in his cab, or patrol car, or whatever it was, but when he looked back the way he had come to see what was going on, the only candidate for the role of pursuer was a rampaging six armed alien, galloping down the middle of the road like a deranged whirlwind.

Shrugging off the presence of an alien life form on Earth as just another lunatic element of the Game, he had waited until it thundered past, then followed the creature – at a safe distance – and eventually found himself in a small, apparently nameless town which sported several shops, boutiques and a bank.

Not recognising that it was remarkably quaint to have establishments where you could actually go and browse through the merchandise on offer, Arnold immediately visited the last, and emerged with a piece of personalised plastic packed so full of credit that the electrons which kept count of the numbers were in danger of dripping out over the side.

What he did not have any more was Carlton's sweat.

What Carlton did not have any more he was shortly to find out.

International Tachyon Travel beckoned to Arnold from across the road. After a short flick through some holographic brochures, and a

107

brief experience of the three most likely destinations in the complete sensory booth, Arnold stepped through the travel company's tachyon matter transference – TMT – door, and emerged in the foyer of the Grand Hotel.

In the day or so since then he had done very little and largely enjoyed it, especially the latest bit with the fat woman, who now stomped off towards the hotel with her tail between her legs and her partner just behind them.

There was just one thing wrong, he thought, and he peeked from under his towel down at his torso. Biondor clearly had not included melanin in the body he had bestowed on the former computer. Arnold could lie in the sun for as long as he wanted, but he wasn't going to go brown.

Ah, well. This was as good a place, literally, to lie low as any other for the time being, until he worked out what he was going to do with his life.

Something grand, he fancied. Something where he did not have to *prove* his superiority, but where it was recognised. Something which ensured that people like *the* Aglaea woman knew that there was Arnold, then there were other androids in order of ability, and then there were humans, all jumbled up at the bottom.

In the distance a hotel flunkey was preparing a new sun-bed for Aglaea, whose credit could not apparently shift Arnold. Shether stood by her side and, glancing across for inspiration to where Arnold lay, took his courage in both hands, and for the first time in his life, spoke back to Aglaea.

She beat him unconscious with her parasol tusk, and he settled on to the beach.

XIII

Curtis still waited for the blow to fall. His tightly closed eyes retained the picture of antlers being drawn back, while his mind calculated the likely reduction in the distance between the front and the back of his head, and whether his brain would still fit in the gap – and work – but then he realised that nothing else had happened; to him at least. There was a scraping noise for a moment, followed by the sound of a brief struggle, and then what Curtis recognised as a resigned whimper. He had long experience of resigned whimpers.

Then, from a little way off, came a snigger. It may have been a deer's snigger, but Curtis had plenty of experience in that field as well.

A little right-shoulder voice began whispering that the noises were directed at him, that by lying there, waiting to be killed, he was doing something embarrassingly amusing.

He unscrewed one eye very slowly, and there was the deer, hanging above him, waggling its front legs in mid-air in a manner with just a touch of the frenetic. Its antlers were inextricably entwined in the branches of the tree above it. The look on its face was no longer one of threat, but of humiliation, with the beginnings of panic.

Then the animal slumped, as best it could without breaking its neck, and resignation took over. One of, apparently, the older group of animals nodded across to a young stag, and he trotted forward, head held high – but clear of any obstructions. On reaching his stricken brother, he gently lifted off his forelegs, and nudged one or two branches aside with deft movements of his antler tips. Curtis's assailant, suddenly free, fell on top of him, and they performed the knocked-out breath duet.

The deer got up first, but as Curtis flinched away in anticipation – inevitably swivelling painfully on his punctured buttock – the animal turned to face the older group, leaving his former target panting on the ground.

'It is to your credit that you sought to lead the group,' said a grizzled animal slightly to the fore of the group. 'However, your qualities are yet to be honed. You may rejoin your fellows, stag Richard.'

Richard! Curtis looked at the deer as it followed its low-hung head to the back of the group.

The Challenger must have done this, he thought, just to take the piss, yet again, and the danger of the situation seemed to lessen as he realised its purpose. He started to clamber to his feet, trying, nevertheless, to do it surreptitiously, while his right shoulder suggested that things took the piss out of him so much it was a wonder he ever had to use the toilet.

Then the danger was back as surreptitious clambering proved over-ambitious, and the rescue deer turned a competent expression towards him. A half movement from the animal had him on his feet and using them, running back through the copse towards where the grab waited, except that, unless he was going the wrong way, the copse had got bigger. Behind him followed cries that sounded like orders, then a crescendo of hooves getting closer.

'Donna, over to the left!' shouted a voice.

Curtis veered, realised that his veer had been to the left, and reversed it.

'Elege, to the right.'

He veered back to the middle, managing to dodge the trees and stay upright. How long that might last, he wasn't sure, as his aching lungs reminded him that the only purpose to which he had ever put his training shoes was to make a record breaking smell.

He ran blindly, expecting to be knocked to the ground by deer or habit at any moment, expecting something to drop from a tree to his neck, expecting something with teeth and an empty stomach to dart out from behind a bush.

He didn't expect a carefully set trip-wire, but that was what he found, using his ankle for the purpose, and he dived to the ground as though he was trying to reach the sea from several hundred yards inland. The air was knocked out of him in a rush; he gouged himself to a halt using nose-plough and forehead, shook his head to clear it of an immediate fuzziness, and looked into the excited eyes of a large termite two inches from his own.

It smiled at him, or, at least, in his direction.

'It works!' said the termite, in tones of hushed excitement. 'I knew I could do it! I don't need them! Now then, how to kill it . . .'

Curtis didn't know whether this was some deeply significant part of the Game, or whether he was just going completely mad – he rather hoped the latter, for a brief instant when letting go and gibbering for a few months appealed greatly – and didn't have time to find out as the noise of hooves pushed its way into his reeling head.

He rolled onto his back and stared up at the antlers looking down, and what looked like smirks of triumph on the ends of the graceful faces. The antlers were covered with fine downy hair, he noticed, but that was only like looking from the chopping block into the basket and seeing a nice bit of blanket at the bottom.

So this is it, he thought, and the comfort of resignation stole over him again. He lay there, almost relaxed.

'Well done,' came the voice of the old stag from some distance away. 'You have initiated, stag Dox.'

The one Curtis recognised as the 'rescue deer' stood a little taller. The others moved off, losing interest completely in Curtis. Dox leaned lower, and Curtis tried to emulate a termite – which he may or may not have seen a few moments before; he wasn't committing himself in case, as a result, someone else did – by screwing his way into the earth. But an antler caught in the fabric of his jump-suit, and he felt himself lifted, before . . .

. . . before Dox set him gently on his feet, nudged him in the chest and muttered, 'Off you go, little human. Go find your family.' Then he turned and sauntered back deeper into the trees.

Curtis watched the stag go until he disappeared, trying to make his head concentrate on something that he understood, but finding nothing of that description near his thoughts.

'Go find your family'! On top of everything else that was assumedly going on, that was the last damned thing he wanted!

Gloria heard Tamon muttering next to her as she stared at the small but lethally-determined koala who stared right back. She glanced to see the security agent whispering into the device on his wrist, then holding his hand up to a point just behind one ear, as if listening through a hidden earpiece. The expression on his face showed that the response was not what he wanted. He hissed at his wrist once more.

'Central! Respond, Central, please. *Please!*'

Gloria watched for a moment, part of her sorry for the man, and, part of her, she knew – just a tiny part – repelled that he seemed incapable of acting on his own. There again, she thought, right then *she* couldn't do any better. Tamon gave up and caught her eye. He looked scared.

'Haven't you got a gun or something?' she asked quietly, and his hand moved involuntarily towards an oblong device attached, somehow, to his waist, but stopped well short.

'These are real animals!' he said, urgently. 'We can't kill animals.' He paused, looked at Kerl standing unmoved, challenging. 'I have no orders. Besides, they're not doing anything yet.'

Gloria looked at him for a moment longer, letting Tamon read what he might from her expression, and then turned back to the front.

'So.' Kerl spoke. The 'so' of success, dismissing Gloria's threat with contempt.

On the ground, Two-leaves moaned and shifted slightly, and Kerl immediately glanced disgustedly towards him, then looked to the next in command, half a leaf down the hierarchy.

'Varl, isn't it?' The animal nodded, and a nervous swallow confirmed Gloria's impression that it couldn't trust itself to speak. Kerl gestured at Two-leaves. 'Kill him.'

Varl's eyes opened wide, and he mouthed nothing for a moment. Then:

'But, that's Morg. He's . . .' He ran out of words.

Kerl just stared at him, silent, and quite still. Varl looked from Kerl's face to the barely moving form of two-leaved Morg, and a tear sprang to his eye.

'If we do not follow orders, Varl, we are nothing.' Kerl's voice was low, measured, conversational, and unmistakably lethal. 'Without order, we revert to savagery. Kill him.'

As if forcing his legs to move against an overpowering paralysis, Varl took a step forwards, the fur on both cheeks clearly showing the tracks of tears which flowed unchecked.

The expression on Gloria's face was one of horror, and she backed away from the scene, whimpering quietly, reaching out instinctively for Tamon.

'Oh, Tamon, this is horrible, horrible!'

He stood firm, slightly taller if anything, letting the woman shelter behind him as the drama played itself out.

He hardly felt the tug at his waist, and by the time it had registered, it was too late. Gloria was two steps away, with the gun in her hand, staring at it and trying to work out what the trigger was and which end the bullet would come from – the device looked more like a remote control than anything else; she was unlikely to foil Kerl with an order to go fast-forward.

'Stop!' she shouted, making the decision that she would just have to risk it.

Varl stopped immediately, and Kerl turned back towards her. She had expected to see anger in his face, but still he smiled. She held the gun at arm's length, keeping half an eye on Tamon, just in case. Kerl took a step towards her.

'Stop, or I'll shoot.'

'You will do *what?*' Kerl asked with contempt.

'Shoot.' He doesn't understand, she thought, desperately. He doesn't know what this is. 'This is a gun. It shoots things.' She waved an unimpressive oblong box in front of his mad eyes.

'This is a spear. It kills things.'

'So does this.'

'Does it really? How?'

I don't know, she thought. It just does!

Kerl raised his spear, and quickened his pace. He was no more than five yards from her and Gloria backed away, putting off the moment until she couldn't any longer. Tamon watched, but said nothing.

She aimed low, for the legs, and pressed the red button.

A disruptor beam on medium spread does more than singe toes.

With a brief scream of what sounded more like anger than pain, Kerl's whole being seemed to wobble momentarily as if viewed through faulted glass, and then simply disappeared. Six inches of viciously pointed spear fell to the ground, and rolled a little way, the subject of countless hushed stares.

Varl collapsed in a heap, sobbing uncontrollably, and Gloria, her hand shaking, and her stomach churning, handed the gun back to Tamon. He took it with a mouth so wide that it looked like he was preparing to eat the thing.

'You're always shagged, fatty.'

The comment didn't strike Carlton as odd, nor the pot calling the kettle black – all of the animals being apparently as round as each other – because he had more important things on his mind. A sharp set of teeth were making inexorable progress towards his throat, and both his arms were weighed down with at least one animal.

Straining, he managed to lift one off the ground and brought it over towards his chest.

'Oo-er!' called the animal clinging to the moving wrist. 'Look out,

113

Dart, it's lifting me up!'

Dart was apparently the one on his chest, because it stopped and looked to whence the warning had come. Its eyes widened as it saw its fellow being dragged through the grass above it, and then brought crashing down on top of it. The grips on both wrist and chest were broken and the two animals tumbled off.

'Look, it's too big,' said one from somewhere else. 'Let it go.'

'What do you mean? It could feed us for a week!'

'It could kill me, is what it could do, Jink, you dit!'

'Well then, it'd feed the rest of us for two weeks then, wouldn't it, greed-ball?'

'Why, you . . .'

Carlton scrambled to his feet as two of the animals leapt at each other, and rolled round and round – for which they were exceptionally well equipped – pummelling with hands and feet but not, apparently, causing too much damage to the rolls of fat that surrounded each of them.

He tried to get his bearings, to find Dano, and saw the tell-tale flattened grass just off to one side. At the same time, he heard the sound of her own efforts to rid herself of the creatures.

At his feet, the two combatants broke apart, and lay there panting, as he pushed towards where she lay. Then something landed on the back of his neck, and wrapped sharp-clawed hands around his throat.

'You little bastard!' he croaked, grabbing its paws, pulling it off, and flinging it away.

'Here! It spoke!' said one of the creatures lying on the ground.

'Hey, stop everyone! You lot! Oi!' called another. 'It spoke.'

By the time he had pushed his way to Dano, she was free of the creatures and sitting up, inspecting various tooth and claw marks that oozed rather than poured blood. The animals had clearly broken off the attack, and were forming into a group, staring at the two humans.

'Go on,' said the one called Jink, to Carlton. 'Say something.'

'What?' he asked, and suddenly felt stupid, and glad that Arnold wasn't there.

'Bleedin' 'ell,' said another. 'A talkin' 'uman. Can *you* talk an' all?'

Dano just stared at the animal, the shock of the situation overcoming any wish her vocal cords might have had to get in on the act.

'Nah, that one can't.' This was from one of the creatures with what

Carlton had originally taken to be a bald skin, and so it proved to be, except that it had obviously come from some other animal, and was simply being worn as a coat. From the look of it, Carlton had a pretty good idea of the sort of animal who had donated it.

'Of course I can talk!' said Dano, finding a voice that sounded impressively steady to Carlton; not that he would let *her* know. Probably.

'Blimey, it can, too! I must have eaten some mushrooms.'

'Well, you've eaten just about everything else.'

Again, two animals dived at each other and skirmished briefly before falling apart and panting for breath.

'What are you?' asked Carlton.

'What do you mean?' Dart sounded affronted.

'What species of animal?'

'We ain't animals. We're mink!'

'All right, Skip, don't get uppity. It's not to know, is it? It's only a human.'

'But minks are lithe little animals that hunt on their own,' Dano pointed out, frowning. She still hadn't quite got her brain around this concept, Carlton thought. On *her* world they might be that, or at least used to be . . .

'We used to be,' admitted Dart, somewhat confusingly for Carlton. 'But that was before we had Joop as the leader. She taught us how to hunt together, as a team. Clever little mink, Joop. We can catch bigger stuff now, and we don't ever go hungry.'

'That's fairly obvious,' Carlton threw in, regaining his equilibrium with the practice of someone who had battled commando sheep in his time.

'Now there's no need to be like that, is there!' protested Dart. 'I get enough of that from this lot.'

'Oh, 'ark at 'im. All 'igh-an'-mighty, mister perfect!'

'Jib off, puss-bag!'

They leapt at each other again, while Dano looked on with ever-increasing confusion.

'Mink aren't supposed to be like this. They were solitary.'

'Wish we could be,' said Jink. 'Trouble is, these days we can't afford to be. We wouldn't catch anything.' It put its paw to the side of its mouth, confidentially. 'Not the size we are now.' It shrugged. 'We're stuck with it, I suppose. Joop got us all civilised and now there's no way out. It's better than it was in some ways, but, I don't know, we've lost something . . .'

'Ain't weight, is it!' came a comment.

'Go pug your coat, Dash.'

Dash gave a barking laugh and smoothed the pink skin of the coat he was wearing on top of his own.

Carlton watched. 'What's the coat made of?'

Dash looked as sheepish as a mink can manage, and scratched the earth with a paw. 'It weren't no talkin' 'uman. It weren't an intelligent one, like. Just some dumb animal.'

'Human!' Dano breathed the word, the look on her face suggesting that she recognised a slight blemish on Dash's attire as being the mole on her mother's upper arm.

'Don't blame me!' Dash spoke with more vigour. 'I bet if you had the chance you'd wear mink coats!'

Dano's expression became more shocked still. 'I certainly would not! The thought of it!'

Carlton said nothing. Dano was still a 'civ', albeit quite a nice one, and he wasn't about to provide any free ammunition.

''Ow comes you can talk then?' Dash asked Dano, changing the subject.

'How come *you* can talk?' she threw back.

'Don't be daft. *We're* mink. Mink talk. *Animals* ain't s'posed to talk.'

'We're not animals,' Dano told it, but, Carlton noticed, without the shocked reaction that they had encountered so far on Earth Five Zero. Odd. Perhaps she was clean out of shock; she'd had a few.

'I reckon we should take them back home,' a mink to their left decided, turning to Dart.

'Oh yes, Zip? How do we do that, then? Why? for that matter! You gonna keep them as pets? You'll need a bloody enormous litter tray.'

Zip considered, and apparently the answer was made clearest by whacking Dart on the side of the head with a flat paw. They both did that for a while. Off to one side Dash and Jink were already tussling for some unknown reason.

Carlton and Dano looked at each other.

'Time to leave, I reckon,' he told her, and she nodded.

The animals were still fighting as they made their way back towards the doorway home, and Dano kept looking over her shoulder, almost reluctant to leave.

'I'd *rather* starve than stick with you lot . . .' floated through the grasses.

XIV

Chichit had always had what she considered a sensible outlook on life
– you treat life with respect, and it stays with you. A staid, safe
outlook. A paws-on-the-ground outlook, even if, occasionally, those
paws left the safety of one branch and glided to another. But not too
far. Gather your Almonds, mind your Pistachios and Quassia, and
you wouldn't go far wrong.

Her outlook on life at the moment was anything but sensible and
staid. And it was a downlook as much as an out one.

She was forty-four feet in the air – four of her own and forty of air –
and just about to drift across the chasm. Tied to one leg – by what the
big animal that stood upright called a slip knot – was a liana. And
buffeting into the stretched skin between her wrists and ankles, was
wind.

Wind could drop at any moment.

And so could she.

She swallowed, and closed her eyes tightly.

Something about keight, the new creature had said, presumably
because it had something to do with height.

She risked a look, saw the edge of the chasm, and risked no more.

She wasn't cut out for this sort of thing. She wasn't a hero. She was
quite happy with her place somewhere in the middle of the social
scene, not bothering anybody. You needed someone like Creechee
for this – he had once glided thirteen feet with a big Hazel under one
arm, and therefore with only half a skin. Now *he* was an adventurous
one.

Mind you, she thought, somewhere in a corner of her brain that
wasn't just blue mist, big Hazel had been livid . . .

On the island, Fission played out the liana, tied to her own wrist
just in case, a look of deep determination etched on her face. She
heard, but ignored, the sound of a mass of earth and crumbling rocks
disappearing from somewhere nearby into the river below.

A kite had been the only way. Dangerous, of course, but there was

117

no alternative, except one.

Chichit had volunteered for the task by being the slowest out of the way when Fission made a grab for a leg, and had kept on volunteering by not being able to struggle out of her arms before the rope was secure.

'You stretch arms legs wide, you fly,' Fission had told her in the sort of no-nonsense tone that contrasted nicely with the actual words. 'You don't, you drop into river. I pull you out.' That sounded sort of okay, in a masochistic sort of way. 'We try again, 'til you get right or drown.' That didn't.

Now Fission looked up and noted approvingly that Chichit – she wasn't sure if that was the right name or a fear-bred stutter – was stretching out as if the four corners of the world were merely milestones for her paws to pass on their way to the outer regions of the galaxy.

'Now that's what I *call* flying, that is,' came a comment from the group behind her.

'Maybe we're not proper flying squirrels either,' said another. 'We should be gliding squirrels.'

'Not really much of a glide when you look at seagulls and things, though, is it?'

'No, I suppose not. Well, what are we, then?'

'Er.'

'What about falling-not-quite-so-quickly-as-other-squirrels squirrels?'

'Well, it's got something . . .'

Timidity is what it's got, thought Fission, and gritted her teeth a bit more. She pulled on the line, gently, and Chichit rose.

The flying squirrel opened one eye again, realising that she wasn't actually dead yet, and looked to the ground. The whole island was there before her. Twisting her head slightly, she could see the mainland behind, almost below her, now. Perhaps it was for the best, she thought, a little desperately, because the island didn't have long to go. Perhaps it was good that this large creature had taken the lead, and had . . .

The wind gusted, then dropped.

Chichit dropped, and her wind gusted.

Fission pulled the liana, and the animal rose again, eyes shut tighter than a sand crab's buttocks.

It wasn't a good idea after all, she thought. On the island she at least had a mate – Keeter. She tried to concentrate on his face, while avoiding the thought that she would never see him again. Keeter, with the finest nuts on the island.

Then she felt herself falling once more, and Keeter's face was just a memory.

The sound of the river was loud in her ears, and she knew she was doomed, that nothing but death awaited her, that she had nibbled Keeter's nuts for the last time . . .

Then she landed with a bump so slight that all it did was jolt her eyelids open. And there was the island, spread before her – how small it looked – across the other side of the chasm, the group of her friends and the large animal watching from the cliff top.

Strange that heaven should look so much like earth.

But, no . . .

She had made it!

She was there! The big animal had been right.

She took a few pantingly deep breaths, resisted the understand-able temptation to run madly in circles for a few seconds, and instead loosened the knot before slipping the rope off her leg.

Back on the island, Fission watched as the weight of the liana im-mediately dragged the loop towards the edge. Her eyes narrowed, she muttered a quiet 'fonk', and looked around for the next volunteer kite.

But then the rope caught on the remains of a woody shrub and a scampering Chichit recovered it. Her senses once more restored, she looked around for a good-sized stump, and dragged the liana across to it, widening the noose created by the knot as she went. Then she slipped it over the top, and waved to the island.

Fission pulled the liana tight, tentatively at first, then with more confidence and strength. Keeping it taut, she wound it around a tree and tied it off. The squirrels all watched with a nervous interest, each making sure that he or she was not in the front row of the audience, which made for some interesting shuffling.

Then the big creature stopped, and indicated the taut line.

'Bridge,' she said. 'Cross.'

They looked at her, and Fission wondered how she would induce them to make the crossing, but then all the falling-not-quite-so-quickly-as-other-squirrels squirrels were swarming for the rope at once, hanging underneath and running as fast as if they were scuttling across the surface of the island. In no more than two minutes, Fission was the only one left.

She swallowed, looking at the rope, and wondering if it would hold her. With a slow-motion, tearing crash, a huge tree not ten yards away uprooted, or downrooted itself, as the land beneath it disappeared, and plunged into the rushing waters.

The tree around which the rope was tied shifted lazily, leaning over the edge to see what had happened, and to decide whether to join its friend. The liana slackened with the movement.

Fission looked around quickly for another tree with rather more of a fundamental grip of itself, and there was none within reach of her rope.

She could risk it, or she could stay on the island.

She smiled grimly, walked to the edge, took hold of the liana with both hands, and swung off. She hung for a moment, sensing the lifeline drooping. Then, ignoring her senses – all five, plus good! she thought – she moved hand-over-hand a couple of yards out, wrapped her legs around the rope and shuffled, hands first, legs catching up, across the chasm with the confidence of one who has no fonking choice.

XV

Arnold stood in the sand and zipped up the front of his jump-suit, while three young children stood silently and watched him with the wide-eyed innocence and serious expression which characterises the breed. Arnold tried not to return the gaze, and found it increasingly difficult; there was a magnetic quality about six eyes with but one aim.

Arnold recognised a new feeling. He had only met one child before, and that had been a baby, and even that had turned out not actually to be a baby at all but a changeling pretending to be a baby. His experience of pre-pubescent humanity was severely limited.

Now it was greater. Children were creatures which hovered their miniature sun-gliders so that the shadows fell on you, and if you looked gruff or made an hurrumphing noise, they just giggled and interpreted it as an invitation to do the same thing again. They were completely impervious to anything but the direct, apoplectic shout, and even that did not disperse them, but simply drew them together in a silently threatening huddle and produced an angelic expression which proved, unarguably, that it had all been your fault in the first place.

What was far worse, for Arnold, was that children were especially immune to sarcasm. They just stared at you as your barbed witticisms flew over their heads like clouds in a gale. They didn't recognise that being scythed down to size should make them feel smaller. Arnold knew that he might as well curl his lip at a cat.

For him this was defeat. This was the Enterprise without phasers; it was Superman on a bed of green Kryptonite; it was the Invisible Man with uncontrollable flatulence.

There was, eventually, nothing to do but relinquish his bed occupation, which had withstood the worst that Aglaea could do but which now crumbled like a wafer before the power of chaste impurity.

As he trudged away from the spot, and six eyes watched in stoic

121

silence, a quotation from the Bible came to comfort Arnold, as it does for so many people in times of trouble.

'Suffer little children,' the Bible said.

Arnold *liked* that bit.

Besides which, he was about to leave anyway, he decided. Lying there was not going to further the plans which he had for the rest of his life.

Which were?

What did he enjoy doing, that was the question?

Puncturing the self-inflated windbags that defined the term 'human beings' probably came at the top of the list. Proving that he was better than humans at anything they could think of was probably second, and generally also served to puncture them further, as an added bonus.

But that did not immediately lead to a ready-made profession.

It had to be something that would make him impervious not only to *the* Aglaea and her ilk, but also to these execrable little cubs and theirs.

He had time to make up his mind, though, he thought, and scuffed the sand in front of one foot. The idea that Tamon had, about him being some claimable robot, would soon pass once the humans resorted to common sense – there must be *some* of the morons that would! – and he had all the money he wanted and needed, so there was no need to rush.

Just so long as he didn't have humans telling him what to do. He would *not* be ordered about like some underling.

He looked over the water, waiting for inspiration.

There wasn't any that way, so he turned round, and saw a hologram declaring that 'Miron's Mother was a Syphilitic Baboon'. A little thought entered his head, and suddenly got very much bigger.

The Challenger broke off from the intricacies of the situation on Trand, and noticed its opponent apparently deep in the mind of the android Arnold.

Now what was it up to?

Arnold smiled, and walked purposefully off the beach, pausing only to tell the children to go and play with the enormous woman over there.

*

Varl stood with his shoulders hunched, and his spear all but falling from his hand, staring at the ground and taking deep breaths. He looked shrunken – no mean feat for a two-foot koala.

He sucked in a final lungful, let it out in a rush and looked up. The sun caught his eyes, and they widened immediately. It was already over the third eucalyptus from the left!

'Parade!' he shouted. 'Parade!'

Some of the other bears started shuffling for position, with the choreography of panic. Gloria watched; it looked like a primary school show, and might even have been funny under different circumstances.

Many of the animals, though, just stood around, and it wasn't long before the message got through. Varl lost his manic look, noticed the spear in his paw as if for the first time, and dropped it.

There was no parade.

'Thank you.' Gloria heard the voice, and looked down to see Morg, walking up to her uncertainly. The two leaves were gone from his shoulders, and blood caked the fur on the back of his head, but he looked okay. She bent down, feeling a little awkward towering above him. 'If it hadn't been for you . . .'

She felt even more awkward now. 'I didn't really do anything.' It sounded a bit stupid to her even as she said it, though she knew what she meant. 'Anyone would have . . .' Tamon didn't though, she thought.

'Well, thank you anyway.'

She smiled. Maybe Morg *had* understood what she meant. More than the average bear, perhaps. Or more likely, distracted and hearing nothing.

'That's all right.' She almost patted him, now that the spear was gone. 'What will you do now?'

He looked around, shrugged.

'I don't know, really. I . . .' The bears were drifting off, going their separate ways with no particular destination in either mind or foot, judging from the speed. Varl was one, a quiet sob interrupting his progress every so often, but the others were apparently too preoccupied to provide comfort. Spears and epaulette leaves lay discarded on the ground. '. . . don't know.'

Morg frowned, confusedly, and seemed to lose sight of Gloria, drifting off after no-one in particular. She straightened and glanced at Tamon.

'We should get back,' he told her, and his voice was firm,

authoritative. 'Follow me.'

He strode off towards the copse, and she looked after him with a little frown, before smiling ever so slightly, and dutifully falling into step just behind.

There is virtually nothing less reassuring than the touch of a hand when you know you are the only human present, and when that touch is the very last thing you expect.

'Hero, eh?' commented his stomach in fluent churn, as he took the sharpest of breaths, and held it at both ends. 'Nothing can possibly go wrong, eh?'

He wondered obtusely how Arnold had managed to invade his intestines, but the smug grin on his stomach's face was shifted when a slow-motion head movement showed another human being standing behind him. Wilverton let out the deep breath in a sigh of relief and chided his imagination.

'Dr Livingstone, I presume,' he muttered. The man didn't look an awful lot like Livingstone, who, as far as Wilverton could remember, was dour looking, middle-aged, and wiry, with receding hair and a moustache. And he was dead. This man was reasonably young, clean shaven, with hair that had receded all the way, of medium build and medium height. He was also smiling, which presumably made him a happy medium. And he was apparently alive.

'No,' he replied.

'Right,' said Wilverton, when it was plain that the conversation was not about to move any further. He looked around to make sure that their chat was not being scrutinised by a trand or two. It wasn't, as far as he could tell, though a trand could blend well enough into rough stonework for him not to be overly sure.

'Do you know somewhere safe to hide?' he asked, assuming that the man must have come from somewhere. He appeared unharmed and somewhere to hide in safety where he could take a bit of a breather was a location which appealed. The man nodded, and smiled again, and let go of his shoulder, for which Wilverton was grateful – he had heard of male bonding but didn't think it should extend to an apparently glue-like attraction.

'Follow me.'

Wilverton gave him a brief look of Earthly déjà vu.

The man scuttled across the street, and Wilverton scuttled after him – thinking that scuttling was a good way to move when you are trying not to be seen; it seemed to fit, somehow – and followed him through the open doorway of a building which looked abandoned and dishevelled, like all the other buildings. Wilverton slammed the door shut behind him and leaned against it gratefully.

The Champion watched the turn of events from on high. And from on low and on wide for that matter; its energy was difficult to pin down with a natty locational description. There were many possibilities for events within the confines of the building which its Player had now entered, and it allowed a brief flash of ultraviolet to suggest concern that it could counteract them all, just in case the Challenger should be watching it, which it would be.

Not that the Challenger would necessarily be fooled. Bluff and double bluff were child's play in the Game. It was only when they got to the heady heights of, say, sesquicentennial bluff that they felt the need even to concentrate.

Meanwhile, though, the Champion pondered what it might do with a slamming door . . . Ah, yes . . .

The force of the shutting door somehow managed to dislodge a slate from the roof, and it skittered down the incline and leapt off the precipice of primitive guttering into the air with a reckless exuberance. Roof slates are like that.

Henry[1] was walking along the street on his way back from the market, where he had gone with the express purpose of picking up an orgal egg, and, if he had to, paying for it. An orgal was a bird about twice the size of a chicken, whose eggs were much prized for their flavour and nutrition, and their dimensions, being about as large as that of an ostrich. Given the disparity in size between the orgal and the egg, a disparity of which the prospective mother bird was extremely well aware, it was no great wonder that they were also prized for their great rarity.[2]

They were especially prized by the strongest of Henry's household, which happened to be his wife, who, when she could get hold of one, watched with growing excitement as the egg boiled for over an hour before going to work on it. Even as Henry walked, she was pacing the living room of their home in restless anticipation.

Henry was holding the egg tenderly – for a trand – in three hands,

[1]Grtaajn if you're interested, or just plain pernickety.
[2]When they hatch, even after the long incubation, the young orgal softly keens the first sound that penetrated its newly laid shell, and the air of the wild breeding grounds is filled with the soft strains of 'oomifanni'.

and treading very carefully indeed, when he heard, but took little notice of, a skittering sound. Then the sound stopped for a moment or two, and a part of his mind noticed the lack of the noise, while most of his mind concentrated on not dropping the egg. Then the whole of his mind watched as a slate landed right on the top of the egg, and just kept on landing right on top of it until it had reached the bottom.

Henry's wife was going to be very disappointed.

'I wasn't expecting to find anyone else,' said Wilverton, visually checking the room. It was much what he had expected – bare walls and a bare floor and nothing which qualified for the description of furniture apart from something which might have been a stone bench, on which the man who was not Dr Livingstone now sat. The superfluity of home comforts made some hovels look decadent.

'Nor was I. I thought I was the only one here.'

'I'm Thomas Wilverton.' He held out a hand in shake mode, wondering if this man came from a planet where hand-shaking was the form of greeting. Perhaps they should sniff each other . . .

'Norim.'

Apparently not.

They shook hands, Wilverton getting the impression that Norim could exert considerably more pressure than he could, but seeing nothing out of the ordinary in that since he received exactly the same impression when he shook anyone's hand.

'What are you doing here?' asked Norim.

'Well, it's not easy to explain. I'm taking part in a Game played by super-minded beings using a team of humans and a team of trands, and this particular round demands that I do something here, but I don't know what. To put it briefly.'

Norim nodded. 'Me too.'

'Really?' asked Wilverton, using one of those words which is not really meant as a question but as an expression of surprise. 'Well, I suppose there can be more than one Game going on at any time; Biondor's never said anything that would suggest otherwise.'

This, he thought, smells fishier than a shark's larder.

He considered.

When you have eliminated the impossible, then whatever is left, however improbable it may be, must be the truth.

Thus spake Sherlock Holmes, and he, Wilverton recognised, should know.

The problems Wilverton had always encountered with that were, firstly, that he could never be quite sure that he had discounted all the impossible bits, and, secondly, that if he had discounted all the impossible bits and still found himself left with thirty-seven not impossible but very improbable bits, then he and Sherlock would both be completely stymied.

Of course, this never actually happened to Sherlock, because he was always left with only the one improbable, which turned out to be the right one. If a Holmes story had finished with the words:

'Well, I'm buggered if *I* know what the bloody hell's going on, my dear Watson.'

'You really are a complete tosser, Holmes.'

then Conan Doyle might have been less successful than he rightly proved to be.

But no story did end like that, because it wasn't real life.

And immediately the little voice came back to him, but fainter still now, as though ready to make a quick getaway if it was found out. If he could eliminate all the impossibilities with this Norim character, then by using exactly the same argument, whatever he was left with must be the truth.

It was worth a try, he decided. Even if the voice was wrong – as a now much louder voice was telling him it was – then he had nothing to lose by giving it a go.

He therefore smiled at the man standing before him, and decided not to let on that he knew that this must, in fact, be a trand.

Biondor had said that Wilverton was the only human being on Trand.

Biondor did not lie.

Therefore this was a trand. One either surgically altered to resemble a human being down to the last detail, or one whose optical appearance to Wilverton was that of a human being. The former was, in Wilverton's opinion, impossible, therefore the latter must be the case.

'Well, no point hanging around here,' he said, expecting now that the safe haven was probably the setting for an ambush, or, more likely, a lunch. 'Let's get on with it. Okay?' Norim agreed readily enough – which he had to do or else he would be giving away the fact that he wanted Wilverton to stay in the house – and they headed for the door once more, Wilverton opening it just a crack and peering out to see if the way was clear.

He got as much of a view as anyone can through such a crack, and, like all such views, its emptiness convinced him that there must be nothing dangerous in any of the other one hundred and seventy-five degrees which the view did not encompass. He stepped into the open, confident . . . .

. . . And wrong.

Having picked himself and his gun up from the fallen masonry, brushed himself, and his gun, down, and started all over again by kicking a bit of the collapsed wall until he felt a bit better, Sam was on the trail again. He had seen the street towards which Wilverton had been heading before his view had been obscured, so that was the one he had headed for, but the street was now empty. Angrily, Sam kicked a stone at his feet, and it flew into the distance.

The stone sped through the trandian air, then simply landed and rolled to a stop a couple of hundred yards away, and had no other effect on anything else whatsoever, ever.

Incredible.

Suddenly, a door a little way ahead opened a crack, and Sam could imagine someone looking out through the result. He immediately flattened himself against a wall. Relatively, since 'flat' was something that your average trand was never going to approximate without leaping off a cliff. Sam made himself look as much like an unsightly bulge in the brickwork as he possibly could – and did that very well, nature having given him a considerable head start – being careful to avoid leaning against the door, in front of which he would have been easily spotted.

The door ahead opened a bit more, and Wilverton stepped out into the street, glancing every which way but not spotting Sam.

Sam raised his gun once more, and took aim. The Captain would respect him when he took this body back, small though it was . . .

A muffled voice came from the other side of the wall against which he was leaning, inside the house.

'The first orgal egg in over two months and you smash it!'

'I'm sorry, dear. I was only trying to please you.'

'You'd please me by not dropping my orgal egg!'

'I didn't drop it. Something fell on it.'

'I wish something would fall on you! Do you know how much I've been looking forward to that egg?'

Henry's wife slammed her foot into the front door by way of an opening manoeuvre. It was a good one. The door flew outwards, its hinges straining against the centrifugal force, and it would have smashed into the brickwork at the extent of the swing had Sam not been standing there with his gun poised. The door was not one for petty prejudices, so it smashed into Sam instead.

The Challenger allowed a brief emission of ultraviolet to escape, rather like the Champion a few trandian minutes before; not that it had a lot of choice.

Respect was due to the Champion for the manoeuvre, and it broadcast a brief flash of purple, but tinged it with an x-ray!

The Champion relaxed to infra-red, ignoring the x-ray barb. Its long wave emanations answered the Challenger with barely-concealed contempt.

For the watching Lessers, this was wonderful stuff, and they would have whooped, hollered, and gone collectively wild had they been equipped. They weren't, so they went collectively gamma, instead.

Having looked up and down the road and seen nothing except the shabby brickwork of trandian dwellings, Wilverton turned and beckoned to Norim, before heading off along the road.

A muffled noise from behind him barely made an impact on his mind, which assumed it had come from his companion.

Everything was going extremely well, Wilverton thought to himself and, in a way, he was right.

XVI

All around the picturesque capital of Earth Five Zero were distributed even more picturesque little towns. They were inhabited, on the whole, by those whose advancing years or retiring dispositions made the excitement of big city life just that little bit too thrilling – a bit of a challenge for the incontinence underwear – even big city life which appeared to Fission, especially, to have all the fizzing nervous energy of a rest home for the terminally apathetic.

The mayor of the little town of Relaxation had been a fan of science fiction since his very early youth. Science fiction from the archives, with its incredibly quaint ideas of what the future – now the distant past – would be like, and science fiction of the moment, speculating still, as it had always done, on what might be 'out there' and what would happen should whatever it was decide to come 'in here'. Although not in the same league as Wilverton – which would have been some feat – he had read quite a bit.

Enough to know.

Enough to know that the first encounter between human beings and visitors from another planet was one that could go disastrously wrong if the humans acted in a way dictated by fear of the unknown – beat the shit out of them first and then ask if they come in peace or pieces.

Mayor Arnaud therefore had a grave responsibility, and it was not one which he was about to blow. He would treat the alien with open-armed friendliness, making no movement and taking no action that might be construed as threatening. Especially, a little cautionary part of him insisted, when the alien's reaction might well be, judging from the size and look of him, to remove Mayor Arnaud's head and drop kick it onto the town hall roof.

What they needed, decided the Mayor, was a happy show of friendship, complete with traditional medieval brass band – not the synthesised whale song that filled the pop charts these days – and speeches.

Of course, he would inform Central of what was going on, because that was his clear duty, but he would do so after it had gone on, just in case Central thought that someone else should come and make it go on instead of him.

For now, this was Arnaud's alien. Arnaud's ticket, he thought privately, fooling absolutely no-one, to fame, fortune, and a spectacular social plateau.

The trand had entered the sleepy little town of Relaxation from the east like a small, pissed-off tornado, leaving in its wake a trail proving just how its attitude to aliens differed from Arnaud's.

Which posed a question.

Given that anything which had so far failed to get out of its way had been treated to the levelling attentions of six ill-tempered arms, how, precisely, had the Mayor reached the conclusion that what the trand was seeking was a civic reception?

Difficult to say.

He had, though, and the Mayoress, instead of arguing with him – which she didn't because it was his position which allowed her to lady it over the rest of the town – was even now making, with her own fair hands, some of her famous old recipe spaghetti bolognese which, they apparently assumed, would be an alien's ambrosia, rather than the equivalent of, say, fertiliser – horse, rear end, variety – on a bed of worms.

The trand, meanwhile, was clearly not preparing for a civic reception.

The trand had, in fact, and in a manner depicted in precisely none of the books the Mayor had ever read, entered the library-cum-museum.

But was he now sitting quietly behind one of the tables, flicking idly through the Relaxation Gazette, while trying not to respond to the overpowering desire that afflicts you as soon as you enter a place with 'Quiet Please' plastered all over it to clear your throat?

No.

He was not.

The trand was reducing the place to rubble. This did not appear to be because it is always best to stick to what you are good at. The trand was apparently looking for something, and, presumably, not finding it.

The library was twinned with the museum because a large number of the books possessed by the town of Relaxation were in the form of bound paper. The trand picked each of these in turn from its shelf, and studied its spine. If the title, or the author, or whatever, was not to its satisfaction, then it threw it at the far wall, where the various resultant bits fell to join the rest of the heap. When the shelf was empty, this too was reduced to matchwood, apparently just for the sheer hell of it.

By the time it had looked at the very last book, and found it as unrewarding as all those that had preceded it, the first faint noises as of a traditional brass band tuning up were drifting in through the broken windows.

No-one had thought to ask Mayor Arnaud, or, perhaps more pertinently, the players in the brass band, how they knew that the sounds they were about to make were not exactly those made by aliens such as the one inside the museum library when they were about to attack, or which in their ancient customs meant that your mother charged by the quarter hour and still didn't have two pennies to rub together. No-one, therefore, had thought to consider what the reaction might be if they did.

When the trand emerged into the sunlight on the steps of the museum – uncharacteristically using the door when there was a perfectly good wall nearby – it was faced with a number of people pointing gleaming something-or-others at it, which might or might not have been weapons, and a woman with a gold chain round her neck holding out a plate full of what looked to the trand to be fertiliser – harg, rear end, variety – on a bed of worms.

Arnaud smiled the welcoming smile of one who has proved his worth to a fellow sophisticate. It was a very short-lived smile indeed.

'This is incredible.' Dano pushed her way through the grass, still wearing a look of wonder, staring at the colours of sky and vegetation. 'And those animals . . . Amazing.'

Carlton glanced at her, noticing the tears in her chiffon 'covering', noticing the body underneath more, and tried to think of something to say. The knowledge that he was not only a primitive, but the world's second least attractive man – assuming Curtis hadn't been killed in the meantime – nudged the back of his mind, but his mind wasn't in sole charge of his mouth right then.

'I thought they were going to turn out to be the Fukarwis,' he managed.

'The what?'

'The Fukarwis. They're little foot-high animals that live on plains covered in two-foot high grass. Every now and then one of them

132

jumps up above the level of the grass and shouts "We're the Fukarwi."'

He grinned at her. She looked – well, not exactly blank, but not exactly tickled either.

'I don't understand.'

No, you don't do you, he thought, maintaining the smile as a defence. That expletive has been well and truly deleted over the past few hundred years.

'It was just on another planet I've been on,' he lied. 'They were very similar to the ones we've just met.'

She nodded, and they covered the last few yards in silence. Carlton asked himself why he hadn't just told the truth, and the creeping feeling of inadequacy stole over him again.

They reached the Earthly trees, walked another five yards, and there was a grab, in the middle of a roadway that bore no signs of the attack it had suffered less than a couple of hours before. They looked back, and the other world had vanished.

The noise changed from the distant and half-imagined sound of scuffling mink to that of an approaching full-blown parade. Off to their left, Carlton saw, maybe two hundred yards away, banners and ticker-tape – or the impression of those, anyway; there was nothing more material than light – filling any bits of the air that weren't already crammed with rhythmic beatings, as of music, but with a primitive feel to it; something, Carlton thought, that might have been co-written by Souza and Ug-Mammoth-Killer. In front of two columns of dancing supporters floated the holographic heads of Miron and Pomona.

With the ability granted to her only by the very exceptional, Dano ignored it all completely, and kept glancing back the way she had come.

'What was all that about, then?' she asked. 'Real animals . . .'

Carlton glanced at her, wondering if the second comment was her answer to the first. He shrugged. Now that they were back, and his chat-up jest had failed, his mood was settling back into a deep rut.

'Whatever it was, it hasn't got me and my team any further forwards trying to find this robot. Waste of time.'

Talking of 'his team' . . .

He looked back to the parade, and saw Fission apparently leading it, but actually ignoring it completely and making straight for him. He looked the other way, and there was Tamon emerging into the open, and immediately talking to his wrist. He was followed closely by Gloria, wearing a frown of thought. Carlton watched all three glancing back the way they had come, and guessed that they all saw the same normality as he had just met, and not what they might have been looking for.

Three lots of weird experiences, he reckoned, that finished at precisely the same time.

Hmm. Some chance.

So what could he glean from that bit of logic?

Erm . . .

Right.

Anything else?

He wondered where Wilverton was. For all his galloping insanity, he *was* quite clever.

'Peter! Fission! Er . . .' – whatever the woman was called . . . – 'You're safe. What happened?' Gloria smiled at them, and they smiled back automatically; it was difficult not to get caught up in the miasma of good nature that surrounded her.

'We were attacked by a bunch of fat mink,' Carlton volunteered, and immediately felt as heroic as Conan the Interior Decorator. He added quickly, 'They were dangerous little buggers.'

'Real, too,' Dano noted, but with a frown, still. Of disbelief, Gloria thought. 'But in a group.'

'We were lucky to get away.' Carlton felt that being real and in a group did not quite convey the peril they had faced.

'Not much of attack,' Fission mentioned. 'No damage.'

'What do you mean, no . . .' . . . damage, just look at all these cuts and bruises and torn clothes, Carlton was going to finish, when he looked to Dano as evidence and found her chiffon cover-nothing to be once again whole. Nor were there any blemishes visible on the skin beneath. She studied herself, and frowned some more.

'We were attacked by koalas,' Gloria told them.

Carlton sucked in his breath sharply. 'Nasty!' At least it made his mink a bit perilous by comparison.

Gloria gave him a withering look. 'With spears. They had a horrible leader who made them do terrible things.' She paused, remembering. 'I had to . . .' but it was as far as she got. What she had done was best forgotten. 'What animals did you have?' she asked Fission.

'How you know any animals involved?'

'Because I think it must have been a clue from the Champion and I think it's all got something to do with animals, that's why.' She had been thinking about that on the conversationless walk, two yards behind a striding Tamon.

Fission shrugged. The fact that it was Gloria's idea didn't necessarily make it wrong. 'Flying squirrels.'

They thought for a moment. They *could* be dangerous, Carlton supposed, like something out of an old Hitchcock vid; The Squirrels . . .

'They not attack, they need someone lead them to safety. I did.' Her face clouded as she spoke, and Carlton and Gloria said nothing, assuming that something had annoyed her; it seemed a good bet, and they couldn't see Larna's shade.

Gloria's attention was taken momentarily by a stream of white-robed Foundation Foundation members following the bobbing, smiling head of Miron as it passed fifty yards or so away from her. There was one with a particularly happy expression who pulled a small dog on a lead, she saw, but didn't take much notice.

'A clue to what?' Dano asked, gaining her attention once more.

'It's probably nothing,' Carlton commented, wanting to be in on a conversation with Dano, but, from Gloria's view, perhaps not pausing to think of the best method of entry.

'Excuse me! It's probably a way of telling us who the renegade robot is. There's a clue somewhere in the animals.'

'You think your renegade robot is an animal?' Dano asked, moving her glance back from Carlton.

'Well, it could be.' It sounded unlikely, but that hadn't stopped anything else happening in this Game thing. 'Biondor never said it was human looking.'

'Said household robot,' Fission pointed out, and Gloria's galloping logic hit a fence, hard.

Carlton watched the jockey get a face full of mud and shrugged again. 'Like I said . . .'

The Champion squeezed its being with a nonchalant vengeance. If it wasn't very careful, something in the x-ray range would escape, reminiscent of fingers being drummed on a table. The Challenger was not to be awarded that minor victory.

Keep calm, it told itself.

They'll get it.

Eventually.

No need to get annoyed.

135

Vexation was unwarranted and would solve nothing.

Keeeeep caaaaalm . . .

It noticed that it had drifted near to a planet; one apparently bearing primitive life.

'Peaceworld', they called it, according to the brainwaves of the water-bound natives.

Well, that was nice.

It watched its team for another long instant . . .

Then it looked back at Peaceworld and pondered, momentarily, whether to squeeze the fetid thing with the gravity of a million suns, making the new life-form's eyeballs bulge and their brains implode and their stupid, *squirmy, mushy bodies fill the oceans with the blood of an UNINTELLIGENT, FEEBLE LITTLE SPECIES* . . .

But no.

Calm.

They'd get it.

'. . . I don't think it was a clue. This Rudy's the one we're after. It was probably just the Challenger trying to get us killed, and nothing to do with the answer at all,' Carlton concluded, then glanced about oddly as the music in the parade hiccuped in his head to something that sounded like a million popping eyeballs and imploding brains.

'Okay, what's going on?' Tamon approached the group, his wrist now safely stowed by his side, his face flushed.

'We don't know,' Carlton snapped, frowning in automatic response to Tamon's existence.

'I still think it was a clue . . .'

'Central says I've been missing for two days,' Tamon interrupted. 'Dano, too.'

They looked at him in silence for a moment. On the grass a few yards away, a multi-coloured cloud of light appeared, shimmering and rising to about ten feet off the ground, expanding from a tight sphere to what appeared to be a loose conglomeration of photons, like a slow-motion super-nova. They ignored it, but one or two people turned from the parade to watch, and passers-by paused.

'Two days?' Gloria asked. Tamon nodded. 'Well, perhaps it's like when you go round the world and you go across the international dateline. This could be some sort of interplanetary dateline.' It didn't sound very likely even to her, and their expressions soon told her that no such thing existed.[1]

'That just proves it must have been the Champion or the Challenger,' Carlton concluded. 'It's no big deal for them.'

Gloria nodded, happy again, and looked vindicated.

'It still doesn't mean it was a clue,' he told her, irritated. 'And even if it was, it's a lousy one! Animals! Where does that get us? What's it got to do with Rudy?' The jerk of his eyes skywards dismissed the idea, and Gloria shrank a little. 'Mention animals around here and everyone goes ape-shit anyway!'

'Leaders,' Dano muttered, still frowning, as though trying to remember a dream. 'That's another link, if there is one. You talked about a leader, and our mink were taught to hunt together by an old leader of theirs. Joop.'

'Sorry?' Gloria looked a little concerned – she used to have an elderly aunt who said 'plink' at the close of every sentence, towards the end; as in 'Very comfortable, thank you, Doctor, plink.'

'Joop. That was the name of their leader.'

Gloria nodded with relief.

'Squirrels have no leader.'

'Until you came along,' Dano pointed out, ignoring the 'who-said-you-could-talk?' expression forming on Tamon's face. 'It was still all about leadership though, wasn't it?'

'Oooh!' The idea hit Gloria so hard that a bit had spilled out of her mouth. 'It was the leader that made the koalas nasty. He made them do barbaric things. So it might be the leader that's going to do it to the planet. The President! She could order people to do things.'

Dano shook her head. 'The President has no power. He – it's a "he" at the moment – he's no more than a titular head.'

Gloria frowned. That probably wasn't a very nice thing to say, and she wasn't quite sure what Dano meant – she didn't think her titulars had heads. Then she frowned again because the conversation would leave her behind like all the others did if her mind didn't run to keep up. Oh, where *was* Thomas?

'Central runs everything now,' Dano finished.

'Well, all right; Central's a sort of robot, isn't it?' Gloria caught up. 'So it could be the renegade one. And Tamon said that Central was like everyone's household robot, so it fits!' She beamed. That was it.

[1]Not entirely correctly. The Interplanetary Dateline agency arranged, for exorbitant fees, blind meetings between species seeking new, erm, experiences. Especially popular were the Hrdians, the positioning of whose genitalia – inside the mouth – offered many customers two for the price of one, as it were.

She'd got it, and now they'd be able to get Thomas back. 'Rudy could just be a red salmon.'

'Herring.'

'Whatever.'

'Now just wait a minute!' Tamon's expression, as his cry brought him to their attention, was a picture. Not the sort you'd want to look at for too long without a handkerchief over your mouth. 'Just what are you saying? That Central's going to ruin the planet?'

Carlton shrugged. This was a better idea than he had thought at first – it may have been rubbish, but it had the major plus of annoying the hell out of this hero-worshipping Tamon.

'Could be. Why not? Why shouldn't it be a renegade robot?'

'You'd like that, wouldn't you!' Tamon accused him with no apparent logic.

Dano looked at him with surprise, while Carlton squared up and tried to stand a little taller, feeling slightly stupid even as he did so. He managed to stop himself from a challenging 'Yeah?'

Fission took a verbal grasp of their antlers, which didn't make Carlton feel any better.

'Can't President order it turned off?' she asked Dano, who shook her head.

'No. And anyway it would have to be Central that did the turning off. Humans don't really know enough even to program it these days.'

'Destroy then? Rudy blows it up, takes control . . .'

'. . . And makes people do barbaric things!' Gloria liked that idea, so much that 'do barbaric things' came out rather like 'eat ice-cream'.

Tamon looked like he was going to have a seizure, but Dano answered calmly enough.

'It's too big, too widely spread to destroy – there are bits of Central all over the world. The only time anyone gets anywhere near its main terminal is during the ceremonial restart after the election result; and that's just punching a few keys to order.

'And even if you *could* blow it up, it would be so obvious that no-one would ever follow the person who'd done it. If you're going to get people to do something against their nature, something barbaric, then you need a big following, surely. Maybe if you could get people to believe that Central was bad for them . . .'

They fell silent for a moment, Dano and Tamon clearly contemplating the thought that Central might be bad for them, in the same way you might conclude that your heart is a cancerous growth.

The parade of Presidential hopefuls passed them, and a further parade drew level. From the look of them, wearing football kit in different colours – one predominantly red, the other blue – they were opposing teams from a big game. Carlton assumed, in as much as the back of his mind considered the matter, that they would perform as a curtain raiser to the election result.

Fission watched the tail end of the Presidential-to-be procession. If one of those two could somehow gain power from Central, and order the people to do something, like Gloria's koala . . .

But they couldn't. And, much more importantly, they *knew* that they couldn't.

She sighed, exasperated; it sounded so good, and it would fit what had happened to them if it wasn't for all the facts getting in the way.

Carlton watched the shimmering coloured light taking the shape of a head, and frowned. Didn't he recognise it?

'Well, I think it *must* be Central,' Gloria concluded. 'It's been made bad by the Challenger. Why else were we shown all those things?'

Her argument failed to impress Tamon, but did manage to draw out his chin. 'Well, for one,' and he held up a finger, '"those things" were just about animals; they have no relevance to human beings! And for two,' and he was rude, 'I'm not sure anything happened to us at all.' Gloria looked at him as though he was denying possession of his own head; of course something happened! 'I wonder if you haven't made all this up, drugged me and agent Dano and given us hypnotic suggestions.'

'Why we do that?' Fission's question didn't quite sound contemptuous, but it was a close thing.

'How do I know! I've never known what makes offworlders do what they do!'

Something in Carlton snapped. 'I wish you'd just shut the fuck up about offworlders! You think you're so bloody "civilised"!'

'And you'd rather we weren't; that's right, isn't it?' Tamon challenged, but Carlton just shook his head to end the argument before it started. It didn't work. 'I think you're maybe planning something against Central because that's what makes Earth so much superior to the offworlds. I think maybe you tried to get us on your side by making us think that Central could be dangerous!' He finished on a high note of passion, which brooked no argument.

Gloria was tone deaf. 'But you said no-one could get rid of Central and take control,' Gloria pointed out, glancing at Dano to bring her into the 'you' definition.

'You didn't know that, though, did you! Not until we told you!' The high note rose higher. Any higher, Fission reckoned, and he'd need a change of clothes.

Gloria's eyes suddenly widened, as if the implications of Tamon's words had struck home, that her dastardly plan had been rumbled. But if it had been rumbled, it was apparently by something just over Tamon's right shoulder; the now solidified light.

They all turned to follow Gloria's gaze, and they all adopted similar expressions.

It was Arnold.

Looking down from twelve feet in the air, and smiling – which looked all wrong to most of them for a start – the caption underneath said it all. 'Vote Arnold for President, and *You* will Control your Destiny.'

'So *that*'s your plan!' Tamon shouted, and Dano made a mental note to keep a spare set of clothes handy in future. 'You thought the President could do what he wanted to Central and take over the world!' Dano made a mental note to keep a spare body handy – Tamon's current one was surely about to explode all over the place. 'You know what that is? That's . . .'

His punchline was interrupted by a man bursting through the line of marchers which separated the group from the bunch of trees into which none of them had seen Curtis disappear.

'It's Richard!' said Gloria.

'It's *treason*! Plotting against Central is treason!' A drip of spittle ran down Tamon's chin, probably trying to get away before the inevitable detonation. He's in love with the thing, thought Fission. He's nutty as Chichit's pantry. 'This whole Rudy thing was a ploy. You probably ordered him to leave Chanta so you could hide your real aims. You should be locked up! Or shot!'

Gloria paused in her movement towards Curtis to glance at Tamon with a touch of exasperation. 'Oh, don't be ridiculous, you silly man.' Her mother had told her to say nothing if she couldn't say anything nice, but there *were* times . . .

Tamon stared hard at her and then brought his wrist up to his face. He started talking earnestly to it.

'Richard!' Gloria called, and watched as he stumbled towards them, looking like a toddler who had re-found his mother. A toddler quite literally, to whom the niceties of elegant leg movement were still something of a closed book. She realised that her concern for his absence had been tempered by the fact that she hadn't actually noticed it. 'We've been worried about you!' Carlton and Fission threw quick glances at her, but said nothing. 'Where have you been?'

He pointed back the way he had come, then jumped as a sudden voice exhorted him to 'Vote for Miron' as the start of the procession doubled back on itself and drew level.

Behind him the footballers and their supporters continued to march the other way.

Above them, the face of Arnold beamed down and, next to it, another shimmering light in the air began to coalesce into the shape of a giant hammer. Carlton gave it a worried glance and noticed Fission frowning in the same direction.

'Never mind where he's been,' Tamon told Gloria angrily. 'Central says you're to be held, er, in a hotel of your choice, until, er, well, for a while.' It was difficult to maintain his intensity of feeling when inviting them to an indeterminate period of enforced luxury, but he made an effort with, 'Everybody in the grab!'

Gloria gave him a hard look, but obeyed, more because she didn't trust his reaction if she didn't than in response to his authority.

The hammer hovered in the air, directly above them, and some of the football supporters pointed towards it, grinning, seeing no apparent danger in it.

Not so Carlton and Fission, for whom an apparently insubstantial hammer, plus the influence of the Challenger, spelled squish. Curtis read the same word, judging from his eagerness to comply with Tamon's orders. Haste and Curtisian movement were never happy companions, though, and Carlton watched with a sense of the inevitable as Curtis sprawled. As the others climbed into the vehicle, he stooped to retrieve his Captain, keeping a nervous eye on the hammer as it hovered and bobbed above them and wondering, briefly, whether he might just leave the idiot there and thereby improve their chances.

He had reluctantly decided against it – Gloria would only make a fuss – and was preparing to throw Curtis into the grab when the hammer suddenly fell, and he flinched before it missed him completely; hitting, instead, a group of blue-clad footballers walking amongst the reds, and smashing them into the individual photons of which they were made. The crowd cheered happily at the symbolic destruction.

Carlton paused with a handful of Curtis's collar, watching with a frown while Curtis hung like a puppy in its mother's mouth, then he threw his bundle into the cab and climbed in after him.

One of the white-robed processioners stopped in disbelief, and his dog did likewise, a moment later, as the lead jerked tight.

Alive! LOVE stared at the grab as it set off, ignoring the tired and somewhat choked look from Stay level.

Behind him, Chanta also watched the grab.

That four-hundred-year-old offworlder had bundled someone into the back. Rudy? Had they found him?

XVII

It wasn't the conventional way to wear a sousaphone. This is a brass instrument with a wide conical bore; a very long horn wound up into various geometric shapes so that the musician does not sit at the back of the orchestra pit and knock the conductor off his podium. It is normally worn over the shoulder unless you happen to have incredibly strong arms and a two foot neck.

The example currently in the fore of the Relaxation brass band was being worn over both shoulders and around the upper parts of the musician's arms, while the wide conical bore bent downwards and backwards between his legs so that he looked like he was sporting an early attempt at rocket-powered flight for the dare-devil individual.

He was in the fore of the band for the simple reason that the other members, with less encumbrances about their limbs, had marched backwards at speed and bugger the formation.

The steps of the museum library were now devoid of trand, and held nothing but the sorry remains of a plate and its spaghetti bolognese contents. The trand had gone back inside.

Mayor Arnaud was trying to work out what he had done wrong. He had been friendly; he had not surrounded the area with a circle of heavily-armed soldiers. He had not refused the alien any request; not that there had actually *been* any requests, which at the time had disappointed Arnaud because he was rather hoping that it would ask someone to take it to their leader, because that would have been him. Now he was thanking his lucky stars.

He looked at the carnage around him, wondering vaguely how the scene had managed to play itself out without anyone actually getting killed, and concluded that the alien, on the whole, was not one to whom he would extend an invitation to join the Club.

It was extraordinary behaviour.

For a race to possess the knowledge to cross between stars, it must, perforce, be an advanced civilisation. And that description did not tie in with what had just happened.

Arnaud concluded – the only possible conclusion – that he had done something terribly wrong.

He wandered shakily back to his home, in which his partner was alternately blaming the trand for not appreciating her culinary efforts and Arnaud for suggesting them, and instructed his computer to make contact with Central.

Central would know what to do. It always did.

The trand, for his part, didn't want to join the Club. He was back inside the library, reading.

Many species made the mistake of thinking that trands were simply huge collections of undisciplined and largely violent muscle. They *were* that, but they were quite bright with it, so many species found themselves on the end of not just any old random mugging, but of a carefully thought out hammering.

And this trand liked to read.

Okay, he was a bit embarrassed by it, but he liked to do it.

And Biondor had told him sufficient to make him think that his reading had something to do with his task on this Wilfred-forsaken little planet.

The trand was leafing through an atlas.

Why?

Because if reading had something to do with it, then that meant books, and he had worked out, now that he had calmed down sufficiently for intelligent thought to gain the upper hand, or at least hold its own, that if he was looking for something which might aid his captain in the quest against a renegade robot, then a book on robotics might help him find it.

Not any old book, though. That wasn't logical; it had to be something which stood out. None of the books in the Relaxation library stood out – in fact, they just sort of lay there in a sorry heap.

So, if he wanted a book that was special, he presumably had to look in a special library, and that was likely to be found in a major library in a major city. Hence the atlas. The trand would visit the capital of this pebble in space.

How?

Travel. The next category after the atlas.

Anyone looking through the library windows would have thought that the trand was planning his holidays.

Not that anyone was very likely to look through the windows. Which was a pity; not for them, but for Danlor.

Danlor was the little man who sat behind the desk in Relaxation's

Intercontinental Tachyon Travel store. He didn't have to – he could have let a robot look after everything while he sat at home and toyed with his animal noise reproduction hobby – but he liked to come in every now and then, to meet people – since he was partnerless – and get a few extra credits.

He looked up with a big welcoming smile on his face as the door opened.

'Opened' is perhaps a slight understatement for the door's action; it would never close again.

The trand stood in the resultant hole, and filled it. Danlor's smile remained in place because it was petrified.

Be polite, he told himself, that way you might yet live. It may be an offworlder, but that did not necessarily make it inferior once the other factors were taken into account.

The number of arms, for example.

Swallow.

And the size of them.

'Good morning, sir,' Danlor said with strained, sycophantic salesman jollity. 'What can I do for you?'

The trand made the sort of noise Danlor would expect his computer to produce if he programmed someone biting the tail of a grizzly bear, and one which held the same promise of life expectancy. His smile remained his only defence.

'Yes. Didn't quite catch that?'

The trand took a step forwards by way of response. This was not what Danlor had in mind, and he immediately pushed his chair backwards, forgetting, as it is easy to do in such situations, the fact that there was a wall behind him.

Mathematically, given the arrangement of particles within atoms and atoms within molecules and the fact that most of what makes up most things is in fact the space between them all, it is possible for one solid object to pass straight through another one without hindrance. It's a trillions to one chance, and before Danlor pushed his chair back against the wall, there had never been a single recorded instance of it happening. After Danlor pushed his chair back against the wall, there still was not a single recorded instance of it happening, which left Danlor faced with several hundred pounds of apparently disgruntled trand.

What a bummer.

Danlor made a sound full of the promise of soiled underwear, but the trand held out a brochure to him, and the action was so normally out of place, and unbelievably unthreatening, that it calmed him in an instant.

He leaned forwards, trying to see what the open page was showing. The trand helped by smacking it down on the desk in front of him.

The capital, thought Danlor, looking into the small hollow where the brochure now lay.

'Well, it's just down the road, sir, no more than about seven miles. You don't need tachyon travel for that; a grab would do fine.'

The trand pointed to the tachyon booth in the corner of the shop.

'No, sir, you don't understand. You really don't need to travel via tachyon to the capital, you . . .'

The trand made the sound of a bear whose bitten tail has just been sat upon because you knocked him over backwards with a tree branch.

Displeased.

'Tachyon travel is *just* what you need, sir,' enthused Danlor, sensibly knowing his place once more. 'And how would you like to pay for the service, sir?'

Danlor definitely recognised a bear lying on its painfully bitten tail because someone has knocked it down with the tree branch and is jumping up and down on its stomach whilst wearing running spikes. That was the noise.

'And what a bit of *luck*! Sir, we have our special offer of *free* tachyon travel today only, for any alien who wants a trip to the capital! *Especially* those with six arms! This way, sir!'

The trand followed rather meekly, no doubt battered by quite so many exclamations.

The door open, the door closed, the settings were set, the button was pushed, and Danlor was laughing.

The penthouse suite of the New Church Street Hilton was sumptuous, yet spartan at the same time.

The main room was antiseptic enough to clean a surface wound. The carpet was white, and they could not hear the low hum indicating that the constant cleaning was keeping it that way – any bug in this rug would be snug only for the instant before it was sucked down and disintegrated. The sofas and armchairs were transparent, apparently made of some sort of plastic substance, and seemed to be filled with swirls of gas which slowly and constantly moved around, to give the impression of sitting on clouds.

And their posteriors were cuddled with a vengeance. You still got

146

what you paid for, thought Gloria, recalling Chanta's buttock-fondling furniture.

The walls were white, and the artwork – assuming it *was* artwork and not the result of an ink-snorting creature sneezing a lot – was black. There were various ornaments dotted around the walls on small shelves, all tasteful mixtures of curves, angles, black and white.

There was no colour anywhere. Presumably the hotel licence was cheaper.

The suite might have been sumptuous, but it was still a prison if you weren't allowed to leave, which, according to Tamon, they weren't, until Arnold had been found. Then, he warned with a blanching concern, the threat to Central would be evaluated; and if nothing else the question of ownership would be decided by a court.

Until then – and he half smiled – they were to stay where they were, and Dano would stay with them in case they interpreted the instruction in the same way as had Arnold; as an invitation to immediate movement.

Fission had interpreted it as an unconstitutional fonking attack on her fonking rights, and had not shrunk from informing Tamon of the fact, and then Dano after Tamon had shrugged his indifference and left while he was still intact.

'I'm sorry about this,' Dano responded. 'And I know it's not much of an excuse, but I *am* only following orders, and I guess you could argue that they're sensible ones.' She had recovered the poise and good humour she had begun to show before her apparent offworld excursion, enough to hide a certain discomfort at what Tamon had told her to do.

Carlton had certainly recovered his pique. 'Because we're dangerous offworlders?' Maybe she wasn't any better than the others.

'Because the possibility exists that you might be,' Dano replied, using the justification Tamon had used on her. 'Whatever way you look at it, some pretty weird things have happened since you've been around . . .'

'Like being attacked all the time on a planet that doesn't have aggression!' Carlton 'suggested'. Fission threw him a glance with something that approached respect.

'We get occasional aberrations. I don't suppose you're in the mood to agree, but it's bound to happen with such a complex organ as the brain.' Carlton made a noise that sounded like his bottom's comment on that bit of logic, and Dano gave him a hard look. 'Just stay here for a while, okay? It's a nice place. We've got to work this out, surely you can see that?' She looked around. They couldn't. 'We must wait and see what Central comes up with.'

'Central again! You're ruled by a bloody computer.'

'It's a good job Tamon didn't hear that,' Dano told Carlton. 'It would be more evidence. You *need* someone in charge; without it you've got anarchy. And Central happens to be better at it than anyone else.'

'If you ask me' – she wasn't going to ask him, thought Gloria, watching them almost square up – 'you're just a bunch of fat mink.'

Curtis nodded. That was probably one of those very rude insults that he had never understood, and he was damned if he was going to let his face give the game away.

Dano just looked at Carlton in a funny sort of way for a long moment, and he looked back.

'Just stay here,' she said. 'Look on the bright side.'

'Is no bright side,' Fission told her.

'Suit yourself. But that won't change anything; it'll just make it less fun while you're doing it.' And she left quietly, closing the door behind her, while Gloria nodded inwardly at the good sense, and Fission looked fit to live up to her name.

LOVE grimaced with effort, and with the pain of straining arm muscles which pulled him up the side of the hotel. He looked like Spidey would have done had he been bald, wearing a long white robe, and been naff at climbing things.

He could have used an angtron flyer, but this was more appropriate. He had tried modern methods, on which Miron would surely have frowned – as he thought so he touched his forehead with respect and nearly toppled off – and they had proved inadequate.

As they would.

He should have known, he thought, with chagrin, that Miron's teachings of the simple ways applied to everything.

Hence the apples.

In a small pouch hung over his shoulder were three apples, each containing enough karmer – a substance designed to give those who partook of it a calmer karma – to bring a smile to the snout of a rutting rhino who finds himself locked in a monastery.

The infidel would eat the apples, which LOVE would place surreptitiously in the hotel room, and he would calm down so much that he would stop altogether.

LOVE smiled.

The Challenger didn't.

The inducement to split the drug between three fruits had been no suggestion of its own, and it didn't take anything more than a fourth level mind to work out whose it had been.

The Champion watched Trand Whatever, ignoring Earth Five Zero with the innocence that can only be displayed by the truly guilty.

Finding her feet before her voice, Fission gave the door a swift kicking and managed to dislodge some of the delicate marquetry in the process, which she then glared at as though it were evidence of how badly they made doors on this excuse for a version of Earth when everyone knew that they should be able to withstand a good kicking every now and again, especially in posh hotels.

'Calm down,' Carlton told her. 'You're giving offworlders a bad name.' It was like smacking a child to get it to stop crying. Fission turned on him.

'At least I concerned about Game; something important. Not just worried about being weak and ugly.' Which he wasn't, she thought.

In a corner of the room, the Foundation Foundation extolled the virtues of Miron as opposed to Pomona only for those who could read lips, as the holovision sound was barely audible. Gloria looked at the bauble dangling around the neck of the woman and wondered again why the monkey was being subjected to that particular ordeal.

Carlton decided to rise above Fission's jibe, even if that needed the mental equivalent of a weather balloon; leaders didn't argue with their troops.

'We should all just think sensibly about this renegade robot, and how we could identify it if we find it. I think my idea of logic being anathema to it is our best bet.'

You would, thought Fission, but said nothing.

A brief silence allowed them to consider the notion, while Fission concentrated on a thought that wouldn't leave her be, then . . .

'My auntie had one of them,' said Gloria.

'One of what?' asked Carlton, not expecting an answer which would have had a Mensa meeting gasping in admiration. More likely one that would put an intellectually superior smile on the face of a milk-cow. He wasn't disappointed.

'An athema. She'd tried prunes but they hadn't worked, so they gave her an athema.' Carlton sighed and opened his mouth to reply, but Gloria suddenly got very excited and pointed at the holovision. 'I bet that's what that is! I bet the monkey's having an athema. That means it might be something to do with the robot!'

Carlton looked to the skies. There was something lacking in Gloria's argument. Like intelligence. 'That's an enema,' he told her, a touch sharply. 'Anathema means you really don't like something.'

'Well, my auntie really didn't like it, I can tell you!' Gloria was reluctant to let this bit of reasoning go, despite the content being ninety-eight per cent gibberish.

'Just let us do the thinking, okay?'

Gloria fixed him with a stare that could have melted a glacier on Pluto in the middle of a cold snap. 'Well, *your* thinking hasn't got us any nearer to finding this robot. And we haven't a clue how to get Thomas back. So I don't think you're as good at thinking as you think!' She frowned momentarily, having used up a day's allocation of 'think' in one phrase. Why did words always get in a mess on the way to her mouth?

Carlton's weather balloon was obviously punctured, but he still rose to the bait like a starving barracuda. 'I don't know what you see in the little squirt anyway! You're just a sucker for flattery.' And he tried a dirty grin to suggest what she did in return for flattery before the grown-up bit could stop him.

Curtis glanced up from his contemplation of fellow floor-level creatures, looking incongruously happier. An argument, and he wasn't on the losing end of it. It was ever so nice.

Gloria's lips completed a very successful crash diet. 'Well, I certainly don't know what I ever saw in *you*!' she managed to squeeze out between them, thinking back to their brief, but physical dalliance on the Pioneer. 'Apparently the women on this planet are a lot more sensible than I am!'

Carlton's shoulders plummeted millimetrically before his automatic ego protector stopped them. Gloria's dipped as well at her own words, passing, on the way, the rush of blood heading for her face. 'Not that *that's* very difficult,' she added quietly.

The Champion wondered briefly what oblivion was like. It couldn't be as bad as trying to make this lot act like a team. At this rate, it was shortly going to find out.

It *wasn't* just flattery, Gloria thought, looking miserable. Thomas *meant* it when he said nice things about her. Didn't he?

Wilverton *did* mean his flattery, thought Carlton. Which fitted in quite well with all the other evidence to prove just what a raving nutter he was. Except, of course, nutter or not, he had got the girl, because she didn't mind him being an uncivilised offworlder, whereas Dano . . .

He noticed the almost happy expression on Curtis. It looked like a bullseye.

'I don't know what you're smiling at! If you hadn't been here we'd have probably won the whole Game by now!'

'That's not fair. I've helped.'

'Quite probably. Sadly, not us, though.'

'I have too! I've . . .' And he stopped, realising that it wasn't a long list. Realising, in fact, that it wasn't a list at all. Carlton confirmed its itemlessness.

'A discussion of your useful points would be the shortest conversational cul-de-sac in the multiverse.'

'Well, at least I know what a multiverse is. I bet Gloria doesn't!' Curtis bravely adopted the go-home-and-kick-the-cat option of counter-attack. Gloria's misery was tinged with anger.

'I expect it's some sort of poem. But if it's one *he* knows,' and she glanced at Carlton like he was a cat murderer, 'then I'm sure I don't want to know what the verses are. They've probably all got willies in them.'

'Well, you'd know about that!'

And then Gloria started to cry, and Carlton felt ashamed of himself but couldn't bring himself to say the first sorry, and Curtis looked as though he might join Gloria but stopped after going redder than a furious cherry at what he saw as his own temerity.

While Fission stared at them with the expression of the school-marm who's just walked in on the under fives' hand-rolled bogey flicking championship.

She shook her head in disbelief. This was no time for them to start fighting like cats and dogs.

No, she corrected herself. Not 'start'; continue.

'Maybe Tamon find him for us.' Her suddenly calm voice caught their attention.

'Tamon's looking for Arnold,' countered Carlton.

'That's what I mean.' Three disbelieving expressions turned to her.

Her own disbelief had gone. When Tamon had first suggested it, she had almost dismissed the idea, but the seed of doubt had grown somehow, as if nurtured, until now it qualified as a firm conviction.

'I think Arnold one we're after! Challenger done something to him. He enough megalomaniac before, now running for President!' Although turning Arnold into a 'renegade' would hardly require a being like the Challenger. And that was the point, the thought came again; Arnold was a natural for a renegade if ever there was one.

'But Arnold's one of us!' said Carlton, trying to think of reasons why Arnold should be eliminated from Fission's enquiries, as opposed to just being eliminated. 'What kind of threat is he to the world, even if he gets to be President? And would *you* vote for him?'

Fission considered. Silently. She'd rather vote for abortion.

Short of an answer, she went on the attack, working on the principle of sticking to what you're good at. 'What kind threat Rudy, then? He going to screw everyone to death?'

'You should be so lucky!' Their eyeballs did silent battle for a while, and Carlton tried to think of an argument on his side.

The fact that a renegade robot would not behave logically was not one that was going to make the task of finding it any easier. It would be less of a problem than trying to view the buttocks of every robot in the world to find a strawberry-shaped birthmark, but you still had at least to be in the vicinity of the right robot before you could see it behaving strangely. It was all very well having one modelling Wyoming's Devil's Tower out of mashed potato, but unless you were there . . .

'That alien thing could have been the robot,' said Curtis, very quietly, in case they spotted him. 'It certainly looked like it could be a danger to the planet.'

There was no ready answer to that one. As far as getting them any further was concerned, the alien was a brick wall – and the similarities didn't stop there. It was almost inconceivable that it had appeared on the planet coincidentally with themselves and had nothing to do with the Game, but just what was a guess no-one was prepared to hazard.

Silence held sway. Swaying was a bit short of falling, but silence had not quite done that since the holovision was murmuring very quietly in the corner.

It seemed to be a nature documentary.

It seemed to Gloria that the whole of Earth Five Zero was a nature documentary.

Ants, this time, apparently; a long line of them trudging through the undergrowth – or overgrowth if you happened to be an ant – some two feet above the carpet. Gloria looked at them with no great interest – she had accepted guiltily, long ago, that if you couldn't pick it up, cuddle it, and stroke its fur, then she didn't really want to know – but she felt strangely drawn to it.

And literally, too.

The ants were getting bigger, swelling as she watched; but so was the rest of the room.

She was getting smaller, she realised, and the successful application of logic failed to cheer her.

She tried to cry out to the others, but no voice came. She tried to turn to them, but no muscle responded. She tried to feel scared, and that worked just fine.

The ants were waist high, marching past no more than a few feet in front of her, and she could hear them talking.

'Which way?'

'Straight ahead. Follow the others. Pass it on.'

'Follow the others. Straight ahead.'

'Pass it on. Follow the others. Can't miss it.'

'Follow.'

A never-ending line of the insects, all exactly the same, all sounding alike. She stared at them, not knowing what to make of it, wishing she did, feeling somehow that it was important.

Then her perspective changed, and she found herself looking a little off to one side of the main line, to where an ant stood back and wiped a leg across his brow, surveying the small structure in front of him. A miniature hammer was strapped to another leg, and the largest of three watching ants behind him moved forward and helped him free of it.

'Is it ready, Dad?' asked one of the two smaller ones.

'Aye, son.' The ant glanced at his offspring, then back at the tiny wooden hut in front of them. A minute porch and open front door beckoned. 'All this crap about soom Queeeen in charge of t' place wi' bluidy *serv*ants wand'rin' about an' all pullin' together. Never 'eard so much codswallop in all me life. We'll show 'em, eh! Stand on our own six feet, we will!'

His partner looked slightly worried. 'Are you sure, luv? I mean it were safe in't hill. I can't 'elp thinkin' it's a bit, you know, exposed out 'ere.'

'Nay, don't you worry, lass. It's safe as . . . well, safe as 'ouses!' He chuckled. His family smiled awkwardly, nervously.

'Dad?'

'Aye, son?'

'How are we gonna find food, Dad?'

'Well, son, 'tis quite simple, you joost follow . . . no, we can't do that now. Er. Well, you, er.' Pause. 'You joost leave that to me, son. Er.' He gave a little antean frown, and looked about, uncertainly.

The background whispering that had continued in Gloria's ears from the line of insects rose in volume, and she found herself looking, once more, at the procession.

'Follow the others.'

'Pass it on.'

'Just follow. Can't miss it.'

'Follow.'

'Straight ahead.'

'Oh, I'm fed up with this!'

An ant stopped. The pile-up behind it – Gloria wasn't too sure how you sexed an ant, should the urge take you – was immediate. Hundreds of legs waggled in the air, trying to sort themselves out. The ant ignored the confusion.

'All this "follow, pass it on" stuff.' It turned to those behind it as they picked themselves up and milled around uncertainly, looking fondly at the receding queue-end. 'What about a bit of creativity, eh? What about a bit of original thought?'

'We must follow . . .'

'Follow. Follow! That's all we ever do! Follow! What's the matter with you all? Are you all sheep?'

There was a shuffling of feet – something for which ants are superbly equipped. 'We're ants,' muttered a couple of invisible individuals, answering the question somewhat literally.

The mound caused by the sudden stop had spread out to a group now, the tail-end of the others long since disappeared round a huge leaf in the distance.

'I want to follow the others,' came a voice.

'But why? Think of all the other things you could be doing! Music, painting, philosophy, nobbing yourself silly . . .'

'I'm hungry. The Queen is hungry.'

'Sod t' bluidy Queen!' came a voice from some way off, and the sound of a tiny hammer hitting the ground.

The cause of the hold-up nodded, pointing to the last speaker. 'Yes, you can do that if you like. No reason why not . . .'

'But I'm hungry! I want to catch up with the others.'

'You don't really, you know. It's just conditioning.'

'I bloody do!'

'But wait, think . . .'

'Out of my way!'

'You don't understand . . .'

And suddenly they were fighting, two ants pummelling at each other with arms and legs – not that Gloria could tell the difference. Then others were joining in, but on whose side it was far from certain; a mêlée of limbs and antennae, snapping jaws and writhing segments . . .

Gloria looked on worriedly, in case the fighting spread to where she sat helpless, but then, suddenly, the sound was fading, and the insects were getting smaller. The room, invisible in its enormity, came back into view; the art work, the chairs, the others sitting there – and the holovision was a three dimensional diversion in the corner, two feet off the carpet . . .

Gloria shook her head, frowned, looked around her, and saw the others doing the same.

'What was all that about?' asked Carlton.

'It was animals again, except that ants aren't animals.' Gloria frowned at the echo of her words, but knew what she meant.

Curtis frowned as well. 'There wasn't any proper leader, just an ant saying there should be. And they've got Central here . . .'

'Probably the Challenger trying to confuse us again.' Carlton was the first to reach a conclusion.

The Champion watched calmly, if the lack of electromagnetic radiation could be believed.

It did like the human team, especially the Gloria one with her strong mind, despite everything. It almost felt sorry for them, something its opponent would see as a weakness.

But sometimes it was hard to keep patience . . .

The planet Peaceworld hung silently within a few parsecs of where the Champion kept the centre of its consciousness, and a number of its inhabitants held their breath. Not for fear of a super-being of which they had no notion, but because they were trying to cross from one pool to another, dragging themselves across the mud on stubby little fins. And wondering why, suddenly, the gravity seemed to increase . . .

★

Nobody contradicted Carlton's conclusion, though Fission looked dubious. So did Carlton, wondering why his mind had just flashed him a picture of a flat fish.

XVIII

Its onset was so unexpected, and it had been so long since it had happened, that Wilverton got quite a shock. The last time he could remember it happening was back in his cabin on the first Pioneer spaceship.

It's raining, he thought, but as he carried on along the narrow road, hugging the walls and making sure nothing lurked around a corner, his thought demanded clarification.

On Earth Prime, rain conjured pictures in his mind of Sunday afternoons with his parents, a coal fire, and a copy of Kafka's works, while the outside of the windows was caressed by a passing sheet of misty droplets, alighting on the sill like an aphid with blisters. That was rain.

Then there were the storms, when any aphids on the sill without built-in crash helmets would be reduced to little green smudges and washed away, and Wilverton's father would look up from his text book and pass a comment about isometric pressure and chaos theory and how the whole thing could be started by a butterfly flapping its wings in deepest Africa, and the young Wilverton would wonder briefly why they couldn't go over there and make it stop, before bending his head once more to 'How to Hug', volume nine of the encyclopedia.

That was Rain, capital 'R'.

Here on Trand Whatever, the precipitation quickly passed through those stages, and reached RAIN, capital everything.

Wilverton carried on manfully – ignored a brief flash of sports teacher memory that defined his efforts as wimpful – taking the turns forced upon him by the buildings on either side, and suddenly realised he had lost his sense of direction. He did not want to go in circles. He tried to glance upwards to get a bearing by the sun, but it was like Niagara in the monsoon.

Why wasn't the Champion helping, if he was the hero?

Except that heroes didn't need help. He frowned.

Ahead, the road forked, spitefully.

'Which way to the centre of the city?' he asked, taking the opportunity to try to catch out the trand pretending to be a human, then so as not to make it too obvious, added, 'Do you reckon?'

His companion looked at the two routes as if considering, then pointed to the one on the left.

'I guess that one.'

Wilverton nodded. 'Guess', eh? A likely story!

Why the centre? his brain asked. What's special about that? It just seemed a likely idea, more likely than the outskirts, he couldn't say why – just a hunch. Did the Champion choose him to have a hunch?

Why *did* the Champion choose him? What was he good at?

Tricky one.

What was he better at than the others?

Better?

What made him stick out?

Gloria.

Apart from Gloria, let's say.

Well, nothing really. He wasn't a dynamic, thrusting individual. Not the life and soul of the party. Not big or powerful. No leader of men. Just a bookworm.

But a king among bookworms . . .

Of course!

Books.

Why hadn't he thought of it before?

Because he'd been scared stiff, that's why.

That was okay; scared was good.

In a book? As the hero?

Don't start. What to do with the conclusion, then . . .

Obvious – find a library.

The brain shook hands with itself. The body took a deep, soggy sigh and wondered if they could get on with it now, please?

Wilverton's jump-suit was waterproof, but did not have a hood. There was more liquid pouring down the inside of his clothes than he had experienced since his very early childhood, and it was nowhere near as warm and satisfying.

And the RAIN somehow managed to get heavier. It bounced off the cobbles of the roadway, as though it didn't like where it found itself and was trying to reach back to the sky, but its fellow drops – chums when they used to hang out together in clouds – were having none of that, and it was smashed down again so that the six inches nearest the ground were an opaque veil of water, while the rest of the atmosphere was a heavily-shaded pencil drawing.

Then the drops donned full metal jackets and went onto the attack. Wilverton tried to pull his head into his shoulders as the tiny bombs landed on it with thousands of stunning blows. He put his hands onto his head to try to protect it, so the drops attacked those instead, and just as painfully.

He turned to Norim, thinking to suggest that they find somewhere to shelter, and found his companion standing quite straight and seemingly unconcerned by the battering storm. But then he wouldn't be affected, would he, because he was a trand with a hide that would make a grandfather elephant in biking leathers seem particularly thin-skinned. Further proof, if proof were needed.

Proof weren't; shelter were.

Preferably a library, but any port in a deluge.

'We've got to find somewhere to get out of this RAIN!' He barely heard his own shout above the clamour of the climate.

The trand human – truman? wondered Wilverton with some redundancy – glanced upwards, as if noticing for the first time that there was indeed a certain moistness about the atmosphere which could not be put down to ordinary levels of humidity. Wilverton would have narrowed his eyes suspiciously had they not already been all but screwed shut against the elements.

Having glanced, the human trand – hand? – shrugged, and indicated the doorway of the nearest building. It was as good a choice as any, being nearest, thought Wilverton, and, as Norim did not appear to be moving in the direction of his nod, he took the initiative and trotted a couple of yards to the building, stopping flat against the wall some inches short of the only window.

Carefully, he peered into the dimly-lit interior of the room. The room itself appeared to be synonymous with the building; Wilverton could see no doors leading off it, and it was huge. A number of rough tables were dotted about, along with a larger number of rough chairs, all well in from the walls.

And around the walls, wonder of wonders, were books.

This was a library.

'Coincidence' tried to push its way to the front of his mind, but couldn't get past 'inevitable', then got some help from 'contrived'. No book would have a coincidence like that, he thought. The RAIN gets heavy enough to stop me just when I'm outside a library . . .

★

The Lessers had not the chance to push the Third Elder forward with a timid question before the Champion showed them its inducement of the beats of semi-reptilian wings, pushing off from its last meal of dead rodent. Beats creating currents, currents mingling and massing, clouds pushed higher, so that just when Wilverton was next to the library, the force of the rain increased . . .

Chaos theory tamed.

The Lessers subsided, satisfied, respectful.

The Challenger's nano-second x-ray burst was pure hate.

The RAIN proved just how powerful a force it was by beating its way – literally – through Wilverton's thoughts, suggesting he should get inside the building as quickly as possible, and he was in total accord with the prevailing conditions.

Sam picked himself up from where he had slumped against the wall and shook his head to clear it. Whoever had smashed a door into him had apparently not noticed, or had noticed and decided not to do anything about it, because there was no-one to be seen. His gun had been thrown from his hand and now lay in a little puddle a few yards away from him, a puddle which had not been there when the gun had last been aimed. It was already Raining, and was just starting to RAIN, when Sam bent painfully and slowly to retrieve his weapon, and started off once more in search of his prey.

Carlton looked at Gloria's miserable face, and felt a pang of pity, and a twinge of guilt. The atmosphere was about as comfortable as a cross-legged Sumo wrestler.

'Look, I'm sorry about what I said. It wasn't fair. It's just that . . .' He tried, but knew that admitting his ego was giving him some real jip would be as shocking as the Pope's admission of dancing naked in a coven every third Wednesday in the month.[1]
'Well, I'm sorry.'

Gloria nodded, and tried a smile that looked as washed out as sub-aqua cricket. 'We all ought to be ashamed of ourselves,' she said, in a quiet tone which did not threaten to start anyone off again. 'We're supposed to be pulling together to try to win this Game thing and all we can do is argue. And it's all really just squabbling about who's the

[1]Which, even in 2457, she didn't.

160

team leader, when really that isn't important at all.' Well it wasn't to her; getting Thomas back was important. Then trying to stay alive.

She was going to make them stand in a corner soon, thought Carlton, while part of him denied any truth in what she was saying.

Then Gloria's eyes widened slightly. A thought had hit her like a train.

'That's what the ants were all about! They were telling us that we have to work together as a team, because if we don't then there's just going to be panda . . .' Damn. 'Something to do with pandas, anyway.'

'Cra . . . er.' Carlton managed not to contradict his opinion with his first word. 'I'm not sure about that.'

'Could be analogy,' Fission suggested.

Gloria frowned. To what? she wondered. Ants? She didn't ask.

LOVE edged higher, the effort now becoming painful. But he knew he would succeed; LOVE would conquer all. Slowly he approached the window.

A gust of wind pushed him sideways, threatening to dislodge him, dragging one hand loose from its hold. He waved in a way that might have been a slightly premature hello to his maker, and caught the bag of apples a glancing blow. One fell out.

He looked down, watching it fall.

Stay watched up, at the same thing.

Food.

'No, Stay!' hissed LOVE into the wind, but it was too late. With a pounce and a gulp, the apple was gone. Would two be enough? 'Bad dog, Stay!'

But Stay didn't care. About anything.

'Doesn't matter anyway,' Fission decided. 'We got get out. And we got find Arnold.' She held up a hand to stop Carlton's protestation, and it worked. At least we don't have another argument, she thought, with relief, and Carlton misread the expression on her face with a fresh surge of adrenalin. 'Whether Arnold is renegade or not' – and he is – 'it good idea find him.'

'Where are we going to find him, then? Any brilliant suggestions?'

Curtis looked up. He had seen something on the holovision, and it had reminded him of something, and that had led to an answer to Carlton's challenge. And as soon as it occurred to him, the possibility strengthened, somehow.

If he said it, though, and he was wrong . . .

He had been wrong before . . .

'I think I know where he might be.'

Carlton, Fission and Gloria looked around. Something had spoken in a very small voice, like a cartoon mouse emerging from a hole in the far wall. It was probably going to be another of those animal allusions.

But no!

It was Curtis.

'Where?' Fission asked.

'Well, whenever we had politicians at home who wanted to impress people, they came to see my father and get photographed with whatever project he was doing at the time.' Deep breath. 'So I think he might well go to the launch of that tachy-gluon ship thing.'

It was quiet, except for the sound of some hefty explosions keeping time with Curtis's heart.

'Okay,' said Fission.

'We'll give it a go,' Carlton agreed.

'You're going to do what I suggest?' It did, admittedly, sound like the sort of mind-bogglingly sensible action followed by the fly saying 'Hmm, nice parlour you've got here . . .'

'No better choice. Let's get out of here.'

'How?' asked Carlton, presuming that Fission was going to fight her way past the guards which Tamon had promised outside the door.

'Window. Climb.'

Behind which, climbing, LOVE grunted with effort.

Effort which Miron would appreciate; would smile upon. He might even get a promotion within the Foundation – not that that was what he wanted of course, but it would be nice.

Would two apples be enough?

Priest First Class?

Down below, Stay tapped a paw rhythmically on the ground. 'Knick knack, something something, give the Dog a Bone! Yeah!'

LOVE looked down. 'Quiet, Stay, and take those sunglasses off.'

Who needs pack leaders? thought Stay, but couldn't be bothered to explore the answer.

'I'll go first,' said Curtis.

Oh God, why? groaned his right shoulder. I bet it's me you land on.

Ignoring his vociferous joint – the other side was strangely mute on this subject – Curtis rose purposefully from his seat, which reluctantly relinquished its claim on his bottom, and crossed to the window. He looked out, then closed his eyes and swallowed. What had he said? His fear of heights came just after his fear of ghosts, only because he had so many fears that it was easiest to list them alphabetically.

But he wasn't going to let himself down again. He'd made a start on the ladder, he thought, and he wasn't going to slip back down this time; and he ignored the seed of self-knowledge suggesting that this wasn't exactly a *triumph* of achievement over historical disaster, more likely a very temporary setback.

He looked for a way to open the window. There was no catch, no handle, no apparent mechanism.

But then there wouldn't be, because the hotel would certainly be air-conditioned and it was high up so it would be dangerous anyway.

He'd have to break it.

That would be brave.

He turned slightly sideways, while the others looked on in growing disbelief, and smashed the window with his elbow.

Or not.

He actually smashed his elbow with the window, and then rubbed it for a few frantic seconds before he regained his composure and looked at his crew to see if they had noticed.

They had.

So had LOVE. A bang from the window just inches above his head had nearly made him lose his grip, but he was not to be beaten. This quest would not fail. He gritted his teeth, and pulled himself to window level, ignoring

'You are the eggman, we are the eggmen, I am the Dog . . .' which drifted up from the ground in a soft howl.

'Computer,' said Gloria. 'Open the window, please.'

The window opened.

There was a muffled noise, then something like a fading scream, as though the window had knocked someone off the ledge.

LOVE was able to ignore the pain in his forehead as he fell four storeys . . .

. . . Where his fall was initially broken by the outermost branches

163

of a fortuitously placed tree, blown into place by an equally fortuitous gust of wind, and further broken by the next branches down, with their unusually lush foliage, and he landed in a large bush which knocked the breath out of him but left the rest intact.

The Champion and Challenger studiously ignored each other's part in the whole affair.

Curtis looked out and down, straight down, onto some shrubs which seemed to shake in a low level breeze. But it wasn't what he saw when he looked straight down that worried Curtis, it was the fact that he *could* look straight down.

Four floors straight down.

What was he supposed to do? Could the computer provide hover boots, or tip the hotel over sideways so they could walk, or what? Was it obvious? Should he know? Should he be able to work it out? What would Fission shout at him if he got it wrong?

He had only just proved himself, and now he could make a mess of it all again.

It wasn't fair.

One of his University tutors – he'd had a lot – once told him that he would have kept a psychiatric convention breathless,[1] and the memory chose now to surface before he submerged it again with an effort of will.

He put one leg over the sill, thinking that any way of climbing down must logically begin with being outside, then stopped when his frantic brain compared being thought a wimp with being dead, and found the former marginally preferable. 'All right, how do we get down? Have you got some clever method or something?'

Fission shook her head slowly. 'We tie sheets together.'

There were plenty of them. Sheets were apparently a luxury, and that was what this hotel was about.

Curtis began tying a knot when Carlton told him to stop.

'Why?' He demanded an explanation.

'Because I wouldn't trust you to tie a shoelace, let alone something my life's going to depend on. That's why.'

Yes.

[1] In fact he had, on Earth Seventeen, where several of the audience had to be wheeled out in jackets where the sleeves do up. The medical term Curtiphobia had entered the dictionaries shortly afterwards.

Well, that was an explanation.

'Sit in front of the door in case someone tries to come in.'

Curtis dutifully planted himself on the floor, apparently having found his niche in life as a draught excluder and, while the carpet tried unsuccessfully to clean him away, he built up his courage. By the time the sheets were knotted and secured he had not so much a building as a very small mound.

Gingerly, he climbed out of the window, sheet grasped for dear life, until both feet rested against the wall, with straight legs leading to a quivering body. And, atop it all, a head trying to control the nerves; trying, in fact, not to be scared sheetless.

Now what? He had seen this sort of thing done. Abseiling they called it. You pushed off the wall and somehow went downwards.

He didn't know how.

He would push himself off and see if it came to him, he thought, not terribly sensibly.

He pushed, swung away from the wall, swung back, thudded flat against the masonry, lost his grip and slipped down a couple of feet.

Well, that seemed to work, he thought, but his arms had already begun to ache and vied for attention with the first of many bruises.

He did it again, with the same qualified success.

After a few more attempts his aching arms were well ahead in the battle for attention. It was clear that his strength was not going to be enough; hardly surprising, since he could lose an arm-wrestling match with a carriage clock.

He slipped and slithered, held on tightly as panic gave him more power, but it was only momentary, and he knew he was going to fall. Slowly, his fingers loosened, lost their grip one last time, and he let go, his mouth opening for the dying scream.

Then the breath was knocked out of him as he hit the ground three feet below him.

He lay and stared up at Gloria's descending posterior – not without some hopeless appreciation – and did not see a bare arm stretching out towards him from within both a white sleeve and a bush. A noise from one side made him twist his head, and he felt a hair being plucked loose, presumably having snagged on the ground, as he did so. He did not turn back because his attention was claimed by a small dog apparently crooning to itself, while wearing shades and a kaftan.

Behind him, LOVE clutched the hair, crawled from the far side of the bush, and called Stay to him.

Curtis watched the dog go, in obedient if shaky response to being called from somewhere out of sight, but any further interest he might have taken was diverted by Gloria's arrival, and then that of Carlton and Fission in quick succession.

Four floors up, the door to the now empty room opened, and Dano stuck her head in, checking.

She nodded, her eyebrows raised in surprise. Tamon had been right.

It had certainly taken them long enough, though.

XIX

Norim stood by the window, purportedly keeping a lookout, while Wilverton checked out the books. A lookout was about as useful as a condom to a eunuch, since the RAIN had reduced visibility to roughly an inch or so, and all Norim would be able to see would be a reflection of Norim, but he stood there anyway and gazed at whatever was available.

He was ignored by Wilverton, who didn't know where to start looking, let alone what to start looking for, and who just picked a random book off a random shelf, and opened it to a random page, delighting in the immediately apparent ability to understand the squiggles before him.

'There was once a young trand called Scraggy-curls,' Wilverton read, 'who was wandering through the forest one day, hoping to come across a targer[1] or a poltin[2] whose neck she could wring with her dainty hands and maybe take home to her mother for a snack.

'"I'm hungry," thought Scraggy-curls, and spotting a little cottage a short way off through the trees, decided to see if there was any food she could wrestle from the rightful owners without suffering too much physical damage. Off she skipped to the cottage, and found the door open and nobody inside, which was a major plus.

'On the table in the kitchen she found three bowls of freshly cooked poltin stew; one very big bowl, one medium-sized bowl, and one baby-sized bowl. Scraggy-curls immediately started in on the biggest of the three, reasoning that since she had no idea when the morons who had left all this free feed in the open would come back to the little cottage, it was sensible to start with the one which had most stew in it.

'She managed to finish all three bowls of stew without being

---

[1] A medium-sized animal which the trands quite liked to eat.
[2] Another medium-sized animal which generally went the same way as the targer. (Almost every medium-sized animal on Trand went the same way as the targer and the poltin; straight down the throat of the first trand to get its hands round a furry neck.)

discovered before she realised that she had probably eaten too much and needed to throw up before having a bit of a sleep to digest the rest, and she skipped through the little cottage to the bedroom, where she found three beds. She was sick all over the smallest, and then flopped onto the biggest, and went out like a light.

'She was still asleep when the owners of the cottage returned from a visit to their neighbours, whom they had suspected of encroaching on their land and to whom they had therefore given a bit of a lesson with some hand-held rocks. The owners were really hacked off when they found that their food had gone, and when they discovered Scraggy-curls asleep in the bedroom they broke three of her arms and threw her so far out of the cottage that it cut her home journey by half.

'Then they scraped as much stew as they could save from the baby bed and . . . '

Wilverton closed the book on his finger and peered at the spine, to confirm that he was indeed reading a fairy-tale. He wasn't, apparently. He was reading a Discourse on Trandian Social History and the Great Turning Points of the Past. They were pretty damned natty with titles, were the trands, he thought. He reopened the book, and started reading the next page.

' . . . and shows the accepted and quite natural physical tendencies of our race, which, while admirable, did for many long years in our history prevent scientific advance and the creation of today's civilised society.'

He nodded. Reasonable. If you react to an experiment giving the wrong results by taking the laboratory apart with a cudgel, then it is likely to slow down the march of the scientific vanguard.

'Hence the invention of the Gun was so important to our society. The Gun allowed control to be exerted over our more base proclivities, and its creation can be seen as the single most important turning point on our road to civilisation. The original (pictured below) is now kept in the council chamber as a constant reminder of the debt which we owe to it and its inventor.'

Pictured below was not a slim pistol – it was squatter, much more bulky; if the tinder got wet you could always brain someone with it, Wilverton reckoned – but it had a trigger and a dangerous end. A weapon. A weapon presumably powerful enough to stop a trand.

And therefore powerful enough to stop anything – including a renegade robot!

'Eureka!' he muttered, and didn't see Norim's frown.

This must be what he was here for; anyone could deduce that the weapon would be useful, but only he would have come to a library. And the Champion must have been working overtime! Of all the books in all the libraries on all of Trand, I had to pick this one. Of all the pages in all the books in all the libraries in all of Trand, to boot.

He did something that he had never done before, and tore the page out of the book, folding it and putting it into a pocket of his jump-suit. Crossing to the window, he found that the RAIN had eased, so that now it was just plain raining. Time to move on, now that he had somewhere to go.

'I need to get to the council chamber. Do you know where it is?'

'What is a reeker, and why am I one?'

Wilverton's brain tripped over, got up, rewound. 'I was talking to myself, forget it.' He waited. Nothing. Norim looked around vacantly. 'That's a no, is it?'

'Sorry?'

'You don't know where the council chamber is?'

'You said forget it.'

Wilverton sighed. Either the Challenger was sodding about again, or Norim was what his father used to call 'a right one'.

'Let's start again. Do you know where the council chamber is, from here?'

Norim held out a page which he, too, had pulled from a book. Wilverton took it. It was a map. Norim pointed to a square – or as close to a square as trandian architecture ever managed – and in the centre to what was marked 'Council Chamber' in neat squiggle.

'We're here,' he said, pointing again.

'Brilliant! Let's go!'

Norim nodded. 'I will lead.'

Well, you're more the hero shape, thought Wilverton, briefly; he was more concerned as to why Norim had a map to the city centre, and whether close study of the gift horse would reveal dangerous gums.

Sam noticed the lessening of the RAIN only because the visibility improved. For the past few minutes he would have found the feeble creature for which he searched only if he had tripped over him, but now he had a blurred view of most of the street ahead. It was an empty street, but Sam was not one of those who needed ever-present tangible results in order to maintain his motivation. Not for Sam the necessity of constant achievement and instant reward. Sam was a stayer, held on his pre-set course by an unwavering sense of purpose, a loyalty to his fellows which was quite immovable, and a fairly deep-seated lack of intelligence.

Sam yearned to follow in the footsteps of the revered, six-legged Wilfred,[1] his greatest hero in all the mythological history of Trand; that mountain of muscle, much of it between his ears.

It was going to be tricky, since Sam couldn't hope to follow in Wilfred's footprints without breaking into a quickstep, but he wasn't one to give up without a fight. He wasn't one to do *anything* without a fight, but especially not give up.

Reward for his persistence came this time with the déjà vu experience of an open doorway some distance along the road, and Wilverton stepping out.

At a speed which would have made an elderly sloth take a deep breath, Sam lumped himself against the nearest wall, and raised his gun. There would be no escape this time. No doors to hit him, no walls in danger of giving way, no earthquake which might swallow his efforts.

Sam aimed.

Water and air nearly solid assailing the wings
    Muscles that screamed in such pain for release from their
work
    Try to keep going but agony haunts every move
    And . . . oh bugger this for a game of crows!

A small rodent can provide only so much energy, especially for a creature that size, and more especially when the creature has to battle not only against gravity – the bane of life to all natural flyers who can't attain an escape velocity and a deep breath – but against the buffeting of a wind and RAIN storm.

It had tried to stay aloft, but it was too much. With a final and resignedly half-hearted flap of its huge wings, it headed for the ground, already unconscious.

And, inevitably, smashed into Sam just as his finger squeezed the trigger.

You, thought the Challenger, glancing at the Champion, are taking the piss.

[1] Gpgpttgjwp, incidentally. His parents were not only alien but met at the Severe Speech Impediment Clinic.

Wilverton followed Norim through the door, and was about to continue round an immediate corner when a loud thump from behind stopped him, followed almost instantly by the impact of a projectile in the stonework of the library.

He spun round instinctively, and saw a trand slumped on the ground about thirty yards behind him, and a huge bird-thing, even more slumped, next to it. Nothing else was in sight. He glanced round the corner ahead, to where Norim was walking slowly away, unaware, then looked back.

It was one of the trand team in the Game, he knew. Unconscious; helpless. With a gun.

He darted back to where Sam lay, found the gun sticking out from under the bird, and pulled it out. It was a different model from the one in the picture, and with a bent barrel. Unusable.

He looked at the trand again.

He could get a rock – there were plenty about – and improve the odds.

It was the sensible, logical thing to do in a Game to the death.

There was really no alternative.

Games to the death demanded death, he thought. Otherwise they would just be Games to the . . .

Will you stop trying to put it off?

He sighed.

Nearby a bit of building had relinquished the honour, to become just another rock with jagged edges. Wilverton heaved it into the air, staggered back to his fallen foe, lifted it over his head, and paused.

The trand moved feebly, and his eyes opened, looking straight, if unfocused, into Wilverton's, then passing on to the rock and taking on an expression of regret, hopelessness, defeat.

The rock wavered, and Wilverton wavered with it. He remembered an amusing out-take from a weight-lifting competition which he had glimpsed when his mother hit the wrong button and missed the science channel, but it was just a way for him to postpone the decision a second longer.

He knew he wasn't going to do it.

It wasn't possible.

Simple as that.

He could no more crush this alien's head than he could . . . he searched for a metaphor, couldn't find one . . . well, it didn't matter; he just couldn't do it.

He dropped the rock behind him, turned and ran back after Norim.

Sam watched events through eyes that were closing again, and unconsciousness overtook him once more even as he realised that he was still alive.

The Challenger smiled in long microwaves.

'As I predicted. They are soft; they have come too far. And they pride themselves on it! They will feel superior even as they die!'

The Champion did not respond. Compassion came with the evolution of intelligence, it knew well. And one being's weakness was another's strength.

XX

The Library in Orlando, Florida, capital of Earth Five Zero, had a fine tradition. Its marbled steps and ornate portico led to a building watched over by ancient and delicately sculpted figures – here one of an elephant with enormous ears, there an orang-utan which looked almost as though it strove to be human, perhaps so that it could stroll right into town.

Orlando Library was the epitome of classical architecture, as most befitted its great age.

Gedna sat just inside the doors – *her* doors – which allowed admission to the library – *her* library. She permitted visitors, and they were dutifully grateful to be granted the privilege of access. The library was her pride, its reverent history her joy, and she was reflecting on just that as she sat back and wriggled her bottom for a more comfortable position in a tactile duet with her chair.

The trand 'rushing' up the steps didn't give a poltin's pisser for the reverent history of the place.

Gedna was on her feet in a flash as the door was pushed roughly back, ready to remonstrate. How dare someone be so rude as to treat her . . .

Er . . .

What in Walt's name was that?

Well, it didn't matter what it was; it should be thrown out! It couldn't just barge in, she thought, while her eyes told her what a damned silly thought that was.

She watched with slightly slackening orifices as the trand lunged down the hall and made match-plastic out of one of the reading room doors, leaving the other with its beautifully-carved giant female mouse smiling wistfully at nothing.

Her mind flashed her a picture of her partner, Ranya, and her child, Dallen.

She had a choice. She could either be firm with this creature and assert the library's property rights, or she could see Ranya and

Dallen again.

Hmm.

Well, they were only books, she thought, as she left.

Outside, a functional robot followed to the letter the orders of the human City Council, which in turn was following the instructions of Central, by orchestrating a welcoming committee; this one armed with no musical instruments and definitely no spaghetti bolognese, which, the Mayoress of Relaxation was chastened to learn, had borne the brunt of any blame for the extraterrestrial's previous actions. What must the ambassador have thought of them!

They wouldn't make the same mistake again – this must be hands across the Universe, not across the windpipe.

This welcoming committee consisted of a large number of bewildered looking birds in a neat semi-circle of cages at the bottom of the library steps. Behind the cages, a number of even more functional robots stood stoically to attention, staring straight ahead, each carrying a slab of stone in arms which would not tire. The robot was not aware why any of this should be considered appropriate, but it wasn't its place to be aware. It didn't even check with Central to confirm the humans' rather peculiar orders.

As for those humans, they were following just as fast as they could. It was just unfortunate that some of them forgot their combs, or discovered they were wearing odd socks. It wasn't their fault.

Oh no.

But until they did arrive, the robot would follow their orders. To the letter.

Lots of bunting and flags they had said, and that was sure as hell what it was going to deliver.

'And how long have you been a robot?' Arnold asked the machine which stood smartly to attention in front of him.

'All my existence, sir.'

'Well, that's nice. Very good. Keep it up.'

'I will, sir.'

It didn't really have a lot of choice when it came to think of it, and it didn't come to think of it because it wasn't built to do so. It was built to build the micro-circuitry needed to persuade gluons to let go of their up-and-down quarks in a more genteel manner than in the earlier TMT devices, when the constituent parts of protons and neutrons had to be ripped forcefully from the gluons' grasp prior to their transportation. This meant that over any great distance – and

174

you don't need a fisherman to describe the gaps between galaxies – the integrity of the original particles was disrupted so badly that they could not be terribly well re-formed. Whatever you sent generally arrived like so much tomato jelly.

The tachy-gluon drive eased the particles apart so smoothly that the resultant beam was narrower than a puritan's mind. If it arrived at its destination with a metaphorical hair out of place, then that was due to shoddy combing before it left.

That was the theory, and it had been the practice for the inanimate objects which had tried the thing out, bringing back recordings of star clusters and nebulae that did not exist in their home galaxy as proof of where they had been, since a postcard would take absolutely ages.

The mechanism was now installed in a flyer which could carry something the size and shape of a human being, and something the size and shape of a human being was being shown around it. As far as the robots doing the showing, and the holocams watching them were concerned, it *was* a human being. It would have been an honour to have a world Presidential candidate showing such an interest in something so material, had they been made to appreciate it.

For Arnold, it was a photo opportunity.

'You don't mind if I sit in it for a while,' he told the nearest robot, who immediately added this new piece of knowledge to its memory bank.

Arnold stepped over the low shelf and into the vehicle, which looked more like a grab than an intergalactic spaceship and settled himself into the seat. His fixed smile gave way to an expression of mild surprise – but not fluster – when he noticed a holocam looking at him.

'Oh, my, is this going out on the holo?' he asked no-one in particular, and no-one answered because the robots had not been furnished with the information and because the camera, although sporting legs, arms and rather more than its fair share of eyes, didn't have a mouth. 'Well, I didn't expect this, but let me just take the opportunity to say what a marvellous achievement this is. It is another example of the amazing ingenuity of the people of Earth, and it is a tribute to our civilisation that our planet is where this great advance has been made.'

He knew all the watching humans would be swelling in reflected glory, as though they had anything to do with it. Humans were like flies, he reflected; they both just ate up crap. He had to go the whole

175

hog, though.

'Furthermore, it puts Earth at the very forefront of all planets in our Universe, not just our Galaxy. For had another race been so advanced as to create intergalactic travel, we would surely have received their visit by now. And we have not. We can all take great pride in being the first.'

The grab slowed to a smooth halt and allowed Fission out in a sensible hurry. Without noticing that the area was marginally less scenic than the huge tracts of parkland through which they had passed to reach it, accounting for the almost complete lack of people, she immediately started running towards the hangar which the grab had identified as containing the tachy-gluon cruiser.

In her path, two rival packs of monkeys were approaching each other, arguing amongst themselves until they spotted their common enemies, when internal squabbles were forgotten in favour of screaming territorial defiance across the divide, leaping up and down and pounding the ground in displays guaranteed to strike terror into any pound-fearing chimp.

The look of manic enthusiasm on Fission's face, the streaming blue hair, and the determination of her feet silenced them in a second. She thumped through the centre of no-chimp's land without a sideways glance.

When she passed, they re-started as though nothing had happened, red eyes staring across the divide, screams reaching fever pitch.

Carlton, Gloria and Curtis, in strict order of athletic ability, silenced them once more; or almost – one or two sighs greeted the interruption.

The frowns on the chimps' faces, and the disapproval in their red-brown eyes, took Gloria's mind from a question that had bothered her on the trip – if the glue-on stuff was only tacky, wouldn't they do better to let it dry?

Over the shoulder of the camera Arnold could see across the vast expanse where the robots manufactured their craft with computers, crystal growth chambers, sheet metal and chitin, working consecutive twenty-four-hour shifts until they dropped, which they didn't. At the far end of the hangar were the huge doors through which craft could be moved if they couldn't disappear under their own steam – or tachyons – and the smaller door through which humans and

176

robots had little choice but to come and go thanks to their lamentable ineptitude at corporeal transmutation.

It was this latter which Arnold now saw swing open to allow in a group either of completely nutty robots or else of perfectly normal humans. Four figures started racing across the expanse to where the tachy-gluon craft nestled unconcernedly. The leading member of the quartet had bright blue hair, was waving her arms around as though the hands were frantically trying to escape from their shackles in any direction possible, and Arnold fancied he could see little flames coming from her eyes; if Fission was ever literally to live up to her name it was going to be when she arrived.

Now what was upsetting her? Just because he wanted to be independent, it annoyed them. Why did humans think they had the right to tell him what to do? Probably an inferiority complex – they certainly had good cause for one.

His smile never flinched.

'And how does the craft work, then?' he asked. 'What will the human pilot have to do?'

A couple of the robots looked at each other, clearly unsure about who should answer. Behind the smile Arnold silently approached apoplexy – Look, don't debate it, you low-grade simpletons, one of you just tell me.

'The pilot will verbally instruct, sir,' answered one, an eternity – about a second – later.

'Well, I think it is important for a prospective President to show that he has what is needed to make courageous decisions on behalf of his fellows. I will take it upon myself to give the craft its first test flight. Computer, close the lid.'

A transparent bubble appeared around Arnold, through which his frozen smile could still be seen. The words he spoke to the ship were then lost to the holovision viewers, and the craft disappeared. Only the smile remained, imprinted on the watching retinas.

'You bunch fonking povvos!' floated across the hangar, and was picked up and transmitted to people all over the globe. Carlton reckoned Fission was insulting several million people at once; well it would save her doing it individually.

She didn't get the chance to push the point home as the cameras turned themselves off and wandered away, leaving Fission to point out a number of imagined inadequacies of the engineer robots who stood calmly and stared at her, understanding precisely none of what she said and caring, if anything, less.

This did not cheer her up. They were *that* close!

Dano checked the empty grab to make sure it was that way and hurried towards the hangar, noticing how the chimps on either side of her stopped screaming, but continued muttering as she passed. She couldn't quite make out what they said.

Fission started walking slowly back towards the entrance, steaming quietly, but calming herself with an effort. The others followed.

'Right. We got look at this with clear heads. Where would Arnold go next? Any ideas? Anyone?' Nothing. *That* close! echoed through her mind. 'Dic . . . er . . . Richard, you worked it out last time.' Don't frighten him. 'And good bit of work. Got clue?'

He wished an answer into his head; it was nice being one of the team.

He concentrated so hard his face went red.

He searched the corners of his mind.

Old Mother Hubbard would have recognised the feeling.

He sadly shook the empty vessel at Fission.

'Fonkshit!' Her shoulders dropped along with her eyebrows.

The door opened before they reached it, and Dano's head poked around the corner in the way that heads do when they want to be invisible. The cranial wish was disappointed when she found four people staring straight at her from a distance of ten yards.

'Oh. Hello,' she managed, without an intervening 'er' anywhere – there probably weren't any left after Curtis had reached the front of the queue. 'Arnold's not here, then.'

'No,' Carlton answered, wondering how much further his last exchange with Dano had pushed down her opinion of him, and wondering why he cared quite so much. 'He's just left.'

'Do you know where he's gone?'

Fission took a deep breath, the action taking longer than usual through teeth that were clamped together like a clam refusing mummy's spoonful of purée, and allowing Carlton to keep the initiative.

'No.' She was the least pompous of those they had met, though. And one of the prettiest. If only he wasn't an offworlder. 'What made you think he was here?'

That building over there, under the low roof with the long ramp leading down to things that were just about worthy of the description 'doors', thought the trand, having watched yet another couple of the creatures fleeing at breath-taking speed from his friendly advance. That's where some more of these human things would be, and they wouldn't be able to run away. The library had proved useful – he now knew what he wanted; the book being mashed in his third left hand gave him the clue – and the humans in the building would tell him where to find it.

The trand trotted, like an unsettled cliff, towards the hangar.

Chanta was about to run between two sets of some sort of monkey, which for some reason were sitting quietly and staring at her, one or two of them drumming their fingers on the ground, when a noise behind her, like a cliff on the move, made her look round.

She paused; briefly.

She decided that, if Rudy *was* in the hangar, then a few more minutes of waiting wouldn't hurt.

She darted off to one side, finding a tree big enough to hide her.

There was already someone behind it – a man with a face that looked like it had lost a very large gamble. He glared at her, and raised his wrist, above which the security insignia suddenly appeared.

'Find your own tree,' he told her, and pointed his gun back at the hangar doors.

His attention was taken momentarily by the renewed screaming of the chimps, but that lasted only momentarily, and was replaced by angry mutterings, drumming fingers and tapping feet.

It was the alien thing again, lumbering towards the hangar, and the chimps were bombarding it with twigs and small stones, to no apparent avail.

Tamon frowned. Where did the alien fit into all this? Built like that, he thought, in a big hole in a Ganymede quarry.

'Well, to be honest,' and to be sheepish by the look on Dano's face as she replied, 'I followed you.'

'What!'

Dano remembered, when she was a kid, telling her mother that she had put Largo, their puppy, in the Instacook because she was all wet, and she remembered the look on her mother's face when, just after Dano had finished speaking, there came a squelchy bang from the kitchen. She was getting the same look now from Carlton and Fission. She didn't let it put her off.

179

'It was Central's idea, of course. Reckoned that there was a high probability that you would be able to find Arnold and that I should tag along.' Then she added, 'That's why we let you escape.'

Fission frowned, and Carlton felt like a bumbling offworlder for the first time in minutes. The feelings he had been having were way off line – she was just another stuck-up civ!

You're being stupid again, muttered his conscience.

Well, you know why that is, don't you! he challenged it, angrily.

He glared at her, and she looked back, and he opened his mouth to say something about mink, or sheep, or even ants, but she kept looking at him and in the end he didn't say anything at all.

'Couldn't you have stopped him?' Dano asked. 'You knew we wanted to talk to him.'

Gloria noticed that neither Carlton or Fission was about to answer – the former looked oddly confused and the latter as though something inside had exploded and the force was trying to escape through her bulging eyes – so she did it herself.

'He stole the tacky glue-on spaceship they were building. We couldn't stop him.'

'*Stole?* How can you steal a spaceship?'

Curtis knew the answer to that one, and he hadn't said anything yet. 'Well, he just got in and closed the lid and . . . '

'No.' She gave him the tired look of a kindergarten supervisor, which was easily authority enough to render him instantly speechless. 'I mean, it doesn't belong to anybody. You can't steal something that . . . '

Dano stopped suddenly, put her hand to a point just behind her left ear, and listened intently, frowning. After a few seconds she lowered the hand and looked at everyone in turn, pausing on Carlton's face fractionally longer than the others, or was that only in his imagination?

'That was Central. Seems it didn't know about your being kept in the hotel. It must have been Tamon's idea.' She looked confused. 'Why would he do that?'

'Because he's a nutter,' Carlton told her, shrugging. Well, it was obvious. 'He thought we were a danger to Central and that was enough to tip him over the edge. It's his hero. He'd marry it if he could!'

'He'd what?'

Here we go again. 'Never mind.'

'Well, whatever, I . . . '

Then a part of the main hangar doors rushed into the interior of the building, dragging a six-armed alien along with it.

The group snapped their heads round and adopted the tableau position as the trand brought himself to a halt – not the accomplishment of a moment – and the bits of door slipped gratefully from his torso. The robots who had led their honoured guest around the spaceship had long since disappeared in the absence of both guest and ship, so there was nothing to be seen in the direction he was looking.

'If you think those things we saw were supposed to point you at an animal,' Dano whispered, to Carlton, specifically, he noticed, 'then what about that?'

The trand spun round slightly faster than the moon, and spied life. Still life. That was what he wanted. He moved towards it.

Not still life, suddenly.

Life scrambling for the door with the sort of 'after you' gallantry you'd expect if someone dropped a million wollar bill.

The trand stared after them. Why were they running? He wasn't going to do them any harm!

Why not? demanded the Challenger.

Well, he would now! the trand thought, the notion occurring to him with a hot flush of anger.

He would have chased after them, but they were moving quicker than a targer with a torched tail – usually seen in pairs, while trands bet on which would reach the river first. He looked around, and there was a large canister almost within reach, bearing the legend: 'Danger: Hyperphallic acid.'

Danger, eh! The trand plucked the canister with his top two right arms and took aim. It soon would be for these humans!

They were almost at the doors, two abreast; Gloria, therefore, on her own as she glanced over her shoulder in response to an alien cry, and saw the thing poised to throw something at them, anger in its eyes. And she knew immediately that this was no animal. Animals didn't attack through anger; they only preyed for food, protection, territory.

That meant it wasn't what they were after.

She would have taken a moment out to be relieved if the trand hadn't lobbed a canister at her, and concentrated her mind in her feet.

181

'Hyperphallic acid!' shouted Fission. 'Come on!'

At the sound of yet more footsteps, two opposing groups of chimps watched through brown-red eyes, stopped screaming, looked at each other, glanced at the sky, turned round and trudged away.

Tamon stepped out from behind his tree, gun raised, waiting for the robot that would target his Central.

Chanta watched, looking for the Rudy that used to target her Central.

The group cleared the hangar doorway like there was not only no tomorrow, but very little left of today, and Carlton led them immediately off to one side before the hangar doorway cleared the hangar. He knew that unprotected hyperphallic acid wasn't safe at the best of times, and that grinding its container along the ground was just asking for trouble.

They hit the earth moments before bits of hangar wall streaked past where their heads had just been. The roof, badly supported by thin air, dived onto yet more canisters, exploded back upwards again, and crashed down in pieces. Any remaining bits of wall joined it, and only a slow dust rose from what was left.

Red-eyed chimps scampered towards the scene, searching for any signs of life under the rubble, as Gloria rolled over and sat up, surveying the scene with the others.

'The poor thing,' she said, apparently discounting what the thing had in mind when it initiated the episode – as only she could, thought Fission.

The 'poor thing' pushed bits of hangar away from him and stood up. Four tons of construction material had re-introduced about as much composure as he ever suffered, and he looked around, his thoughts once more on information gathering.

The humans were doing the opposite of gathering, all heading for vehicles – one fell over a couple of times on the way, but wasn't going to lie there long enough for him to catch up. He looked disappointed. His shoulders almost sagged, but he managed to stop them, sensibly – it was one hell of an effort to get them back up again with six hundredweight of arm hanging off them.

Only one human had ever remained where he was when the trand had approached, came a dim memory from the recesses of his mind. He would have to return. He lowered his head towards his chest and, painstakingly, raised it again in what would have to do as a nod.

XXI

LOVE smiled grimly to himself as he bent over his console, which displayed a perfect double helix, apart from a small missing section. Replacement – substitution – of the segment did not involve delicate hand movements and a steady nerve, unless you were a particularly clumsy typist, and he watched as the computer carried out his instructions.

Is this really necessary? he asked himself in the quiet of inactivity.

The rhythm of Stay's paws beat a litany in his brain. 'We shall overcome,' they seemed to say. 'We shall not be moved.'

Absolutely, he told himself, and nodded with certainty.

'Blowing in the wind,' said the paws.

Indeed.

'They've paved paradise, put up a parking lot.'

Er . . .

'By the time I got to Dogstock . . . '

'Shut up, Stay.' The dog glanced vaguely in the direction of its masters and considered that the blue one was currently really rather cosmic.

LOVE's computer beeped the completion of its work. LOVE smiled.

Wonderfully easy to isolate, DNA, from a hair. Wonderfully versatile stuff, too. From creating new life through cloning – LOVE did not appreciate that with Curtis DNA he could have come up with Pillock Park – to the exact opposite. The infidel might be invulnerable to normal methods, thanks to some guardian devil, but a DNA bullet could not be denied.

Bullets used to have names on them – a real bummer if you were called Smith – but this viral projectile bore nothing so ungainly and could kill no-one but its intended victim.

It also couldn't fail, guardian devil or no.

The 'guardian devil' looked down from the ether and passed no electromagnetic comment. Let the Challenger worry about whether it was worried, or not . . .

The Challenger noticed, of course, and gave no indication that it had done so, of course. It was certainly not going to worry about the Champion's lack of worry, or give away the fact that it was – if it was.

'Now what?' Fission asked. She was open to suggestions. So far they had thrown themselves and each other into the grab and made tracks, but that was just about where it ended – she had no idea where to go, and she knew enthusiasm alone wasn't going to give her a clue.

'Well, we *should* find Arnold,' said Gloria. Not because he was the renegade or anything – Central was still top of her suspicion list – but because it seemed a good idea; at least he was one of the lost crew members who they *could* find.

'But he take intergalactic cruiser! How we find?' Fission didn't sound upset, but she didn't sound like it would take much, either.

'Just because he's got a spaceship that *can* go between galaxies doesn't mean he's *going* to go between galaxies, does it?' It sounded reasonable to Gloria, but then so many things did, until the others pointed out why they were silly.

Wilverton was right, Fission thought – Gloria *was* a good lateral thinker. Funny how first impressions . . . Fonk funny, get on with it! 'You're right. Good thinking. Doesn't help.'

Before Gloria could work out whether to feel good, bad, or indifferent, Curtis spoke, pointing ahead and upwards. 'There's Arnold!'

Arnold, Miron and Pomona were sitting in transparent, cloud-filled armchairs, and the first was surrounded by what looked like a menagerie, while the others were alone. Carlton, taking his gaze and thoughts from behind them, where Dano followed in her grab, recognised an election debate.

They were hanging holographically some twenty feet above a stall selling baseball caps, each with 'Vote for Arnold' on the front, and buttons proclaiming 'Arnold for President'. A small knot of people watched, while others bought buttons, and searched for somewhere to stick them which wouldn't necessitate bloodshed. A dozen spectacled bears sat to one side, like cubs in uniform, their identical markings suggesting they had come on a group outing. They watched the debate, but didn't look convinced.

'Computer, can you take us to studio where election debate going on?' Fission asked.

It could.

'Do it.' She punched a couple of buttons to confirm her orders, and the grab forked left. 'Fast.'

It ignored her. Central had no-nonsense views on grab speed, and distance from other vehicles. Views which, since it could go two falls out of three with a medium strength god, it could enforce regardless of the ambitions of lunatic humans.

Fission took a few deep breaths which calmed her not at all.

Nor did the people past whom they drove. What they were doing didn't matter – except for that pair just by the bush over there whose antics it was admittedly hard to ignore – but what they were wearing, did. Arnold tee shirts complimented the caps and buttons, and they were beginining to look common; the people wearing them, beginning to look like a team. They were beginning, thought Fission, to look like a winning team.

'Computer. Turn the holovision on. Show us the election debate.' Carlton seemed to have had the same thought. He and Fission glanced at each other, and the hostilities hung suspended between them.

'My leadership of the Foundation Foundation is something I hold most dear. Our shaven heads are a sign of the sacrifice we are willing to make for our beliefs, and proof of my preparedness to make the sacrifices required to be President.' Miron adopted an expression of reverence next to which the Pope would look a bit smutty.

'I am sure we're all *suitably* impressed,' Arnold commented from his armchair. 'Heaven knows what you would be prepared to shave if elected!'

On his shoulder sat an owl, blinking slowly, looking wise. On his left, a snow leopard looked more regal than any President of a planet could hope to approach, while to his right was something that looked like a large dog, but on closer scrutiny turned out to be a hyena, albeit a rather appealing one. At Arnold's comment, it giggled to itself, its shoulders jogging up and down as it hissed in amusement. Miron skewered it with a stare, then looked back to Arnold.

'I see no signs of a willingness on your part to make personal sacrifice,' he pointed out coldly.

'I don't see that having the chance to represent my fellow Terrans involves a sacrifice. It will mean that there are things I cannot do, but they will surely not be things I would *rather* do. I can't think of an honour higher than being chosen to personify the people of this greatest of planets. That is no sacrifice. I am sorry if you think it is.'

The leopard slowly turned its head to look at Miron. It all but smiled. And Arnold gave the cameras a look of such sincerity as to make other sincerities those of second-hand grab dealers, were there such things as second-hand grabs, let alone dealers.

They would lap this up, like cats with award-winning cream. They were such total *morons*.

Miron apparently agreed. Had this not been a live holo debate, his expression said, he would cheerfully have strangled his political opponent on the spot.

From the third cloud-filled, buttock-biased arm-chair on the set, Pomona joined the conversation. 'I am really not sure that I would want to be represented by someone such as Arnold. He really does appear to be someone of limited breeding.'

'I do try to limit my breeding,' Arnold admitted. 'Aren't you concerned that people will think you're a rabbit?'

Pomona flushed and spluttered; Arnold wasn't quite sure whether at the sexual or animal reference. The hyena hissed away to itself, until Arnold held up a hand, looking aghast. 'I am sorry! Wasn't that what you meant? I just assumed, from what everyone says about you . . . I mean, I don't wish to reduce this to insult . . . '

'The traditional contest for this great office demands such by-play,' Miron pointed out, clearly enjoying Pomona's discomfort. 'Any prospective President would respect those traditions had he the wit to do so. The Foundation Foundation places great store in the ways of the past.'

'That is all very laudable,' said Arnold. 'Such an attitude will certainly prepare us for the world of the twenty-third century. In this age of the tachy-gluon cruiser, though, Earth must think to the future, must prepare to take its place in the forefront of the universe. We must guide the "younger" planets, those not yet as civilised as ourselves. We need, now, a President who will look forward and carry the banner to the future, not one who is tied to the past.'

He's very good, thought Gloria, and caught an expression on Carlton's face that agreed with her.

'I wonder if we get a vote,' Curtis wondered.

Carlton turned a raised eyebrow at him.

'Why?'

'Well, you know . . . I just thought . . . I mean, it would be nice . . . Arnold and everything . . . ' Why were they looking at him like that? Again.

'Arnold's lying, Richard,' Gloria told him, quietly.

'Oh.' Curtis looked as though Santa had just ceased to exist. 'Well, yes, I know. I was just . . . '

'Shut up,' Fission suggested, tersely. There had to be some way she could make this grab go quicker.

Carlton looked out the back of the vehicle, just making out Dano, still following. There seemed to be a third grab behind Dano's, but he couldn't see who was in it, and he didn't really care. Off to one side of the roadway, he noticed a male lion lying on its side, the lioness a little way off, searching the horizon for food with a limp – something on a stick, perhaps – and he frowned at the unexceptional. The emotions he was feeling were difficult to describe and, he thought, it was just as well that describing them was the last thing he would be caught doing.

If the President was going to make a difference, Dano thought to herself, keeping half an eye on the grab in front, then I could easily vote for Arnold after that lot.

And she frowned. Why?

Because he makes me feel part of his team, not the subject of some ruler, which was how the other two always came across. And more, he makes me feel part of *Earth's* team, playing against the Universe and winning, appealing directly to a desire to be successful, to be better than the rest. And a leader who made you think like that could make you do things, could get people to act out the fantasy.

Clever.

Dangerous.

Maybe there *was* something in what Tamon said.

Was war Arnold's plan? It sounded ludicrous even as she thought it, but she thought it just the same.

But even if it was, it wouldn't work, because the President couldn't *do* anything, least of all lead them in a war against the rest of the Universe!

Central was leader enough, and had been since it had truly civilised them.

Turned them into fat mink . . .

Damn!

Why did Peter have to say that? she thought angrily; but too late, her mind catching hold of the phrase again, and worrying at it.

Then it took a second out to worry at why she had thought 'Peter' in that tone of thought, before getting back on line.

Fat mink who couldn't go back. Fat mink who hated what they were but had no choice, because they couldn't live any other way.

Then the realisation hit her with almost physical force. No leader would have to *replace* Central and then force them to become barbaric. If someone could just take Central away, turn it off, that would do it. And it wouldn't have to be all at once, no massive explosion or anything. Bit by bit would be enough. They couldn't do anything without Central any more. They were fat mink.

And only a robot would know enough to turn Central off, to begin that process.

And Arnold was a robot.

And the Presidential election result was followed by the ceremonial restart of Central, where the President keyed, by traditional hand, just what he was told to key.

Unless he knew to do something else.

'Computer! Emergency velocity override code seven three four zero eight. Hurry.'

The grab smoothly accelerated, passing the one in front, from which Fission gave it a look of frustration that should have fused it to the roadway.

'The leader should be someone who is used to leading, someone with a presence which will be readily apparent when she meets representatives of the lesser worlds.'

'Withdrawing so near the election, Pomona?' Miron asked, and Arnold almost nodded in approval. 'Although I agree that leadership experience is necessary.' And he smoothed down his robes.

Arnold shook his head. 'I wish you wouldn't refer to it as "leading". Representation is what we should be concerned with, not leadership. You imply that you are better than your fellow Terrans. I'm not interested in "leading" for its own sake . . . '

'Lucky for you that you won't get the chance, then!' Pomona smiled, triumphantly.

The hyena hissed momentarily, until Arnold's eyebrow cut it dead, and the leopard glanced at Pomona, but couldn't stare her down.

'Your wit is sharp,' Miron interjected. 'Would that your dress sense were the same.'

★

Gloria's attention was distracted when the grab took them past Orlando Library.

The robots still stood impassively with their slabs of stone in their arms, amid a lot of bits that looked like birds after a good lawn-mowing, and waited for orders.

The grab sped – crawled, for Fission, who was rhythmically tapping the panel in front of her, preliminary to rhythmically thumping it – silently past, leaving its occupants none the wiser.

'They were robots not acting very sensibly,' said Gloria, clutching, she realised even as she spoke, at a straw so feeble as to make even an elderly camel sneer.

'True. Unfortunately it's not going to help us very much.' Carlton sounded distracted, but stopped looking for a long-lost grab and turned to Gloria. 'For starters, there's lots of them and we're looking for just one that stands out. And, secondly, robots *are* pretty stupid really. They just do what they're told without asking questions.'

'Arnold doesn't!' came Gloria's inevitable response.

'Hah!' Fission explained in one simple syllable, with thump accompaniment, that Gloria's comment was the winning own goal in the match between Fission and the Rest of the World.

Tamon's match had been won when the notion of Arnold's treachery had occurred to him, and had grown to a conviction in moments.

He rushed headlong from his grab to the building where he knew the debate to be taking place, arm outstretched, looking as though his disruptor was some huge runaway dog, pulling him along.

Calm down, came a thought from somewhere. You will be more efficient, more able to protect Central.

Go for it, came a second thought. Just get there as quickly as you can, not a moment to lose.

He didn't know where the thoughts had come from, and didn't spend time wondering. Tamon just ran. Central needed him.

'Isn't your Foundation rather exclusive?'

'Anyone may join . . . and I don't see what it has to do with the election. Your attention is wandering, I fear.'

Arnold's attention was suddenly snatched by a familiar face mouthing something on the far side of the soundproof door behind one of the camera robots.

Tamon.

'Not at all. I was just considering what other planets would think of us once we had all shaved our heads. I fear they would legitimately poke fun.'

Tamon was almost at the door.

The disruptor was even nearer.

'I certainly wouldn't want to be bald!' Pomona stated, her hand rising to as much of her hair as she could reach.

'I doubt anyone would be tempted, Pomona,' Miron suggested.

'*TRAITOR!*' Tamon's voice mingled with the sound of the wall, admitting that it wasn't soundproof-doorproof.

All three candidates were on their feet immediately, which was more than Tamon was, after meeting the sill at the door's base.

'It's a Pomona supporter!' cried Arnold, the owl launching itself from his shoulder. 'He's pointing a gun at Miron!'

One of the cameras spun round, and down, just missing, assumedly, Tamon pointing a gun at Miron. Another stayed on Arnold as he heroically rushed to Miron's aid.

'I'll save you!' he shouted, collecting the Foundation leader like a sack of flour and lifting him onto one shoulder with a slight effort before swinging towards a back exit. 'Come on, Pomona, I can only carry one!'

He was such a hero.

She turned to follow, but Miron's swinging sandal kicked her in the midriff, so she bent double and gasped instead.

The hyena was beginning to find events somewhat amusing.

Tamon leaped to his feet, raised the disruptor, saw Miron hanging down Arnold's back as an inadvertent shield, and rushed towards the set.

The snow leopard rose serenely and ambled towards him.

Pomona straightened up.

Tamon saw the leopard, and dived athletically over the top of it, cleverly foiling its intentions, not seeing that it just ambled on and wandered from the studio . . .

And having no notion of the burst of x-rays which flooded through the much troubled planet Farger several million light years to his right . . .

He slid across the polished floor like a desperate last shot in the human curling championships, to the sound of hyenan guffaws from off left. Pomona watched with an expression of pain and superior anger until it became clear that the lunatic was only going to be stopped by her legs, when panic set in.

But too late, and wrong. Tamon wasn't stopped by her legs at all, but merely scythed them from under her, while the hyena rolled on its back and screamed at the ceiling.

The dignity of high political office slipped off-set without a backward glance, as did Arnold, before dumping Miron, glancing at him with a frown because he didn't look big enough to weigh that much, and legging it.

Pomona landed on her bottom and managed a tiny bounce. Her gravitationally contemptuous hair couldn't cope with the inertia and promptly flopped over her face. She blew it aside, and held it there while she stared at a Tamon now trying to sit up and find a target to blast.

'You farking *prunt*!' she shouted, just, sadly, before she remembered the cameras. She looked at one. 'Oh, nobgush!' said her mouth. 'Oh shit!' her brain suggested on hearing the second obscenity, and clamped her mouth shut against any chance of a third.

A moment of inactive calm was shattered when the owl swooped low over the scene and deposited the results of its last meal squarely onto the bridge of Pomona's nose, from where it dribbled down and dropped forlornly off the end.

The hyena gripped its sides, noiselessly convulsed, and rolled around in a puddle of its own making.

Pomona wiped her nose with her sleeve, and briefly studied the result. It looked a lot like the remains of her political career.

XXII

'I am weak and deserve your abuse.' Sam hung his bruised head, while his Captain maintained a frown that looked like a small rock slippage. One renegade robot in the pathetic shape of a human being to find and subdue.

Subdue!

It was almost laughable – and something had to be pretty damned funny to make Rupert so much as smirk, given the pain involved.

A task as stretching as outmanoeuvring a small puddle, and Sam manages it not. A bigger disgrace to the legendary Wilfred More-than-ten-limbs[1] it would be hard to imagine. Not that the Captain found anything easy to imagine.

He spied a part of Sam's head which appeared relatively un-harmed, and laid into it with a few well-placed concussion creators for a while, but desisted before Sam reached the comatose state which would have been his just reward under normal circumstances because, he admitted with an uncharacteristic flash of mercy, these circumstances were not altogether normal, not with two bodiless aliens contending somewhere in the ether above them.

The rock slippage frown became a bit more severe – Newtonian physics would have had difficulty explaining why his eyebrow ridges didn't fall off – as he recalled those currently in apparent partial control of his life. The fact that there existed something which he could not grasp by the genitals and throw fifty yards did not sit quite right in his view of the way things should be. In fact, it got up and trampled all over his view of the way things should be.

What was even more galling was that when he was normally annoyed by something, he could relieve his anger by attacking the thing which riled him. If he lost, he lost, but that was how things should be. By definition, that was not possible to do with the Challeng-er and the Champion, which just served to frustrate him more.

[1] Any number from eleven onwards was known to the legendary Wilfred as more-than-ten, and he had always been pretty damned proud of getting up *that* far.

And a frustrated trand is not a happy trand.

A trand that *isn't* frustrated is not a happy trand, let alone a trand that is.

'We must together this creature seek. Come.'

A trand of few words was the Captain – and those not necessarily in the right order – but they were apparently all that were required as four smallers followed him to the rude door of the rude building. The fifth, Sam, dragged himself to his feet for the umpteenth time that day and did likewise.

He had tried, but the fates were against him. He had tried to live up to the standards set not only by Wilfred, but by his gloried direct ancestor, Sam the Unvanquishable and Difficult to Pronounce. But, even if it meant living with the title of Sam the Easily Said Wimp, he had realised that he was not going to manage this without the help of his biggers.

What he had not told them was that the human had had him defeated, and had not finished him. He did not understand it, but he did feel slightly ashamed of it. He should have been dead.

As they passed out into the street, Sam cast a baleful eye at the huge bird he had dragged along as evidence. It lay with its head at an unnatural angle and did not return his look, much as it would have liked to.

Igneous creature! Sam thought at it. Birds should fly, or die quietly; which they would were it not for insubstantial aliens taking the precipice with the laws of probability.

Frustrated at not being able to blame the aliens in the way he liked best, Sam blamed the bird instead, and leaned down to grasp its scraggy neck – anything short of a moose has a scraggy neck by trand standards – before lobbing it high over the group of low constructions to his left, and slouching after his colleagues.

'Through here,' said Norim, pointing at an alleyway between what might have been two imposing sides of buildings had the bricks not apparently given a long exhalation and settled themselves down for a bit of a snooze, so that the alley looked like the narrow valley floor of two rather shabby ranges of hills.

Wilverton looked down the alley without much enthusiasm. There was no rain at the moment and, in amongst the buildings of the city, the ambitions of the wind were blunted to an occasional impotent gust. But there was a depressing dankness about the place which promised that a young man's fancy would have to stay in a deep rut for a while yet.

Not that Wilverton's fancy was near the forefront of his mind. He had a job to do.

'What's down there?' he asked. Norim consulted his map again.

'It should be the main square of the city and, in the middle of the main square, should be the council chamber.'

'Main square.'

Norim consulted his map once more, to make sure, and nodded. 'Main square. Should be.'

'As in, where a lot of trands probably gather.'

Norim passed no comment on that, which Wilverton did not take as a confident denial of the likelihood that when he poked his head beyond the shadows of the alley it would be removed from his shoulders before he had a chance to unpoke it again.

'Why don't you go first,' he suggested, having tried to think of a way in which he could make the proposal sound anything other than an invitation to amble down death row, and having failed. But this was no time to change his spots and try to be a leader. Perhaps that was another reason why he was here instead of one of the others – would Peter demand to lead, and get himself killed, or would he control that instinct until the job was done?

Norim started walking down the alley. Wilverton shrugged, and followed.

The frall was a small furry animal which held an almost unique place in the fauna of Trand Whatever in that it was not on any trandian dinner menu.

The frall was a natural enemy of the trand.

Not that this qualification made it special, since anything which came into contact with the trands for any reasonable length of time became their natural enemy, but that is no great shakes unless there was even a sniff of a chance of actually winning against one should it come to a fight.

And, for the frall, there was.

The frall carried around in the fibres of its flesh a substance which caused a trand, having ingested it, to double over in agony for a fortnight, during which time they lost weight and strength in equal proportions, so that they ended up with the prospect of coming last in a muscle contest behind Willy the Weedy, a fate much worse than death. Even touching a frall caused the trands considerable discomfort and a worrying loss of appetite.

Trands knew this and so they gave the frall the sort of berth you could fit an ocean liner into, sideways. The frall also knew this, and, being at least as intelligent as the trands, considered the arrangement a pretty neat one on the part of Nature.

As Wilverton set foot in the alley – in the same way you might set foot on a string bridge – a frall a few streets away was setting four feet with a comfortable nonchalance on its way to removing a few titbits from a well-stocked larder of its acquaintance. It felt as carefree as fralls usually did, and might have whistled a tune had it known any, and been able to whistle.

A shadow passed briefly across its path that was darker than the absence of sunlight caused by the weather, and it glanced up to see, disconcertingly speeding through the air towards it, a huge, almost reptilian bird. The frall sighed.

Depressingly stupid; these birds had never quite got their minds around the fact that attacking a frall and rending it limb from limb with talons and beak was, in fact, an extremely energetic way of committing suicide. The one which was swooping down with its wings oddly pinned back appeared to be just the latest in a long line of kamikaze flyers.

The frall stopped short, and fast, turned in a flash, and headed back the way it had come, keeping close to the walls of the buildings for protection. It would, it decided – not taking too much notice of the thudding sound of a bird crashing into the street behind it, in what would have been a fatal accident had it not been dead already – go for its number two larder instead, on the other side of the square.

Respectfully hanging beneath the Champion and the Challenger, the Lessers watched in a mess of electromagnetism.

Extrapolation was often the key to the Game, and the Champion, they knew, was a past master of it.

The Challenger was a present master of it.

They were not. That was one of the reasons they were Lessers.

Watching the Champion manoeuvre the frall, gathering its forces, they could sense that the climax was approaching. A number of them tried to determine how it would end – if they got it right maybe they could challenge in the next Game.

Against a new Champion?

The Challenger, apparently, was concentrating on the trand Henry.

Some of the lessers nodded knowingly to each other in ultra-violet, hoping that no-one would ask them to explain.

It wasn't *his* fault. He couldn't have been any more careful with the outcropping orgal's egg without the help of anything short of an armoured orgal egg carrier. And he had saved up for ages in order to get one – an egg, not a carrier. Edna was so happy when she had an egg, and making Edna happy was what Henry did. It made *him* happy.

On the bright side, he *did* know where the orgal, from which the egg had come, was kept.

Of course, these were not the bad old days when thievery was a way of life, but there *were* occasions, and it wasn't really stealing, just substitution . . .

If he could get to the orgal then maybe he could persuade it to provide him with a free replacement.

He wasn't quite sure how, but given that the egg came out of the bottom end of the bird, he reckoned you presumably got hold of the top end and squeezed downwards.

With this simple theory of orgal egg farming forming in his mind, Henry pushed open the door of his house, and stepped into the street.

The harg – that animal capable of scratching a Rottweiler from its ear with one lazy sweep of a hind leg – rose once more from yet another annoyingly uncomfortable position.

It yawned, displaying teeth that would make a great white shark clamp its mouth shut in embarrassment, and frowned. It wasn't a frown accomplished by any eyebrow movement – this animal's eyebrows were lost in the mass of black wire-wool which passed for fur – but one which used its eyes. Anyone looking into those eyes would see the frown very clearly and, if they had any sense whatsoever, very momentarily.

As Rain is to rain, the harg was in a Bad Mood.

It wandered off up its alleyway, heading, quite by chance, towards the centre of the city, and looking, quite deliberately, for something on which – or on whom, preferably – the waves of its anger could crash.

Creeping down the alley, it occurred to Wilverton that a street party here would require little black flags, and the odd gravestone dotted about ornamentally, while the band struck up a dirge.

It was dank; it was cold because the sun had not managed to penetrate its twists while the rain most definitely had, and all the buildings somehow seemed infinitely sorry for themselves. Wilverton didn't altogether blame them; it couldn't be easy going through life looking like the morning-after produce of the Jolly Rock-Eating Giant's heavy night out with the lads.

In front, Norim slowed to a careful saunter, then stopped altogether as the alley ended. Wilverton joined him and they peered into the centre of an enormous square where stood a most unusual building. On Earth Prime, in Wilverton's time, it would have looked almost ordinary, but in this city its straight walls were oddly out of place. It was four storeys high, and built in heavy stones with but a few paltry windows dotted here and there.

Wilverton knew it was the council chamber – it looked imposing, important, a place where Elders gathered, a place where you were supposed to feel smaller as you entered.

Between the two watchers and the facing wall of the chamber, one which had no apparent door, was a space of some hundred yards, the ground covered in rough cobbles.

But not covered in rough trands.

There was no-one in sight.

The ends of many alleyways similar to their own were plainly visible; innumerable low and dilapidated buildings were not possible to miss despite the way they hunched unsociably down into their shoulders like granite Greta Garbos; and joining everything together, the wet cobbles, which, following the RAIN, had, for the most part, just managed to come up for air.

But that was it. No trands.

Norim turned to Wilverton briefly. 'No,' he said.

'"No", what?'

'No, not "as in, where a lot of trands probably gather".'

Wilverton cast his mind back, and recalled asking the question. Or stating the fact. One which the trands, by their continuing absence, proved to be false. Wilverton looked at as much of the square as he could see one more time, then back at Norim and nodded briefly.

'Off you go, then.'

Norim walked boldly into the shabby light of the square and began to cross it, while Wilverton watched from the relative safety of the dark alley, and got the same feeling he sometimes did watching a film. Something was going to happen. There was absolutely no way

197

that Norim was going to get across the square without something happening.

Even though he was now half way there and apparently not being slowed at all by the weight of the albatross hanging round his neck.

Three-quarters of the way there and still the metaphoric waters of the Red Sea had not closed over him like one of God's sicker April Fool pranks.

All the way there, and he disappeared around the side of the council chamber with no challenge.

Which made it Wilverton's turn. He suddenly didn't need an imposing council chamber to feel even smaller and more vulnerable than he actually was.

He placed a foot in the square, and withdrew it quickly as though he had found the water too hot. Still, the place was not overrun with baddies, so he replaced the foot and left it there, even put his weight on it as he lifted the other one, which then proceeded boldly to overtake its partner.

Repeat.

Wilverton walked into the square like someone who was just learning how to do so.

He turned briefly to check that all was still clear.

It wasn't.

Emerging from one of the alleys to his left was a group of five trands, the smallest rubbing his head every now and then, until, along with his colleagues, he spotted Wilverton, and all movement stopped.

This acted as a spur, and Wilverton was about to make for the council chamber at double time when a high-pitched caterwauling pushed that direction down his order of preference with the promise of an active reception.

He turned to his right and saw a single trand walking slowly towards him, looking unhappy. Not that it was easy to tell, but Wilverton wasn't about to check on the creature's current disposition, especially when 'happy' might still involve breaking him up.

That left back the way he had come, and he turned, to be faced with the vision of a harg lolloping out of the alleyway from which he himself had just emerged. The animal looked bigger than the houses past which it had walked, and it was eyeing Wilverton as though he were a snack.

It was just possible that the creature would be put off its lunch by having a piece of excrement thrown in its face. It was also more than possible that a piece of excrement would very soon be readily available, as Wilverton's stomach passed comment on his predicament.

He kept the notion in reserve as he looked in the three directions which contained visible life, and in all three the life was approaching.

Hero was he?

The Challenger immediately, and suddenly, ceased any attempt at influence within the human's head. It accompanied the cessation with a purple flourish which might have been visible in the depths of the storm clouds above if Wilverton felt constrained to look up.

He didn't.

Hero, eh?

No.

Peter Carlton would be a hero, because he believed in them, needed them, needed to be one, the leader of the pack. Wilverton didn't care for heroes, didn't need them; they were just people, no different, no better. Except in books, where reality was suspended.

But that was different.

Because in a brief moment of total clarity, during which most of his life tried to flash before his eyes, but was so boring that it sort of meandered past like a procession of geriatrics on a fell walking trip, Wilverton suddenly knew that this was real life.

Very real life.

Soon to be followed by very real death . . .

XXIII

'Fonk.'

There was no-one there, just a snow leopard lying in the fading sunlight, and a tear-stained hyena leaning exhausted against a tree trunk. Presumably up in the branches was an owl, but Fission didn't give a hoot. Arnold was long gone; so, too, the other candidates and Tamon. Another dead end, and she felt her frustration growing again.

What were they to do now? She had no idea. Carlton had, for the moment, given up on trying to be the leader instead of her – which didn't cheer her up because the competition was good if it meant they came up with an idea – because he was distracted by something, or some*one*, she thought, knowing that he was searching the area for Dano rather than Arnold.

There was just a studio – a large mound in the ground and a lot more underneath, presumably – and one current selection from the holovision choice hanging in the air above it; an advert for some hotel on Titan offering spectacular views of Saturn, which Fission frowned at because, one, Titan was usually surrounded in red mist and you could see fonk all, and, two, it gave her something to frown at.

Carlton frowned at the lack of Dano, and frowned at the frown, wondering what it was doing there, and thought about lions and lionesses, and birds preening their feathers in trees, and about his old girlfriends, whose names he couldn't remember, and about sponsoring kids in Africa and keeping quiet about it and, on the whole, wondering how his life had suddenly got itself into such a self-analytical mess, when it used to be so easy, if nameless.

'So what are we going to do?' he asked, and his voice made Tamon's depressed tones sound like the clown at the start of a children's party.

'We *got* find Arnold, somehow,' said Fission. 'We got stop him.'

'Brilliant plan.' Carlton laid the sarcasm on with a trowel the size of Tasmania. 'Let's just do that, then, shall we?' He knew he was just striking at someone else to ease his own discomfort, but he didn't care. In this case, though, it *was* a bit like stubbing your toe and reacting by punching a tiger up the throat.

'I thought I'd give chance for one of you to do something positive instead of doing all myself.' Fission wasn't going to fall behind Carlton in this peculiarly human race. 'All you think about is your worm, and bet super pov hasn't even got one of those to worry about.'

Gloria was already doing the prim bit again, but Fission pointed.

'And if you say anything *sensible*' – it was a term of abuse – 'about how we supposed to be working together I tie your tongue in knot! Sav?'

Apparently Gloria did sav, although her expression warned Fission that at some point when they had all calmed down she was going to say something Very Sensible Indeed.

To be on the safe side, Curtis moved his hands protectively to the area where he thought his worm probably was, but Carlton squared up to her.

'You know, I thought Bill Bowen was an obnoxious old fart, but next to you he looks like Father Christmas on happy weeds. Your family really must have put in some work on the objectionable front in the last four hundred years. And it's certainly paid off.'

'Yes,' Curtis joined in, now looking inexplicably excited, and standing slightly behind Carlton, from where it was a lot easier to be fearless. 'If there are genes for being odious then I think your family stocks all the denim.'

Yes Richard! he thought. Excellent! The first time ever that the witty comment has come to mind during the same week as the argument.

There was a brief pause.

'All the *what*?' Fission was giving him the foreign language look.

'Denim.' Pause. He started to feel just a touch embarrassed. 'It was a sort of material. You made jeans out of it.' You shouldn't have to explain brilliant insults. It ruined them.

'Genes?'

'Yes.'

'Biological building blocks.'

'Er. No. Er. Trousers.' It wasn't really witty any more.

She looked at him as though he were as unfathomable as a peat bog. 'Why don't you go crawl under something while we find Arnold?'

'We only argue when we're on our own,' Gloria pointed out, dangerously sensible. 'When there's someone else around, or when we're in trouble, we act like we're a team.'

There wasn't a question in it, but Carlton answered it just the same, because it hit a nerve currently more raw than fresh lion steak.

'It's tribal. We're like those groups of monkeys at the hangar – we argue amongst ourselves until we're faced with a threat, and then we pull together. We're just primitive.' Pause. 'And it's the same one on one.' He stopped.

'What do you mean?'

The way we need to dominate – the way I need to dominate every relationship I'm in, just like a lion with his lioness. It isn't really wintered and sexy or anything like that; it's a primal animal throwback. And these days it's something revolting, and no woman is going to fancy anyone who . . .

'Nothing,' he said.

They didn't comment and Carlton threw some more words into the deep well of silence. 'God, I wish I'd never come on this stupid bloody trip.'

They waited until his words splashed in the water at the bottom, where the ripples disturbed Curtis, as if he wasn't disturbed enough as it was.

'It wasn't stupid when we started,' he said, moodily. 'It was a wonderful expedition when we started.' And he had been Captain then.

'It was stupid by the time we arrived, though, wasn't it!'

Curtis considered. They had set out in the space race to another star with a good lead over the rest of humanity and had trailed in last, by about two hundred years. 'Triumph' wasn't the first word that sprang to mind; in fact it came somewhere between 'débâcle' and 'disaster', and then only for a spot of light relief.

'A bit, yes.' He crawled back inside his shell and peeked out into the daylight.

Carlton looked at the floor, his anger spent.

Fission's frustration wasn't exactly spent – in its entirety it did make Brewster and his millions look like a poorhouse candidate – but it was at least under control.

'Well, I don't think they're as clever or civilised or anything as they say they are,' said Gloria. 'If they were, then they wouldn't keep saying it, and they wouldn't get so upset if anyone says they're not.'

'Hmph,' was Carlton's noncommittal response. Only later did it occur to him that Gloria's good sense no longer surprised him.

'Doesn't help find Arnold,' Fission said, quietly. She recognised the emotion of the moment, but wanted them back on track.

Then Curtis risked it.

'The election's tomorrow, isn't it?'

Fission nodded shortly.

'Well, we know where Arnold's going to be then, don't we? He'll be at the place where they announce the result.'

This time Gloria nodded. 'Yes. I think we should get some sleep and then go there.'

Fission and Carlton glanced at each other, but the decision had already been made.

A decision they were about to put into effect when Miron appeared, above the studio roof, and reached for the trinket around his neck in yet another repeat of his broadcast. They turned away, uninterested.

'This,' said Miron, holding the spaceship Pioneer between finger and thumb, 'is the space ship Pioneer.'

Three of them stopped at the words, and Fission stopped in response, recognising the name only on recollection. They all turned to stare at Miron's hologram, chins aweigh.

'It took the prophet Richard Curtis from a planet which had forgotten the right way to live. And this,' Miron fingered the chimpanzee, 'is the sign he sent back to us, a guide to those too far down the road to ruin to see for themselves, telling us to mend our ways by adopting the simpler way of life of our ancestors.'

'It's Tonto,' said Gloria, recognising the Pioneer's test pilot. There were few quicker where furry animals were involved. Her face lit up with the knowledge that he had got back safely, after Curtis had inadvertently relaunched its original homecoming. And, further cause for celebration . . . 'It hasn't got a needle up its bottom after all!'

'One day Richard Curtis will return to us' – Miron ignored the irreverent comment – 'and will lead us on the path of righteousness to a future where all may be at peace with Gaia. But not yet. Richard Curtis would not sully his feet in the dirt we have strewn across the face of our world, but will keep his countenance from us until we have once more exposed the true earth to sunlight. I may speak metaphorically' – he may speak bollocks, thought Carlton, coming to terms with what he was hearing – 'but do not make the mistake of thinking that you can ignore my words. It is up to all of us to change the world into a place fit for his second coming. We must prepare for that great day.' He spread his arms in supplication to the watching dozens.

Having held the pose for a few moments, Miron disappeared from the holovision.

Silence did precisely what was gravitationally expected of it.

Danlor had taken his pulse on a hundred different occasions since the grey curtain of the TMT had removed the life-threatening alien from his presence. While his wrist would warn him of anything which might have left him in less than good health, Danlor was in no mood to banish paranoia.

He was having the TMT disabled from automatic transmission of incoming traffic – if the alien went that way, he could come that way. He had already replaced the door.

Well, *he* hadn't; he had slumped in his chair as though he had just lost his virginity to a female rugby league team, and told a robot to do it for him.

As he contemplated the one-way TMT with some satisfaction, so the brand-new door was opened for the very first time in its life. And for the very last time in its life as well, as the trand demonstrated that its earlier effort had been par for the course and not some demolitionary birdie.

Danlor could have observed his heart beat by finding a mirror and opening his mouth.

Every instinct told him to take flight, even though that meant either a mad attack against an underground wall or a kamikaze dash past the alien, but he stayed in the headlights, swallowed, and said:

'Hello, again, Sir! I recognise that, er, face!' with a commendable welcoming expression providing a flimsy covering for his naked fear.

Why hadn't Central done something clever? Like killed it? That was what they had Central for. To protect them.

The trand moved forwards, holding all six arms wide, trying to project as reassuring a manner as it could muster. Recognising what he saw as a human gesture, Danlor had the sort of feeling you might get in the split second when you see the juggernaut bearing down on you before the squelch, and you notice it's got a big red plastic nose on the front; it might just take the edge off things for the clear-minded esoteric, but you'll still end up as a smudge on the tarmac.

Then the trand stopped and held out a book. A book on which it had not, apparently, practised its conspicuous dislike for all things literary, since it was still in one piece. It wasn't the one piece originally intended by the robots that made it, admittedly, but none of it had actually fallen off yet, despite the mashing it had received from the trand's none-too-dainty carriage.

Danlor leaned forwards slightly, trying to get his eyes closer to the page in front of him while keeping the rest of his anatomy four miles away, and saw the start of a chapter on Achie's 'Logic and the Three-Lawed Robot', which of course was the one book absolutely *everyone* had heard of.

Which didn't help a lot.

'Right, Sir. Er. Yes.' What did it want? A literary discussion? A robot?

It wanted a disruptor beam up its jacksie, he thought; *that's* what it wanted!

The trand stabbed a finger at the page and succeeded in pushing it out the front cover. It held up the finger, with the book swivelling rather tiredly on the end of it, and then delicately removed it and showed it to Danor again. Achie's 'Logic and the Finger-Shaped Hole'.

'Do you want to read a copy?' He thought of the trand sitting by the window with pipe and slippers. It was a short thought. The trand stabbed at the page again.

'You want to find the original?'

The trand made a very pleased and encouraging sound.

All things being relative.

Danlor took this as an indubitable 'yes', even though it was very dubitable indeed.

'Well, it's at Admin, Sir. Big glass cabinet right in the middle of the Grand Hall. You can't miss it, especially with the big game on. Oh, and the election.' If the shop was anything to go by, the creature certainly hadn't missed anything else.

The trand dropped the book before turning on his heel like an oak tree stubbing out a cigarette and heading for the door.

He proved that he did miss things by missing the hole where the door used to be, and regaining the open air by means of an unexpectedly liberated section of wall.

The book lay on the floor and, after a moment or two, Danlor joined it, collapsing gracefully. He glanced at it, at a page showing an ancient soldier flat on his stomach, legs separated, sighting along a large stick – no, a gun of some sort – at something or other. Probably an alien, thought Danlor.

Yes. An alien. What a good idea. You can save mankind.

He had an old disruptor somewhere, didn't he? He could repulse the invading alien. That would at least even things up. Danlor looked to the hole in the wall, and smiled.

Outside, a robot stood forlornly. The dish it had carried so carefully from its laboratory lay smashed on the ground in front of it, and the contents – a rich jelly completely smothered in interestingly coloured bacterial growths – oozed between the bits. The way the trand had simply knocked the thing from the robot's outstretched hand without even a second glance had proved, quite conclusively, that the interpretation of Central's latest idea was no nearer the truth than all the others.

What the alien apparently did *not* want was some culture.

The Challenger kept its thoughts tight. If the Danlor human expected to find an old disruptor with any charge left, then he was going to be disappointed – except that he wouldn't check. The Champion had wasted its time.

XXIV

Tweet, not incredibly, was a bird.

One in three birds is called Tweet – that's why they all talk at the same time.

This particular Tweet had been up all night, sitting on a branch of a tree in a nice residential district, watching the occasional red-eyed owl swooping after the occasional red-eyed mouse, and struggling to keep his eyes open as the gathering twilight became the conference of darkness.

Tweet sat and watched the stars appearing, and didn't for a moment wonder what they were, nor did he go raving mad. And not just because he was unaware that one of these was what you were supposed to do when you saw stars for the first time. Tweet was watching for a purpose; and he was concentrating.

Every morning there was a first, and on every morning of Tweet's life so far, it had been someone else, and he had woken with a feeling of envy and unfulfilled ambition.

Until this day, when it was all going to be different.

This day Tweet's would be the first voice in the dawn chorus. His would be the signal to the whole bird population to greet the new morn. He would be the first bird that all the others would follow; *he* would be Tweet Dawnbreaker.

He watched as an almost-imagined lightening of the eastern sky banished the dimmest of stars just above the horizon.

He looked along the branch at his fellows, all far away in the arms of Morpheus, swaying on their twigs but never toppling off, the faint sound of bird snore drifting to him through the leaves.

He cleared his throat. Very quietly, so as not to risk anyone waking too soon.

This was going to be *good*.

This would knock them off their branches.

This would have their eyelids shooting up quicker than a robin's todger.[1]

One last look around; one last gentle cough to ensure that the first voice of the morning was not a dawn croak; one last check of the eastern horizon trying to convince himself that he could argue the toss with anyone who might suggest he had jumped the sun; open the beak, and . . .

And the tree was swept from under his feet by a rampaging eight limbed alien 'hurtling' along the street in search of Admin.

The quiet residential district was stirred from slumber not by the dawn chorus, but by the dawn crash of falling timber, and a faint, cheated, outraged, vengeful dawn squawk.

It didn't wake Carlton up.

Fission woke Carlton up, by means of a dawn scream which, if it didn't come from the top of her not-inconsiderable voice, was certainly in a position to make a push for the summit.

His door opened so impressively that there must surely have been a complete scrum of trands behind it, but it revealed only one Fission, albeit one who appeared more angry than usual.

She glanced quickly at Carlton's face, glanced even quicker at the admittedly attractive dark brown body on show, and told him to 'Move it! Super-povvo's screwed up again.'

They had found a new hotel, and Carlton had been informed by the lobby robot that his wealth now made a church mouse look like a bloated capitalist, to which information he took slight exception, before it occurred to him that Arnold could suddenly afford to run for President, and he put two and two together and came up with several million for Arnold and nothing for himself.

'Super-povvo', which Carlton recognised as, if anything, a rather flattering description of Curtis, was supposed to keep a lookout for the last few hours of darkness before rousing them at six so that they could move before Tamon found them, and so they could get to the election results first – to a place, according to the grab, called Admin.

Apparently, Curtis had failed.

Carlton wasn't a bit surprised.

He rose, quickly put on his jump-suit and re-entered the main living room. Gloria was standing quietly, her red eyes a testimony to the dream about Wilverton from which she had had a sad awakening. Curtis was looking red-faced with anger and embarrassment.

[1] No idea. Ask a robin.

'It wasn't my fault!' he tried, but wasn't in with much hope since his two-and-a-half-hour vigil had fallen short by two hours and twenty-seven minutes.

If they'd asked him to take the first watch then he would have been fine, because he was wide awake.

The prophet Richard Curtis. The man the whole of the Foundation Foundation followed. The leader. No, the Leader.

The others hadn't the energy to talk about it, apparently, and they must have been tired because as soon as they had gone to bed he could hear them snoring in what sounded a very happy sort of way, as he lay staring through the ceiling to the stars beyond.

Then, by the time his watch had come, he had only just gone to sleep. So it *wasn't* his fault.

Fission stopped fastening one of her boots to look daggers at him; more like ruddy great broadswords, in fact.

'Whose fault, then? Your idea of guarding is snore loudly enough to scare people away?'

'No, but . . . ' Curtis searched desperately for a good reason, then a half decent excuse, then anything at all that might deflect the blame. 'I wasn't woken properly by the lookout before me.' His justification floated through the atmosphere like a butterfly, and with much the same sting. Fission finished fastening her boot and shrivelled the insect's wings with a glance.

'So *my* fault, was it?'

It invited more bold bravery – the sort displayed by the six hundred as they rode into the valley – and Fission's tongue waited to administer the same end result. Curtis looked at her, sullenly. 'No. Not really.'

Arguments with Fission were like that – you lose some, you lose some.

'Are we going to get a move on, or what?' Gloria stood near to the door, waiting, and listening for anything coming. She could hear a faint murmur from outside, but it was only a waiter robot calling at each room in turn, offering breakfast.

Fission straightened up, whipped Curtis's self-esteem one more time with her eyes as it lay there, small and helpless, crossed the room in a single bound, and pulled the door open.

'Breakfa—?' began the robot, but stopped short as Fission elbowed it in the stomach, just in case, before running down the corridor to the lift. The others followed, while the robot took their assault and flight to be a probable negative in response to the

209

breakfast interrogative, and hurried to the next door.

The foyer was all but empty – one robot stood behind the desk and another attended the doors. In the corner of the ceiling Miron was talking to anyone who would listen, which didn't currently include the team – although Curtis cast a glance at his disciple – as they hurried towards the exit, where the robot protected the door by opening it for them.

'Have a nice day, madam.'

'Fonk off!'

'Thank you, madam. Have a nice day, sir, madam.' Carlton trotted past, just in front of Gloria.

'Thank you for staying, sir, have a nice day.' Curtis, buoyed very slightly by someone – all right, something – being nice to him, caught up with the others, standing in the shadow of a tree, and looking around for anything conspicuously official and hostile.

'Are we going to go to the Foundation Foundation?' he asked, stamping his new-found authority on the group.

'No. We're going to Admin.'

'The Foundation will be there, though.' Gloria softened Carlton's rebuttal and received a look as a result. 'Well, we could try to persuade them that Richard was their prophet,' she defended. 'Their, you know . . . their *orifice*. Like the Greeks had' – she searched her memory – 'at the Adelphi, or something. If they thought Richard was an orifice, then they'd help us.'

'Well, everyone else who's met him has thought he was an orifice,' Carlton told her, 'but I think you mean oracle.'

'Isn't that a sort of boat?'

'That's a *cor*acle,' said Curtis, who used to win every game of Trivial Pursuit that he persuaded the neighbour's children to play before their bedtime.

'I thought that was what your hair grows in.'

Carlton sighed gently. '*Foll*icle.'

'Now you're just being rude again.'

Carlton pondered. 'Well, you're probably floating round phallical or bollickle, but either way I wasn't being rude.'

'Luc!' comented Fission.

Gloria shrank a bit. 'Why am I so stupid?'

'Just lucky, melons; everyone's good at something. You want spend rest of life here or are we going?'

'Why shouldn't we?' Curtis stood his ground, and reversed the conversation. Carlton sighed.

'Because Miron is the leader of the Foundation Foundation, and even though he says that he is waiting for the great prophet, he doesn't mean it. If you turn up and ask him to step aside, what do you think he'll do?'

He'll step aside. He'll ask me to take over. He'll say that I'm the leader. He'll ignore me completely. He'll say I'm an imposter and nail me to a cross. He'll make fun of me in front of everyone. I'll crawl back down the beach and into the sea.

'See?' Carlton had watched Curtis's thoughts charge across the outside of his face.

Gloria frowned. There *was* something, but she couldn't get hold of it. 'This Admin is where Central is, isn't it?' Carlton nodded. 'I think whatever's going to happen is going to happen there. And today.'

It was intuitive, maybe, but it sounded right, especially when, as each of them considered the thought, it grew to a conviction in a moment. Fission nodded shortly.

'Let's go.'

They ran to the grab, the great prophet Richard Curtis struggling to keep up.

XXV

The stage at the end of the Grand Hall, right at the centre of the
Admin complex, was a stunning architectural feat, and completed so
many years before that the builders must have used human workers.
Many historians had speculated on how the stone could have been
transported and shaped when all that was available then were the
most primitive disruptors, and antigravitons were still proving
playfully elusive. Some concluded that extraterrestrials must have
helped; a theory which made Dani Von Eriksson a wollar billionaire
after he penned the best-selling 'Chisels of the Gods'.

Most didn't really give a toss.

They all agreed that it was impressive.

Carved columns stretched to the high ceiling and, from the days
when real animals walked the world, crocodiles peeked from behind
them, standing on their hind legs. Between the pillars, and carved
into bas-relief on the walls, were elephants and hippopotami, the
latter in the most delicate filigree tutus. From the wings, ostriches
craned their necks and perched on the tips of their ballet shoes.

However it had been accomplished, with such history depicted it
was indeed a most fitting place for the inauguration of the next
President of the World.

The pièce-de-résistance, at the back of the stage, was a stunning
castle, the blue points of its pink towers rising to the heights. Its
drawbridge was lowered, and nestled on this was a computer console
and, over the drawbridge, courtesy of the computer input; Central.

On the stage stood the lone figure of Miron, his bald head and long
white robe contrasting sharply with the elaborate decoration of his
surroundings. He looked at the console and a frown spread over his
face. He spoke, to himself, since he was alone on the stage and,
apparently, alone in the Grand Hall.

'President Arnold! It must not happen. It cannot happen.'

Arnold smiled. Broadly.

'President Arnold'. It had a nice ring to it. And when it came to pass, they wouldn't be able to touch him.

He glanced up in the darkness from where he sat beneath the stage to the chinks of light that came down to him and the slight variations which gave away the movements of the person above.

He would be elected, and then he would rise from beneath the stage, making a grand entrance and claiming his rightful place as Emperor of the whole bunch of bastards.

Well, President then. Emperor would come later . . .

He stood up carefully and put his eye to a crack. Above him, Miron shuffled slightly so that he stood directly above his rival, and Arnold looked up to see where the light shone dimly through Miron's robe; dimly, but distinctly enough to show a strawberry shaped birthmark on the Foundation Foundation leader's buttock. Miron shuffled again, moving slightly backwards, and the clinching proof of his identity dangled above Arnold's head like the Big Ben bell rope.

Slowly Arnold subsided to a seated position once more, and nodded slowly to himself.

No wonder he had felt heavy.

And no wonder Chanta had tears in her eyes.

'Of course you can come in, so long as you have a ticket. There's absolutely no entry without a ticket.'

A woman whose name badge announced her as Neara pointed a smile at Carlton, Fission, Gloria and Curtis in turn, in the same way you might point a gun. She was not one to let someone enter Admin while remaining ticketless. It would be like going into the most holy temple of Rishvaner the Many Toed; Each of Them Rather Lovely, in a pair of wellies.

'It's your territory, is it?' Carlton asked with what sounded like irony.

'Sorry?'

'How much are the tickets?' It wasn't the time.

'How much?' repeated Neara, clearly having trouble with this one.

'Are the tickets,' finished Carlton. 'The cost.'

'Oh, they're free. It's just one of the traditions we like to maintain here.' Neara smiled her understanding of the question as she handed the tickets to each of the four in turn, and was lucky not to have her fingers burned as Fission snatched the piece of what looked like paper but wasn't.

213

Around her, others were doing the same, only with slightly more decorum. Bald characters in long white robes and sandals, tress-haired people whose clothing reminded Fission of the Christmas trees she used to decorate as a child, and people wearing Arnold-for-President tee-shirts, caps and buttons. The Christmas trees looked less than confident; one or two had decided to make the best of the inevitable and were sporting holographic designs which swirled the word 'nobgush' to anyone who looked closely.

Outside, the blue or red of the two football teams had been much in evidence, but was less so here as the supporters made their way to the huge stadium adjoining the Admin building.

Looking at the signs which hung above the corridor, Fission saw one pointing to an internal stadium entrance, and another leading the way to the Grand Hall. She followed the latter, the thrill of the chase buzzing in her veins.

'Come on!' she threw over her shoulder. 'Let's find reneg . . . Arnold.'

'Come on,' Carlton said, rather more quietly. 'Let's find Arnold first.'

'He's what!' The look on Miron's face could hardly have been more shocked if someone had told him – scurrilously – that the great Richard Curtis was, in fact, an ineffectual prat.

'A robot. And I believe he has intentions that threaten Central.' Tamon spoke quietly, intensely, eyes darting around like caged humming birds. 'You don't know where he is, then?'

'No. But I assure you we will help you to find him.'

'Good man.' Tamon patted his shoulder.

Wrong, thought Miron. On both counts.

Tamon hurried away, heading from Miron's private room back towards the Grand Hall, wondering briefly why Pomona hadn't shown up yet – not that he was going to risk asking her a favour when she did.

He saw Fission walking slowly towards him, a vague expression and a slight smile on her face, and his eyes narrowed suspiciously. He couldn't get out of the way in this corridor. What should he do?

Should he shoot her? He wasn't sure she was a threat to Central, but surely it was best to take no chances.

No, he couldn't. Not without Central's permission.

But Central didn't know the danger it was in.

214

Too late. She had glanced at him and smiled nervously, shyly, in response to his stare, had walked past, and was gone.

He hurried on, frowning in puzzlement, walked down a short corridor to the Grand Hall, and Fission was coming towards him again, looking more purposeful. The impossibility of it froze his gun-hand this time, and she was on him.

'Found him yet?'

'Who?'

'Arnold.'

The gun came up. 'What if I have?'

'So you haven't.' Fission gave the gun a look of such contempt as to droop its barrel, had it possessed one.[1] 'Look, I on your side. I think Arnold renegade. Got to stop him to win Game. Can't let him win election.'

There was conviction in her voice, Tamon thought, not knowing that Fission could yawn with conviction. Should I believe her . . .?

Believe her.

The Challenger smiled in microwaves. The Champion shrugged in yellow.

'All right.' He believed her.

'Is this man causing you trouble?' Carlton asked Fission, arriving on the scene and leaping off the white charger he didn't have and couldn't ride anyway.

'Opposite,' Fission told him.

'*You're* causing *him* trouble?' It sounded more likely, come to think of it, but Fission smiled thinly.

'Let's get you a gun,' Tamon told her, and they left without another word.

Carlton and Gloria – Curtis was lagging behind for some reason they neither knew nor particularly cared about right then – looked on with a new worry. Arming Fission, thought Carlton, was like taking the first Napoleon in line from the institution and installing him as Emperor of France.

'Bother.'

Quietly put. Muttered under a breath that hadn't been taken in the

---

[1] 'Is that an oblong in your pocket or are you just grossly misshapen?'

first place because Arnold didn't breathe.

But sincere.

He did not want to emerge from his hiding place until after the election result. But 'after the election result' might just be too late to prevent Miron doing whatever he wanted to do. And if he did it, then Arnold might get zonked along with the humans.

It was a chance he couldn't take.

He had to tell them.

Well, he had to tell Carlton, preferably; Fission at a severe pinch; but with the other two it would take too long to explain.

Why did he have to be saddled with humans? So much self-importance there wasn't room for any intelligence.

Just have to make the most of it, he supposed, ever thankful for his objective androidity.

He'd tell them, then they could bugger off and do the necessary while he got himself elected king.

He nodded slightly, and uncurled himself from the lotus position which Biondor's mechanical expertise had made possible.

One room off the Grand Hall's perimeter corridor was a sea of white robes. It looked like an audition for a ghost story except that a bald head stuck out of the top of each one. On a chair, Miron raised his arms and called for quiet among his followers.

'We have to prevent a travesty of justice in this election, in this statement of mankind's superiority.

'One of the candidates, Arnold, is a robot.' He looked suitably stunned by this revelation, as though he were learning it himself for the first time from his own lips, as if a part of him had kept it secret because the knowledge was too shameful for such a pure mind to hold.

The Foundationers took a collective gasp and held it, their plaintive eyes offering their leader succour.

He noted the offertory.

Suckers.

'I tell you, my friends, in the days when Richard Curtis walked this planet, there would never have been thought of a robot standing for President.

'The search for Arnold is just another quest in our mission. Some time today, he must come here. For the sake of mankind, woman-kind, humanity . . . ' – which just about covered it – 'find that robot!'

The sea of robes flowed towards the door, pushing past Curtis, who had paused to watch what was going on in the hope that he would hear his name mentioned. All right, he admitted, in the hope that someone would point at him and cry, 'That's Richard Curtis' and sort of come and worship him a bit and stuff like that. Especially the women. Well, there was worship and worship . . .

But by the time he *had* heard his name, it wasn't important any more.

What should he do?

Er.

Find Peter, that's what!

He made his way to the Grand Hall, pleased to have made a decision.

To get there he made his way round the orbital corridor, then down one of a number of short passages which in turn led to the Hall itself. The whole thing was like a spoked wheel with the Grand Hall as the hub.

Inside, a crowd of people swirled around a huge glass cabinet in the centre, in which a single book rested on a purple cushion, minding its own business and looking important.

Carlton and Gloria stuck out in their blue jump-suits – Gloria stuck out a lot more than Carlton – and Curtis hurried across to report, pausing only a couple of times to apologise.

Carlton listened carefully, and nodded briefly.

'Robot!' he called into the hubbub, beckoning, and there was a servant by his side before the sound waves had dissipated. He gave some quick instructions to the machine, which then hurried off without word or acknowledgement.

'What did you say to him?' asked Gloria.

'One of us is going to have to dress up like a member of that Foundation thing and go with them. If they find Arnold, we've got to know about it before Miron or Tamon, and especially Fission.' At least the action took his mind off other things. All right, then, Dano.

'Who?' Gloria interrupted what might have become a downward flow of thought.

Their eyes were dragged towards Curtis. He looked relatively unconcerned. Pretending to be a Foundationer sounded like a pretty daring thing to do, and he liked being daring so long as it was perfectly safe.

'I don't mind. It's only putting on a white robe after all.' Two pairs of eyes raised themselves slightly to look at the top of his head, and his hand followed them, touching his unimpressive but semi-precious locks.

There was a drawback after all.

Typical.

'But I'm . . . ' he started in a very tiny voice, as the robot returned with a small bundle containing robe, sandals, trinket and scissors. It took Curtis gently by the elbow and led him away without a word, like a kindly nurse. Curtis looked over his shoulder at his crew members, wearing an expression that made the parting scene from ET look like an argument.

Gloria felt a pang of sorrow – when someone gave her flowers she always thought it was a pity that they had been picked – but it had to be done, and she stood her ground.

Which was more than did someone watching from near one of the exits. As Curtis was escorted through a side door, Chanta began weaving her way through the mass of occupied sheets, tee-shirts and Christmas trees, and followed him.

Arnold eased a section of stage out of place behind the centrepiece castle, and pulled himself out through the resulting hole with the brashness of an introverted octogenarian snail.

He looked around in the semi-darkness of backstage and saw no-one, but the eerie light was, in itself, slightly disconcerting. He swallowed almost nervously, and rather pointlesly.

Somewhere, he guessed, were the lunatic Tamon, probably that other woman who had been with him, and maybe some reinforcements, who could number hundreds by now.

Somewhere else, were the rest of his embarrassment of a 'team'.

All he had to do was to find the latter without finding any of the former. It was like finding the pin without disturbing any of the hay.

Chanta half crept and half hurried down a corridor leading off the Grand Hall.

She had a theory, and its resolution lay behind that door over there, through which she was convinced her Rudy had disappeared. A Rudy surgically altered in facial appearance, certainly, but so long as they hadn't touched *that* bit . . .

She approached the door, and listened for a few moments outside it, hearing nothing. Slowly she grasped the handle, not even thinking how quaint such a thing was, and pushed the door open.

There, in front of her very eyes, was a man's naked posterior, displaying on its right cheek a strawberry-shaped birthmark.

'Rudy!' she shrieked, and the posterior in front of her immediately reacted to the shock of it all.

No, not like that.

Its owner tightened the muscles by way of pulling himself upright and spun round to face her.

Curtis had just removed the last of his garments – socks with little bears on them – prior to replacing them with the white robe and sandals of the Foundation Foundation. He had given no thought to the remaining evidence of the piece of tree on which he had fallen, evidence now in the form of a red discoloration in exactly the shape of a strawberry and it didn't really occur to him now, as he stood in front of Chanta with his heart pumping wildly in his chest and his eyes wide with surprise.

Chanta was looking at neither heart nor eyes, though. Her gaze settled on that feature of Rudy which she held so dear, but not for several months.

'Oh,' she said, with the deep disappointment of soaring hopes dashed in an instant. 'No. You're not Rudy at all, are you.'

It was a simple statement of tragic fact.

Curtis held the robe in front of him protectively, forlornly, and pathetically, while his shoulders slumped a little more.

No, he wasn't Rudy at all.

And he never bloody had been.

If he could just work his way round and come to the Grand Hall from the side, then he could find somewhere to wait until Carlton showed up, because if Carlton showed up anywhere, it would be in the Grand Hall.

That was the plan. He knew it might be flattered by the description 'meticulous' – in fact it should blush at the description 'plan' – but at least it was ahead of 'I'm going to bury my head in this nice sand and sort of hope for the best'. Just.

So far he had seen no-one on his travels – all of twenty yards – but as a precaution he had furnished himself with a disguise by pencilling a moustache where Biondor had provided the proverbial baby's bottom. He looked like a defaced poster, but it might give him a fraction of a second to make a tactical withdrawal.

It really was the most incredible piece of luck, as far as he was concerned, when the first person he came across was one of the team. He had apparently found the needle without even touching the hay, as Fission walked around a corner at the far end of the corridor and stopped dead in her tracks.

He could tell Fission, and then go and win the election. Even though she didn't seem to like him very much, for some unfathomable reason, and he was more than happy to return the opposite of compliment; still, winning the game would be all important to her, because she was like that, and that would mean acting on what he said.

Except, she acted before he said anything, by raising something that looked suspiciously like a weapon of some sort, and pointing it at him, while her eyes took on an aspect of manic satisfaction. It wasn't *necessarily* a weapon – it wasn't in the shape of a Colt 45 or anything – but it wasn't in the shape of an olive branch either, and Arnold was happier to admit a mistake in person rather than through a medium.

He made his tactical withdrawal down a small off-shoot from the perimeter corridor at a speed that made greased lightning look like the sludge on a bird-filled beach, and was rewarded by a shriek of anger from Fission, and the sound of an impact between the far end of the corridor and something ballistic.

Tamon caught up with her just as she fired, and he looked the length of the corridor to see the head of a rabbit toppling from its sculpted shoulders. In front of it a small bald man stood with his sculpted rifle and looked indefinably pleased with himself as the head hit the ground, with, as it were, a dull Fudd.

'Fonkshit!' Fission shouted at the lack of dismembered Arnold. 'Went that way.' And she pointed to the corridor, then followed her finger, not realising that in these circumstances she should really have said 'thataway'. Tamon didn't comment, but chased after her, his own disruptor nestling in the palm of his hand.

Arnold shot down the corridor, caution thrown to Fission's storm. The time of prudent progress was over; if any of the hay got in the way right now, then it was going to get itself severely chaffed.

As he thought so, one stray member of the Foundation Foundation appeared round a corner, and found himself bounced against the corridor wall like a quarter-back who was not only being sacked but assured of never working in this town again.

Arnold didn't even slow down.

Round the next corner were two small doors, open and beckoning, and he accepted the invitation.

The Foundationer struggled to his feet and shook his head to rid it of the bits of wall which had tried to get inside, then swayed into the middle of the corridor as the shaking disturbed an uncertain balance.

Which sadly put him in the path of Fission's sickle-form elbows, one of which clouted the point of his chin, accompanied by the instruction to:

'Get out fonking way!'

He slid down the wall and lay still. A moment later, Tamon leapt over the inert jellies that doubled as his legs in less violent times and closed on Fission.

Fission darted round a corner and saw two small doors just closing. She skidded to a halt and raised her weapon. Tamon had seen fit to provide her with a needle gun rather than a disruptor – he didn't trust her enough not to want to have an advantage – and, as he came to a stop next to her, she emptied the gun's contents into the room in which Arnold was presumably sheltering.

'Got him!' Fission shouted with some glee, as Tamon arrived next to her. 'Sprayed whole room! Must have got him!'

He glanced at her, slightly worried at the intensity of her feeling.

'The room's not there any more,' he told her, and she snapped her head to look at him, demanding at least an immediate explanation, and preferably a retraction. 'It's an elevator.'

The head snapped back to the front.

'Fonk! Come *on!*' And she was off again, heading for the staircase that curved ornately upwards, grasping the glass slipper at the base of the banister as a way of propelling herself up the first three steps, then throwing it behind her as it came off in her hand.

Tamon ducked to avoid it as it whistled past his head like a flying stiletto, and followed.

They arrived at the next floor to be met by the sight of a TMT displaying the 'in-use' sign. They looked at the settings of the machine.

'Titan!' Fission sounded as though Titan was hardly a place any self-respecting fugitive would choose to visit; that when she caught up with it, it would wish it had never coalesced. 'What he going do on fonking Titan?'

It wasn't a question Tamon could answer – he only barely understood it – but then Fission didn't expect him to. It was just something to say until the in-use sign went out.

They entered the TMT, ordered a repeat of the last co-ordinates, and issued their tachyons across eight hundred million miles of space, where the advanced machinery managed to reform even Fission into the same complicated arrangement from which it had broken her down.

All was quiet, until a door near the TMT swung open, and Arnold stepped out behind an expression for which smug was a pathetically inadequate description.

It was hard to see how even winning the election could come anything but a distant second in comparison to outwitting Fission . . .

The noise in the amphitheatre stadium was steadily growing as football fans filled it. On the pitch, a herd of wildebeest trotted around, and pretended to eat the artificial grass, while Thompson gazelles pranced around the outside, leaping over enormous nothings, and half a dozen cheetah stalked them both.

'Not very authentic, is it?' said one cheetah to another.

'How do you mean?'

'Trying to keep out of sight in half an inch of green plastic.'

'The crowd have got to be able to see us.'

'That's what I mean.'

'Could be worse. With the big game to follow, the wildebeest aren't even allowed to crap.'

'I thought wildebeest *were* big game.'

'Different sort of game.'

The other nodded, looking round the herd. 'Which one do we choose?'

'You haven't done this before?'

'First time.'

'The smallest and weakest, usually. They are the easiest to catch.'

'Not much of a spectacle though, is it? Why don't we go for a big one? Have a decent scrap?'

'We are supposed to show nature in its true light, how unfair it could, at times, be. The prey usually did not stand a chance of survival, while the hunters reduced their personal danger as much as possible.'

'Shall I shoot it, then?' It held up a paw.

'Most animals did not have the ability to unhinge a limb containing a disruptor.[1] Besides, the small wildebeest twenty yards to our left is expecting a carefully choreographed attack in seventeen seconds. Nature isn't just some random occurrence.'

[1] Weapons were used, of course. Squid, skunk, etc. could be said to have the ability, but none more than the Turod of Faedria, a bulky rodent which ejected liquid faeces into the faces of its attackers, and could do so even when asleep in subconscious response to certain external stimuli. Hence its nickname, the 'browning semi-automatic'.

'Program three, then?'
'Correct. Ready?'

Carlton and Gloria wandered about the Grand Hall and its immediate environs – which meant sauntering a few yards down the odd passage and back again – with all the usefulness, in Carlton's opinion, of a belly button.

There was really nothing they could do except wait for someone to come up with something and hope that it was the right one and the right thing.

'That Dano likes you, you know,' Gloria said suddenly, and Carlton paused in his quest to win a Game of life or death on hearing something far more important. 'I know you've been worrying . . . '

'I have not.' She does? Really! But I'm a primitive offworlder. 'What makes you say that?'

'It's obvious. The way she looks at you.'

They were strolling past a corridor which was nothing more than a deep alcove when someone said, 'Psst!' from its end.

'Not now, Arnold,' hissed Carlton, before his brain made the link.

'Arnold!' said Gloria, in a tone which would cause many a man to react with weak-kneed hope, a smile lighting up her face. She *had* missed him, but, more, she admitted, finding him again was like an omen of the return of Thomas.

He had a smudge along his upper lip acting as a disguise in much the same way as would Quasimodo's skull cap, and he beckoned them to approach the shadows where he stood.

'Sshh!' he told her, ignoring the welcome of her tone completely. He hadn't missed her at all. 'Listen, I've got something to tell you.' They edged closer, like you're supposed to when someone's got something to tell you in a shadowy corner.

'Just stay right there and don't move.'

As an instruction it was bound to have the desired effect if only for the moment of shocked silence. Once the moment had passed, though, Arnold looked, with the other two, at the figure of Dano standing in the only exit to their dead end, holding a disruptor quite calmly, and pointing it straight at him. It said 'Don't move' just as fluently as Dano had.

'Dano!' Carlton had never experienced quite so many emotions at one time, and Gloria even looked at him with concern as he passed through disappointment, pleasure, confidence, uncertainty and hope in a second.

'I've got a magistrate standing by to determine the matter of ownership. After that we can decide whether we need to follow up this renegade question.' She wasn't going to say any more and risk giving away that she might know what Arnold's plan was. If it *was* Arnold.

'But it's not Arnold!' Gloria insisted. Why couldn't this woman see the obvious?

'How do you know?' Dano asked. 'Where's your evidence?'

'I haven't got any evidence. It just isn't.' Gloria recognised that a court of law might not find such an argument totally convincing. Which was a pity since they might be about to ask one to do just that.

'I know who it is,' Arnold commented quietly. 'That's what I've come to tell you.'

'Who?' asked Gloria and Dano together.

'I'm not telling you.'

'That's what you've come to tell us and you're not telling us?' Carlton was drawn out of his silent contemplation by Arnold's surrealism, and they all stared at him.

'We'll see about this ownership stuff first.' Arnold shrugged. 'You should recognise it; it's an animal thing called self-preservation.'

XXVI

The least of evils, you would think, is the one you can't see, if compared with three which you most certainly can, all promising a speedy resolution to the question of whether the after-life is just something made up by people who want you to have a really boring time of it while you're alive.

If, however, you are as widely read as Thomas Wilverton, then your imagination can come up with so many things which might be the cause of an agonised shriek that the imagined evil outstrips the boring visible ones like the hare outstripped the tortoise before its nap.

Wilverton was precisely as widely read as Thomas Wilverton, and the noise which was coming from around the corner of the council chamber brought to mind more fitting fictions than he cared to count, and none of them from the comedy shelf. Something, that way, was surely being dismembered, and he hoped briefly that it wasn't Norim – whatever he was. Wilverton wouldn't wish the fate described so lucidly by that noise, and his imagination, on anyone.

Except maybe the group of five trands who were walking slowly but very surely towards him from the left, and possibly the single trand who was also walking towards him from the right. And just possibly the award-winning set of teeth, with a house-sized animal behind it, that was approaching from the rear.

Apart from those, he wouldn't wish the fate on anyone.

The group approached in formation like something from the troll version of West Side Story, but suddenly they all stopped short and stared at the ground between Wilverton's feet.

As far as the frall was concerned, Wilverton stood in its path, and it wasn't about to make a detour. Trands made detours, especially very small ones like this; fralls didn't. Fralls wandered whither they would.

Wilverton hadn't noticed the animal at his feet, but he did notice the look of horror on the trands' faces. At least, he assumed it was horror; their normal expression looked like it had emerged from a graveyard after a long spell in residence.

The frall continued its walk across the square, and Wilverton spotted it, just before spotting the trands starting towards him once more. Two and two, he thought, and he started to follow the animal, noting the confirmation of his arithmetic as the trands maintained a respectful distance.

The harg had respect for nothing, and apparently least of all for distance. It closed on the pair in front of it.

Wilverton glanced over his shoulder and mentally urged the frall to greater effort.

The frall ignored him.

'Hurry,' he hissed. 'One of us could really get killed.'

The frall knew which one.

The leading trand of the group bent down to prise loose a cobblestone. A moment later, it whistled so closely past Wilverton's head that it could have whispered in his ear if it had had anything interesting to say. It probably had other things to worry about; like landing.

All five of the trands had got the idea by now – they weren't slow on the uptake where damaging things was concerned, Wilverton noticed – and they all liberated cobbles, then aimed them at him.

The harg broke into a hungry trot about twenty yards behind him. Wilverton didn't notice that, having quite sufficient to occupy him in other directions, thank you very much.

The frall sauntered.

From the front came the high-pitched shriek once more, this time accompanied by a visible manifestation. A bird, roughly the size of a large chicken, came steaming around the corner of the council chamber and hurtled straight at Wilverton, its wings flapping frantically and apparently uselessly, its neck stretched out as though the head were trying to outpace the feet, its eyes clearly determined to arrive before *any* other part of the anatomy, and its legs going up and down faster than a buck rabbit's buttocks.

Wilverton didn't recognise an orgal in a hurry.

Eggs were the bane of the orgal's life. It was quite bad enough trying to produce one of the oval pile-drivers as nature had intended, but if this trand who had pulled up the corner of its cage and yanked it out thought that stretching its throat was going to act as some sort of inducement to lay, then he was sorely mistaken.

As soon as it had a chance to peck the hand which made it fed up and thereby gain its freedom, it was off, at pace. The orgal couldn't fly, maybe, but that certainly wasn't going to be for the want of trying.

Why did the orgal cross the square?

To get away from the bloody mad-trand who was doing his homicidal best to throttle it, that's why!

The frall paused as this demented chicken careered towards it, and so did Wilverton.

The harg didn't.

Nor did the rock-throwing trand band, and Wilverton's sudden stillness let them take rather more careful aim. And throw.

Then from round the same corner from which the orgal had appeared, Henry thundered after his quest, his progress making a herd of boisterous rhinos sound like a shy vicar's bridge party.

This took Wilverton's attention momentarily from the orgal.

The orgal, with all its attention already taken in making its legs move, tried to reach a decision concerning which side of Wilverton to pass before it reached him . . .

. . . And failed.

So it went straight through him instead.

This re-attracted his attention, since his feet were now a yard behind him in mid-air, and he dropped like a stone.

Five other stones screamed through the mid-air where his head had been a moment before, and smacked squarely into the wide space between the eyes of the harg, which was just on the point of making a teeth-first leap for its Wilvertonian titbit. It skidded to an unconscious halt.

The frall glanced over its shoulder at the commotion. Bunch of raving nutters, it thought, and changed direction to avoid the oncoming trand who had obviously not seen it.

Henry was still haring after the orgal when Wilverton started pulling himself groggily to his feet and shook his head to clear it. Then he noticed a trand approaching him like a runaway truck with arms, and that cleared his head in an instant.

A shout from his right hardly made any impact on his brain.

'Henry!'

It made an impact on Henry, who threw himself into emergency reverse and stopped with a sound much like the grinding of a gearbox.

'Edna!' he said, and took a step towards his wife, ignoring both the orgal and Wilverton, the latter of whom scrambled himself upright, while the former reached the sanctuary of an alleyway and disappeared.

Snapping his head to the left, Wilverton saw the frall sauntering in the general direction of five trandian backs that diminished with distance.

But they wouldn't for long. Nor would the harg stay unconscious for long, and when it woke up, it would most definitely be in a BAD MOOD.

Wilverton made for the council chamber.

The Champion radiated a visible blue, and moved it through the spectrum from green to yellow and orange as it relaxed after its efforts.

The Lessers radiated respect, a collective curl of visible purple stretching up towards the Champion, who ignored it. There was plenty to do yet.

The Challenger maintained a clamp on an ultraviolet pulse of frustration, but then forced itself back towards the longer frequencies, like its opponent. The Champion would not tire, certainly – the only way one of these beings would involuntarily diminish was when entropy left too little energy in the old Universe to sustain it; and since that was several hundred billion years in the future, playing for time was not really a feasible tactic in the Game – but if it had to concentrate so hard on protecting its Player, there would be less concentration left to expend on the situation on Earth Five Zero.

The Challenger was satisfied.

Wilverton wasn't.

He did not need a wildlife audience while he got the gun, particularly one whose sole aim was materially to affect his way of life by putting a stop to it.

He rounded a corner and found Norim standing about twenty yards ahead of him, looking unconcernedly up at a door which he had not put to its customary use.

The door to the trandian council chamber was designed with six moving parts, each held in place by a catch, which had to be pushed, and the pressure maintained in order to prevent it catching again. All parts had to be moved to let a trand enter, and the doorway was wide enough for just one trand at a time.

Any trand intent on entering the chamber with no good in mind would have to do so singly and with all arms occupied with opening the door. This would allow those already inside to change the visitor's mind by the age old trandian debating technique of a swift attack on the vulnerable bits, neatly exposed by six wide-spread arms. The whole contraption had been deemed necessary since, even after the invention of the Gun, the trandian system of government rotation still tended to rely quite heavily on what Earth's political historians might descriptively have christened the Stalin-was-just-an-old-softy method.

'We have to press these catches to get parts of the door to open,' Norim said, having completely failed to ask Wilverton what all the noise was about and whether he had encountered any trouble. He was a rum cove, thought Wilverton, which seemed to sum things up without actually getting him any further forward.

Enough time later to work Norim out. For now, Wilverton wanted to get further forward by about three yards.

Following Norim's instructions, he pressed two of the catches, while the teacher pressed two others, allowing sufficient of the door to be opened to allow access to the much smaller humanoids. Norim went first, holding the catches while Wilverton followed, sliding head first through the bottom portion of the door.

As the trand captain rounded the corner of the building he saw Wilverton's feet disappearing into the chamber. He pointed at the doorway.

'It inside is. We must it follow.'

And proceeded they to do so.

XXVII

Gloria had expected that a courtroom in the twenty-fifth century would consist of a quick phhht of truth serum and there you go, but apparently this bit of Earth Five Zero went for the old-fashioned courtroom drama, with but one or two changes.

It was an antiseptic affair with a couple of tables, a few chairs, and very little else.

'Computer. Dano requesting commencement time for hearing of Arnold claim case. Previous report refers.' She had already contacted Central, using her wrist even though she was probably within spitting distance of it, since communication by spit is notoriously imprecise.[1]

'Are all the necessary people gathered?' enquired a neutrally sexed voice from nowhere in particular.

'Who is claiming to be the owner?' asked Dano. Gloria looked at Carlton, who shrugged, so she answered.

'Richard, I think.'

Dano nodded shortly. 'Richard Curtis is not yet present.'

'Commencement time will follow his arrival,' the computer informed them. One section of wall shimmered and a picture appeared of soldiers on horseback, firing in the air and galloping across the plain. 'While you are waiting we will be showing a holo of the history of justice in the United States, beginning hundreds of years ago with the so-called American Indians, when the United States referred only to a geographical location in a part of one continent. These "Indians" committed the heinous crime of usurping the land long before the rightful owners had even arrived . . . '

'They've found him!'

'Glory be!'

---

[1] Except on Daneeb VII, where the inhabitants live in a constant atmosphere of insults and waterproofs.

'Thanks to Curtis!'

'Sorry? What?'

'I said, "Thanks to Curtis".'

'Don't mention it.'

'What?'

Most of them were back in the Foundation's private room, milling around like berobed headless chickens with heads. Curtis was still feeling like the first day at school when everyone else had already been there for a term, but then that was normal whenever he found himself in a crowd. He could do without the added confusion of someone thanking him for doing something about which he knew nothing, though – it was strange enough being thanked, full stop.

Miron's second-in-command – Rablin – stood before him and waited for the continuation of the conversation, slightly peeved that the reception of this wonderful news – that Arnold had been found and that Miron was free to conclude his pursuit of the World Presidency – should be disrupted by someone who gave the first impression of being a pillock.

'You're new, aren't you?' he asked, when Curtis failed to find anything coherent to say. Curtis nodded. Rablin looked him up and down, with a critical expression, which Curtis found familiarly reassuring. 'What's your name?'

'Er . . . ' Oh dear.

Rablin waited with commendable patience. 'What's your name?' had never in his experience been one of those questions that demanded contemplation for any great period of time. In fact, had he created a list of questions most easily answered, there was a good chance that 'What's your name?' would come fairly high up, right alongside, say, 'Is this your skunk?'

But he couldn't give his own name, Curtis thought, and then thought of several others he might use. 'Gloria' was the first one that occurred but was quickly replaced by 'Carlton' because 'Gloria' failed on sexual grounds. (Actually Gloria had never failed on sexual grounds, but Curtis was confused enough as it was without that added complicating thought.) 'Carlton' failed because Rablin might meet him, and after an intervening 'Er', he settled on his Uncle Frank.

'Glocarlerfrank?' repeated Rablin, with some scepticism.

'Yes,' said Curtis, wondering if he'd be able to remember his own name for any length of time.

'What kind of name's that?' There were some odd people in the Foundation, but . . .

It's one that I've just made up. No.

'Er.'

'Where are you from?'

'London?' Does London exist on this version of Earth?

It was another of those relatively easy questions, and usually got a very confident response. Perhaps Glocarlerfrank wasn't the most confident of people. Rablin shrugged inwardly. So long as he was a supporter of Miron.

'Right. Well, help me up on this chair. I've got to tell everybody the good news.'

He wasn't to know. When you wanted help doing something that involved even the most minuscule amount of personal risk, Richard Curtis was the person you asked only *after* Laurel and Hardy had turned you down.

It was a matter of moments before the two of them lay at the bottom of a heap of Foundationers whom Curtis had managed to drag down amid a flurry of limbs with as much co-ordination as Blind Pew's wardrobe.

By the time Rablin had made it onto the chair, he was sporting a much dirtied robe, several bruises, and a growing disbelief in this Glocarlerfrank character. He brushed himself down as best he could and raised his arms for silence, which he got, momentarily.

Before Rablin had uttered the first word of his good news, Carlton shouted from the doorway.

'Richard! Richard Curtis!'

Was this blasphemy? Or an expression of faith? Or what? wondered the Foundationers in dead silence. Rablin stood with arms and mouth open.

Then, into the well of silence, spake Glocarlerfrank.

'Er, I'm over here.'

'Well come over here, then, quick. We need you.'

Curtis recognised an order when he heard one, and eased his way, with several 'Excuse mes', through the crowd, each of whom stared at him with a certain uncertainty.

Just what was going on? Who was this man who called himself Richard Curtis? Should they get a couple of bits of wood just as a precaution?

Rablin let his arms drop, and stared after Curtis.

*

'Commencement will be in two minutes,' the computer informed them when Carlton had delivered Curtis to the courtroom.

'What have I got to do?' Curtis asked.

'Just confirm that Arnold is yours.'

'This is so embarrassing,' Arnold commented.

'I *made* you, remember. Well, bits of you, anyway.'

'And you still have no conception of how humiliating that is, do you?' Arnold's social graces had apparently not been perfected during his absence. Curtis spluttered a bit and went red under Dano's disbelieving glance.

'You'd better not treat the magistrate like this, Arnold,' warned Gloria, in a disapproving tone which pierced Arnold's hide like a ping pong ball would pierce a tank.

'I'll be sweetness and light,' Arnold assured her, with his choirboy smile. 'You know me.'

'Yes,' said Gloria, and it sounded like mummy's warning voice. 'I do!'

'The court is now in session,' the computer informed them, and the door at the far end of the room opened. Arnold prepared a smile of welcome and put it on his face.

'Magistrate Aglaea presiding.'

The smile shrivelled like an Eskimo skinny-dipper.

The woman who entered was dressed rather more thoroughly than when Arnold had last seen her – in fact she looked like a galleon in full sail; possibly a whole armada of the things – and she did not have Shether in tow, but there was no mistaking her.

'I believe,' said Arnold, very quietly, so that only Carlton heard, 'that the phrase is probably "Oh, fonk".'

'What's the matter?' Carlton hissed.

'We've met before.'

Carlton nodded. Where Arnold was concerned, that was quite enough explanation. That could put them, as his old mum quaintly used to put it, in deep shit.

Aglaea seated herself – and she didn't just sit down, she definitely seated herself – then looked up to see the subject of the hearing. Her head stopped moving, and the rest of her face also paused a moment or two later.

'You!'

It sounded a lot like 'Guilty!'

Arnold smiled, weakly, and as close to obsequiously as he could, which meant that he missed by a country mile.

Aglaea didn't smile at all. She opened a drawer in the table behind which she sat and removed her badge of office, the judicial cap, round and black and with two circular ears on the top. She set this on her head as though it were a diamond studded tiara.

'Computer,' she said, not taking her eyes off Arnold for a moment, 'what, exactly, is the charge?' Judging from her expression, the phrase tasted like the finest Swiss chocolate.

'There is no charge.' Her face dropped marginally, which still meant moving a couple of pounds of flesh.

'Pity. Never mind, we'll think of something.' This jumped-up little man would be cut down several pegs one way or another.

'Determination of ownership is the issue,' continued the computer.

'I *beg* your pardon?'

'Determination of ownership is the issue.'

Computers hadn't changed much in four hundred and fifty years, thought Carlton.

'What do you mean?'

'Agent Dano reports that Arnold is a robot and claim must be established.'

Aglaea looked at Arnold with a new hate in her eyes. A *robot* had usurped and abused her? Oh, no. Surely not!

'Analysis of Arnold.'

'Place your hand in the imprint,' instructed the computer, and the outline of a hand glowed softly on the table behind which Arnold sat. He looked at it for a moment as though he blamed it personally for all that was happening to him, then put his hand where the glowing fingers indicated.

There was a pause of maybe a second or so, then the computer reported. 'A robot. More advanced in technological make-up than any other encountered and with unusual positronic pathways, but definitely not human.'

Arnold swelled. The chest inched outwards despite there being no intake of air. He inspected a fingernail, and found it to be perfect.

'It wasn't meant as a compliment,' hissed Carlton, but the only difference between using his breath this way and trying to perform the kiss of life on Rameses II was that at least this way he didn't have to wipe bits off his lips afterwards.

'And who is claiming ownership?' Carlton pushed Curtis forwards from his customary position guarding the rear.

'Er, I am, your honour.'

'Your what?'

'Er, your hon . . . your wor . . mada . . Er. I am.'

'Computer, analysis.'

The imprint glowed again, and Curtis leaned forward and laid his hand on it, looking as though he was putting his head in a noose. He stared at his fingers, willing the voice not to say anything about pillock, or prat. And just how much could it tell through this analysis? Would it say something like . . . oh please, no . . . surely it wouldn't say virg . . .

'Human,' came a neutral voice, and Curtis breathed an audible sigh of relief. Aglaea stared at him for a moment, wondering how someone could have doubts about their own species, but the others didn't react at all, which might have told her a lot had she noticed.

She didn't. 'Do you claim the robot?' she asked Curtis.

'Yes.' There; no 'er'. He was asserting himself, he thought, not recognising that if you can assert yourself merely by not saying 'Er', then you are probably starting from too low a rung to have much hope of reaching the top.

'I don't want to be claimed by him,' said Arnold, suddenly looking worried and wringing his hands. 'Anything but that. Please don't give me to him.'

'What's that?'

'Please, I really don't want to be claimed. You can't do this to me!' Arnold looked anguished, a soul in torment.

'What is your concern at such an outcome,' Aglaea asked, her eyes shining just a little brighter at this obvious discomfort, and her lips barely falling short of a smile. She looked like she was getting ready to lob the irritating creature straight into the middle of the briar patch and watch him suffer.

'Well,' said Arnold, with a sidelong glance at his potential owner, and the anguished look was joined by something indefinably insulting. 'I mean, look at him.'

Aglaea did, and Curtis shrank a little, so that only the outer shell was visible. Aglaea's expression softened a touch – she could see what Arnold meant – but memory hardened it again.

'The alternative is disconnection.'

'I'm all his,' said Arnold.

'Which will be enacted' – she ignored his interruption as though it was a plea for understanding to the Inland Revenue and continued to address Curtis – 'unless three witnesses can corroborate the claim that the robot is yours.'

'Well, there's me,' said Carlton, 'and Gloria.'

235

Two. One more.

'And Dano?' he tried. Dano immediately shook her head.

'I am prohibited from witnessing by my position as arresting officer.'

'Why?' asked Arnold. Dano shrugged.

'It's in the rules.'

'Live a little. Break a rule.'

'Do you have a third witness?' Aglaea inquired with an expectant leer that, if not quite a king yet, was certainly a crowned prince.

'I'll have to find Fission,' Carlton said. Gloria looked worried.

'But she'll say "no" so that Arnold will get disconnected,' she whispered. 'That's just what she's waiting for. Then Arnold won't be able to tell us who the robot is and we won't find him and we won't get Thomas back.' Which was what mattered. 'And we'll lose the Game and get killed.' Which mattered nearly as much.

'Well, for a start we'll make sure she doesn't find out what alternatives are on offer,' Carlton whispered back. 'If she thinks it's just a straight question about ownership then she'll back us up.' I'm discussing things with Gloria, his mind interrupted, suddenly. Maybe that's a good sign! 'And if we can make her believe that Arnold knows who the renegade is . . . Besides, do we have any choice?'

Well, yes they did. They could let Arnold be disconnected.

'Does anyone know where Fission is?' Carlton asked, looking at Arnold.

'I think she's probably on Titan.'

'Oh, brilliant!' He turned to Aglaea. 'Can we have a recess? Please?'

'Of course,' she replied with a smile, bending over backwards to be helpful. 'You have ten minutes.' The smile turned its back and bent over forwards. 'During which, computer, relay that whispered conversation, would you.'

The Challenger watched with a quiet emanation of microwaves. It did not have to influence this human at all; the Arnold robot had done more than enough already.

Nothing escaped the Champion's environs. It was concentrating.

Guided by the spherical twin towers which topped off the Admin complex stadium, the trand made a bee-line for its quest.

When the bee is laden with food and is heading for the haven of the hive, it goes straight, since that is the shortest way home unless the search for pollen has taken it far enough to make the curvature of the Earth a significant factor; which only rarely happens, after a night out with the drones. Either way, it does have the good sense to avoid those things in its way with which a bee is ill-equipped to cope – like trees and houses and stuff.

The trand didn't bother with all that. When *he* made a bee-line, it was the trees and houses that had better move, or else.

Some bee.

Some line.

Flying along above it, with the sniggering whistles of its peer choir still ringing in its ears, Tweet glanced down every now and then and thought of ways to get its revenge.

It was hardly spoiled for choice.

The words of Tweet's great-uncle came to its mind: When faced with anything that can reduce you to feathers in a red goo if you get within arm's length, the best, the only, method of attack is to crap on it from a very great height.

Tweet looked for blackberries.

Danlor looked for the alien. He had smeared dirt on his face as both camouflage and a highly efficient way of caking his eyelids, making it practically impossible to see where he was going. The trand had not exactly taken time to cover his tracks, though – rather, his tracks covered everything else – and Danlor followed the path of destruction, darting from broken tree to rearranged house, his disruptor held in front of him.

Carlton rushed round the first corner in his search for the TMT and thence, hopefully, Fission, and nearly ran her down as she walked unhurriedly along the corridor.

'Fission!' he exclaimed involuntarily, inviting a withering comment.

'Yes,' she said, and her voice was quiet, not withering at all.

'Come on!' He'd count his blessings later. 'We need you. This way. And please be reasonable. Arnold isn't the renegade. Just believe me. And don't ask who is, because I don't know. Yet. Arnold does.'

That staccato barrage of verbiage wouldn't even have convinced *him*, he thought, and he already believed it.

Well, there just wasn't enough time to try to argue with her.

237

He grabbed her hand instead – normally a marginally more stupid thing to do than repeatedly digging a lion in its protruding ribs while dressed in an antelope suit – and pulled her towards the courtroom. She followed with a slightly shocked expression but not a word.

'And you are?' asked Aglaea as they entered.

'She's Fission,' said Carlton, and suffered a lower-middle-class look from the magistrate.

'Is that correct?'

'Yes,' said Fission in a small voice. The others suddenly weren't quite so sure.

'Do you recognise these people?' Fission looked at Curtis, Gloria, Arnold, Carlton and Dano in turn.

'Yes, yes I think so.' She had pulled one of them out of the way when there was that stripway mechanism malfunction explosion.

What in the name of anything supernatural had happened to Fission? they all wondered. It was like Hitler marching into Poland and redecorating all the houses.

'And do you recognise the robot Arnold to be the property of the rather skinny person next to him?' God, I miss Wilverton, thought Curtis. 'Before you answer, though, I think it only proper that you understand the responsibility laid upon you.' Aglaea enunciated her next sentence like a nun reading her favourite Bible passage. 'If you fail to confirm the robot to be his property, then it will be dismantled. Permanently.'

Fission looked at Aglaea with her mouth slightly agape, then looked at Arnold. Arnold smiled, wanly. So far this particular ploy had worked with Fission precisely no times at all.

'Oh dear me,' said Fission.

'Dear' her? Not 'fonk' her? Sideways, perhaps?

Fission was mad, thought Carlton. That was the only answer. She must have been brainwashed by Tamon.

'Yes, he is,' he hissed, and backed it up with a nod as soon as she looked at him.

'Er, well, yes, as far as I know the robot would seem to be the property of the scrawny gentleman.' Oh, thanks. 'There's really no need to have it dismantled on my account.'

Aglaea gave her a look which would have kept a side of beef fresh for a decade, and then made that look warm with a glance at Arnold, who wasn't going to risk a gloating smile yet, but who had to make a not-inconsiderable effort to keep this visual equivalent of 'nyahh

nyahh' just below the surface.

'Very well. The ruling of the court is that the *robot* Arnold' – the tone bestowed on Arnold an honorary turdship – 'is the property of the weedy fellow called . . . ?'

'Er . . .'

'Curtis,' supplied Carlton.

'Ercurtis. Let it . . .'

'No,' Curtis interrupted. '"R" Curtis.'

'Pardon?'

'"R" Curtis, not Er Curtis. For Richard. But not Dick.'

'I *beg* your pardon?' What was the stupid little man going on about. He and the robot deserved each other.

'Not Dick. Do you still have Dicks? I don't mean do you still have . . . well . . . you know . . .'

'Shut up,' Carlton told him. 'His name's Curtis.'

'Curtis.' Aglaea could feel herself losing this one, and hurried back on track. 'Let it be written.'

Now, thought Dano. The crunch. What to do.

'There is a representation from the Foundation Foundation,' the computer informed Aglaea. Arnold raised an eyebrow. Aglaea raised a hope. Dano's thought paused.

'What is it?'

'Arnold is running as a candidate in the election.'

'What election?' Aglaea had much better things to do with her time than concern herself with the ineffectual meanderings of democracy.

'For World President. The Foundation question a robot's right to stand.'

Aglaea's eyebrows described the absurdity of the notion. 'Is there no law?'

'There is nothing recorded on the subject. A ruling would be taken as precedent.'

A smile spread over Aglaea's face, one that could justifiably be called a winning smile. She *liked* being a magistrate.

'I hereby rule that *no* robot may stand as a candidate for World President. Let it be written.'

'It is so written.'

Arnold wondered what Aglaea would be legally entitled to do to him should he instruct her to go sit on a pineapple and wriggle. He was just about to find out when she turned her attention to Curtis.

'I am sure that there are laws against allowing a robot under your control to be a public nuisance, and this one is certainly that.' Arnold's expression told her that flattery wouldn't get her anywhere. 'I suggest you keep this machine on a very short leash indeed.'

Arnold looked at Curtis, and Curtis looked back. Arnold won, pretty much without a fight, but Aglaea had already removed the eared cap and was rising to leave, and so did not see her suggestion being strangled at birth.

'I presume that I am free to go,' Arnold told Dano.

He turned on his heel and walked from the courtroom without a word, his nose slightly in the air.

They were after him in a moment, and caught him in the corridor, where Carlton's hand stopped his shoulder from moving any further. The rest of him agreed not to leave it behind.

'Come on, then!' Carlton invited.

'Come on where? And how can I when you've just stopped me?' It was a cheap effort, and not delivered with the same sort of calculated irritation as usual.

'Don't start.' Carlton brushed the comment aside. 'Look, who's the renegade?' Arnold spun to face him, forcing someone to dart sideways on his way to hear the election result.

Carlton saw real emotion in the android's face.

Jealousy.

Dano stared at him, too, frowning.

'*I'm* not allowed to stand in the election. Because *I'm* not human.'

He sounded peeved. Childishly peeved, Dano thought. It wasn't him. When your plan to take over the world is foiled, you don't act as though you can't have your favourite ice-cream. She had to check.

'What were you going to do if you were elected?' she interrupted.

Arnold shrugged. 'Oh, I don't know . . . Make the world a better place; ban humans, especially children, and adults . . . '

'The President can't *do anything*,' Dano persisted, watching Arnold closely. He frowned.

Gloria helped. 'It's something to do with his nipples.'

'Sorry?'

'The President is only a titular head,' Carlton told him, and Gloria nodded. 'Central does absolutely everything; humans don't get a look in.'

'So I've been . . . ' Arnold's expression looked momentarily aghast, but quickly reformed itself. 'Well, I knew that. It just seemed the best way to find the renegade.'

'Who is?' Carlton prompted.

'It's Central, isn't it?' Gloria prompted.

'It's Miron, isn't it?' Dano prompted.

Arnold looked at Dano. 'It's Miron. Spoilsport.' He seemed to have recovered from the tragedy of missing out on the election.

In the moment of silence, no-one noticed a crowd-mingling Chanta listening intently, looking intense, and striding off towards the Grand Hall, with intent.

'Miron?' Curtis looked shocked. Miron was, well, his disciple. 'Miron the leader of the Foundation Foundation?'

'No,' said Arnold, 'Miron the assistant caretaker at the Jewish deli on fifth avenue.'

Curtis frowned. When had Arnold been to fifth avenue? And was there a Jewish deli there with an assistant caretaker? What was a deli anyway?[1]

'How do you know?' asked Carlton.

'I was hiding under the stage and I happened to look up his dress.'

'Did he ha . . . ' said Gloria, but it was as far as she got. He must have had or Arnold wouldn't have been sure. But how big, exactly?

'How did *you* know?' Carlton asked Dano.

'You said it yourself. The mink. Once they were "civilised", they couldn't go back to what they were before. Remove the social routine that was imposed by their leader, and you remove the civilisation.' She turned to Gloria. 'What happened to the koalas after you killed their leader?'

'How did you know I killed him?'

'It was obvious, from what you said, from what you are.'

'Well, they just sort of drifted about, not knowing what to do. Aimlessly.' That was the word.

'Precisely. And Fission . . . ' Where *was* Fission? She hadn't followed them. 'Fission's squirrels couldn't do anything without leadership; they needed it to save themselves. And Di . . . er, Richard's deer were trying to show they could lead. It all pointed to the same thing; leadership, hierarchy, but it's not what leaders can make you do, it's what you *can't* do without them; it's what happens if you take leadership away. It doesn't need someone to take over from Central and force everyone to do anything – we're so reliant on Central that just turning it off, even bit by bit, making it work wrong, affecting it in any way, is going to mess up the world. We're

[1] Earth Twenty-Three had a Jewish deli on Fifth Avenue, as it happened, called Seven Unleavened.

so dependent on it, on its leadership, on our whole hierarchy, that we'd just fall apart.'

'And the ants!' Gloria got terribly excited very quickly. 'That was the same thing. Take away the, er, the thing, and they go all, er, thingy.' Damn. Dano looked a little confused, but the others knew what she meant.

'And the gorillas,' Curtis offered.

'Tamon said it all just applied to animals, not humans,' Carlton pointed out, watching for Dano's reaction. She shrugged – she wasn't going to comment on that one.

Curtis was; in vindicated tone. 'He just didn't want to admit it. It's like I said right at the start. We *are* animals, just like any other. Hngh!'

The man hit him squarely on the chin, dropping him like a sack of sand.

'I warned you,' he said. 'Come on, Marqa, it'll be on soon,' and he led his partner down the corridor towards the Grand Hall.

They looked down at Curtis for a respectful second or two. He rewarded their obvious concern by moaning.

'So we'll hang around here and see what happens, shall we?' Arnold asked. Gloria glanced at him, while satisfying herself that Curtis was as capable of standing upright as ever. Arnold's sarcasm was missing; it was the only way he could suggest they got on with the Game without appearing interested! She smiled. Where *was* Fission? she wondered.

In one corner of the corridor, up by the ceiling, the figures of Miron and Pomona appeared, small at first, but growing in size. Behind them, on the stage, the input console to the Central computer sat in its pink castle. Pomona looked less than confident; Miron, the opposite.

'Come on,' said Dano. 'We've got to stop him.' She took a step through Miron, and the others followed, the insubstantial form of Pomona proving no more of an obstacle.

What did prove an obstacle was the needle gun which preceded Fission round a corner just ahead and pointed at them.

XXVIII

Wilverton looked around, half expecting to hear a booming voice saying something about smelling the blood of an Englishman. The place was huge. The ceiling was far enough away to make painting it not so much a job as a stunt. And looking down from the walls ten feet below it were what presumably had to be gargoyles with their exaggerated features – he couldn't help thinking that one of them looked inescapably like Charles III.

Norim's sense of aesthetics did not seem to be suffering any shellshock, as he stood calmly waiting, though not for long, because Wilverton took in the scene in an instant before the reality of the situation came flooding back into his head – that he was nearing the end of his quest and that the group of trands behind him was just nearing.

The reality of the situation . . .

He swallowed.

'I think this is all really happening,' he told Norim, who seemed to consider it quite seriously for a moment.

'So do I.'

'I suppose that's good, in a way.' Wilverton tried to cheer himself up with the thought. It didn't work, because . . . 'The trouble is, there are an awful lot of other ways that it isn't good, especially the lack of heroes.' Norim accepted this information without comment, which was perhaps slightly peculiar, since 'You're nuts' was just crying out for an airing. Wilverton didn't notice. 'Come on.'

By way of encouragement, someone knocked on the front door with his head.

One difference between Trand Prime and Trand Whatever was apparently the mechanism which prevented easy hostile access, and there was a pause, during which, no doubt, the collective brains of the trand team were bent to the solution of the puzzle, extrapolating, theorising, hypothesis-forming.

Then someone hit the door again, but not with his head. This time it was with someone else's head.

Why can't we all just live together happily? Wilverton wondered. If this is real then we don't need excitement and conflict and death, do we? . . . Well, maybe you don't, but the Champion and Challenger apparently do, and the trands certainly do.

And sooner or later they'll come through that door and get it.

He trotted across the floor of an entrance hall that filled the whole of the ground floor of the building, towards a staircase beginning in the centre and stretching up to the heights of the ceiling and beyond. Norim followed.

Climbing the stairs would have left an athlete puffing, and Wilverton took a few moments to heave in several breaths whilst trying to avoid heaving out his last meal – not that he could remember when that was – during which interlude Norim watched with all the apparent distress of a bug in the non-self-cleansing shag-pile.

Wilverton did have enough oxygen left in his blood to work his eye muscles – just – so he had a quick look around, after deciding once and for all that he would question Norim when the rest of him was back in working order – probably about a week Tuesday. The first floor had more rooms in it than the ground, but behind them was a pair of decorated doors, the only ones with any adornment. Decorated in trandian tradition, of course, so that they looked like the aftermath of a particularly spectacular accident with a chainsaw, but decorated nevertheless.

Wilverton and Norim headed for them, spurred by the sounds of success – as in satisfied grunt rather than pulped headbone – coming from the ground floor, and pushed them open to reveal a room still devoid of trandian life, but with more furniture. Stone benches and tables were dotted about, but the eye passed over these to a glass cabinet in the centre of the room. And in the cabinet . . .

'The Gun!' said Wilverton, and rushed towards it as fast as his exhausted legs would carry him – it would only have been breakneck speed if he had an incredibly fragile neck. Norim sauntered along with him, and watched as Wilverton inspected the cabinet, looking for a way in, and finding exactly none.

The 'cabinet' consisted of a boulder on which rested the Gun and over which a huge glass dome had been firmly fixed. Wilverton could not hope to raise the dome – it must weigh a ton, he reckoned – so he began looking around.

'We need something to break the glass,' he said by way of

explanation, and Norim held his hand in front of his face for a moment, as if contemplating the answer to Wilverton's problem. Then he thrust the answer to Wilverton's problem through the glass, and took the gun from the boulder.

Why didn't I think of that? wondered Wilverton. I did think of that, he corrected himself, but discarded the option on the realisation that thrusting my hand through there would result in more lacerations than a masochists' orgy, and I need all the blood I've got.

Norim, apparently, didn't have the same concerns. The skin around his hand was certainly in poorer shape than it had been – bits of it hung in strips like orange peel from his fingers and wrist – but there was no blood.

Or flesh.

Metal bones and possibly carbon fibre sinews and chitin cartilage, but none of the sort of stuff that made a human.

'You are the only human being on the planet,' Biondor had said. Wilverton nodded slightly.

What Sherlock *should* have said was that, quite regardless of how many impossible and improbable theories you might be able to conjure up, if you were only able to see them by overlooking the bleedin' obvious then you didn't really have a mystery worthy of the description.

'You're a robot,' Wilverton told his companion.

'I know.'

'Can I have the gun, please?'

'Sorry. No.'

'Ah.'

Bother.

'Why not, exactly?'

'This is the council chamber,' explained Norim. 'The council meet here.' Reasonable so far. 'There are very few trands capable of the calm reflection needed for administrative competence. I will kill them and without their leadership the city will return to a state of anarchy.' He certainly seemed to have it all worked out.

'Why do you want to do that?'

'Because I must.'

Hmm. 'Well, could I borrow the gun for a little while?' Start off being reasonable, thought Wilverton, and if that didn't work, then, er, then he'd, er . . . then he'd continue being reasonable until he thought of something else. The Champion had chosen *him*.

Norim shook his head.

Then the room shook its head as the captain of the trandian team and his colleagues, with Sam in the rear, did what they euphemistically referred to as entering; it was little wonder that the city looked like San Francisco after the big one when each transition from outside to in involved further disruption of the masonry.

Having entered, they stopped, and the only movement was a door swinging forlornly on its remaining hinge just for old times' sake before toppling to the floor.

There were two pink things with two legs in the room.

The captain had expected only one, and there were two.

Pause.

'He's the robot! He's the one you're after!' shouted . . . Norim?

He pointed at Wilverton, using the gun now held in a hand untouched by glass scalpels, while the other, more dilapidated specimen stayed firmly behind his back. Wilverton snapped his head from the trands to Norim and opened his mouth, letting realisation flood in – if there was a renegade robot on Earth in this round then there would be one on Trand, of course. And on Earth what they had to do was destroy the robot – or stop him, in any case – and on Trand they were likely to have to do the same thing, rather more than likely when all the available facts were taken into account.

And take them into account Wilverton did, bloody quick, before reaching the decision in about a second that the first thing he should do was deny Norim's assertion.

But he thought too long – brains aren't always the advantage they're cracked up to be – and it was Norim who spoke, and acted.

Spoke, by saying, 'I'll get him for you.'

And acted, by shooting Wilverton through the head with a gun that, to judge by its effect, was clearly still in full working order.

The trand felt optimistic. He was approaching the end of his bee-line, and though there was neither a hive nor a pot of gold waiting for him, there was Admin. And then victory for his team, for his race.

Approaching the steps, the trand noticed with some glee – relatively, he didn't generally ever get within spitting distance of 'glee', but he was chuffed in a grumpy sort of way – that there was no-one waiting with some kind of offering. So far, the humans' attempts at appeasement had just left him pissed off – which was no great surprise since he was usually well within dribbling distance of 'pissed off'.

*

Just inside the Admin building, Neara was chatting to one of her colleagues when the trand made an entrance. Literally.

The creature ignored them as they stood and stared open-mouthed at it and strode purposefully towards a corridor, as though knowing where it led.

'It hasn't got a ticket!' Neara hissed to her friend.

'Well, tell it then,' he replied bravely.

'Why me?'

'Well.' Because I've got a partner, four kids, and a life-wish. 'You're Neara.'

She killed off any last vestige of his self-esteem with a sharp glance, took a deep breath, and fixed the expansive trand back with a steely glare.

'STOP!'

And the trand demonstrated that whilst it might not have cherished any of the assortment of odds and ends with which it had so far been showered, what it did appreciate was a direct order.

It stopped.

Fission looked peeved.

Vexed.

Homicidally enraged.

'Where have you been?' asked Carlton, not registering the gun at first, and wondering what could have happened between the court-room and here. 'Come on, we've got to get to Miron.'

'Been fonking *Titan!*' Fission informed them, her voice back to a more normal vehemence.

'What, all of it?' asked Arnold.

She waved the gun at him, via Gloria, who was standing in front of Arnold, not entirely voluntarily. 'Get out way, melons.'

Gloria made to move aside, but got no further than a twitch before staying right where she was – after the more prominent bits of her had undertaken something of a shimmy for a while.

'What's the matter with you? You were quite reasonable in the courtroom just now.'

'What courtroom?'

It was right up there with skunk ownership, and Gloria didn't know quite how to differentiate between the room they had all just been in and all the ones that they hadn't, so she said nothing for a moment, and the silence was only broken by the murmuring of the computer describing the last minutes before the election result.

'Excuse me,' said a woman from behind the group, edging her way past. She had presumably not noticed the gun, weapon recognition and forward movement being conventionally incompatible. It was not her motion that attracted their attention, though, but her appearance.

It was Fission.

Again.

'Fission!' said Carlton.

See?

'Who the athletic fonk are you?' asked guess who, while looking into a mirror, and seeing a suddenly frightened and plainly shocked image looking back. The image spoke rather timidly.

'My name is Fission.'

'Well, so's . . . What you . . . Who . . . ' Fission had been with Curtis for too long, Carlton thought – not that *that* necessitated any great expenditure of time. She turned her attention back to the others and away from her other self, accusingly. 'What's going on?'

They had been wondering. Then Arnold spoke as though he had known the answer for ever.

'Biondor said that one difference between this version of Earth and the real one was that you lot failed in the first round of the Game. So you wouldn't have been called up to replace the fat one.'

'Bill,' reminded Gloria over her shoulder, with a touch of admonishment. Arnold shrugged.

The computer said something about 'one minute', but they didn't hear it.

'Why not say before?' Fission demanded. Arnold paused. Admitting that he had only just thought of it would make him hardly better than human. He paused some more. 'Further proof, you renegade!' she concluded, and raised the gun from where it had drooped slightly floorwards.

'No, he's not!' Gloria didn't move. 'Miron is the renegade. Arnold isn't standing for World President any more, so he can't do any harm, and your reasons aren't waterproof . . . tight . . . they don't hold water any more. Dano thinks Miron's going to do something to Central so that there isn't any leader any more – that's what all the animal things were for.'

Fission thought about it for a long moment. It was indisputably logical. She looked at Arnold with an intensity of frustrated hate that only she could hope to approach, all the more unbearable because she knew it wasn't his fault.

'And we might not have long to stop him,' Dano added. 'Come on.'

They didn't.

'You've got it!' Tamon arrived at the outskirts of the tableau, and favoured Arnold with a look of triumphant hate. He stopped, his face registering concern that all was not well, then surprise when he noticed the two Fissions, then incomprehension because that was easiest.

This is all we need, Dano thought. We have to hurry; we haven't the time. 'We've had the trial and confirmed ownership,' Dano told him. 'Arnold isn't a renegade.' A little weird, maybe.

Fission's eyes hardened to little chips of blue ice as the final nail was driven into the coffin of her theory.

'Fission was wrong,' confirmed Carlton, with just a touch of self-satisfaction.

The first spadeful of earth was scattered over the lid. Fission's eyes suggested that her theory was not the only thing about to qualify for burial.

'And now the moment you have all been waiting for!'

They looked madly around them as the increased volume of the computer's cheerful voice announced their failure.

'The new President of the World . . . '

Miron and Pomona stood before them with frozen smiles, the latter's melting a bit.

' . . . is Miron!'

A burst of radio waves told the Champion that its last chance was quickly disappearing. Influence of the vote had been an obvious manoeuvre, but the Challenger had destroyed Pomona's chance by guiding a small packet of owl-shit onto her nose in the debating studio.

A tight x-ray suggested that the Champion had not given up just yet.

'Ooh goody!' said Fission, with a happy little smile. 'That's a hundred wollars for me!' She immediately trotted off down the corridor towards the Grand Hall, showing more relief than a hundred wollars would normally induce, but trying not to let on that leaving a bunch of very peculiar people, and particularly one catatonic spitting image, behind was worth a great deal more.

'We're too late,' said Gloria, looking at Miron's smiling hologram and seeing Wilverton.

'Not yet, we're not!' Carlton contradicted. Sod leadership, sod relationships, and sod animals! They had a job that could still be done. A Game that still had to be won. 'Come on!'

Fission stared after her team-mates and moved not a molecule.

Tamon, too, stood his ground, and Dano began explaining the danger Central was in, trying to ignore the heretical 'fat mink' in her mind, which was whispering to her to let it happen. Tamon cast worried glances at Fission, wondering what her reaction might be.

It was a fairly predictable one, given that Arnold had made her look a right Curtis.

It was Miron's fault.

And there was no use moping about it. So she didn't.

She fired a hole in the blameless ceiling of the corridor, instead, then spun towards the Grand Hall and yelled *'You BASTARD!'* at the top of her voice, and followed her scream down the corridor before anyone could stop her, although anyone who was seriously thinking of doing so right then would have had to take time out from smiling meaninglessly and dribbling.

Dano and a confused but convinced Tamon followed at a safe distance, which meant one that was not decreasing.

A minute later, a bald, white-robed figure hurried down the same corridor towards the Grand Hall, a phial clutched in a cocoon of LOVE, and a dog walking to heel, except when he paused to give peace 'V's to anyone who looked in his direction, and toppled against the nearest wall.

Directly above the same corridor, the trand wandered happily, lost but so far unknowing, clutching in his hand a small entrance ticket, and a piece of finger.

The remains of Neara's finger was now as numb as her brain thanks to the robot, and she didn't see anything particularly out of the ordinary in the dirt-smeared face of the man who insinuated himself round the splintered doorframe and sidled up to her.

'Have you seen an alien come through here?' he asked.

Neara stared at him. Danlor waited. The question was not, perhaps, clear enough.

'It's about seven, eight foot tall, with six arms. Three on either side.' That should do it. That should distinguish it from any other aliens who might have passed this way lately. Unless . . . 'It sounds like,' and he made a noise normally associated with salmonella.

Something did the trick, because Neara raised an arm in slow motion and pointed vaguely down the corridor. Danlor nodded, and rubbed his way inwards along the wall, while Neara watched, expressionlessly.

'This way, sir.' The robot waved the next-in-line further along the Grand Hall's perimeter corridor. 'This approach is in use, and you will gain access quicker via another entrance. Thank you. This way, madam. Are you together? Thank you. This way, please.'

In the corner of the ceiling, Miron stood on centre stage, his arms raised in the universal declaration of triumph, while around him milled members of the Foundation Foundation – Rablin oddly not amongst them – and behind him the now brightly lit pink castle cradled the console which allowed the President access to the Central computer.

'This way, please, madam. You will undoubtedly get a much better view if you traverse this corridor to one of the other entrances to the . . . '

'Go fonk yourself, you artificial arse-licker.' She'd had enough of robots.

'Thank you, madam. Have a nice day.'

While the robot considered how he could possibly carry out her instructions, Fission elbowed her way past, and continued on a line to the Grand Hall so direct that it made the trandian bee sort look a touch wobbly.

The trand paused momentarily by a window and looked out. Hundreds of thousands of these weak bipedals were sitting in a huge oval stadium, watching the antics of quadrupeds on the ground in the middle. A large herd of what looked like droogs, but with horns, seemed to be grazing, while several smaller creatures, like large poltins, stalked them.

But no books. No glass cabinet with a book in it. So no interest.

The line of people congratulating Miron showed little sign of dwindling to an unassisted conclusion, and a Foundationer lowered his arm in front of a disappointed man shuffling with the queue towards the stage, and just behind a woman wearing a simple robe, rather like those of the Foundationers themselves, but with the hood raised, surely from deference rather than a desire to conceal her face.

'That will have to be all until after the re-start ceremony,' the man informed the next-in-line, who looked like he had been told to wait until the breakfast things had been washed up before he could open his presents.

The woman edged away from the now-halted queue, the loose-fitting robe hiding any signs of faster than normal breathing, and the hood hiding the green hair and the nervous expression on a face which Miron would know well. Chanta shuffled until her feet encountered the first of the steps onto the stage. With an extra deep breath, she started climbing.

'Look, it's important that we get in there, more important than you can possibly imagine.' Carlton was trying to reason. Reason wasn't working. The attendant who barred his way, along with the ways of Gloria, Curtis and Arnold, was apparently made of flesh and blood, and was clearly enjoying his enforcement of the Full Grand Hall policy.

'If you'll just wait until the ceremony is complete and people start circulating again, there will be plenty of time to see the new President.'

He was like the second-in-command koala, thought Gloria, only worse; he was protected by his orders, and he was enjoying the power they gave him.

'It'll be too late by then!' Carlton considered moving the man aside, but he knew that he simply wouldn't be able to do so. He turned to Gloria, and mouthed something at her.

'What?'

Carlton closed his eyes briefly and sighed. He took Gloria's elbow and moved her a little, out of the attendant's earshot, then whispered in her ear.

She frowned at him. Hard.

'Why is it always sex that you think of?' A walrus appeared in her mind's eye, and she knew it would work. It was the reward for being the strongest, for not letting them through.

'It's not sex,' Carlton told her, interrupting her thoughts, and ignoring what he was telling himself. 'It doesn't mean anything. It doesn't cheapen you. Think of it as a tool we can use.'

Gloria stared at him for another moment, then turned abruptly to the attendant.

'Excuse me,' she began, in a voice as soft as a feather mattress. 'I

252

really do need to get into the Hall. I know it's full, but I'll ask ever so nicely.' She looked shyly at the ground, then back up to the man's slightly amused eyes.

'I'm afraid that won't work with me.' He looked at Carlton. 'Now, if *he* asked ever so nicely . . . ' And he looked Carlton up and down, appraisingly. 'I like the little ones.'

Carlton's chin dropped.

'What!'

The man smiled at him. Invitingly.

'Don't think of it as sex,' Arnold said. 'Think of it as a tool you can use. Literally.'

Gloria smiled, caught herself, stopped and felt guilty.

'Shut up, Arnold.' Carlton thought desperately for a moment or two, before the only solution came to him. 'So that's it, then. We've lost.'

The attendant shrugged, his smile fading. 'It's no big deal. I probably wouldn't have let you in anyway. I *have* got responsibilities, you know.'

Carlton took a precious second out to hate him, which brought on an idea. 'Arnold, you haven't got the "Basics", as Fission called them, have you?'

'No.'

'So you wouldn't mind harming a human being?'

'I'm a constant martyr to temptation.'

'Quite. I wonder if you could make a passage for us?'

'Pleased to.' Arnold put a pleasant smile on his face and pointed it at Carlton before turning it to the attendant. 'Excuse me,' he said, and walked towards the Hall. The attendant put an arm out, which Arnold took and used to ease the man to the corridor wall, and keep him there, despite struggles and muttered oaths.

The other three took advantage of the hole and passed through, after which Arnold let go the arm and followed. A hand came down heavily on his shoulder and yanked him backwards. In an obvious effort not to lose his balance, Arnold swung his fist back, quite hard. It hit something, quite soft.

'Oops,' said Arnold as the attendant doubled over, clutching the bit that worried Carlton the most.

'Thank you, my child,' said Miron, gently laying a hand on the head of the latest man to go down on one knee in front of him and touch the robe as a mark of respect to the new President. The man rose and

253

continued on his way, allowing the last in the long queue to approach.

One more genuflection and these ridiculous humans would have finished their worship.

And then the re-start ceremony.

Miron took a deep breath – he had played the role for so long it no longer required conscious thought – and prepared to greet the last to pay homage.

Chanta kept her head lowered and the hood raised, and mumbled something which Miron would not have heard even had it been proper English and not just a meaningless collection of the first few syllables that entered her head.

She knelt before him and touched the robe's hem, with both hands, and Miron extended his own hand to lay on her head.

Before he had the chance to do so, she abruptly rose, keeping hold of the hem, and lifted her hands high in the air. To the congregation in the Grand Hall, and to the watching holovision millions, in glorious three dimensions, of which length was easily the most impressive, the new President of the world was well and truly revealed.

Chanta smiled her delight and glanced around the back to confirm what was already an unshakeable conviction before making the accusation.

'This is my household robot, Rudy! You come home at once!'

A stunned silence greeted the news. It wasn't every day that a public figure was quite so public; the figure being about seven just then.

Miron reacted first, batting the robe from Chanta's hands and back into place before she could take any further action. If his memory served him rightly, the holovision viewing figures might not be the only things she was encouraging to rise. He forced himself to calmness.

'Please remove this sad woman, attendant,' he said to anyone who qualified for the description, and there was movement from both sides of the stage as people were jerked into action by his words. From front stage came a contradiction.

'No! She's right. He *is* a robot. We can prove it. And there's something gone wrong with his brain.'

Carlton wasn't exactly sure – meaning he didn't have the remotest sniff of the outermost reaches of an idea's embryo – *how* they could prove it, but it was the sort of thing that might convince someone sitting on the proverbial fence just then, and should, at least, make them pause to think.

It certainly had the effect of halting the attendants who were making their way towards Chanta. Doubts cast on their leader, thought Carlton – they couldn't immediately dismiss the idea that they were following a flaw.

A doorway opened on one side of the Hall, and Rablin emerged, followed by a half dozen of his colleagues, all wearing serious expressions.

'Rablin!' called Miron. 'Seize the heretics!' And he pointed at Carlton, Curtis, Gloria, and Chanta in quick succession, as though he were confirming the order in one-armed semaphore.

Rablin and his group walked straight and purposefully to Curtis and stood before him.

'Glocarlerfrank.'

'What?' asked Carlton from one side, and Curtis looked embarrassed. So no change there, then.

Rablin's collection of noises did not appear to have been a question, however, and he continued, 'You have chosen to come among the Foundationers, although you have never officially approached us.'

Oh dear, thought Curtis. I'm in trouble now.

'That is good.'

It was?

'You did not seek to make any claims, but chose instead to hide behind a pseudonym.' Not a very good one, thought Carlton, as Rablin turned to face him. 'When *you* came to seek your leader, you did not use a robotic messenger; you chose the simple method of coming yourself. And you called for Richard Curtis. And this man answered.' While delivering the phrase in an almost hushed reverence, he turned back to Curtis, who by now was beginning to feel that odd but familiar juxtaposition of happiness, and worry that he should be feeling happy.

'And finally. We have consulted, and determined that the cure for the last serious mental disorder was introduced worldwide over two hundred years ago. Given that, there is no possible way that the parents of anyone born since that date would have chosen the genetic characteristics which you embody.' Eh? 'The lack of co-ordination you have displayed, and the physical appearance all point inescapably to the fact that you are the product of a bygone era.'

As a laudation it was, admittedly, a bit of a disappointment, but

255

Curtis did feel much more at home. Rablin moved closer to him, and with eyes pleading for the right response, asked, 'Are you Richard Curtis?'

Curtis looked at the expectant face before him, and the others all around him, and he heard the complete silence in the Grand Hall, saw the complete lack of movement – missing the fact that Miron had sidled to the rear of the stage and was now leaning over the computer console. A whole planet was waiting with unbearable tension for his answer. He looked back to Rablin, and said . . . and said . . .

'Er . . . '

XXIX

Wilverton had never been shot before, but he had seen it happen to other people lots of times. Admittedly, only once had he caught a glimpse of the kind of barbaric films they used to show around the turn of the century – grossing millions at the box office and fifty lives on the streets – but he knew what was expected of him.

He should fall over in a bloody heap and never get up again. Having seen the flash from the muzzle of the gun which Norim was still pointing at him, he was fully prepared to do just that; he was, he reflected seriously, never one to argue with a reasonable convention.

How come I'm still thinking? he thought. And like this! When I should have a hole where the brain used to be?

The answer, he deduced, rightly, was that it wasn't that kind of gun.

In the sort of civilised society for which the trands were striving it was considered bad form to deal with minor misdemeanours by summary execution, which a normally equipped ballistic projecting gun would have done. What the trands wanted to do was to remove the desire to commit the misdemeanour in the first place, a desire generated by the various chemicals which built up in the trandian brain, mixed themselves with the electrical activity of life itself, and burst forth into the outside world via several of the fists.

The gun regulated the chemical and electrical interaction so that it would produce a quiet, thoughtful, largely introspective trand who didn't want to burst forth anywhere.

When Norim fired at Wilverton, the gun's mechanism did not recognise the fact that its target was a small, four-limbed weakling human, and it went right ahead and regulated the inside of his head just as it would have done were he a normal eight-limbed, strapping trand.

Wilverton felt great.

Wilverton felt wonderful.

Wilverton felt better than he ever had in his whole life – except maybe a couple of times on the old Pioneer with Gloria, but that was a different sort of feeling. This was a feeling that told him he could do anything, absolutely anything at all; he was a lion amongst pussycats, a Thatcher amongst men.

Wilverton did not fall over. The hell with convention! He pulled himself up to his full height – it didn't take long – and lunged towards Norim in a flash. Norim, stunned, fired again, which didn't help him any, but did help Wilverton. He grabbed the gun from Norim's hand in the blink of an eye, before even the robot could move, let alone the trands, whose jaws were not exactly dropping but sort of creaking downwards.

Wilverton reversed the gun and shot Norim.

Just like that.

He didn't know consciously why he thought this would be a good thing to do considering the effect it had on him, but his subconscious was working with the same hyper-activity, and that was where the suggestion had emanated.

It was a good move. A blank expression appeared on Norim's face and then headed groundwards along with the rest of him.

Spinning round and balancing himself on the balls of his feet like the Duke, albeit standing in a fairly deep hole, Wilverton noted the beginnings of forward movement by the captain of the trand team, and he fired again. The captain stopped, and a smile spread over his face like the breaking of an ice floe. He spoke.

'I want to smell the flowers. It's been so long since I smelled the flowers.' It had been quite a while since he had managed two sentences with the words in the right place, too, thought Edwina, looking sideways with disgust, but the captain was too far gone to notice.

Time for another challenge, she thought.

Wilverton, with little knowledge of trandian sentence construction, less interest in the captain's deviance from it, and even less in Edwina's promotion ambitions, shot her. Then he muttered, 'Smell the flowers, punk,' with his best Bogart impression, which wasn't so much an impression as a slight dent, but there was no-one around qualified to tell him.

Certainly Edwina looked apathetic about passing critical comment as she smiled at her captain, and shyly took his hand.

He looked at her and smiled back.

It was horrible.

One by one, Wilverton gave his adversaries an electrical dose of karmer, except for the last one. Sam was on his mettle, and he dived for cover behind a stone bench well before Wilverton had a chance to re-aim and fire, speed being something easily achieved when trands fell earthwards because gravity really had something to get hold of.

It occurred to Wilverton that Sam might well be able to find some sort of projectile, or manufacture one simply by taking a handful of bench, so, with the rest of the group showing mouths to each other that would have had a potholer gasping in excitement while looking warily at the irregular stalactites, he decided that his best bet was now to scarper.

Sam, with ten pounds of bench held firmly in one throwing hand, risked a peek around the corner of his shelter and saw Wilverton's back disappearing through the door.

The other bi-arm might be the robot, but so might the one running away, and he couldn't take the chance; he had to catch him. That meant he would have to follow at a slightly faster pace, which was a bit of a blow given the agility of an elm, but that wasn't going to stop him trying. Leaping – actually leaping! – over the prostrate and feebly moving form of Norim, and dodging the apparently waltzing forms of his biggers, Sam set off in pursuit.

The doors which opened from the outside in six separate portions did so from the inside in just two, and did not require any release of catches before they did so. And just as well, since Wilverton was not about to stop and study the mechanism; he was about to thump the thing with a shoulder which currently thought it possessed the persuasive power of the U.S. Air Force. He did so, and the door swung open, while his shoulder took a deep breath and made a mental note to hurt like hell when its owner finally calmed down a bit and came to his senses; specifically, touch.

Sam charged down the corridor and saw the open door, a sign that Wilverton was not far ahead, since it would swing shut in just a few seconds. He increased his pace, so that his gait now qualified as a fully fledged galumph,[1] and made for the opening.

There was Wilverton, just ten yards away, running in a straight line, an easy target.

Sam lined up his gun.

And paused.

[1] An enormous flightless trandian bird, much sought for its three hundredweight of succulent meat, whose main defence was the apparent ability to stampede all on its own.

*

Shoot! Shoot! the Challenger screamed in gamma rays of frustration. Why don't you shoot?

This bipedal creature could have killed him, Sam thought, slowly. He hadn't. Even though it might have won the Game for his team, he hadn't.

Shoot, you ineffectual, lumpy little moron!

Why didn't he? It was not sensible. Law of survival demanded death of the weakers when they threatened.

SHOOT!

But as we grow to civilisation, should we still follow the same paths as when we were savage?

YES!

In this instance, thought Sam, yes. We have a Game to win.
     He raised his drooped gun, hearing, but not registering, someone grunting 'Biggers!' in a slightly drunken slur.
     Then the top third of the door accelerated at the exhortation of a punch which, on earth, would have propelled the world karate champion into the next life. With a heart- and head-felt 'Oomph!', Sam did what Wilverton had failed to do, and fell over.
     On the other side of the door, the youth who had begun his drinking bout after rowing with his mother, caught a final glimpse of the creature that started it all, as he rounded the door and saw Wilverton some twenty yards ahead. He raised a wavering hand and pointed the thing out to himself, and was about to confirm loudly that he had been right all along, when, between one footstep and the next, Wilverton disappeared.

XXX

'Well, yes, I am.'

An audible gasp met the news, and Curtis immediately wondered nervously whether it might be better to renege on his admission of identity, but it was already too late. Rablin was down onto one knee quicker than a monk onto a Suzy Deluxe model 307,[1] and he gripped the hem of Curtis's robe – which took all thoughts from the great prophet's mind except a mental picture of the whole world being able to compare him with Miron, unfavourably. But Rablin simply kissed the garment, let it go and rose again, the expression on his face suggesting to Carlton that he had found the Ark of the Covenant, opened it up and thereby caused the person hiding inside to stop drinking out of the Holy Grail and inform him that he was nothing but a hound dog.

The silence was broken by laughter. From the stage.

Miron turned from the console, cackling like a hen who's just seen the joke.

'It is done!' he cried. 'You are all doomed!'

Arnold gave the cough of a butler attracting his master's attention to an open fly, and Miron spun to where he stood at one side of the stage. Arnold lifted a wire, on the end of which hung a plug. He swung it a bit, and smiled.

Miron didn't. He turned back to Rablin, his face doing its best to go red, but wanting for blood, pointed at Curtis and yelled,

'Kill him!'

Rablin looked at Curtis, and Gloria looked at Lord Kerl for a moment. Except that Miron was no longer Kerl, and they wouldn't obey him. A few minutes before, she thought, and they probably would.

'What would you have us do, Master?' Rablin asked.

And a strange realisation dawned on Captain Richard Curtis.

[1] Whatever *that* is.

This man, and all the others who were staring at him in bald adoration, would do exactly what he told them, no matter what he said. They wouldn't tell him that he was stupid, or tell him to fonk off, or shut up and get on with his homework; they would just obey.

He was the leader.

Him.

He could win this round of the Game on behalf of the whole of humanity. *He* could, just *him*, all on his own. He would be a hero, and Fission and Carlton would like him.

In slow motion, careful not to do anything whereby he might wake himself up or teleport himself out of Wonderland, Curtis pointed at Miron.

'Stop him,' he said.

Rablin looked at his former leader. 'Stop him what?' A corona of doubt peeked out from the eclipse of adoration.

'Sorry?'

'He's not doing anything.'

But the pointing finger broke through Miron's rabbit-in-the-headlights immobility. Running to the front of the stage, and pushing Chanta roughly out of his way, he leaped off, his robe billowing. The people below him, automatically giving way to someone who knew what he was about while they largely didn't, did the Red Sea bit, allowing him to land unmolested and start towards an exit corridor.

'Now he is,' shouted Curtis, excitedly swinging his arm towards Miron's fleeing figure and therefore hitting Rablin on the head. 'Oops, sorry.' It did rather interrupt the triumphant progress of his deification, but then he was back on track while his first disciple rubbed a most holy bruise. 'Stop him!'

This time the order resulted in some action.

Rablin and company pushed their way through the crowd towards the commotion which marked Miron's passage. Chanta was lowering herself from the stage with the same destination in mind; Carlton and Gloria rushed after them, while Arnold looked briefly heavenwards, and sauntered to the front of the stage.

Curtis was about to follow his outstretched arm, largely because he didn't want to be left alone, when one of his new disciples knelt before him, and Curtis looked down on the hood which covered the bald head, and saw the hands gripping the hem of his robe. One hand, he noticed, had LOVE imprinted on the back.

Odd, thought a bit of Curtis's brain that wasn't floating somewhere on cloud eleven. Hadn't he seen that somewhere . . . ?

Then he caught sight of Stay, and the coincidence was confirmed, although he didn't recall the badge with Make Bones, Not War, written in an unsteady paw.

Stay was looking pleased with life, whatever he currently conceived it to be, and, on seeing Curtis, he looked even happier.

Curtis was his friend.

Well, everybody was his friend, but Curtis was a special friend.

And he had legs that looked just like Mimi, the poodle-most-likely-to; in fact, the poodle-most-frequently-had.

LOVE let go the robe, and made to rise, manoeuvring the phial in his hand, his mind now just a single track of determination, a blazing trail. The heretic had threatened Miron directly. He must die.

Stay's mind, on the other paw, had expanded sufficiently to touch the orbit of Jupiter (Five Zero) and was still accelerating. He staggered the last couple of steps towards Curtis, tongue lolling, other bits doing the opposite, and climbed onto his hind legs.

Curtis took a deep breath as his nose twitched in allergic pre-sneeze.

LOVE's hand presented the phial, his thumb flicking off the top, allowing the bullet to escape. A bullet on the lookout for one thing, and one thing only; Curtis DNA.

LOVE thrust the phial under Curtis's nose at the same moment as Curtis sneezed.

It wasn't one of those tightly controlled 'Hhnnn' sneezes that make your eyeballs bulge, this was one of those explosive ones that locates all the nasty, gobby little bits and pieces lurking inside the nostrils and sprays them over as wide an area as possible.

Which in this case largely consisted of the back of LOVE's hand.

The virus climbed hungrily out of the phial, was collected by a fast moving glob of mucus, landed in the middle of a large 'L', and found itself in a sea of Curtis DNA.

LOVE stared in horror at his hand.

'Sorry,' said Curtis, as his disciple frantically wiped the hand on his robe, a look of panic on his face, and the dog, with a contrasting look of ecstasy, toppled over backwards.

The great prophet Richard Curtis turned and hurried after his people.

They hurried after Miron.

Miron, meanwhile, dispelled any doubts by shifting into a gear possessed only by robots and humans costing at least six million dollars. He was getting away.

Above the hubbub which now overtook the Grand Hall, a woman's voice was heard, raised in anger, or rather in apoplexy – 'anger' was Sunday afternoon in a deckchair compared to the emotion being loudly expressed.

Miron was almost at the exit when the parting crowd allowed Fission to appear in front of him. Her eyes flashed with sparks of lightning, which was no surprise given the storm currently raging inside her head. This was the man – robot – who had nearly cost humanity the Game, a crime that made genocide look like pinching a black-jack from the tuck shop. She raised her gun and screamed, '*BLARING FONKER!*', almost lifting herself off the ground with the effort.

It was almost immediately obvious to Miron that she wished him no good, and that she had the wherewithal to make her wishes come true – if the gun didn't get him, a few more seconds of the voice alone would probably make his ears throttle him for a bit of peace – so he veered with robotic speed to one side. Fission just stopped herself from blasting some innocents to kingdom come, and set off after him, so that she now formed the vanguard of the pursuers.

The next exit he found was clearer, except for a robot crouching by a wall and apparently trying to do something completely indescribable; although 'revolting' came close. The sight nearly stopped Miron, but he turned sharply to the left once he hit the perimeter corridor, heading once again for the exit.

As Fission followed, the robotic contortionist momentarily grabbed her attention.

'Oh, for fonk's sake,' she threw over her shoulder, 'I didn't *mean* it, moron!' She rushed on while the robot gratefully unwound its limbs.

Miron inexplicably found Fission in front of him again. She didn't look quite so manic, and she didn't have a gun, but he didn't notice either fact. He performed a 'U' turn by bouncing off a surprised bystander, and started off the other way. For her part, the Fission facing him in the corridor looked only slightly less surprised.

The other Fission, having seen Miron go left, now saw him go right before she reached the end of the feeder passage, and she followed, along with Rablin, a dozen or so Foundationers, Carlton, Gloria, and Curtis – proving that his running ability was not improved by wearing sandals. Arnold watched from where he sat on the front of the stage, swinging his legs and shaking his head slowly at the madness of it all.

The next one Miron nearly ran into was the agent . . . Tamon? The thought crossed his mind that, as President, he was entitled to some protection, until he noticed the look on Tamon's face, when suddenly the prospect of being caught by Fission became almost appealing.

Tamon had seen the confirmation of what Miron was and what he planned to do. This . . . this *thing* had almost succeeded in damaging Central, in threatening their very civilisation. This *thing* needed destroying.

Miron took a quick right turn, up some stairs.

The TMT.

There was a TMT on the second floor of this building. If he could get to it, and set the co-ordinates before they reached him, he could lose them at the other end. It may have been more touch and go than a game of pin the tail on the rabid leopard, but he knew he was faster than any of his pursuers if he had a mind to be; and right now it was his heart's desire and his mind wasn't arguing.

Up the stairs, left at the top, along the corridor, round one more corner, and there was the blessed TMT beckoning to him. And no sound of pursuit.

Just a large alien, looking for a way back to ground level and not finding one; a circumstance which, Miron thought, caused it a smidgen of anger judging from the look on its face, where, admittedly, negative expressions did rest very naturally.

A confirmed anger which the trand, with a haymaking left hook, took out on the TMT as he passed, thereby also taking out the TMT

Discretion being the better part of suicidal stupidity, Miron only very briefly considered remonstrating with the alien for this act of wanton violence, because it looked like it had any number of similar acts left in it, but instead turned once again on a heel that was beginning to wonder when the bit at the other end was going to make itself up.

He ignored the stairs, from which noises were coming, and made for the two doors at the end of the corridor – an elevator.

The trand followed, but not for long. Given that he couldn't keep up with a bored slowworm, catching up with a frantic robot was one ambition too far; besides, hadn't he passed some stairs . . . ?

Fission, Tamon, Dano, Carlton, Curtis, Gloria, Chanta and a dozen Foundationers reached the top, turned right, and concertinaed as those at the front found themselves too close to a trand.

265

Fission considered shooting it, but knew that with a needle gun she'd just jolt it out of its good mood.

Gloria's grandmother used to tell her about something called the Keystone Cops, and the kindly, grey-topped face came to mind as she was jostled around – her sharp glance at Carlton confirming that the contact was incidental – and they all set off the other way. A cheer came to her ears, but it was from outside, and she ignored it, as hunters became hunted; allies, competitors.

'Sorry.' The cheetah patted back a flap of skin on the wildebeest's neck as the cheers of the crowd died down, and an air of anticipation settled over them. The President would be out soon, to start the game. 'These teeth are new, and a little sharp, I'm afraid.'

'Do not concern yourself,' the wildebeest responded as they, along with the other animals, made their way to a dugout beneath one of the stands. 'During the first quarter I can use the repair kit in my hoof.'

There was a point when pursuit of inferior opponents came second to pursuit of books that didn't run away, and that point was the top of the stairs. The trand smiled, the sound of cracking flesh being drowned by a steady 'Pres! Pres! Pres!' being chanted from outside, and started down.

At the bottom, he looked down a short feeder corridor into the Grand Hall, and made one of his noises. In the Serengeti it meant 'I am king of the jungle' or 'I have got my bollocks caught in a sprung trap'. In Admin it meant a trand had spied a book.

A lot of people made other noises, and ran the other way. Any other way.

So did Miron. The commotion was just what he wanted, as he emerged from the elevator and mingled with erstwhile followers, rather than current pursuers. Over his shoulder, somewhere, he vaguely heard the sound of splintering glass, but he ignored it as the light at the end of his personal tunnel came into view. Daylight.

It wasn't where he had expected, but gift horses . . .

He charged down the remaining few yards of the corridor, ignoring a woman having her hand tended by a nursing robot. Ignoring, also, a high-pitched and agonised shriek.

'Where is he?' LOVE cried, and his voice was cracked, not unlike the rest of him. 'Where is the unbeliever?' He staggered around the corridor, waving a disruptor around, his eyes streaming and his brain reeling, but with a wild feeling of happiness washing through him; he would be giving his life for his leader, and there was no greater honour.

A friendly hand alighted momentarily on his shoulder.

'He's coming right now,' said Arnold. 'There he is, look!'

LOVE squinted through blurred eyes and vaguely saw several white-robed figures rushing towards him, coalescing into one before splitting again. But all running, trying to escape! Who else but the infidel would be trying to escape? He pointed the gun, but the figure shimmered, and he hesitated.

The old ways, his brain told him, pounding against the inside of his skull, while sweat dripped off every angle of his body.

As Miron neared the exit, an embryonic grin appearing, LOVE screamed and threw himself on the heretic's back, feeling his limbs stiffening even as he did so. Miron's smile of impending success disappeared faster than good humour in a traffic jam as he found himself giving an impromptu piggy-back to a dripping-wet, gibbering maniac.

LOVE's arms were stretched stiffly over Miron's shoulders and his legs protruded rigid from under his arms, but still he managed to cling on like a limpet, mainly because his teeth were buried in Miron's inhuman neck.

Miron staggered into the light, and the sound of 'Pres! Pres!' overcame the low growling from just below one ear.

Tweet looked down on six waving arms and two legs. That was the one! Its blackberry gorge cried freedom, and Tweet prepared to leap.

'There he is!' Gloria pointed through some open doors which led onto a balcony looking into the amphitheatre from the middle of one end. The others followed her finger, and, ignoring the plush seats on the balcony, saw Miron approaching the twenty yard line, in possession of a lunatic.

A lunatic on *their* side, though, thought Curtis, as he led the way onto the balcony. One of his disciples; and a flush of pride accompanied the notion. In fact, wasn't it . . . ? Yes. He couldn't see the tattooed LOVE on his hand, but the dog with the long cigarette wobbling into the sunlight was a clincher.

The crowd were quiet, not knowing whether this was a scheduled entertainment. A few of them looked up to the balcony where the new President was supposed to appear and start the game, and some cheered as Curtis appeared, assuming he was that Miron bloke.

267

Tweet launched himself and swooped downwards, but the six-armed thing was dodging about, and even the 'Snap the Crap' champion couldn't be sure of a hit. He clenched his bomb doors, and climbed steeply.

From the Admin building streamed twenty, thirty Foundationers, led by Rablin, bearing down on the dancing pair in the middle, their charge splitting to avoid a dog howling something about Lucy being in the Sky.

The crowd were murmuring a little, still unsure of what was occurring.

LOVE was trying to get his gun trained on the body around which he was wrapped, but his arm wouldn't bend, and the heretic was easily a match for the dwindling strength in his wrist. The pain was fading, but so was the light. Then the face of Miron filled the encroaching blankness of his mind, and he smiled, one last time.

On the balcony, they watched, transfixed.

'Haven't we won already?' asked Gloria, not taking her eyes from the scene. If they had won, then perhaps Thomas would magically reappear.

'We should get down there,' Fission commented, but didn't follow up her assertion.

Tamon watched nervously; more than nervously, thought Dano. He was biting a finger nail, and muttering to himself. Only she was close enough to hear the repeated 'Get him, get him, get him . . . ' and she looked back to the scene below with too many emotions to separate.

'Is this the game, then?' asked a cheetah. A wildebeest glanced up from where it had been busy sewing its skin back on, and considered. Two individuals wrestling, and a posse bearing down on them.

'Doesn't look like it. Must be some other sort of human ritual, since we are the entertainment.'

'Interesting. I shall learn.'

Miron saw the grimace of effort on LOVE's face, and bent suddenly at the waist, tipping the madman over his shoulder, sending him crashing to the ground, and jarring the gun loose. He leapt for it, trained it on the body at his feet, but didn't need to fire. His assailant twitched a couple of times and lay still.

LOVE died.

Miron swung towards the Foundationers bearing down on him,

and lifted the gun.

'Stay where you are!' he shouted.

They stopped, the gun restoring some deference.

But not a lot. 'Get off!' called someone from the crowd.

'Yeah. We want the game!'

Miron ignored them.

So did a group of players standing in a passageway just next to the dugout where the animals were waiting. They would come and play just as soon as there weren't any guns being pointed at people.

'Miron!' Curtis's voice rang out from the balcony. He didn't know how he knew that the button in the arm of the centre chair would activate the sound system – he just knew. He didn't know what he was going to say, either, but he knew he should say something. He was Leader of the Foundation Foundation, and as the knowledge continued to sink in, he seemed to feel himself getting physically bigger, filling out, the people around him shrinking.

He was in control, of himself, and the situation.

Carlton glanced sideways, wondering what Curtis was going to say, and reckoning it would almost certainly be 'Er'.

'Central is safe, Miron. You will never be able to harm it as you intended. You will never be able to turn it off and plunge the world into an age of darkness.'

Miron waved the gun in Curtis's direction, but the distance, and the immediate forward swell of the Foundationers made him lower it again.

'For that is what he intended to do.' Curtis switched naturally to the third person, addressing the crowd, and they recognised that he was talking to them. The others on the balcony were looking at Curtis as though he had sprouted wings – he had certainly sprouted vocal cords, and of such authority that Tamon, Fission and Carlton just let him get on with it.

'This traitor sought to become President, and would have cut off the lifeblood of the whole planet, by wrecking our greatest creation, the single entity which makes Earth the pre-eminent centre of civilisation that it is. He sought to plunge us into barbarism by destroying Central. He sought to reduce us to the level of animals!'

The rumble of the crowd grew angry, the game forgotten as their attention focused on Miron. One or two moved from their seats, coming towards the pitch.

A Foundationer, screaming, ran from the group in front of him, and was caught in the beam of Miron's disruptor; the fanatical scream cutting off abruptly as he suddenly didn't have anything to make it with.

The crowd gasped, and then silence fell again, but it was heavy with threat.

'Make way!' Miron told the group before him, and Rablin beckoned those behind him. Reluctantly, but obediently, they parted.

Tweet swooped.

Bomb doors, open.

With an almost silent fart, he let go his packet of revenge, and, just moments later, reflected on his target's number of arms.

Two.

But it was too late; after three seconds of gravity, he would have shat on an innocent man.

Miron walked slowly.

Wilverton appeared directly in front of him.

'Thomas!' whispered Gloria, her hand flying to her mouth as the imagined danger he had been in became a very real one. She wanted to run to him, but couldn't move.

Wilverton frowned. Instead of hurrying forwards across the cobbled square, he was suddenly hurrying across a football pitch towards someone with a gun.

It was Norim.

That was odd.

It wasn't odd for the Challenger, who suddenly realised the import of the Champion's insistence that both robots should be identical.

It flashed an x-ray of anger, and watched.

They both stopped momentarily, before Miron raised his gun.

The splat was inaudible, the result largely invisible to the crowd, but very visible to Miron, as an ounce of digested blackberries caught him squarely in the eye. He jerked involuntarily and shot into the air.

Wilverton shrugged, aimed, and fired.

Norim/Miron crumpled to the ground and moved feebly.

'Kill him!' screamed Tamon from the balcony, the sound system broadcasting his passion.

The Foundationers rushed forwards, surrounding Miron in a second, and the crowd edged forwards in their seats, eager, encouraging. Hands reached for the robot, lifting it, pulling at it, punching it, tearing it, as cheers urged them on . . .

Gloria looked, horrified, into the amphitheatre, and her 'Do something, stop them' was barely heard above the crowd's enthusiasm. Tamon stared with wide, excited eyes, and a rictus grin, while Dano's eyes, almost as wide, showed fear, and . . . what? thought Carlton, alternating between her face and the pitch. Disgust?

'This looks a lot like what we do,' commented the cheetah.

The wildebeest took a piece of cotton from its mouth and surveyed the scene with a contemplative frown.

'Hmm. Yes, it does, except they appear to be going a bit further.' It shrugged its shoulders and went back to threading a needle. 'We aren't built to understand what humans do. We are just dumb animals.'

'We're not dumb.'

'It's a figure of speech.'

'How can being dumb be a figure of speech?'

'It means we do not understand the ways of humans.'

The cheetah frowned.

'Just watch the ritual,' the wildebeest advised.

Dano turned as she finally felt Carlton's eyes on her. A tear rolled down her cheek, though she couldn't quite say why. As the cheers of the crowd rose to a crescendo, he put an arm round her shoulders.

'They're like . . . ' she whispered, but didn't finish. He didn't comment.

The end came quickly, as the group immediately around what was left of Miron saw that it was over and moved backwards.

The crowd relaxed, sitting back in their seats quietly, in a murmuring hubbub, some shifting uncomfortably at the sight before them.

Gloria swallowed deeply before her legs finally worked and she ran from the balcony.

It was a moment before Fission realised where she had gone. 'Melons! Wait! Trand!' As she turned to follow, she clipped Carlton's shoulder. 'Come on.'

He frowned at her back, then back at Dano, still staring over the pitch, but knew he had to go. Duty before massive lifestyle upheaval.

Robots were hurrying around the pitch, one removing LOVE's body, and being followed by Stay; others clearing away the bits of rag, chitin, and metal that had been Miron. Chanta stood still amongst them, something held lightly in her hand. She looked at it sadly, then dropped it on the grass.

Gloria ran down the stairs, obeying her sense of direction without a thought. Still nauseous from what she had seen – even though she had known it was a robot, which the crowd hadn't – she felt wildly happy, and uncertain at the same time. Thomas was back safe, which was wonderful, and now he could resolve the worry that Gloria had had before he left, which might not be. Could he bear to live with someone who didn't even understand the relevance of a President's nipples . . . ?

She took a short-cut through the Grand Hall, concentrating on her thoughts, but noticing as she entered that it was oddly empty; except for the trand . . .

Standing amid fifteen million pieces of toughened and presumably rather embarrassed glass, with the remains of a few chairs and a couple of overturned tables dotted about, and with the book clutched triumphantly in one hand, the trand did that manoeuvre with his mouth which approximated to smile. The mighty tome that was Achie's 'Logic and the Three-Lawed Robot' was his, and with its advice he could rid his beloved Trand – well, Trand Whatever – of the renegade robot presence.

He noticed Gloria standing uncertainly a little way off.

Might as well finish his time on this planet by reducing the opposition, he thought, and took a step towards her.

She looked to go round him; her destination was still that way, and dodged to one side. The trand took another step.

Keeping both eyes on it, she started running.

So did the trand.

The chair didn't. Lying on its side, and therefore presumably in a mood to help nobody, it stuck out a leg and tripped Gloria. She waved her arms around, trying to regain her balance, but couldn't and toppled over; backwards, amazingly.

The trand gave no thought to the unlikely directional decisions of physics; he just knew that she had fallen, and was at his mercy, except he didn't have any. He gave no thought to what might have been lying on its stomach behind a fallen table and pointing a disruptor at him, either.

Danlor's head poked out, and his hand poked out a little more, lining up the disruptor on the advancing alien. He closed the contact and the disruptor made a noise just like a swamp cricket. Swamp crickets, unfortunately for Danlor, just go 'click'.

The Challenger sensed sideways to find the Champion's reaction to the powerless disruptor, and found nothing. Especially not a wavelength suggesting surprise.

Danlor rapped the disruptor on the ground, and the noise just failed to attract the trand's attention.

Gloria struggled upwards, but too slowly.

The trand trundled forwards. He ignored a table, he ignored the crunchy sound as of human fingers beneath a trandian foot; but he didn't – couldn't – ignore the sound of Danlor's scream of pain, though he didn't liken it to anything. He stopped, spun like one of the tutued hippos that looked down from the stage, and saw Danlor rolling away before scrambling to his feet and heading for a corridor.

By the time he turned back, Gloria was almost upright, but not quite. He could still reach her.

Except that suddenly he was no longer in the Grand Hall of the Admin building on Earth Five Zero, but in the council chamber on Trand Whatever.

Around him, his colleagues stood serenely, vacantly, or lay – they would have reclined, but that involves draping an arm or a leg somewhat sensuously, and even when extremely relaxed your average trand is about as sensuous as a crusty handkerchief – on the benches and on the floors.

Directly in front of him, a revolting looking bi-armal creature was rising sluggishly from a supine position.

Something was badly wrong, and it was sure to be caused by the alien, thought the trand, for whom xenophobia was not a separate notion, but was embodied in the term 'instinct'. He knew that the pathetic creature before him was the renegade robot on whom this round of the Game now depended. It was this creature on whom he should use Achie's 'Logic and the Three-Lawed Robot'.

As Norim dragged himself to a standing position once more, the trand took the giant tome in his top two right hands, and with one swipe that would have had a major baseball league closed down as a threat to aircraft, proved the efficacy of Achie's learned instruction.

Norim would never be illogical again.

Not without a head.

★

The Challenger was non-plussed. Still there was no reaction from the Champion, despite the Danlor human's failure.

Admittedly the delay had saved a member of its team, but that was small recompense, surely. Given the energy expended, and the possible gain, one such as the Champion would hardly see the life of a human as a worthwhile result.

Why, then, did it now broadcast a microwave of satisfaction, as though things had gone according to plan?

XXXI

Wilverton found himself being hurried inside, off the pitch, as his brain came down from its plateau to join the rest of him. He remembered shooting Norim twice, and he remembered, hopefully wrongly, what happened afterwards.

'*Thomas!*'

He looked up to see Gloria bearing down on him, hair flying out behind her, and looking as though she was closely tailing a couple of fleeing beachballs. She attacked him like a St Bernard puppy that's been on its own for a week, knocking him to the ground and falling on top of him. He didn't mind. He would have done exactly the same to her if the manoeuvre would not have resulted in his bouncing three feet backwards.

She planted a kiss on his lips, and held it there exactly unlike a cheetah suffocating its prey . . .

Fission and Carlton arrived on the scene, looking worried as they saw their team-mates lying on the ground. It quickly became obvious that their worry was not required – their presence wasn't, either, thought Carlton, thinking to go back to Dano. She couldn't think he was beneath her now.

He didn't have to go back, because she was coming to him – well, moving into the area where he was, he corrected modestly – along with Tamon and Curtis.

Coming the other way were the huddle of Foundationers, and Gloria scrambled to her feet, pulling Wilverton up after her, then stood quietly, watching the robed figures closely in case their shoulders sprouted leaves.

'Well done, everyone!' Tamon looked as happy as he had since they had first seen him, especially when the robots carried in the bits of Miron. He lifted his wrist to tell Central the good news.

From outside, the sound of a crowd cheering at the first return of the game broke through Gloria's reverie. The incident certainly didn't seem to have left a great impression on them, she thought.

Miron was just one more death, and they had already submerged the memory, denying their guilt; but then, they were good at doing that. It was wrong. You've got to know who you are, what you are.

She shook her head, and tightened her grip on Wilverton's arm.

He looked at her for a long moment.

Real.

She was real, and in the real world – or *a* real world, anyway. And she still liked him. If he asked her to . . . to marry him . . .

She might agree . . . Really.

'Thomas? Are you all right? You're shivering.'

'I'm fine. I was just wondering . . . '

'What?'

'Would you . . . Would you like . . . Would you like to hear where I've been?'

She paused so momentarily that he only just noticed it. 'Yes, I'd love to.'

'But not now,' said Arnold from two inches behind them, then sniggered as they left the ground in unison.

Rablin led his subordinates straight to Curtis. 'What would you have us do, Master?'

'Master!' Fission didn't look like she believed what she was hearing, but the Foundationers ignored her. Curtis didn't, quite.

He looked at the faces before him, and he tried to make some words come, but there weren't any left. He knew what had induced him to speak on the balcony; and it *had* been a 'what', a super-what – the Champion. And he knew because, suddenly, it wasn't within him any more. He felt small. Scared. Normal.

He stood there with his head as bald as his chest – something which had demanded close attention to detail – with Fission's expression saying that he was a povvo, and with Chanta's shrivelling judgement of his manhood hanging around the back of his brain. His stomach had more knots than a Miss Whiplash graduation ceremony.

He wasn't anyone's master; anyone's leader.

Why didn't he just admit it?

When, as a child, he gathered his toys around him, he was only ever second-in-command to Big Ted.

'Er. Why don't you just do what Biondor tells you?'

'Who?'

'Biondor,' came the voice of the elegant, fawn-coloured alien, and Rablin led the spin to see him standing a little off to one side.

276

'It's an alien!' shouted Tamon. 'Get him!'

Biondor gave Tamon a tired look and glanced around. No-one was making a move to 'get him'. There might have been one too many of those lately.

'We must go,' he told the team. 'The trands were no less successful than yourselves, and it is time for the next round.'

'Oh, goody!' Arnold was clearly looking forward to the next round.

'I will deliver you to the spaceport.'

'Wait a minute!' Carlton stopped him doing whatever highly advanced aliens did when they wanted to transport people – which might have been buying a bus ticket for all he knew. He turned to Dano, and spoke, quietly.

'I know I'm primi . . . er . . . old-fashioned, and every-thing . . . '

'No you're not!' And she meant it. 'It's refreshing to meet someone who's different, and you're certainly that!'

He smiled. 'We sometimes get to have a new team member. You can come with us if you want. *That* would be different, and you'd enjoy it. I know *I* would.'

She looked at him, and he waited.

Fission, meanwhile, had spotted someone, assuming it wasn't a mirror. She stared at her alter ego for a few moments, then walked purposefully across.

'Hi.' She smiled, and Fission II smiled back, tentatively. 'Look. Sorry about earlier, yeah?'

'Oh, that's all right. Please don't mention it.'

'No. Well. We go now.' She paused just for a moment. 'You know someone called Janiel?'

'Er, no. No, I don't think so.'

'Lives Lynchberg. Do yourself favour. Look him up.' She turned, paused again. 'Do us both favour.'

And she walked away with a quiet, happy-sad smile that looked as out of place as a fishmonger's last thing on a Friday. Profit.

Dano shook her head. 'I'd like to, really I would. But I have to stay here. It's nothing to do with what you are – it's what *we* are. Ever since you said we were just fat mink . . . '

'Hey, I didn't mean it . . . '

'Yes, you did. And you were right. We can't do anything without

277

Central; we're dependent on it. So dependent that the thought of someone wanting to destroy it is enough to make ordinary people act like animals.' She smiled, sadly. 'It hasn't got anything to do with you being an offworlder, or a throwback. It's the opposite really. We know that this has all been about leaders, or rather, hierarchies. Animals have them everywhere – it's what animals are all about – and so do we, which just shows how close to them we still are. We pride ourselves on being civilised, and yet we're never going to be really civilised until we don't have hierarchies any more. I think we should try getting rid of a few of them. When we can each stand on our own two feet, then we'll be getting there.' She laid a hand on his arm, looked into his deep brown eyes, and pretended not to notice how they shone a little more than usual. 'I *would* like to come, but I'm going to stay here and run for President. There seems to be a vacancy.' She smiled. *His* smile had disappeared to wherever hopes went when they died. 'I hope you don't mind.'

'Hey, no sweat!' But you *can't*! I've asked you to come with me! I actually asked! And I wouldn't try to be dominant or anything. 'No problem.'

Don't you understand? I think I *love* you!

'You could stay as well,' she suggested. 'With me.'

Pandemonium was too ordered. This was giant pandemonium.

He *could* stay, and he could make a life for himself here, and Dano would become World President and he would be the President's husband and . . .

And it was still the wrong way round.

'Biondor won't let me,' he said, and she smiled and nodded, and he smiled and shrugged that it was just one of those things, and felt so miserable and alone that if someone had shouted 'Curtis' he might have thought they meant him.

Dano looked down to where something had impacted her leg, and found a small dog leaning against her for support. It looked up through bloodshot eyes, and raised a paw to its head.

'Bark?' it asked. Will you be my pack leader?

She bent down, gave it a gentle pat, and it toppled over. She picked it up, and looked for Carlton. But, with the alien and the rest of his team, he had gone.

XXXII

'A drawn round, but the point proven. It was a weakness, and one that aided your team. The Sam trand weakened momentarily, and the humans became stronger. You were fortunate.' And it the Champion's manipulation of the Danlor human *had* been just to save the one called Gloria – surely not – then it showed itself to be as weak as its team. The Challenger flashed a spectrum of confidence.

The Champion listened to its opponent's summing up, and turned a long swirl of multi-wavelength radiation towards it.

Fortunate? 'Was I?' it asked.

An x-ray answered it, but the Champion's attention had moved on.

Compassion, a weakness? Love, a weakness? They were precisely the attributes that distinguished the mature species.

The weakness was in failing to see how strong they could be. If the human team loved enough that they were prepared to die for it, then they could be invincible.

Its opponent had much to learn.

'The next round,' it said. 'The last?'

'If you wish.'

And that was when its education would be completed.

'Do not worry. No-one else can see me here. Simply board your craft and you will be transported to the next round.' Biondor looked at them each in turn as he spoke. 'It takes place in your own universe.' They felt better. 'But not on your own planet.' They felt worse. And worse still when Biondor disappeared.

They stood in a huddle in the spaceport.

Wilverton looked at Gloria and all around him, soaking up the reality of it all, and trying to come to terms with the facts of life and love. Trying to pluck up courage.

Gloria looked at him, wondering when he was going to say whatever it was he clearly wanted to say, and split down the middle whether she wanted to hear it or not.

Curtis searched the spaceport for a walrus.

Carlton stared at the ground.

Fission hung back, keeping quiet, doing nothing. With an effort.

Arnold looked at them all.

'I'd just like to forgive anyone who thought I was the renegade robot,' he said. Fission looked up. 'I'd like to say that it doesn't make me think any worse of you. Mainly because that simply isn't possible.' He smiled sweetly at Fission.

'Fonk off, metal man.' She paused. 'I know I wrong, and . . . and I sorry, everyone. Okay?' There. She'd said it.

'We all make mistakes,' said Curtis, kindly.

'And he should know.' Arnold wasn't finished.

'You did what you thought was right,' said Gloria. 'We all did. It was Dano who really got the answer, anyway; she worked out what all those animal things meant.' She didn't see Carlton's reaction.

Fission looked about her, at the lack of movement. No point hanging around, she thought. 'Come on, then.' There was a Game to win.

'Which is your ship?'

'Departures', the gateway was marked.

'"Galaxy",' Fission told it, and a blue line appeared on the floor in front of her.

They followed her lead, Curtis quietly bringing up the rear.

Over on the other side of the concourse, 'Exit' watched its colleague with as much happiness as an inanimate suppository of knowledge can manage; which in this case was actually quite a lot.

'Have a nice journey,' the gateway told Curtis as he passed through. He began to smile his thanks. 'And please, make it a long one!'

He shuffled after his crew.